'If this is your first time reading a book in this series, some of which are yet to be translated, you'll find yourself instantly warming to the strong yet sensitive Veum and the vivid self-reflections that punctuate his perambulations. His ongoing bouts with the tyrannies of alcoholism, which threaten to thwart his investigative efforts, are poignant, and the primal scene that forms the core of the mystery is equal parts shocking and ingenious. Almost forty years into the Varg Veum odyssey, Staalesen is at the height of his storytelling powers' Crime Fiction Lover

'Staalesen has created a sharp and intelligent but also vulnerable PI with whom the reader builds a strong rapport. The end of *We Shall Inherit the Wind* was a devastating blow to both parties and *Where Roses Never Die* is a shared recovery. Staalesen is an expert of his craft and once again he has delivered an absorbing mystery expertly solved by his endearing PI, Varg Veum' Live Many Lives

'Staalesen's greatest strength is the quality of his writing. The incidental asides and observations are wonderful and elevate the book from a straightforward murder investigation into something more substantial' Sarah Ward, Crime Pieces

'Staalesen's mastery of pacing enables him to develop his characters in a leisurely way without sacrificing tension and suspense' *Publishers Weekly*

'Gunnar Staalesen was writing suspenseful and socially conscious Nordic Noir long before any of today's Swedish crime writers had managed to put together a single page … one of Norway's most skillful storytellers' Johan Theorin

'An upmarket Philip Marlowe' Maxim Jakubowski, *The Bookseller*

'Staalesen proves why he is one of the best storytellers alive with a deft touch and no wasted words; he is like a sniper who carefully chooses his target before he takes aim' Atticus Finch

'There is a strong social message within the narrative which is at times chilling, always gripping and with a few perfectly placed twists and turns that make it more addictive the further you get into it' Liz Loves Books

'The prose is richly detailed, the plot enthused with social and environmental commentary while never diminishing in interest or pace, the dialogue natural and convincing and the supporting characters all bristle with life. A multi-layered, engrossing and skilfully written novel; there's not an excess word' Tony Hill, Mumbling about ...

'The plot is compelling, with new intrigues unfolding as each page is turned ... a distinctive and welcome addition to the crime fiction genre' Never Imitate

'A well-paced, thrilling plot, with the usual topical social concerns we have come to expect from Staalesen's confident pen ...' Finding Time To Write

'*We Shall Inherit the Wind* brings together great characterisation, a fast-paced plot and an exceptional social conscience ... The beauty of Staalesen's writing and thinking is in the richness of interpretations on offer: poignant love story, murder investigation, essay on human nature and conscience, or tale of passion and revenge' Ewa Sherman, EuroCrime

'Quite simply, *Where Roses Never Die* is an exquisite work of crime fiction and Staalesen's eye for characters is as finely honed as his readers have come to expect. Beautifully paced and making some wider statements on the repercussions of behaviour on impressionable youths and morality, this is the literary equivalent of manna from heaven!' Rachel Hall

'It's cunningly plotted and kept me guessing right until the end, when I not only gasped but also shed a tear as all was revealed. A perfect choice for fans of Nordic Noir as well as intense, chilling crime fiction' Off-the-Shelf Books

'*Where Roses Never Die* is somewhat lighter in tone than previous instalments in Staalesen's series. It even hints that Varg Veum's lengthy romantic dry spell might be coming to an end. The author also does a superior job of building suspense in regards to both the kidnapping and robbery cases, stitching clues into his plot that leave one wondering about the crimes' connections. His portrayals of the players involved in these puzzles benefit from multiple, gradually unfolding dimensions' Kirkus

'It isn't just (or even primarily) a case of finding out "whodunit". It's not simply a "Where's Wally" exercise in recognising the clues and putting them together with a "Hey, presto – he's the murderer" outcome. The Scandinavian approach also focuses on the aftershocks. The sundering judders, shudders, waves and even ripples that spread out into the lives of people affected by the trauma of the central event. It's at this that Staalesen really excels' The Library Door

'There is a claustrophobic feeling to the story, a sense of unease surrounding this seemingly tranquil suburb. Whilst everything may have appeared normal on the surface, there were secrets just waiting to emerge. This is a well-paced, suspenseful book that keeps you guessing until the very end' Owl on the Bookshelf

'Averse as I am to gushing, with some authors it's difficult to remain completely objective when you have genuinely loved every single book that they have ever produced. Such is my problem – but a nice problem – with the venerable Mr Staalesen, and with *Where Roses Never Die*, which merely compounds my adoration of this series to date' Raven Crime Reads

'A brilliant crime thriller, which I absolutely loved. It reminded me slightly of an Agatha Christie novel, not because of the main character but because of the brilliance of how the whole plot is written and how it had me totally clueless as to how everything fits together and who is behind the disappearance of the young girl. Can't recommend highly enough … this is one author whose books I will certainly be checking out and reading more' By the Letter Book Reviews

'This is really Scandinavian crime writing at its very best. There is something dark and haunting about this novel that will test every sinew of your emotions as the truth emerges' Last Word Book Review

'*Where Roses Never Die* is an exceptionally plotted, well written and hauntingly evocative lesson in Norwegian crime writing. I experienced a wide range of emotions while reading it, and in the interest of full disclosure, this Ice Queen shed some tears reading it! I cannot recommend this book highly enough' Bibliophile Book Club

'This is the sort of crime novel to go for if you like brooding, rough round the edges heroes. The mystery itself takes us down a few misdirected paths, till eventually we see the shocking and sad hidden truth. Staalesen is critiquing the selfish human condition and how it brings about its own downfall. This is a fabulous and very accessible Nordic thriller, with a dark satisfying side' Northern Crime

'There are unexpected twists throughout the story, which are cleverly placed to make sure you keep turning the pages. It's a very enjoyable read about a group of people who aren't necessarily what they seem. Would I recommend this book? Definitely!' Damp Pebbles

'*Where Roses Never Die* is a wonderfully written novel that shows that what goes on behind closed doors is rarely what you would imagine. As long-buried secrets are unearthed, Staalesen takes his time to prolong the suspense about what has happened to this little girl, resulting in an enticing, gripping read' Segnalibro

'Once again, fluently translated from the Norwegian by Don Bartlett, Staalesen's first-person prose is so meticulous, it could have been sculpted out of ice. There's not a superfluous word as Veum edges closer to the frozen core of a truth buried away for decades, revealing as he does so dark and shocking tensions that have split apart the couples living near little Mette's family. Superbly paced, taut and atmospheric, this is a beautifully crafted crime thriller that's always full of humanity' Claire Thinking

WOLVES IN THE DARK

ABOUT THE AUTHOR

One of the fathers of Nordic Noir, Gunnar Staalesen was born in Bergen, Norway in 1947. He made his debut at the age of twenty-two with *Seasons of Innocence* and in 1977 he published the first book in the Varg Veum series. He is the author of over twenty titles, which have been published in twenty-four countries and sold over four million copies. Twelve film adaptations of his Varg Veum crime novels have appeared since 2007, starring the popular Norwegian actor Trond Espen Seim. Staalesen has won three Golden Pistols (including the Prize of Honour) and *Where Roses Never Die* was shortlisted for the 2017 Petrona Award for crime fiction. He lives in Bergen with his wife.

ABOUT THE TRANSLATOR

Don Bartlett lives with his family in a village in Norfolk. He completed an MA in Literary Translation at the University of East Anglia in 2000 and has since worked with a wide variety of Danish and Norwegian authors, including Jo Nesbø and Karl Ove Knausgaard. He has previously translated *The Consorts of Death, Cold Hearts, We Shall Inherit the Wind* and *Where Roses Never Die* in the Varg Veum series.

Wolves in the Dark

GUNNAR STAALESEN

Translated from the Norwegian by Don Bartlett

**ORENDA
BOOKS**

Orenda Books
16 Carson Road
West Dulwich
London SE21 8HU
www.orendabooks.co.uk

First published in Norwegian as *Ingen er så trygg i fare* by Gyldendal in 2014
First published in English by Orenda Books 2017

ISBN 978-1-910633-72-4
eISBN 978-1-910633-73-1

The publication of this translation has been made possible through the
financial support of NORLA, Norwegian Literature Abroad.

Typeset in Arno by MacGuru Ltd
Printed and bound by CPI Group (UK) Ltd, Croydon CR0 4YY

SALES & DISTRIBUTION

In the UK and elsewhere in Europe:
Turnaround Publisher Services
Unit 3, Olympia Trading Estate
Coburg Road, Wood Green
London N22 6TZ
www.turnaround-uk.com

In USA/Canada:
Trafalgar Square Publishing
Independent Publishers Group
814 North Franklin Street
Chicago, IL 60610
USA
www.ipgbook.com

In Australia and New Zealand:
Affirm Press
28 Thistlethwaite Street
South Melbourne VIC 3205
Australia
www.affirmpress.com.au

For details of other territories, please contact info@orendabooks.co.uk

Bergen, Norway

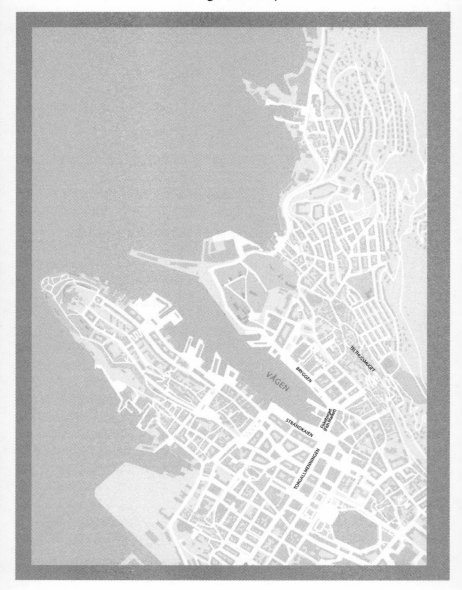

1

They came early – to catch me in bed. At seven I was woken by a loud, continuous ring on the bell downstairs. I staggered to the window, opened it and looked out.

The police car was parked nose to the wall. In front of my door stood Inspector Bjarne Solheim, accompanied by his colleague Arne Melvær.

'Veum?' Solheim said. 'Can we come in?'

'Do I have the option to say no?'

He turned an unsmiling face up at me and shook his head slowly.

I closed the window, threw on a dressing gown, thrust my feet into a pair of slippers and trudged down the narrow staircase. I had barely opened the door before they were inside. Both eyed me warily.

Solheim put his hand into an inside pocket and pulled out a folded document. His look was solemn as he said: 'We have a warrant for your arrest, Veum. And a search warrant. Have you got a computer in the house?'

I stared at him in shock. 'Yes? A laptop. But—'

'It's confiscated. We'll go up with you, so that you can put some clothes on. Afterwards you'll have to accompany us to Police HQ.'

I still wasn't sure if I was awake or if all this was some bad dream. 'Tell me … Are you serious? And what have I been arrested for?'

'We can deal with that at the station. Hamre's already waiting.'

A few minutes later we were heading towards Allehelgens gate. Melvær was sitting with my computer on his lap, his facial expression suggesting he had been entrusted with the Crown Jewels. A few hours ago I had been as happy with my life as I was able to allow myself to be. Now I was sitting in the back of a police car, feeling like a naughty boy being summoned to the headmaster for no obvious reason.

Outside the car, the town was waking up to a dull, grey September day. I could see it was going to be far different from the one I had imagined. I already envied those people getting out of the yellow buses to walk to an office or some other everyday job somewhere in town, anywhere but the police station.

2

Jakob E. Hamre, the section head, was about my age. In other words, he was fast closing in on retirement. Not even that thought made him a cheerier spectacle as he sat behind his desk, observing me with a face gloomier than that of a passport official at the pearly gates. His hair was greyer than when I had last seen him, nearly white in some parts. It was thinner than I remembered as well, unless he had just washed it.

His eyes narrowed visibly as I sat down on the chair opposite him. 'I would never have believed I'd experience this, Veum.'

'We've sat like this on innumerable occasions, Hamre.'

'Not like this.' He looked down and flicked through some papers he had in front of him.

I craned my neck to see what they could be. From a distance they looked like computer print-outs, but internet technology had never been my strongest suit. I was happy so long as my computer worked, I could get online, and send and receive emails.

'I have a print-out here,' he said, rather redundantly. 'It's a summary of the traffic on your office computer over the last six months. If we wish we can go even further back. The laptop we confiscated during your arrest will now be examined by our experts to compare, and perhaps document, similar content.'

I felt my jaw drop. 'Tell me … is that legal?'

He nodded. 'Court order.'

'And what do you mean by "similar content"?'

He sent me a stern gaze. 'I reckon you can work that out for yourself.'

'No, in fact I can't. All I use the computer for is emails, banking, booking the odd ticket and various searches connected with work.'

His eyes flashed. 'And you've been working on cases that involve dubious content recently, have you?'

'Dubious content?' I wasn't so stupid that I didn't suspect where this was leading. Though I didn't understand the how and why. 'Could you perhaps be a little more explicit?'

He heaved a heavy sigh, pushed some of the papers aside, leaned forward slightly and stared at me darkly. 'Child pornography, Veum.' He grimaced. 'Of the most repugnant kind.'

I could feel my body stiffening, the way muscles brace themselves in the face of an assumed danger. I still felt as if I were trapped in a bad dream, as though I had been transferred into a parallel existence where nothing was how it should be; or I was looking into a fairground mirror, struggling to recognise myself.

I gesticulated with my right hand, a denial of everything. 'I know nothing about this. This cannot possibly be right. And if it is…'

'Yes?' He fixed his eyes on me.

'Then someone has got into my computer and left it there intentionally.'

'*Quod erat demonstrandum*, Veum. That's Latin, in case you didn't know, and it means "that which was to be proved".'

'Well, I'll help you in every way possible. You can rely on me!' When he said nothing, I carried on: 'Surely you can't believe that I … that this is something I … that I would … I'm speechless.'

'And perhaps that shows the thin ice you're walking on.'

'Now, just listen here! I understand nothing about computers, except the essentials, as I told you. But surely you have experts who can examine this and … find out what happened?'

'If someone hacked into your computer, as it's called, it ought to be possible to find that out, yes. The problem, Veum, is that you are not on your own. Our raid today wasn't some chance visit. This afternoon you'll hear about it on the radio news. It'll be on TV this evening and it'll be splashed over all the newspapers for days.'

'*What* will be splashed over the newspapers?'

'Hordaland Police District, in co-operation with several other police districts in Norway, other European countries and, furthermore, the USA, in the early hours of this morning uncovered an international child pornography ring that distributes images over the internet. Arrests are being made in a number of countries. As well as you there are three other men in our district awaiting interrogation – either here, or in one case at a provincial police station. Your IP address appeared on this network with incoming and outgoing traffic.'

'Incoming and outgoing?'

'It means you've both received and sent … images that have been shared around the network.'

'But, but…' My face was taut, and all the muscles in my body, from the back of my head to the soles of my feet, were tensed. 'This is absolutely incomprehensible! My God, Hamre. You've known me … for how many years?'

He shrugged. 'Too many, if you ask me.'

'You can't think … you can't believe that I would be involved in this with my background – from Child Welfare officer to private investigator?'

'I don't want to believe it, Veum, but…' Again he showed me the paperwork on his desk. 'The evidence is weighty. And the case has to be examined. In the meantime you'll be remanded in custody. No visitors and no mail of any kind.'

At once I felt a deep fear shiver through my body and I wanted to open one of his desk drawers to see if he had a tiny bottle of aquavit waiting for me.

'I assume you're not going to make a confession?'

'Confession! For Christ's sake, I have nothing to confess. This is madness. Any discerning person can see that.'

'This discerning person can't,' he drawled, then announced: 'Your case will come up today.'

I heard my own voice quiver with nerves as I said: 'I suppose I'm entitled to a lawyer?'

He nodded. 'You are. Anyone in particular?'

'Give me Vidar Waagenes. He knows me well.'

'We'll ring him. For now you'll be put in a basement cell. You can spend your time having a good think. About whether it wouldn't pay to lay all your cards on the table.'

'There are no cards to show you, Hamre. Not in this hand. Can I make a call to tell my family where I am?'

'Only in my presence. Afterwards you'll have to leave the phone with us.'

'You'll examine that too, I take it.'

'What do you think?'

'It's an old model. No camera.'

'Well … are you going to make the call?'

I dialled Sølvi's number. Her phone rang five times, then the voice-mail cut in: *'You have reached Sølvi Hegge. I can't take the phone now, but I can call you back as soon as I'm free, or you can leave a message after the tone.'*

When the tone came I just stared blankly at the phone. I had no idea what to say. So I pressed 'off' and looked at Hamre. 'She didn't answer.'

'Perhaps just as well, Veum.'

3

Bjarne Solheim's scruffy hair, which often stood on end, had always reminded me of Stan Laurel – the thin one from Laurel & Hardy, in my opinion the funniest comic duo ever. But there was nothing comical about him as he stood beside me in the lift, accompanying me to the custody suite in the basement. We didn't exchange a single word, and he stared gloomily at the lift door until we had reached the bottom.

I had my belt and shoelaces taken off me but was allowed to keep my notepad and biro, the latter after much rumination on the officer's part.

'Has anyone committed suicide with a biro?' I asked.

The officer glared at me. 'Spare me the wit. You can use it to stab with, can't you?'

Yes, in my eye, I answered in my head, making sure I didn't say it aloud.

Then the door closed behind me, it was locked and I was alone in a hotel room I hadn't booked, but someone had reserved for me anyway.

Bergen's custody suite is in the basement of Police HQ, which was built in 1965. It didn't appear that any great modernisation had taken place since then. There was no drunk tank, but the sparse furnishings meant the difference was not immense: a bench, a table fixed to the wall, a hole in one corner and a metal sink beside it. No windows, just a hatch in the door to the corridor. Through it I heard the garbled protests of one of the drunk-tank fraternity, but was unable to make any sense of what he was saying.

The shocked numbness I had felt in my body after Hamre had outlined the serious charge against me was now being replaced by something even more unpleasant: panic. It made my heart pound in my chest and sweat form between my shoulder blades and on my forehead.

I gasped for breath as though my respiratory system were on the blink. My body twitched uncontrollably a few times, and I leaned against the wall so as not to fall over; at least that was how it felt.

I slumped down on the bench, leaned back against the wall, rested my head and concentrated on taking deep, controlled breaths, down to my belly: slow inhalation, controlled release; slow inhalation, controlled release.

Gradually the panic attack began to lose its grip, but still I could feel it in my body, like a hollow in the pit of my stomach and a lump in my chest, a kind of collar around my lungs.

I looked around. Bare, greyish-white walls. Not one picture. A few swear words carved into the plaster and some unrefined drawings of disproportionately large, erect sexual organs, head-on, as it were. This wasn't a place people stayed for long. You were taken out relatively fast and released or sent for a longer stay in the luxury accommodation at Åsane – or even further away if it was overbooked.

I had nothing to read. All I had was my pad with a few boring notes on cases I had either cracked or couldn't crack – all two to three months old. I flicked through to a blank page, clicked the biro and sat staring at the white sheet. I had nothing to write. In the end, I jotted down the date, 10th September 2002, and then a big question mark. No matter how hard I concentrated on what Hamre had said, I couldn't understand where all the evidence had come from and why I hadn't discovered it for myself.

On the other hand, there was quite a lot I had only vague memories of in the soon-to-be four years that had passed since Karin had been so suddenly and brutally ripped out of my life. I had a fairly good perspective of the last six months because of the case I had worked on and which had brought Sølvi and me together. The three years or so before that were wreathed in the sombre mists of confusion and intoxication, shame and dishonour, en route from the gutter to the sewer, in the company of men and women I would have preferred not to be seen with, even on the darkest night. I had taken on jobs I wouldn't normally have touched with a barge pole, but I had never been as low as the place where Hamre had put me during the first meeting in his office. There were limits, tattooed inside my heart, and I never crossed them.

Only last night I had been with Sølvi and her young daughter in Saudalskleivane. After Helene had fallen asleep, we had stood above her bed as if we were her parents, and no evil had befallen her or her mother in the past six months. She looked like an angel as she slept, her blonde hair spread out on the pillow like a bridal veil. Helene was ten and a half years old. She was a beautiful little girl with gentle features, round cheeks and a mouth that loved to smile when she was awake. Her eyelids twitched, and I couldn't help but remember how Beate and I had stood over Thomas's bed and looked down on him in exactly the same way, a very long time ago, of course.

After a while we had tiptoed back into the living room, where Sølvi had another glass of red wine and I had a last bottle of Farris mineral water, the idea being that I would drive home.

Once she had finished her wine, we went into the bedroom. Her mouth, so welcoming and soft and open, tasted of red wine. In the dim light we made love with a passion that told us nothing goes out of date so long as the contents are still fresh.

Afterwards we lay chatting.

She tugged at my ear and said: 'I wonder what it was that made me fall for you.'

'I'm probably not the right person to answer that question,' I mumbled.

She chuckled. 'Actually I'm wondering if it wasn't a kind of maternal feeling.'

'Thank you very much,' I said, pulling her to me and kissing her in a way no son would, as if to persuade her there must have been something else.

'I mean it, Varg. You seemed so lost.'

I hadn't convinced her, in other words. But I could live with that. The alternative was a great deal more boring.

It was approaching two in the morning when I got into my car and drove home. We still hadn't reached the stage of having breakfast together; not while Helene was at home. It wasn't a year yet since she had lost her father, and I still had a way to go before I could be promoted to step-daddy, in her eyes. But on a good day I could imagine that I was on my way. And yesterday had been just that: a good day without the slightest hint of what was to come.

There was a rattle in the lock, and I turned to face the heavy door, which was pulled open to let in Vidar Waagenes. He didn't look a bundle of laughs, either.

'Veum,' he declared, holding out a hand.

I struggled to my feet and shook hands. 'Nice to see you again,' I mumbled, although I had no memory of when I last saw him.

He nodded towards the bench. 'We can have a few words here before going back to see Hamre.' He motioned to the prison officer waiting in the doorway. 'You can leave us alone now, Johnsen.'

Johnsen nodded and pulled the door to, without locking it this time.

I looked at Vidar Waagenes. He had become a forty-something, but there was still a boyish gaucheness about him that made you feel he would be easy prey in a court of law. It was a misjudgement many had had cause to regret; and experience had taught me he was the opposite. He was a trial lawyer of the highest calibre and would have been a star in Oslo, if he hadn't preferred to remain in a large house in Fjellveien, within walking distance of the Bergen Law Courts, Wesselstuen – a celebrity restaurant – and other places he had to go for professional reasons or to satisfy other proclivities. If anyone could get me out of the fix I was in, it was him.

His dark hair was speckled with grey, but he still had a forelock and he still swept it to the side with the same flick. He was elegantly dressed in a grey suit, white shirt and a bluish-grey tie that was hardly likely to cause annoyance to anyone. The glance he cast at my outfit – blue jeans and black T-shirt thrown on in haste after the early-morning call several hours earlier – suggested the opposite. He would probably have recommended different clothes if we were going to court.

He sat down next to me on the bench and half turned in what

seemed like a very uncomfortable position. 'Let's hear your side of the story then, Veum.'

'My side? I haven't got one.'

He sent me a measured look. 'That's what most people say, at first.'

I gesticulated impatiently. 'But it's true, Vidar. I have no idea what this is about!'

He sighed. 'Well, what I've been given to understand by Hamre is that they have located extremely incriminating material on your computer. Have you any comment?'

'It came like a bolt from the blue. I've never opened that kind of webpage or gone onto a website of that description.'

He shrugged. 'It could have been in connection with a case.'

'Yes, but that's never happened. Thank God, I've never had cases like that.'

His face crinkled in disappointment. 'We could have used that as an argument in court.'

'I'd opened child porn webpages in connection with a case?'

'Yes.'

'Are you recommending that I lie, Vidar?'

He pouted, the way lawyers do when they are generally trying to avoid the truth. 'Not as such, but … let's say it was your side of the story.'

'Even if it isn't true?'

His eyes gleamed, and he smiled at me. 'Thank you, Veum. That was how I hoped you would react. If we stick to the truth, in principle nothing can go wrong.'

'No?'

'No.'

'We've never had travesties of justice in this country?'

'Well, we have, in fact.'

'But you're sure we'll avoid one this time?'

'Let's not assume the worst. Right now we have two important tasks ahead of us. We have to talk to Hamre and find out how willing he would be to drop charges. From what he said on the phone I doubt we'll achieve that. So either this afternoon or tomorrow morning there will be a review of your case, which could be important. Are you ready for action?'

I spread my arms. 'Ready for everything except staying here, anyway.'

'Then I'll tell Johnsen he needs to get someone down to accompany us.'

'They won't let us go upstairs on our own?'

'Not on a day like today, I'm afraid.'

4

Two officers came to collect us. They looked like brothers: one big and strong; the other slightly smaller. Both had shaven heads, newly pressed uniforms, and they gave the impression that descending into Hades to fetch a depressed Orpheus from the dead-end street where he had ended up was a pleasant duty.

'One each,' I mumbled to Waagenes.

He rolled his eyes and led the way out of the cell. They escorted us to Hamre's office before leaving us in the company of those present.

Hamre wasn't alone any more. With him sat Beatrice Bauge, a surprisingly young woman to have the title 'police solicitor', so young I could have been her father. She had blonde hair pulled back into a bun, a square jaw and the coolest eyes I had seen since I was last in the bank. This lady wasn't going to give much away either, sadly.

We shook hands, but neither of us smiled. There was a sombre atmosphere in the small office, as though none of us actually wanted to be there. At an undertaker's there was a definite tone of friendliness. Here there was nothing. Hamre was grey-faced, Beatrice Bauge had angry red blotches on her cheeks, Vidar Waagenes looked as if he was placing all his bets on the wrong horse, and I wouldn't have been able to perform a somersault if they had paid me a million kroner.

Beatrice Bauge sat there in full uniform, as straight-backed as if she were leading the day's press conference, which in fact she announced. 'You all know what this case is about. The press conference has been called for 1800 hours, and I think I can guarantee it will be headline news throughout the media tonight.'

She deliberately interposed a tiny pause and watched her words sink in. They did, like underwater mines programmed to detonate any second. Again I felt fear grip me, and the room had started to tip.

'Not mentioning any names, I assume,' I managed to stutter.

She stiffened her lips into a caricature of a smile. 'No, we won't go that far, but you never know what the media can find out. They often operate effectively outside our systems.'

'Inside too, I've been told.'

Waagenes gave an admonitory cough. 'Let's hear what they have to say, Veum. They need to have solid proof before they put their heads above the parapet.'

This time she did indeed give a little smile.

'I doubt if there's any proof more solid than this.' She shifted her gaze back to me. 'As soon as we start the hearings you'll be confronted with various links to an international child pornography ring, with primary emphasis on your…' Now it was her turn to cough. '…What shall I call them – colleagues? – in the local area.'

'I don't have any "colleagues"!'

'No? Acquaintances then, perhaps?'

'No, not the kind you're referring to.'

'Early this morning we confiscated the computer you have in your office and the laptop you have at home.'

'In the office! How did you get in?'

'We had some assistance.'

'I hope you remembered to lock up afterwards!'

She sent me a condescending glare. 'This material will now be thoroughly examined by our professional experts. But they've already established that you're an active participant in exchanging images, film clips and comments in this … what shall I call it? … market?'

This was making my head whirl. 'I've never … Film clips? Comments? I've never written a comment in any thread, not even one about Brann FC, however tempting that might be.'

She sighed theatrically and turned back to Waagenes. 'Of course you'll be given all the material we've had to sit through.' She pulled a face. 'For the refreshment and purification of your soul.'

'Amen,' I muttered.

'I doubt you'll be able to object that all the evidence we've gathered isn't enough to formulate a charge. I'm also convinced the court will agree when we ask, initially, for your client to be held in custody for four weeks, with no visitors or access to mail.'

'No visitors or mail?' Waagenes echoed. 'Isn't that a little on the severe side?'

She slowly shook her head. Hamre stirred uneasily in his seat; he'd been conspicuously quiet throughout the proceedings so far. 'Not at all,' she said. 'Any communication within the alleged network must be stopped. We're not ruling out the possibility of further arrests in the course of the next twenty-four hours, but we feel confident that the four people we have in custody now are the main operators in this locality.'

'The main operators?' I burst out, still unable to believe my own ears.

She nodded, without adding anything else this time.

Waagenes looked in my direction with some concern. 'Naturally we'll oppose custody. My client maintains he is one hundred percent innocent of the charges being made. He has absolutely no idea how these images have got onto his computers, and we will assert that they have been planted from the outside – by someone who has hacked into them.'

'We will dispute this. We can wait with the technical data until we're in court, but we are confident that Veum put the images there himself.'

I just shook my head in disbelief. 'What else can I say? Where's the old legal ruling that a defendant should be given the benefit of the doubt?'

'Doubt? What doubt?' Beatrice Bauge answered drily.

'When is the hearing scheduled for?' Waagenes asked.

'1500 hours.'

'Then I'd like to have a full session with my client beforehand. Is there a spare room we can use up here?'

She arched her eyebrows. 'Spare room? Do you think we're running a hotel? You'll have to make do with the custody suite.'

Again Hamre shifted uneasily. 'We need the time we have left, Beatrice.'

'Right.' She stood up as a sign the meeting was over.

Accompanied by Charon and his little brother, Waagenes and I took the lift back down to Hades. I wondered if I should look for a coin or two to place on my eyes, then I remembered all my small change had been taken from me earlier in the day. You weren't allowed to take so much as a fifty-øre coin down into Hades in this part of the world, one early-autumn day at the very beginning of the twenty-first century.

5

With a perturbed expression on his face, Waagenes sat down on the bench and motioned for me to join him while the officer outside locked the door behind us. Through the hatch they could keep an eye on their clientele without having to open up. It was, after all, a place where, if you were dead drunk on arrival, it was easy to suffer a sudden cessation of life.

Waagenes leaned towards me and said in a low voice, 'The first thing we must have one hundred percent clear is the following: Can you, hand on heart, assure me you know nothing about this case?'

'I'll put my hand wherever you want, Vidar, but I can assure you, this came like a bolt from the blue, straight through the roof, in fact, for me too. Someone has gained access to my computers, either directly or externally, if that's possible. I have to admit I know nothing about these things at all. About how you do it. But someone has put this filth on my computers, in which case it must've been intentional. How did the police find it? Did someone tip them off?'

Waagenes nodded. 'I'll try to find out. And you have no idea who this might have been?'

I shrugged. 'Lots of people have borne me some resentment over the years. Not just resentment but deep grudges. But would any of them have the technological expertise to do this? It's just as likely to be a fifteen-year-old as someone of my age. More likely in fact.'

He looked at me sharply. 'Oh? Have you someone in mind?'

'No. That was just an example.'

'Let me try to draw up a list of possibilities here. How has business been for you in recent years?'

I ran a hand through my hair and squirmed. The bench was hard and uncomfortable to sit on, but that wasn't what was making me squirm. I said: 'Earlier this year I solved a cold case, almost twenty-five years old.'

He nodded. 'Yes? Carry on.'

'But it was also the first proper case I'd investigated for ... some years.'

'Oh, yes?'

'I...' Talking about it was still torture. 'I lost my partner in connection with a case nearly four years ago. The time since then has been ... complicated.'

He nodded sympathetically and waited for me to continue.

'It all ... became too much for me. Too many ... too much drinking.'

'Mhm. But you carried on professionally?'

'Yes, but I wasn't very sober.'

His eyes narrowed. 'In other words, what you remember from those days is hazy?'

'Yes, I'm afraid so.'

'Well ... that doesn't make the situation any easier. Let me ask you the following question: Could your fitful memory of these years mean that you might – unbeknown to yourself – have been on some of these websites that the charming *frøken* Bauge informed us about upstairs?'

I looked at him with a feeling somewhat redolent of a bad conscience. 'I'd have remembered, Vidar! I wasn't that far gone.'

'Sure?'

'...Yes.'

I closed my eyes. I visualised some situations, some people, some women I'd encountered during the dark days of my past. Very few of these women were under fifty. If they were, they charged a fee. And I was never sat behind a computer screen; unless I was trying to coax the last drop from my internet bank before the next bill was due. Otherwise the screen remained dark and all the lights were out – at home and in my office.

'Hmm.' Vidar Waagenes looked pensive. 'We have the hearing in a few hours. I'll go and buy you some clothes. You can't appear ... like that.' His eyes wandered eloquently over my outfit. 'In the meantime I think you should consider your situation and see if you can remember anything at all that might help us in court. I'll see if I can lay my hands on a few more facts – any documentation the folks upstairs might be willing to release. Then I'll come back for you. If you had this week's winning lottery ticket it would be crawling with press outside, but this hearing will be behind closed doors, I can promise you that.'

Resigned, I nodded and watched him being let out of the cell. After he had gone I took out my notepad and my lethal biro. Before starting to write, I slumped back against the wall, closed my eyes and probed the past.

6

The first three years after Karin died had been like a peregrination through a Salvador Dalí landscape, seen through the bottom of an aquavit bottle.

The detail was strange, often terrible, and again and again I saw her lying there on the windblown island coast with her head twisted, for no reason, surrounded by long-disconnected clock faces, humanoid figures with grotesque facial expressions, no bodies but enormous legs, like gigantic spiders. Inside a room, there was pounding music, a decibel level beyond anything imaginable, men smashing bottles against glass with such power, like cymbals in a symphony orchestra, and semi-naked women leaning back, pulling up their skirts, spreading their legs and revealing a sunset so murky that the most polluted intersection in Europe – Danmarksplass in Bergen on a cold February day – seemed like paradise by comparison. And outside the wolves howled. When I put my face to the window pane I saw fantasy animals of the most incredible kind: insect legs; a sheep's skin and elephant trunks; dogs with fangs like sabre-toothed tigers; cats with claws like sword points, dripping with blood; and monkeys performing the rudest movements, dancing on an altar in front of a screen filled to the margins with por-nographic images, images so savage I could wake in the middle of the night bathed in sweat and convinced I would never be able to close my eyes again, for fear of experiencing more of the same.

I had staggered in and out of this landscape, with either a bottle or a glass in hand. I remembered trying to cling to my office, where I sat staring at the phone, as if waiting for Karin to ring – or at least a client. I had watched the pile of bills grow ever higher until I could have played Happy Families with them and won every round; nothing was easier than finding four of the same. But recently reminders had been replaced by debt-recovery letters, and it seemed as if I would never win. Creditors queued outside my office door, and on the rare occasion a client did appear they often left frustrated because I had been too drunk to understand what the job involved.

It had been the darkest period of my life, and I had experienced total blackouts, which now meant that I shuddered at the thought: Could I have done what Hamre insisted I did do during one of these? Wasn't I basically guilty?

I opened my eyes and stared at the pale, dirty wall on the opposite side of the room. Once again I could feel my respiratory system malfunctioning, as though my lungs wouldn't take the air I inhaled; instead it wrapped itself around my chest like tape, so strong that I didn't have the strength to tear it in half.

I forced myself to sit properly. I opened my notepad, gripped the biro tightly, stared down at the blank paper and tried to conjure up some images, some names, some moments, from the bleak years.

Slowly the mist lifted and gradually shapes emerged – a few. I jotted down words.

7

When I heard from Nils Åkre, my old friend in the insurance business, one crisp February day in the very first year of the new millennium, it came as a surprise. After an embarrassing and unpleasant case a few years earlier, all communication between us had ceased, with fatal consequences for my finances, business and private. After we finished talking, I sat staring through the office window. The low sun emphasised the saw-tooth roofline of Bryggen's Hanseatic houses on the other side of Vågen bay against the buildings behind, and the silhouette of Mount Fløyfjell was as sharp as a Japanese paper cut-out – greyish-black against the light-blue sky.

As I was already several centilitres down the day's first bottle of aquavit I was obliged to walk to Olav Kyrres gate in order to catch a bus to Nils's office in Fyllingsdalen. Around three-quarters of an hour later I was standing in the reception area at the insurance company, having a visitor's badge stuck to my lapel and the way to his office explained by a woman who was so new there she had never seen me before. I mumbled something about knowing where his office was, and she smiled back in a nice, cultivated way, like a loyal representative of the customer-friendly institution they were known to be – at least until you needed them.

Nils Åkre found it difficult to meet my gaze, but whether that was because he still had a guilty conscience about what had happened the previous time we saw each other or because my eyes were swimming, I couldn't be sure. We exchanged glances like two shy teenagers on their very first date, and then, with a broad flourish, he waved me to the customer chair while he sat down behind the desk.

I wondered whether he had been comfort-eating since our last meeting, because he had definitely swollen up, to the hundred-kilo mark, it looked like, and it wasn't increased muscle mass. He was squeezed into a suit that looked as if the seams might burst at any moment, but had lashed an immense knot in his tie, perhaps to moor himself to life. The tie was the same light-blue as the sky, but there wasn't much sunshine in his eyes, which flitted around, not settling for an instant.

He ignored the opportunity for a chat and got straight down to business. 'As I said on the phone, Varg, I've got a job for you.' I didn't make a comment, and he carried on talking: 'The reason we've come to you regarding this matter is because we have no-one else to turn to.'

It was one of the most dubious compliments I'd had for many years, yet I still refrained from commenting.

He peered out of the window as though the answer to life's mysteries lay somewhere there. 'You might've been wondering why you haven't heard from us for some years…'

Well, actually I hadn't been, considering his Parthian shot the last time we met.

'But in fact we've become as good as self-reliant in what I'd call … your field.'

'Oh, yes?'

'Crime investigation,' he added, as though I didn't understand what he was talking about. 'More and more police officers find employment with us, even before they reach retirement age, and afterwards, of course.'

I nodded. I was aware the market was not on my side any more. Nor did I have early retirement to fall back on. There was no such package for private investigators, I knew that.

'But now one of these is causing us problems.'

'A police officer?'

'A trivial matter, actually, but … we can't sack old colleagues here, we have to turn to others.'

'And of the heavies you know, I was first in line?'

'Heavies?'

'Yes, I assume this is about some outstanding debts? I know all about them, not to put too fine a point on it.'

'Well … yes, it is about something like that. So many bills are due and so little money has been recovered that the bailiff has given up. But we're responsible for car insurance here.'

'All you have to do is confiscate his assets, don't you? Car, house, cabin?'

'That's the problem. He has nothing left – of that kind of asset, anyway. Not even the car in question. Which he didn't pay for in the final years he had it.'

'Nice for some,' I said, envious.

'He's claiming his pension, and that's it. But we suspect he has something up his sleeve.'

'Oh, yes?'

'If I can put it like that. He's got a girlfriend he lives with, in Fusa. This woman has a house and a car, and even more. She has a property in Spain and they spend most of the winter there. In short, there's nothing wrong with their finances.'

'He married wisely?'

'They're not married. A girlfriend, I said. No common property, so nothing we can confiscate from her house.'

'How did she get all the money?'

'Fish farm, which was sold when her husband died.'

'Lucrative business, so I've heard.'

'Not bad.'

'And what do you want me to do about this?'

He leaned towards the edge of the desk, as far as his stomach would permit. 'I want you to pay them a visit and try to get a picture of the possessions they have. See if there's anything that could be said to be his alone. By which I mean anything from expensive fishing equipment to a wristwatch or other valuable items.'

'But you said … It's winter now. They'd be in Spain, wouldn't they?'

'They're back home for … I think it was a funeral. If you're lucky you can catch them before they return.'

'Not close family, I hope.'

'No, it was a neighbour, as far as I've been led to believe.'

My shoulder twitched, which I interpreted as a sign of stress. This was not a case I was looking forward to. 'Let me repeat your words, Nils. This is a trivial matter.'

He clenched his lips and eyed me thoughtfully before continuing. 'We live off trivial matters, Varg. The big cases we take to court.' As I said nothing, he added: 'Don't tell me you don't need the money!'

I didn't tell him I didn't need the money. We agreed that I would take the job. I noted down the name and the address of the people I was to investigate. The police officer, who had served in Bergen, was called Sturle Heimark and, according to Åkre, he was divorced and had no children. His girlfriend in Fusa was called Nora Nedstrand. Heimark was in his early sixties, his girlfriend around fifty. We signed the requisite papers, and I arranged for Åkre to transfer an advance to my bank account, which at the moment was emptier than a football stand on Christmas Day. I stuffed the papers in my inside pocket, thanked Nils, went downstairs, outside and over to the closest bus stop to wait for the next bus back into town.

I tried not to think about it, but the answer was remorseless. If I was going to Fusa the following day I would have to get off the booze as quickly as I jumped on the bus when it appeared.

8

A Toyota Corolla is a patient friend. Even if the owner has barely been in a state to drive more than a couple of times over the last six months, she waits patiently by the kerb in Øvre Blekevei. As soon as I get in and twist the key she starts without a murmur – not so much as a sigh of relief at finally getting some exercise.

The day after my visit to Nils Åkre the clouds had drawn in from the west, the way salmon return to the river of their youth after being away for months. But the thermometer showed around five degrees, so any precipitation would be rain and not snow, which was a plus because I hadn't had any winter tyres put on since my last outing.

The shortest route to Fusa was via Os and the ferry between Hatvik and Venjaneset – a trip that took around twelve minutes; just enough to stretch your legs, go to the toilet or have a quick cup of coffee if you were at the front of the queue. I stayed in my car, examining the notes I had made after meeting Nils Åkre. I noticed I was out of practice and unsure how to tackle the matter. But the advance brought with it obligations, even if in the course of the morning it had disappeared into the payment market of the sky, and I would never see it again. By the time I drove ashore in Venjaneset and passed the large industrial plant by the quay I wasn't much the wiser. And it had started raining.

At the first crossing I drove left to Strandvik, turned into the car park by the local supermarket and took out the road atlas. After studying it I set off again, along Fusa Fjord. On the opposite side I looked across to Osøyro and the stretch of coast between Solstrand and Hatvik, where Mount Møsnuken towered above all the other mountains. According to my notes, Nora Nedstrand had a 1980s detached house. The landmark I had to keep an eye open for was the closest neighbour – a largish building that had previously belonged to a fishing equipment company, now disused and taken over by a local firm importing computer products.

I was there in no time. For some reason I had what was unpleasantly reminiscent of heart palpitations, and my mouth was so dry I cursed myself for not buying a bottle of water at least. I drove as far along the kerb as I could and sat pondering my next move.

The large building had been white twenty years ago. Now the paint was peeling and revealed the greyish-brown woodwork beneath, scarred by the ravages of time, like a stuffed animal. The half-erased name of the original business was still legible at the front: NEDSTRAND FISHING EQUIPMENT A/S. There was a big, blue van parked by the entrance, and a couple of young men were carrying piles of cardboard boxes from the vehicle. They stopped and looked suspiciously in my direction. In town you could pull into the pavement and sit in your car without anyone batting an eyelid. In the country, you stood out like a snail on a racecourse, and not many would risk a bet on you.

I got out of my car, locked it, pretended I hadn't seen them and headed for the green post box that signalled the entrance to the neighbouring building – a grey timber house with a white plinth and a well-established white-cedar hedge to discourage prying passersby. From the corner of my eye I saw the young men by the blue van exchange a few words before continuing to unload.

I checked the name on the post box. The only word there was 'Nedstrand', but that definitely indicated I was in the right place. I looked towards the house. There were lights on in several of the windows. So I shrugged and ambled up the gravel drive lined by rhododendrons and other bushes, speculating which approach I should adopt: the smart one or the stupid one.

To the right of the house there was a garage with the door open, and I saw the front of a popular 4x4 there, a dark-grey Mitsubishi Outlander. The registration number tallied with the number I had been given by Nils Åkre.

The woman who opened the door when I rang the bell was one

of the fairly large kind, with generous curves from the neck down, attractively arranged and camouflaged behind a flowery dress with a dark-blue base, slightly flared at the knee in a way that seemed a tiny bit old-fashioned. Unless it was this year's fashion; I had long given up following trends. She had thick, red hair, combed back and held in place on both sides with dark-green slides before cascading in curls halfway down to her shoulders. 'Yes?' she said, looking at me enquiringly.

'My name's Veum.' I shot a glance over her shoulder, but all I could see was a dimly lit hall and half a wardrobe mirror. 'I was wondering … Are you Nora Nedstrand?'

'Yes?'

I indicated the neighbouring building. 'Do you have anything to do with Nedstrand Fishing Equipment?'

She looked at me blankly. 'It was closed down many years ago.'

'Yes, that's what I thought. You don't know where the owners are?'

She made a tiny moue with her full lips to tell me how sad it was to be asked about precisely that. 'Yes, I do.'

'And…?'

'That is to say … one died exactly five years ago. The other last week.' Without my asking, she added: 'The first was my husband, Oliver. He built up the business together with our neighbour, Knut Kaspersen, whom we accompanied to his resting place just before the weekend.'

'I see. Have you taken it over then?'

'Didn't you hear what I said? The business was closed down many years ago. Oliver and Knut went into fish farming, and that was a lot better, but when Oliver died, I sold my equity interest to Knut and since then have lived off—'

She was interrupted by a voice from inside. 'Who are you talking to, Nora?'

'To…' She looked at me with a vacant expression.

'Veum,' I repeated, with a little smile.

The man who appeared beside her had a lean, vulpine face with a broad forehead, a narrow chin, a high hairline and brownish hair dotted with grey. He was wearing dark-blue jeans, a red-and-white-checked shirt and a worn, brown leather waistcoat.

His eyes narrowed when he saw me. 'What was the name, did you say?'

'Veum,' I said for the third time, and now I had to make an admission. I had chosen the stupid approach.

'Veum? Not as in Varg Veum, I trust.'

I met his gaze. 'Yes.'

He half turned to his partner. 'What did you tell him?'

She appeared even more confused. 'Told him? He asked me about … Oliver.'

'About Oliver!'

'No, I didn't,' I intervened. 'I asked her about Nedstrand Fishing Equipment.'

'Yes, that's right. It was me who…' she gulped and nodded '…mentioned Oliver.'

'Just get back inside, Nora. I'll take care of this.'

She glanced quickly at me and back to him. Then she nodded and, with a gentle ripple under her dress, disappeared from view.

The man I assumed to be Sturle Heimark stepped outside and scrutinised me with such intensity that I automatically retreated a pace, and he partly closed the door behind him.

'I know who you are, Veum. What do you want?'

'You know what I want, don't you?'

He stared at me hard without answering.

'Or have you got so many?' As he still didn't answer I added: 'Creditors, I mean.'

His eyes narrowed to such an extent that I could hardly see the blue irises. 'If someone wants something from me they'll have to write me a letter. I don't talk to the likes of you.'

'Don't you?'

'No.' He came even closer, and I retreated another pace. In the sitting-room window I could make out the figure of Nora Nedstrand, who was looking down on us, following what was happening.

'You say you … I can't remember ever meeting you.'

'And I'm grateful for that. But don't let that fool you. If I see you here one more time I'll ring my ex-colleagues and have them deal with you.'

'Because I came here asking questions?'

He continued his step-by-step advance, but this time I held my ground, so close to him now that I could smell the snus under his lip. In the window Nora put her hand to her mouth as if to stifle a cry.

'Because you're risking a beating, Veum. I know all the tricks and I won't hesitate to use them. You've got nothing on me and if you come here threatening me once more … well, I can't vouch for the outcome.'

'No, very few can. OK … I'll report back to my employer and say it was impossible to talk to you. Perhaps they'll send a more threatening messenger next time. Pay your debts in the meantime, Heimark, and everything'll sort itself out, you'll see.'

With these doubtful and aphoristic words, which would never end up in a book of quotations, I made a quiet retreat down their drive, waved goodbye and see you again to his girlfriend on the first floor and felt his eyes on my back all the way past the post box to my car. I stood looking at him until he made a lunge with his shoulders, turned, went in and slammed the door behind him, as if to emphasise what he felt like doing to me…

Don't bother coming back, Veum. Thank you kindly, and the same to you, Heimark.

But I didn't drive away. Not at once.

9

I got into the car and jotted down the information Nora Nedstrand had given me. As I wrote I heard the sound of a car door slamming. When I looked up I saw the two young men who had been carrying boxes into the old building coming towards me with, for the circumstances, pretty determined expressions on their faces.

I buzzed down the window on my side. Once they reached me they stayed about a metre away.

They were dressed in a practical way: jeans and short leather jackets. The older one had short, dark hair, prominent eyebrows, a set jaw and a smooth appearance. But for his clothes, he could have been an estate agent. The other one was taller, heavier and broader, with close-cropped hair as well, but blond, and he had two- or three-day stubble, not necessarily for cosmetic reasons.

The smooth one spoke. He was clearly from Bergen. 'And what might you be doing, if I may ask?'

I made eye contact. 'And who might be asking?'

They exchanged glances. The same man answered: 'We asked first.'

'I've been talking to your neighbours.' I tossed my head backwards to the house. 'Now I'm making some notes about our conversation. What business is that of yours? This is a public thoroughfare, as far as I'm aware.'

He deliberated. 'We had the impression you were a little too interested in what we were doing.'

'You've definitely made me curious now. Have you got guilty consciences?'

'No, but we … You never know who might … We've learned to be on our guard.'

'Sounds like a useful rule of thumb. Shall we say that's the end of our conversation?'

His friend shifted from one foot to the other, and I saw him lean slightly forwards, ready for action should it be required.

The more eloquent one tightened his lips in something resembling a smile. Then he shrugged. 'Sorry. Don't take it personally.' He nodded to the second man and they moved off the road and gesticulated that I could go. I noticed them make a note of my registration number – at least a mental note. I wasn't convinced they would remember it thirty seconds later; that kind had their own problems.

I spent a bit of time pretending I had more to write down. Then I stuffed my notepad in my inside pocket, with the biro, and searched for a new station on the radio before slowly setting off and waving casually as I passed them. In the rear-view mirror I could see them watching me until I was out of sight. I guessed they would be listening to make sure I didn't stop straight after the bend.

Fusa Church was situated on the Opsalnes headland, and I turned off the main road to go there. In front of the old cemetery, right down by the sea, there was an information board. I got out of the car and studied the notices. The Church Office was in Eikelandsosen and the resident chaplain's name was Per Lillegate. If I wanted to talk to him I could go via Samnanger on my way back to Bergen.

Eikelandsosen is set in an idyllic location at the end of Eikeland Fjord, surrounded by lush pastures and a view inland of Hålands-dalen, with the skiing centre and fishing lakes. It was February-quiet as I parked by the two-storey yellow building bearing the name 'Fjord'n Senter', which, as well as containing various shops, housed several council department offices. A board informed me that the Health and Social Security Dept, Fusa Police Station and the Church Office could be found on the first floor of the mall.

I was there during the stipulated working hours, and Per Lille-gate looked as if he was happy to have a break from staring dismally at his computer screen. His appearance suggested he was the type to hurdle any gate, big or small: He seemed youthful, athletic, ready for a triathlon. The hair around his ears was close-shaven, and the top of his head was shiny and polished, perhaps to reduce any wind resistance.

I said my name, but not my profession, and enquired if he had offici-ated at the funeral of Knut Kaspersen before the weekend.

'Yes. How can I help you?'

'Well, I was just wondering if you could give me any further details.'

'I don't quite understand.'

'Well…' I crossed my fingers – it seemed somehow appropriate. 'I'm a private investigator, and a case has happened to lead me here. My investigation, in fact, concerns his neighbours, but there were business links a few years earlier, and I understand the neighbours came back from Spain for the funeral.'

He inclined his head. 'Yes, that's correct. There weren't many people present, I'm afraid. A few old acquaintances from the village, but Kaspersen had been a bit of a loner, and there was no-one from his family to say a few words, so it was actually *fru* Nedstrand I spoke to for some guidance for my commemoration speech. I assume that's what you're referring to.'

'Yes.'

'His death was a tragic accident, by the way.'

'Oh, really?'

'You didn't hear? It was in the newspapers. He drowned when he fell off his boat while fishing; with the temperature of the fjord now, the fall was fatal. But it took them a day to find him, with the aid of frogmen. He wasn't far from his fish farm.'

'I see. Who'll take it over now?'

'Well, you tell me. I think the closest relative is a nephew, Svein Olav, who runs some kind of business up in the old, disused building.'

It was beginning to dawn on me what he was talking about. 'Some kind of business?'

'Yes, something to do with computers.' He cast a desperate glance at his screen. 'Not my *métier*, as they say in *nynorsk*.'

'Nor mine,' I said in complete sympathy.

'But there was nothing suspicious about the accident, I've been told.'

'No? What about … Did she give you any guidance for your speech?'

'*Fru* Nedstrand? Nothing much. I had the impression her late husband and Kaspersen had more to do with each other.' He gazed into the middle distance. 'That was a personal tragedy as well.'

'You mean … Oliver Nedstrand?'

'Yes, he took his own life.' His eyes met mine. 'Experiences like that leave deep scars, Veum. Finding your husband hanging from a tree behind the house.'

'But that was … five years ago, wasn't it?'

'Yes, but you never quite get over something of this nature. I can vouch for that, as a priest. It's not the first suicide I've experienced and it probably won't be the last.'

'Now at least they'll be laid in consecrated ground,' I commented.

He sighed. 'Yes, thank God. We're not so fundamentalist any more.'

'Nevertheless, it sounds pretty dramatic – two deaths in such close succession.'

'Well. There are not a lot of neighbours to choose from around here, and one is a personal tragedy, the other an unusual accident, so…' He shrugged. 'I don't quite know what you wanted to hear, but have I been of any help?'

'At least you've given me something to chew on,' I said.

Before I left Eikelandsosen I treated myself to a cup of coffee and two halves of a roll topped with brown cheese at the café in the mall. The only other customers were a handful of elderly gents sitting at a corner table and chatting, as far as I could hear, about this, that and ice jigging on Lake Skogseid.

Yes, he had definitely given me something to chew on, good old Per Lillegate. It struck me that Sturle Heimark was not the only person I should investigate; if for no other reason than to have something else to occupy my mind than thoughts about Karin and how much I missed her.

I drove along the still-narrow, bendy road between Eikelandsosen and Tysse until the roads became more driver-friendly; the last stretch through Åsane was like a motorway. Back home in Skansen, I parked the car in Øvre Blekevei, walked down to Telthussmuget, poured myself a glass of aquavit and found enough bacon, eggs and chives for an edible omelette, which I prepared as I worked my way down the glass. After eating at the kitchen table I refilled my glass, went into the sitting room and booted up the computer.

10

In a couple of online newspapers I found some articles about the death in Fusa Fjord the previous week, although I didn't glean any more than Per Lillegate had told me. A sixty-five-year-old man, who hadn't been seen since Friday evening, had been reported missing on Monday and was found drowned by the Venjanes headland on Tuesday morning. There was nothing to suggest there was anything suspicious about the death.

Sitting at my computer, I searched for the names I had jotted down on my notepad. Svein Olav Kaspersen, the nephew, appeared in an article in a local paper under the headline 'Local Entrepreneurs Invest in Fusa'. There was a photo accompanying the article, taken in front of the old Nedstrand Fishing Equipment building. I recognised Svein as the silent one of the two friends I had bumped into. Beside him stood the second one, named as Hjalmar Hope. Kaspersen wore a serious expression for the photographer, Hope the same taut smile he had shown earlier in the day. They said they were offering quick, efficient computer expertise with a special emphasis on business clients, but they were also equipped to take care of any private clients who might need their services.

Then I searched for 'Knut Kaspersen' and 'fish farming', but found nothing except the address: 5641 Fusa.

A search for Sturle Heimark produced some results from a fitness run he had taken part in; otherwise nothing. There were no hits for Nora Nedstrand, apart from on the tax list published annually in Norway, showing everyone's earnings. Hers were nothing special. No fortune, a modest income.

I tried a search for Hjalmar Hope, and there were several hits, most connected with computer news, none of them very interesting; but he had been associated with various firms – possibly the same one that had changed its name, or else different ones; it was hard to tell from what I found online. A couple of names of colleagues ran through some of the articles, and I took note of them as well, just in case, although I had no idea what use they would be for the job I was doing. I did confirm, however, that my innate curiosity was re-awakened, which I took as a sign of health and therefore did not resist.

After this I tried to concentrate on Sturle Heimark. One thing was certain. He didn't like visits, at least not from a private investigator of his acquaintance.

The simplest option was to ring someone who knew him from his time in the police. The most accessible officer on these occasions was Atle Helleve. He didn't exactly sound elated when I gave him a bell at half past eight in the evening, but both he and Hamre had treated me with kid gloves after the events of eighteen months ago, so he listened to what I had to say and seemed to take my question seriously enough.

'You know I can't say much about former colleagues, Varg.'

'Of course. I don't expect any more than a general impression. Was he reliable? Someone who stretched the bounds of legality in his area? Corrupt?' I could hear as I said this that the last question was off limits, blamed the aquavit and hastened to add: 'I know you can't answer the third question.'

'Correct.' He didn't sound particularly pleased to have to say any-thing at all. 'Can't say much about the second, either. I hardly knew him. He was mostly a traffic cop, and for a while was in uniform, whereas my bread and butter has been … well, you know.'

'But did you like him?'

'I didn't have any feelings about him. I didn't know him well enough for that. The only thing I can add is actually positive. Compared with many others of the same age group he was a computer whiz, so good that he held several courses for police colleagues.'

'I see.'

'And what is it that makes you so interested in him of all people, may I ask?'

'There was a death in Fusa Fjord at the beginning of last week.'

'Oh, yes?'

'A neighbour of this former colleague of yours. He drowned.'

'So?'

'Well.' This was my problem. I shouldn't ring someone like Helleve without being absolutely clear in my mind. 'I was wondering if you'd heard anything about it.'

He cleared his throat. 'No, I can't say I have, Varg. If it happened in Fusa the local police station would've investigated it, given due cause. I haven't heard anything at all about it. Can we knock this one on the head and say goodnight?'

'Yes, we can,' I mumbled. 'Goodnight,' I said, but he had already put the phone down.

I walked back into the sitting room and filled a kitchen tumbler full for the third time that evening. The bottle never rested until it was empty and then out came another, if I had one. Which I did, for the next day or two, but the future prospects were far from rosy, in many senses. I needed a more regular income than just the advance from Nils Åkre, and if I managed that I would have to keep my head above aquavit for a few more days before I dived down behind the colourful label again. Outside, the February rain beat against the window panes, and the night couldn't get much darker.

11

When I returned to Fusa two days later, the fjord lay still and pale – a reflection of the cloud cover above us, so high that there wouldn't be any rain for the next few hours, at least.

This time I drove past the old Fishing Equipment building and Nora Nedstrand's house, but slowly enough to confirm there was no sign of life anywhere. A couple of hundred metres further on there was what looked like a logging track into the forest. I turned in and parked the car by an old oak tree, well to the side so that a tractor would be able to get past.

I locked the car and followed the edge of the road back. Before reaching the end I slipped between the trees to try and get the best possible view of the house without being seen myself. The garage door was open this time as well, but the car was gone.

I walked back to the road, turned in by the post box, headed for the door and rang the bell. No-one answered. I walked backwards and looked up at the house front. Not a sign of life.

From where I was standing I could see the roof of the old timber building belonging to Nedstrand Fishing Equipment between the trees. There was a narrow, almost overgrown shortcut between the two properties, perhaps used by Oliver Nedstrand when he was alive and working there.

I walked in his footsteps. There was no car parked outside here either, no lights shone through the high windows, and the front door was closed and locked. Clear signs warned passers-by that the building had security alarms and closed-circuit TV. I looked up and nodded to myself. High under the ridge of the roof there was a camera, pointing at where I was standing, on the front doorstep. I waved pleasantly at it,

like a film star on their way up the red carpet for an award, but my time
was over, no flash lamps went off and no-one applauded.

I walked around the building and saw there was CCTV at the back
too. Of more interest was the path leading out. Between the trees I
could make out a small house overlooking the fjord. I walked towards it.

It was relatively well kept, older – probably dating back to before the
war – and painted in the same white as the timber building by the road.
There were curtains in the windows, and at the back I saw a little red
shack with a padlock. A green post box hung on the door and I read the
name on it: K. Kaspersen. But the deceased wasn't at home.

I strolled past the house. The path led down to the sea, where I saw
the pens of the fish farm. The surface of the water seethed. There was still
an abundance of life in the farm, whoever was taking care of the feeding.

Up by the road a car door slammed. I turned to see who it was. An
old boy in worn, blue overalls and a grey, woolly hat was shuffling down
towards Kaspersen's house. He quickly realised he had a visitor, stopped
in front of me and waited for me to say something.

'Hello, my name's Veum. I was wondering who took care of the
feeding now that Kaspersen's dead.'

'Mm, that's me,' he answered. 'Time being.' He saluted with two
fingers to his hat. His face was broad and good-natured, his skin marked
by a lot of outdoor life. At the corners of his mouth ran a thin line of
chewing-tobacco juice. 'Rasmus Lillegate.'

'Relative of the priest?'

He nodded. 'Yup, vaguely.'

'And you knew Kaspersen well, did you?'

'Nah. We went to school together and lived in the same village for
more than sixty years. But know him? I doubt anyone could say they
knew Knut.'

'No, I understood from Per, when I spoke to him a couple of days
ago, that he was a bit of a loner.'

'We-ell. He wasn't your village idiot, if that's what you think. He was
always well dressed and he shaved every single morning. If you met him
in the shop he was spotless, not a hair out of place. But he kept himself

to himself, or hung out with Oliver, while he was alive. After he passed on, life was probably a bit empty for him. It wasn't the same for that Nora, and when she got herself a new friend afterwards … Tragic what happened to him, though.'

'And now you feed the fish?'

'Yup, for as long as it lasts. But it seems like Svein Olav, his nephew, is going to take over.'

'Kaspersen drowned, didn't he?'

'Yeah.' Rasmus Lillegate gazed across the fjord, his face as expressionless as before. 'It was hard to understand. Would never have thought it could happen to such an experienced ol' bird.'

'Really?'

I waited for him to say some more, but all that came, after a long pause for thought, was: 'That's how it can go though. I dunno.'

'Right.'

'Well, nice to chew the fat. Best be gettin' down to the fish.' Again he saluted before trudging off down to the sea and spitting a long, brown arc of tobacco juice into the heather.

I stood watching him as he walked. He hadn't said much, but I was left with the clear impression that he wasn't at all convinced that Knut Kaspersen's death was an accident, either.

Then I turned around and walked back to the main road. As I passed the timber building, the big blue van drove in. Svein Olav Kaspersen, alone today, had hardly switched off the ignition before he jumped out and ran towards me.

'What the b-b-bloody hell are you doing here?' he stammered, gasping for air, like a freshwater trout coming up for insects. He had shaved since the last time we met, but with a shaky hand, judging by all the cuts.

'What do you know about your uncle's death?' I asked, following the old adage that attack is the best form of defence.

'Eh?' he said, open-mouthed. 'What are you talking about?'

'Such a seasoned boatman falling overboard and drowning – without any help?'

'Don't you dare start on me!' He came closer, brandishing his fists, but he wasn't violent, not yet. 'You'd be better off asking what that guy over there was doing in Norway when Uncle drowned! He was supposed to be in Spain!' He was pointing towards the neighbour's house.

'Sturle Heimark? Was he here that day … and then he went back?'

'You'd better ask him, I said!'

'Did you see him?'

'I saw him; yes, I did.'

'And why didn't you report it? To the local police, for example?'

'I don't talk to cops!'

'But you're the one who stands to inherit, aren't you? From your uncle.'

He didn't answer, just glared at me.

Behind his back I saw Nora Nedstrand's Mitsubishi pass and turn into the house. From the passenger seat she looked nervously in my direction.

'I'll do what you said, Svein Olav. I'll ask him face to face.'

'Doubt you'll get an answer,' he muttered by way of a conclusion, lowered his fists, turned around and walked towards the front door, searching his pockets for the keys.

'Worth a try though,' I mumbled, and set off.

12

Nora Nedstrand and Sturle Heimark were lifting heavy shopping bags from the car as I turned into the gravel drive up to her house. When he spotted me, Heimark put down the bags he was holding so suddenly there was an angry clink.

'Careful,' I said. 'Something might break.'

He rushed towards me while she stayed by the car, watching. 'Yes, you, for example,' he barked. 'Didn't I make myself clear two days ago?'

I applied the same approach as I had with Svein Olav Kaspersen. 'And what were you doing here the day Knut Kaspersen died?'

That stopped him in his tracks. His eyes narrowed, as on the previous occasion. 'Here? What are you talking about?'

'Don't try and talk your way out of it. You were seen.'

'Seen? Who by?'

I didn't answer.

'In which case they're lying!'

'I would assume the opposite would be documented. Return flight from Spain over a day or so? It must be registered. And what was the point of the visit? Flowers needed watering, did they?'

Behind him I could see Nora Nedstrand had taken in what I said. Now she moved closer, with a tense expression on her face. She was wearing an Easter-yellow waterproof that went well with her red hair.

'What's he talking about, Sturle?'

He half turned to her. 'Some bloody rubbish. He claims I was here the day Kaspersen died.'

She paled visibly. 'But that's … that's the weekend you were in Madrid, at the football match.'

'Exactly.' He looked back at me. 'Real Madrid beat Malaga 1–0.'

'And who scored?'

'Erm … not one of the stars. It was … Zarate.'

'You could've learned that off by heart, Heimark. As a policeman, you know all about alibis. Have you got the ticket too, perhaps?'

'Probably. In a pocket, in Spain.'

'Shame you didn't think to bring it with you in case someone asked.'

'And who would that someone be?'

I shrugged. 'The police maybe.'

'Sturle!' Her voice was sharper now. 'He's only bluffing.'

Again he half turned to her, but without making eye contact. 'Of course he's bluffing! What would I travel back here for, just for one day?'

I took a step to the side and looked at her instead. 'Can *you* answer that? Was there any motive for him to wish Knut Kaspersen dead?'

Her mouth opened, closed and opened again. 'Knut and I, we…'

'Yes?'

This time he turned round completely. In a threatening voice he said, 'Nora!'

Her eyes flitted between me and him. In the end, they fixed themselves on me. 'Knut and I knew each other from way back…'

Heimark half turned to me again, hunched his shoulders and thrust out his arms. 'Neighbours, right? What the hell do you hope to achieve with this, Veum?'

I glanced at him then faced her again. 'How way back?'

'We grew up here. He was a few years older than me, but … And he always kept himself to himself.' Her tongue seemed to be loosening now. 'There was something very special about Knut. He always looked good, well turned out, and he read … poems. Olav H. Hauge and suchlike.'

Heimark snorted.

I quickly read between the lines. 'You were fascinated by him, weren't you?'

'Yes…'

'But it was Oliver you married?'

'Yes, he was kind of more direct, he took what he wanted, if I can put it like that. When I fell pregnant it was clear … it would be him and me.'

'I can't understand how you can blather on about all this, Nora, in front of this … halfwit!'

I ignored him. 'But you retained your warm feelings for Knut?'

'Yes, I … did.' Her eyes were shiny, and she tossed her head, swinging her red hair.

I couldn't help but be reminded of what Per Lillegate had told me: that Oliver Nedstrand had taken his own life. Did a motive for suicide lie here? I wasn't sure how far I could go, especially with Heimark present. 'In a sense, if these feelings were still the same, there's a conceivable motive here.'

'A motive for … what?'

'What happened to your husband five years ago?' I waited for a reaction and read her face: a mixture of nervousness, fear and a guilty conscience. 'And what happened just recently, to Knut Kaspersen.'

She looked at me in astonishment. 'Knut? Oh, no, no, no!'

'No?'

'They had diminished over the years.'

'Your feelings?'

'Yes.'

'But they hadn't disappeared?'

'No.' She sent Heimark a despairing glance. 'Not completely.'

He drew himself up to his full height, but I noticed he was a lot less overbearing than he had been at the beginning of this conversation. 'Well, I don't see that this has anything to do with you, Veum. We're not doing much more than making the most outrageous allegations, that's all. I'd strongly advise you not to take them any further. If you do, you might have reason to regret your actions.'

'Are you threatening me?'

'I'm warning you. Don't do anything unless you're a hundred-percent certain what the consequences will be. If you understand what I mean.'

'Not completely, but I'll make a mental note of it, for the time being.'

'So this is goodbye.' He impatiently waved me on to the gate. 'Otherwise we'll be contacting the police and making a complaint about you, for breach of the peace.'

I smirked. 'I can see you feel confident you have everything under control, Heimark. People have made that mistake before. We'll talk again, you can be sure, in a day or three.'

'Not by choice.'

'Nor for me. Perhaps by lack of choice.'

We stood like that for a few more seconds. Nora Nedstrand wiped her eyes, then walked back to the car and the plastic bags waiting for her. Sturle Heimark sent me a final warning glare and followed suit. I stood like an abandoned scarecrow until they had carried all their shopping into the house and I was left alone with difficult questions of my own: where Sturle Heimark had been ten days ago, and who had scored for Real Madrid on the Friday Knut Kaspersen drowned in Fusa Fjord.

13

Arriving at Fjord'n Senter for the second time in a couple of days, I almost felt at home there. I noticed the same group of old boys sitting at the corner table in the café and got a friendly nod from the woman behind the counter, who had freshly made *sveler*, Norwegian pancakes, on a dish in front of her. Tempting – both her and the pancakes.

I took the stairs up to the first floor and found my way to the police office, next door to Per Lillegate. The priest and the police weren't far apart here if you had a complaint.

Behind a counter and a glass partition sat a young woman tapping away on a keyboard. She looked up as I entered, got to her feet and opened a hatch in the partition. I introduced myself and asked if the Chief was in.

'I'm afraid not. He's at a meeting in Bergen today. But you can talk to one of the officers.'

She opened the door beside the counter and let me through. In one of the offices with a view of the car park sat a uniformed officer with curly fair hair, youthful pimples on his forehead and the appearance of someone who had just left police college. When I entered the room he put aside the folded newspaper he had in front of him, but not quickly enough; I just caught sight of the crossword he was working on. That seemed to be in line with the crime rate in Fusa on a Thursday in February. It was probably busier at the weekend, when there was a dance at the local community centre and people travelled in from all the surrounding villages.

We made our introductions. His name was Petter Larsen, and when he spoke it transpired that he was an Østlander, from the east.

'Yes?' he said. 'Is there anything I can help you with?'

I wasn't convinced he could, but presented the case as well as I was able. I told him about the ostensibly accidental drowning in Fusa Fjord, and he nodded in recognition. When I enquired whether they had investigated the case he replied that they hadn't, beyond the routine procedures. He had himself spoken to the Fire Service's team of divers who had found the deceased, and there had been no suggestion of anything suspicious about the death.

'So you left it at that?'

'Well, the case wasn't deemed a priority,' he mumbled, stealing a glance at the unfinished crossword.

'And you didn't talk to any of the neighbours?'

'Not beyond routine procedures,' he repeated like a kind of mantra.

'Who reported him missing?'

He looked at me blankly. 'I'm afraid you'll have to wait a minute while I find out.' He swivelled the chair and roused his computer from its slumbers.

He scrolled down the screen, tapped a few keys and seemed a great deal more confident when he spoke. 'Here we are. It was one of the neighbours, it appears. Rasmus Lillegate. He hadn't had any contact with the deceased – hadn't seen him for several days – so went to his house and became worried when he saw his boat wasn't moored. Then he got in touch with us.'

'And you organised a search?'

'Yes, together with Search and Rescue and eventually the Fire Service in Bergen.'

'When he was found were there no signs of … no external signs of violence? Had he been held underwater or anything like that?'

He had started to become curious now. 'No, nothing. But the water was cold. You don't survive for long in such temperatures if you can't get ashore or back into the boat.'

'And if someone shoved him overboard … ?'

He had turned round from the computer now. 'Do you have anyone in particular in mind?'

'In my opinion, you should do at least two things …'

'Yes?'

I nodded to the notepad he had on the side of the desk. 'Perhaps you could take notes?'

He nodded, moved the pad and grabbed the biro he had been using to solve the crossword.

'There are at least two people you should talk to. One is Kaspersen's nephew, Svein Olav Kaspersen. He has a business near his uncle's and is, from what I've been told, the sole heir.'

He nodded and scribbled.

'The other is a neighbour, Sturle Heimark. I suspect there may have been some entanglement between him and Kaspersen, without wishing to go into too much detail. But let's say it's about a woman: Heimark's partner, Nora Nedstrand.'

He was taking enthusiastic notes now.

'If I were you I'd examine Kaspersen's boat for fingerprints, among other things. It's not so unlikely that you'll find the nephew's. But if you find Heimark's I would be suspicious. Then I think I'd bring him in for a little chat.'

He finished off his notes. Then looked up at me. 'Fine. I'll discuss this with the senior officer when he's back.'

'And then?'

'Well.' His eyes roamed around. 'Then it's up to him, of course, to make a decision.'

I took out my business card. 'He can find me here, if he wishes to take the case further.'

He held it in his hand, read it and looked up again. 'Private investigator?'

I smiled wryly. 'Wouldn't recommend it if you were thinking along those lines. You're better off where you are, becoming a crossword expert.'

He blushed like a teenage girl on her first date. Then he answered curtly: 'As I said, I'll bring this to the attention of the senior officer.' Without further ado he turned to his computer and pretended to be busy with something or other.

I leaned over his desk, peered down at the crossword and said: 'Doctrine? Could be thesis.'

As he didn't answer I wished him a pleasant day and the same to the young woman at reception. Downstairs in the café I allowed myself to be tempted and ordered a cup of coffee, accompanied by two of the fresh pancakes with raspberry jam and a sweet smile from the woman behind the counter. Both were so warming that I walked to the car park in a much better mood and drove back home to Bergen in an elated frame of mind. Sometimes that was all it took.

I heard nothing from the Fusa Chief of Police, and a week later, now one of the first days in March, I took the initiative and called him.

'Klyve here,' the Chief said when I was put through to him.

'Veum,' I said. 'I'm ringing regarding the case I spoke to your officer about last week.'

'Yes, I made a note of that. Knut Kaspersen.'

'Have you got any further with it?'

I heard the sound of documents in motion. Klyve belonged to the paper generation and didn't trust the computer screen's captivating reality. While searching he answered: 'Yes, we've done some investigation work. It was you who suggested we look for fingerprints on his boat, wasn't it?'

'Yes.'

The piles of paper fell silent. 'Yes, here it is. Well, we did. Don't tell me we don't respond to requests.'

No, I wouldn't do that, not on this occasion anyway.

'But we didn't find any. Apart from the deceased's, mostly. The others were so faint they were impossible to identify; and as for the two people you'd said we should concentrate on … no matches there either.' For some reason he was chuckling.

'Something funny?'

'No, no, not really. But they weren't very happy to see us. It turned out … You didn't mention that one of them was a former colleague of ours. His prints were in our police files, of course. When we spoke to him he didn't have very nice things to say about you, Veum.'

'No, I can imagine.'

'The other one refused to give us any prints at first.'

'You mean Svein Olav, the deceased's nephew?'

'Yes. He'd got it into his head that you'd tipped us off, so you're warned. We'll have a closer look at him, but in a different context.'

'I see.'

'I don't know how much I should tell you, but, as he kicked up such a fuss about having his fingerprints taken, we went to the trouble of getting a search warrant for his business, and I think I can say that his accounts were extremely dubious. As was the documentation for the provenance of the immense stock of computer equipment he had. In short, that case is still under investigation.'

'And what did you mean by "you're warned"?'

'I can't rule out the possibility that we're talking here about, at best, receiving stolen goods or, at worst, the illegal acquisition of computer goods.'

'And that means break-ins and theft?'

'For example. And in such circles they have their own form of justice, as I'm sure you know. So if I were you I wouldn't go down any dark alleyways or back streets in the near future, and if you should see young Kaspersen or any of his pals there, I would turn around on the spot and leg it.'

I felt an unease spread through my chest and said: 'Are you saying I need police protection?'

Again he chuckled. 'If so, you'd have to take that up with my colleagues in Bergen. But thanks anyway for your help, Veum. We need alert civilians in our society too.'

I guessed his calling me a civilian was not chance. 'And you're not going to take the drowning any further?'

'Unless something new crops up, I think you can regard that case as shelved.'

The following day I rang Nils Åkre and told him about my failed attempt to make Sturle Heimark pay what he owed, and I recommended he send a heavier heavy next time. We agreed that the advance covered the expenses I'd had and so that matter was shelved too, at least in my office.

Two or three weeks later, what the Fusa og Tysnes Chief of Police had prophesied came true. After a two-day beano I ended up in bad company in one of the town's back streets and was beaten up so viciously that it took me several days to struggle to my feet. When they had finished the brutal going-over, I received one last kick to the ribs, and one of the assailants leaned over, exhaled bad breath into my face and said: 'Greetings from Fusa, Veum.'

With the greeting came two massive black eyes that took two weeks to lighten enough for me to be able to pass children on the pavement on the way to my office without frightening the life out of them. I had hoped that was the end of it, but now – two and a half years later – I was not so sure it was.

14

The heavy cell door yawned open. I blinked and saw Johnsen, the warder, letting Vidar Waagenes back in. In one hand he was holding a plastic bag bearing the name of one of the town's most reasonable clothes shops.

He lifted up the bag to show me. 'These clothes will suit you well, Veum.'

'If you could get me out of this nightmare, that would suit me better.'

He smiled encouragingly. 'All in due course. Initially we have the hearing. When we know the result of that we can start the wheels turning. I've already been in contact with a computer expert I use on such occasions: Sigurd Svendsbø. I'm going to demand a complete copy of both your hard drives so that Sigurd can go through them with a fine-tooth comb and see whether there's anything we can find out.'

I nodded.

'Have you remembered anything in the meantime?' He pointed to my notepad, which lay next to me on the bench.

'I've made some notes and written down a few names. But there's bound to be more out there in the mists. As I said earlier today, these last three or four years haven't been good for me.'

'It's definitely too early to take this any further now, but as soon … when the hearing's over we'll know more about where we stand.'

Suddenly I felt immensely tired. Any expectations of a positive outcome from the hearing had long since evaporated. As Waagenes started taking out the clothes he wanted me to wear I was reminded of my early childhood and my first day at school, when my mother had done the same.

Afterwards I felt like an unwilling bridegroom who was to be presented to the magistrate with his future spouse, to be given a life sentence with only very limited opportunities of appeal, at least for the first part of the term. I could hardly squeeze into the grey trousers he had bought and I gave up on the button on the waistband. I didn't feel very comfortable in the matching jacket either, but the shirt was alright, so long as I didn't do it up the whole way, which I never did when I wore a tie. Of course, he had bought one of those as well. It had a discreet, grey-and-black checked pattern and wouldn't have looked out of place at a funeral; very suitable in other words.

Waagenes went through the court procedure point by point, and I nodded my head in acknowledgement at each one. After all, I had attended a few over the years, sitting in the audience.

'But this will be in camera, as requested by the police and out of consideration for the ongoing investigation.'

'Fine by me,' I sighed. 'So there'll be no press either?'

'There are no reports taken of the hearing, but there'll be enough scribbling. The first articles have appeared in online papers, so…' The dot-dot-dot was in his eyes as he looked at me.

Before we were transported to the Law Court I was handcuffed. In the backyard we were led into the police vehicle that would take us through Bergen, but from the side street next to the Law Court, named after an old tavern – Fortunen – it was open season for anyone who wanted to see the unfortunates being led to an uncertain fate.

Luckily there was limited attendance in the courtroom. Beatrice Bauge greeted us in measured tones from her position on the left of the room. On the bench beside her sat Hamre, stony-faced. The atmosphere was strained, tense, and it didn't get much better when the judge entered, closely followed by a registrar who would take the minutes, as Waagenes explained to me discreetly in one ear.

Everyone stood up. The female judge, her hair well groomed, nodded graciously to us all, and we sat down. After some introductory remarks about the nature of the case, she gave me a stern glare over her glasses and said: 'Do you plead guilty?'

I shook my head. 'No.'

'Then I'll have to ask Barrister Beatrice Bauge to present the prosecution case.'

Which she did, briefly and to the point. The case had international ramifications, it was still being investigated, and for this reason it was of immense importance that the accused was held in custody, initially for a period of four weeks, and that access to visitors or mail should be denied.

The judge nodded sympathetically and asked if the defence had anything to add.

Waagenes rose to his feet and said the accused refuted the charge, rejected any possible association with it and was innocent. He therefore asked for him to be set free with immediate effect. Then he added: 'But should the court come to the contrary conclusion, I will have to insist – further to my legal right to visit the accused in custody – on permission to take with me a computer expert, for whom I can vouch, since some insight into this particular field of knowledge could have substantial significance for how we tackle the case. In addition, we must seek from the court a ruling that a complete copy of the contents of both hard drives seized by the police shall be supplied to us so that we may undertake an independent examination.'

The judge looked as if she had to ponder long and hard what he meant by that, and to be on the safe side she conferred with the registrar, a relatively young man, to be sure she had understood correctly.

'Do the police have any objections to the defence receiving these copies?' she asked.

Bauge and Hamre conferred on the bench. They didn't appear to be wholly in agreement, but in the end Bauge gave in to Hamre, turned to the judge and said: 'No. We can accept that.' But she couldn't refrain from adding: 'The defence counsel has so few other pleasures in life.'

The judge sent her a sharp look. 'Spare me the levity in such a serious case. Has anyone else anything to add?'

No-one had, and she didn't spend long reaching a decision. She upheld the prosecution plea. The accused was to be held in custody for four weeks without mail or visitors. He would have restricted access to the press – all material surrounding the ongoing case was to be removed – but no access to the radio, TV or internet. The judge did, however, give permission to the defence counsel to take what she called the 'requisite expertise in computer matters' to meetings with his client. Afterwards she banged the table with her gavel, declared the session closed, got up and departed the courtroom, bearing a royal mien, followed with alacrity by her young registrar.

I slumped back down on the bench. Hamre made eye contact, gloomier than I could ever remember seeing him, while Beatrice Bauge tidied up her papers with an arrogant toss of her head in our direction.

I looked at Vidar Waagenes. He appeared to be more concerned than I would have liked, but when he noticed my gaze he straightened up, sighed and said: 'At least she supported us on one point. As soon as we have the copies I'll have Siggen get cracking. If there's anything to find, he's the right man, I can promise you that.'

I watched the police officers at the back of the room get up, one with handcuffs at the ready. 'What happens now?'

'Now I'm afraid Åsane is the next stop, Veum.'

'And I've always done my very best to keep a safe distance from IKEA.'

'OK, but we have to travel further than that, you know.'

He was right. I knew. As we passed IKEA on the way out, for the first time I felt a sudden urge to go shopping, but we continued on our inexorable journey to Bergen State Prison and the tall, grey walls that surrounded it, like concrete city ramparts in the wilderness between Haukås and Hylkje. Not a place you would wish to go. Not a place you would dream about if you weren't having nightmares and the alarm clock would soon be telling you it was morning and nothing dangerous had happened. But I wasn't so lucky. When the third iron gate clanged shut behind us there was no escaping. Good advice was expensive and my account had been empty for years.

15

During my first days in Åsane I was left in peace. As I was supposed to
know as little as possible about the ongoing investigation, I received
neither post nor visitors and was kept in isolation from the other
inmates. I had my food served in the cell and had access to the library
after normal opening hours. I grabbed a large number of books without
checking much, except to see whether I had read them before; there
were a couple I fancied re-reading. For one hour every day I was taken
to the exercise yard, accompanied by one of the warders. I could only
fantasise about what the police were doing in the meantime.

When I wasn't reading I paced the cell floor nervously. I peered
through the bars of the window to see what the weather was like; it
changed from sun to rain and back again with no effect on my mood
whatsoever. Low-pressure cyclones were queueing up in the cell.

My sole visitor, apart from the warders, was Vidar Waagenes. He did
what he could to cheer me up. At present they were waiting for the
copies of the hard drives to arrive so they could get started, but 'Siggen's
raring to go', as he put it. Also he had, at my request, had a long chat
with Sølvi and he brought her 'warmest wishes'. 'She's looking forward
to you getting out, Varg.' I was happy he used my first name. We were
on a personal level then. As soon as he switched to my surname, it was
formal, and that unsettled me.

I thanked him and asked him to ring her and say hello. 'I wish I could
talk to her myself.'

'Yes, I know. We'll have to see how long this is going to last. There's
no-one else you'd like me to contact?'

'There's my son and his family in Oslo. We don't talk a lot, but he
might be worried if he's tried to call me and I didn't answer the phone.'

I gave him Thomas's telephone numbers – mobile, home and the university – and he promised to take care of this as well.

'As my defence counsel, are you allowed to say anything about the case I can't read about?'

He gave an affirmative nod. 'But there's not much in the papers. No more than we already know. The press ban is just nonsense, but as the judge accepted it, there's not much we can do about that now.'

'My name hasn't been revealed?'

'No, no, not yet anyway. You're referred to as a man of fifty-nine from Bergen, and the same applies to the others: man (thirty-eight), Nordhordland; man (forty-seven), Bergen; and man (seventy-two), Bergen.'

'Wide age-range, in other words.'

'My guess is the police will confront you with some of these names when you're called in for an interview again.'

'Will you be present?'

'Naturally.'

After a short pause he resumed: 'Have you remembered any more people who may be harbouring a grudge against you?'

'No. I can't concentrate in here. But I'll try and pull myself together.'

'But you had remembered some, you said, last time we chatted?'

'Yes.' I told him about Sturle Heimark and my failed mission to Fusa. I also mentioned what I'd regarded as a suspicious death there and the possibility that both Heimark and the deceased man's nephew, Svein Olav Kaspersen, were in cahoots. I told him about the computer business owned by Svein Olav and his friend from Bergen, Hjalmar Hope, and what the Chief of Police in Fusa had said.

He noted down the names and said he would see what he could find out. 'That's good, Varg. Keep it up. Try and put everything else to one side and concentrate on this.' He deliberated, then added: 'If you need it, I can arrange for a visit from a doctor or a psychologist.'

I nodded. 'I'll try without first.'

'Fine.' He looked at the books on my table. 'You're getting stuck into some reading, I see.'

'Yes, and I'm getting a bit of exercise. With luck that'll keep me going until they realise what a dreadful mistake they've made.'

He smiled wanly. 'Good. I'll be back tomorrow, whether there's anything new or not.'

'Thank you.'

We shook hands, and he was conducted out of the cell. I heard the door being locked and stood staring at it. After a while I sat down on the chair in the bare interior. I turned to the table attached to the wall, took out my notepad and gripped the biro tightly, as though this ritual would facilitate searching back into the murk I had been stumbling around in for much too long.

The wall was an eggshell colour. I sat staring at it, trying to focus on the task Waagenes had given me. Gradually I felt the pressure lift from my shoulders and neck. My eyes lost focus, my eyelids half closed, and from my consciousness a scene appeared: one afternoon in early October two years ago, Nicolai S. Clausen visiting me in my office with an offer I should have turned down, bearing in mind the consequences.

16

When you receive a client it might be advantageous if you are as sober as possible. The well-dressed man in the grey suit and light-brown coat came in through the waiting-room door while I stood behind the desk with nothing to lean against. I motioned him to the client's chair and plumped down, a view of Mount Fløyen and Bryggen at my back, no other light in the room except for the desk lamp. If he had been sceptical at the outset he didn't seem reassured now.

He remained standing in the middle of the floor. After an inspection of the office he looked at me disapprovingly and said: 'Nicolai S. Clausen. I need a private detective. But I'm not convinced you're right for the job.'

I let that seep in and made another vague flourish towards the client's chair. 'Won't you sit down?'

He was around fifty years old with dark, wavy hair, brushed back, shiny, not the slightest hint of grey, which made me suspect some of the colour came from a bottle. His nose was long and straight, his eyebrows were arched and his eyes blue and sceptical. Under the suit he wore a white shirt, open at the neck, where you could glimpse some steel-grey masculine hairs that had not yet been dyed.

I was having trouble focussing. In an attempt to disguise what I had been imbibing I lunged at a tin of throat lozenges I had on the desk, took one myself and passed the tin to him. He stared at me with disdain, holding up both hands, as though I had offered him a deadly poison.

I closed the tin and put it back on my desk. At the same time I shifted a letter-opener to the pile of unopened window envelopes, as if opening them was the next point on the agenda.

Nicolai S. Clausen coughed impatiently. 'Erm, aren't you interested in hearing what my visit is about?'

'Yes, yes, of course,' I said, waving my right arm again. I used the other to maintain my balance on the chair.

'I need some discreet surveillance of my wife's movements on nights when I'm travelling; or at any rate when I'm busy with other matters and not at home.'

Almost on automatic pilot, I started to trot out my fixed rule never to take on such cases, but he interrupted me before I had got further than 'such cases'.

'And I'll pay well.' He glanced at the window envelopes with a sardonic expression. 'Probably a lot better than you usually earn.' He leaned forward. 'On condition that you bag a result.'

The window envelopes were like sirens; they lured you onto out-of-the-way paths and sent you crashing down cliffs as soon as they saw an opportunity. The sirens sang so beautifully in my head that I gave in without any substantial resistance. I took my notepad and pen and articulated as carefully as I could: 'Then I'll need some factual information about you and her.'

Nicolai S. Clausen was the owner of a company that specialised in financial advice: Nico Vest AS. His wife was called Åsne, and they had one child, a boy who was now fifteen. 'Yes, Åsne was no more than twenty when we met,' he added, as if that had any relevance. She worked for a computer firm in Sandsli – SH Data – as an office manager.'

'SH?'

'Yes, it's supposed to stand for Sherlock Holmes, a famous problem-solver. You may have heard of him.'

'Older colleague,' I mumbled, mostly to myself.

'Bit of a stretch, if you ask me.'

Clausen's own company had an office in Valkendorfsgate, and the family lived in Kalfarlien; neither of these addresses told me anything.

'And what makes you think your wife's … ?' I let the word hang in the air.

'Unfaithful? You just know, don't you?'

I shrugged, so imperceptibly it was hard to notice.

'I've noticed it in the way she behaves … sexually, if I can put it like that. And there are other signals.'

'Such as … ?'

'Well … she used to like coming on trips with me. Now she prefers to stay at home. If we're invited out somewhere – professionally, that is – she always asks if it's absolutely necessary. And then there are the phone conversations that suddenly stop when I appear. Things like that.'

'Well … in cases like these …' I sighed. 'You might …' I couldn't finish what I had intended to say. 'You need to give me more to go on. You said your wife's thirty-five or thirty-six. Did I understand you correctly?'

'That's correct. Thirty-six. We met when she was twenty and the following year we were married and … became parents. But we didn't have any more after him. Severin.'

'Your son's called Severin?'

'Yes. After his grandfather. My middle name.'

I mumbled as I wrote it down. 'Nicolai Severin Clausen.'

He glared at me. 'But this has nothing to do with the case!'

'No, it doesn't. It's just good to have all the details clear right from the word go.'

'Then I'll give you some more specific details. Tomorrow at lunchtime I'm going to London and I'll be there until Monday evening. Various meetings.'

'At the weekend?'

'In our line of work there are no weekends, Veum.'

I made a few illegible squiggles on my pad. 'I've made a note of that.'

He sent me an indulgent look. 'I'd like you to find out what Åsne does while I'm away and then report back when I contact you on Tuesday.'

I sighed. 'But then I need at least a photo of her. Have you got one?'

He put a hand in his inside pocket and took out a wallet that was so slim it suggested there were more cards than cash. He fished out a newspaper cutting and passed it across the table to me. 'I happen to have this.'

I looked at the cutting. It was an article about new appointments in the business sector. Åsne Clausen looked young and attractive, with a pronounced jaw and short, practical hair.

'Her hair's a bit different now. Longer fringe and a lighter colour.'

In this family they had 'his' and 'hers' bottles, I gathered.

'And how does she get to and from work?'

'She has a car. A red Toyota Yaris.' He gave me the registration number, and I wrote it down.

'So you think I should drive to Sandsli, park at a suitable distance and see what happens?'

He shrugged. 'Something like that.' He added, sarcastically: 'You're the pro.'

'I'd like to say that this is not what I do normally.'

He had taken a credit card from his wallet and held it in his hand. 'You're a private detective, aren't you? With a diploma and so on?'

'Diploma?'

'Obviously you don't have a sense of humour. How much do you want as an advance?'

I gulped. 'This'll take a few days.'

'Five thousand, is that enough?'

'And it's the weekend.'

He raised his eyebrows ironically. 'Then let's say ten. Have you got an account number you can give me?'

I took one of my business cards from the holder on the desk and passed it over to him. He put it in his wallet without even a glance.

'I'll transfer it from my laptop in my car. It'll be there in ten minutes.' He rose to his feet and buttoned up his jacket. 'I hope you understand this is not something I do with a light heart, Veum. Nothing would please me more than the result of your surveillance turning out negative.' He walked towards the door. 'You'll be hearing from me on Tuesday.'

'Have a good trip to London,' I mumbled.

As soon as he had gone I flicked through the pile of bills to see which needed paying first. From memory, ten thousand wasn't the biggest advance I had ever received, and it wouldn't take long to spend it. If nothing else, it deadened the bad conscience I already had about taking the job. But I carefully averted my eyes as I passed the mirror over the sink on my way out.

17

That night I drank only water. However, I still wasn't sure if I ought to be driving until well into Friday. Recently I had felt that there was more alcohol than haemoglobin circulating through my veins, and the red there was lay like a thin fruit soup over the whites of my eyes.

During the morning I tried to gather as much background information about Nicolai S. Clausen and his wife Åsne as I could. One of the searches revealed an article about their son, Severin: a newspaper interview discussing a middle school's early use of computers. Regarding the parents, I found out that Åsne's maiden name had been Kronstad. She was the daughter of Kåre Kronstad, a well-known name in Bergen shipping circles, who did a lot of business in the country, but less outside its borders. *Dagens Næringsliv* suggested Kåre had invested quite a lot of money in his son-in-law's company, Nico Vest AS, owning a shareholding of forty percent. I didn't find much else about Åsne I didn't know already from the text, accompanied by a photo, that Clausen had given me the day before. Although, from various fun-run race results, I gleaned she was an enthusiastic participant. Notably, she had run the uphill Stoltzekleiven Opp in under fifteen minutes, which I considered a very good time for a jogger. It would have taken me close on half an hour if I had tried, and that was on one of my better days.

In the end I contacted Geirmund Granerud, a peripheral acquaintance who had given up trying to sell shares to me, but who was chatty enough whenever we met. He didn't have much more to tell me than I already knew either. However, he said there were rumours in the business world that Nico Vest was being investigated by the Fraud Squad because there was some suspicion of insider dealing in connection with a large share issue earlier that year, but he didn't know how much truth there was in this. Nicolai Clausen was generally known as a cunning fox, he said, and someone who had 'married well'.

'And by that you mean … ?'

'He brought a name with him – from both of his grandparents – but moss had grown over the old money he represented. At the time it had been a smart move to marry Kåre Kronstad's only daughter and have a finger in the in-laws' financial pie.'

'So they didn't marry for love, is that what you're saying?'

'When did they ever, in those circles?'

'Well, you know more about that than me.'

'Nic isn't known as the kind to reject a woman who offers him the goods.'

'Really?'

'He's bound to have some skeletons in his cupboard. I bumped into him in New York once a couple of years ago; he was in the company of a very curvy so-called escort. And it didn't look as if it was international finance the two of them were discussing at the bar.'

'Hmm. Interesting.'

'But of course, don't quote me, Varg.' He already sounded as if he regretted what he had said.

'No, no. I'm as discreet as a Catholic priest.'

'That doesn't sound very reassuring any more.'

'You can trust me, Geirmund.'

'OK.'

If what he said was true, why was Nicolai S. Clausen so uneasy about what Åsne was doing while he was on his travels? Was it something to do with sauce for the gander being forbidden to the goose? Or was there something else behind it? Something to do with money?

'Kåre Kronstad, is he well off?'

'All things considered, yes. He's invested wisely and doesn't take great risks. His ships sail as they always have done, although not with the same profits, nor with a Norwegian crew, apart from the captain and a couple of the officers. Otherwise it's Poles and Filipinos. However, he has salted away a substantial part of his fortune in investments in oil, computer technology and other areas where the stock quote is still rising. No danger signals on the horizon, as far as I know.'

Armed with this I got into my car and drove to Sandsli well before the working day was over. I had found the address of SH Data in the Yellow Pages and had, as always, my road atlas with me, even though in this case it turned out to be unnecessary. SH Data shared the building with several other companies and the logo of the biggest one lit up half of the front wall, visible the second you turned in from Flyplassvegen.

I drove into the large car park and slowly passed the lines of vehicles until I found Åsne Clausen's gleaming-red Toyota Yaris. I cast around for an empty space not too far away and found three or four in the parallel line. So, I would have a good view of her car whenever she appeared. There was nothing else to do but switch off the engine, lean well back and unfold the first in the pile of newspapers I had bought. Experience is the best teacher. Surveillance jobs can soon become tedious, and it didn't take long before boredom became so overwhelming that it was hard to stay awake. On the seat beside me I had a little camera ready for use if need be.

Even though it was a Friday afternoon few people left their place of work until it was time in Sandsli. It was past four before anything started happening at all and the biggest rush came between half past four and five. By then it was difficult to distinguish one person from another, and I had to stare hard at the red car to make sure Åsne Clausen wasn't suddenly there and moving off.

I recognised one person: Hjalmar Hope, whom I had come across in Fusa six months before, was clearly still at large. He was chatting cheerfully with a colleague across a dark-blue version of the latest Audi, and there was nothing to suggest he had anything to fear, either from the authorities or from any other quarter. They finished their conversation, and Hope got into his car and reversed, while his colleague walked further down the lines to his own car.

Åsne wasn't on her own either when she rolled up at ten minutes to five. Her fringe might have been long and untidy, but it was the hair I recognised first, and then the face with the strong jaw. She was wearing a colourful jacket of twisted wool, with bright strands of red, blue and green, and elegant light-blue jeans. The man who was accompanying her was dressed in more everyday clothes – a short outdoor jacket, dark trousers and a grey scarf tossed casually over his shoulder. They walked together as far as her car and parted company without a hug or any other intimacy. After she got behind the wheel he continued down through the rows of cars. He had an idiosyncratic way of moving, a kind of jig with expansive arm movements, like a middleweight boxer on his way into the ring before a defining title match.

I glanced down at the camera. I hadn't decided on when to take a shot and when it was too late. That spoke volumes about how good I was at this work.

Her car turned out of the parking space. After a shortish wait I set off after her. I didn't want to have too many cars between us in the traffic hell customary at this time of day. At the roundabout by Flyplassvegen she indicated for the Bergen lane, and I moved up to two cars behind her. We dawdled along at a speed of ten to twenty kilometres an hour, and even more slowly as we approached Lagunen, which was reputed to be Hordaland's biggest shopping centre, surrounded by what seemed like boundless chaos. At a snail's pace we moved along what was supposed to be a motorway, but which, in fact, functioned as an airport travellator. Even at my age I could have run the same distance in half the time.

Sensibly, she turned off at Hop, drove down Storetveitvegen into town, turned off again at the end of Lake Tveite and entered Nattlandsveien, into the traffic leaving the centre. In the process we had lost the cars between us. If she looked into her rear-view mirror, we would have eye contact over a distance of less than five metres.

When she turned into Kalfarlien I decided to do the same, but then she pulled in to park, so I continued past without a glance in her direction. I parked on the slope where Forskjønnelsen met Leitet – two street names that told Norwegians something about classic urban renovation and old rural settlements on the mountainside above the town.

I strolled back, saw that she had left her car tucked nicely into the kerb and in the, approximately, hundred-year-old white building behind the hedge, glimpsed her fair hair as she shuttled backwards and forwards in what I assumed was the kitchen: straight from the computer industry to modern domestic service. I continued almost right to the end of Kalvedalsveien, where a lanky boy with a fashionable rucksack rounded the corner and passed me. I checked both directions, then turned round and walked back whence I had come.

The boy in front of me opened the gate and walked up the garden path of the same house that Åsne Clausen had entered. When I passed it this time he had already gone, and so had Åsne from the kitchen window. I was fairly confident this was Severin returning home from school.

At the end of Kalfarlien there are some narrow wooden steps going up to where you can follow a path leading to Leitet. I took them and went behind a bush for a pee. If there was one thing I disliked about jobs like this one it was the stress it put on the bodily functions of a man in his late fifties. But that wasn't what I disliked most. From the day I opened my agency in the mid-70s I had consistently rejected the so-called marital cases. The main reason had been that I considered such cases private, and the longer I could make ends meet without resorting to them, the happier I was. Now this time had clearly gone, creditors were more ruthless and ever-ready Varg was more ever-ready than he used to be.

In a way it made me feel like a beginner again. I was much more at home with cases where I could call on people, talk to them face to face and try to find out what was lurking behind their smooth facades. Actually I would rather have been investigating Nicolai S. Clausen, for example, in a business context.

But I had to be satisfied with the crumbs from the table. There wasn't much else I could do but get in the car, drive up to Leitet, turn round at the intersection there and drive back to Kalfarlien, where I shot into a free parking space – miraculously there was one – switch off the ignition and wait for something to happen.

Kalfarlien is not one of the town's busiest streets, even if there is a lot of traffic going to Skansen, through one of the gaps in the toll ring around Bergen. A lot of people walked as well, and sitting behind the wheel I felt as discreet as a modernist installation in a Munch museum.

Dusk turned to night. If this job was going to continue I would have to remember to bring sandwiches next time. My stomach had been rumbling for some time when mother and son appeared by her car. She sent a glance in my direction, then another, but she was too far away for me to be able to read her expression. Then they got in the car.

They drove down to Kalvedalsveien and turned right towards the centre. I followed them. Down the hill to Stadsporten, I was no longer in any doubt: now I saw her eyes in the rear-view mirror more times than traffic safety normally required. At Bergen Katedralskole she pulled in and dropped off her son. Luckily I had been held up by the lights at the Nygate crossroads, but I set off on green and turned into Lille Øvregate, which was the only option she had in this traffic lock step. She went down Øvre Korskirkeallmenning, left again into Kong Oscars gate, and was heading back home, for all I knew. But at Nygaten she took a right, and not long after we were going down Bryggen in convoy. We passed Bergenhus Fortress, the big Bergen Fiskeindustri building in Bontelabo, the old timber houses in Skuteviken and carried on. In Sandviksveien she suddenly pulled in and parked in front of the large brick building known locally as Sing Sing. I did the same, about twenty metres behind. She got out of her car, slammed the door and strode in my direction with her eyes firmly focussed on my windscreen.

I wound down the window on her side and tried to appear as innocent as a confirmand caught red-handed with a porn mag during high mass.

She leaned down, studied me and shouted: 'Who the hell are you? And what the fuck are you doing?' Hard to fault the eloquence of her vocabulary.

'Super Sleuth they call me,' I answered in my last attempt to be funny that month.

18

In my younger days I used to circle in red the days on the calendar when something nice happened. A first kiss, first sex and so on. At my current stage of life, my instinct was to put a black line through most of them. That Friday in October was a case in point. After the verbal assault by Åsne Clausen – I didn't offer a single protest or answer one of the questions she asked – I drove back home with my tail between my legs, feeling like Inspector Clouseau in *The Pink Panther*.

At home, I unscrewed the top of the half-full bottle of aquavit I kept in the kitchen cupboard for emergencies; there had been no shortage of them in the last year. Before the evening was over the bottle was empty and I didn't feel the slightest bit comforted.

The weekend was a struggle to get through. I managed to get down to the Vinmonopolet before they closed at midday on Saturday and breathed a sigh of relief that there was still enough money in my account to avoid my card being confiscated on the spot. I walked home and stayed there for the rest of the day and the whole of the following one. I had enough cans of food in the cupboard. It took me until Sunday evening to snap out of this mood, put trainers and a tracksuit on and do the Fjellveien trail – the whole way there and back, which was about eight and a half kilometres in total. After a long, hot shower I felt relatively restored, but not exactly ready for the following day.

I had barely entered the office when the telephone rang. Warily, I lifted the receiver to my ear, extremely nervous about what was awaiting me.

She hadn't softened much over the weekend, but I recognised her voice at once. 'Veum?'

'Yes.'

'This is Åsne Clausen. Are you free now?'

'Yes, in a sense.'

'I'll be there in ten minutes. Don't move.'

'No, OK,' I said, but she had already rung off.

I took a seat at my desk, more or less unable to act. There wasn't much I could do. I brushed the dust off the desktop, but decided to leave the pile of bills. It functioned as a kind of excuse: I hadn't cleaned the place for weeks, but there hadn't been much going on, and no money coming in, so it didn't really matter.

She was true to her word. Exactly ten minutes later she knocked on the waiting-room door. When no-one answered, she opened it, passed through and studied me from the doorway.

She was a little more elegantly dressed this time, as though she were on her way to an important conference: a half-length, black jacket cut in at the waist and beneath it a charcoal-grey skirt. In one hand she held a briefcase, solid enough to act as a weapon if need be. Her face was twitching, she had dark bags under her eyes, so dark that the light make-up couldn't camouflage them, and her eyes looked moist and angry, such as after a long, sleepless night. I knew all about that. It was like looking at myself in the mirror most mornings of the year. But she was attractive. Much more attractive.

'Come in,' I said, standing up behind the desk. I nodded to the client chair. 'Please take a seat.'

She looked around with the same contempt as her husband had a few days earlier. Before sitting down she examined the seat carefully to make sure there was nothing nasty on it. When she did finally sit down she perched on the edge with her legs at right angles to the floor, graceful yet on her guard.

Then she met my eye. 'I have nothing but disdain for people who make their living as you do.'

'How—?'

She interrupted me. 'I wrote down your registration number. As easy as pie. And I'm aware it was Nicolai who employed you.'

'I can't—'

'No, of course you can't. But I'm not a complete idiot, even though you must have assumed I am from the way you tried to – what's the word? – *tail* me on Friday.'

'I admit—'

'Of course you do, but in fact I have something to show you.'

'Oh, yes?'

She looked at me with what seemed to be triumph in her eyes, but I suspected she had nowhere near the control she pretended she had. There was a nervous energy inside her that I knew, from experience of similar situations, could explode at any moment.

Then she opened the briefcase, took out a large brown envelope with foreign stamps on, opened it and produced a handful of A5 photos. For a moment she seemed to hesitate. Then she threw them on the desk in front of me with such force that I had to place a hand on them to prevent them from skidding onto the floor.

I laid them out across the desk and leaned over them. They were graphic enough, if not outright embarrassing.

I soon recognised Nicolai Clausen. In all the photos he was accompanied by beautiful young women with elegant hairstyles; a couple of ladies with bare shoulders, a couple with plunging necklines. There seemed to be several of them, and Clausen wasn't always wearing the same suit, which told me, Sherlock Holmes that I was, that the photos had been taken on several different occasions. The surroundings were, generally speaking, opulent, glitzy bars with a selection of bottles I wouldn't have refused if someone had asked me to test the quality. In a couple of the pictures Clausen and the woman were in such deep conversation a kiss would have been the next step.

One photo stood out. It had been taken from a distance, probably from a window on the opposite side of the street. A somewhat grainy shot showed what I assumed was the inside of a hotel room, where Nicolai Clausen was in a hot clinch with a woman, and her dress was sliding off, the way a chrysalis falls away from a butterfly as it emerges in full flower, beautiful and perfectly formed.

I looked up at her. Her eyes were wet now, and there was a red flush high on her cheeks.

'Who—?'

She anticipated all my questions before I could articulate them. 'I employed a … colleague of yours…' The last phrase she almost spat out. 'In London, after seeing various signs and with increasing suspicion about … what he got up to in the evenings on these business trips of his. This was the result, as well as a full report.' Then she added, 'Professional enough though,' with an expression that suggested she didn't believe I was capable of anything similar.

I sighed aloud. Then I gathered the photos into a pile and pushed them towards her side of the desk. 'And why are you showing me these?'

'Why? You ask me why?' An explosion was imminent. 'So that you can see what sort of man I'm married to and so that you…' She seemed to implode in front of me. She sobbed, took out a packet of tissues from her briefcase and began to weep. Her shoulders shook, so much so that for a moment I was scared her clothes would fall off too.

I sat watching her. I didn't feel I was in a position to go round the desk, put my arms around her and whisper some consoling words in her ear. All I could do was sit tight and wait to see how she would bring this to an end.

Eventually she pulled herself together. The shaking subsided; she wiped the remaining tears away and took out a mirror, which she used to adjust her eye make-up before turning to me again. With a frosty stare, she said: 'In short, I'd like you to terminate the job you were given by my husband this minute, Veum. If I see you in my vicinity one more time I'll call the police.'

'But—'

'I'll take care of my husband.'

I didn't doubt that. He had something to look forward to.

She got up, tossed her head, turned without another look in my direction and left. I never saw her again.

The following day I received confirmation from Clausen himself that the job was over. He phoned this time, and his voice was so full of anger that I was glad he hadn't appeared in person. If he had, there was a good chance I would have landed on the pavement four floors down, following a swift exit through the office window. The Clausen couple had, in the course of two days, given me a harder time than I had experienced since Dankert Muus retired, and I hoped I would never hear from either of them again.

However, a shock went through me when three or four weeks later I read her obituary in the newspaper:

My beloved wife, my loving mother, my dearest daughter, Åsne Clausen, née Kronstad, who died suddenly on 18th November. Nicolai, Severin, Kåre. Funeral at Solheim Chapel, 27th November, 12.00 a.m.

A remorseless sense of guilt grew in me. Was this in any way connected with the job I bodged in October? And what did it mean, 'died suddenly'? A sudden illness? An accident in the home? Something else?

There had been nothing in the news about her. Murder had probably been ruled out, as the funeral was taking place with the normal lapse of time after the death. But an accident at home could be so many things. Falling down the stairs, a variety of everyday mishaps ... According to the experts it was probable that most murders were concealed in this way. But so what? If the police hadn't questioned it, was it appropriate for me to do so?

For some reason or other, which, later, I could never explain to myself, I went to the chapel for the funeral. I arrived just before the service started and sat right at the back. The chapel was far from full, and when the female priest started the commemoration I understood why. Although she expressed herself in very vague terms, it wasn't so difficult to understand that Åsne Clausen had chosen to end her own life, which only magnified the bad feeling I'd had about this case from the very first moment. But there was still something I couldn't make add up. In the two short meetings I'd had with her, Åsne Clausen had not stood out as a suicide candidate. Quite the contrary, she had seemed determined and dynamic, like a woman who would definitely not be pushed around. I found it very difficult to imagine she would have committed suicide. And the blame for it didn't lie with me. Nicolai Severin Clausen would have to carry that burden.

When the procession filed out of the chapel, with the family at the front, he saw me, and I noted his face went even greyer than it already was. Outside, I was making my way around the gathering of people paying their condolences when he marched towards me, grabbed my shoulder and spun me round. 'How dare you!' he snarled. 'You, after messing everything up!'

'I didn't mess anything up. She was already on your trail.'

He wasn't listening. 'But it was you who egged her on. And let's be clear about one thing, Veum! I'm going to destroy you! Do you hear me? Destroy you!'

He raised his fist, as if to punch me, but some people came and dragged him away before he could carry out his threat, glaring at me as though I had caused all this.

Afterwards I wasn't bothered by the threats he had made. I was used to this. What seared itself on my retina was the sight of his son, Severin, who was staring at me with eyes full of hatred. I had never seen anything like it. And now, almost two years afterwards, *that* was what occupied my mind. The shock I had felt at that moment.

19

Vidar Waagenes came alone the following day as well. But now he was able to tell me that the police had handed over all the material from both hard drives and Siggen was at work.

'What about Svein Olav Kaspersen and Hjalmar Hope? Did you find out how their case went?'

He nodded and produced a document from his bag. 'A minor punishment. They were charged with not keeping proper accounts and failing to produce purchase documents. They had to pay a fine of a hundred thousand kroner, which, incidentally, they appealed against and had reduced to seventy-five thousand. But the company was closed down and young Kaspersen has now taken over his uncle's fish farm and, to my knowledge, lives off that.'

'This Hjalmar Hope. I remembered seeing him six months earlier, in the car park outside a computer firm called SH Data.'

'SH?'

'Sherlock Holmes.'

'Elementary, my dear Veum.'

'There are, of course, several firms in that building, so I don't know for certain if that's where he works – or worked. It's quite a while ago now. But it's a computer firm anyway.'

He made a note. 'I'll see what I can dig up. Have you remembered anything else?'

I told him about my bodged job for Nicolai S. Clausen, Åsne Clausen's sudden death and their young son, who, according to reports, was supposed to be a computer whiz.

'You mean Åsne Clausen and Hjalmar Hope could have been colleagues?'

I shrugged. 'It's a possibility of course. But … this isn't a case that gives me particularly good vibes, Vidar. To this day I think back on it with great reluctance. I've never really been able to get rid of the sense that I bore some of the blame for the case developing in the way that it did.'

'If so, there's a clear motive … for someone,' Waagenes said, making another note. 'I'll check that out. I think I might have a colleague who was a legal consultant for Nicolai Clausen for some years. I'll find out if he can tell me anything about how she died at least.'

'Fine. When do you think your computer man will be able to have some results?'

'Siggen? Perhaps by the weekend.'

'Have you heard anything else from the police?'

'No contact except for the delivery of the hard-drive copies.'

'And the other matters?'

'Those … they're being fully investigated. I asked when they were intending to call you in for another interview, but they wouldn't give me an answer.'

'And … the press?'

'Their interest's on the wane. So long as no more information is leaked they don't have a lot to say, apart from writing complicated articles about child pornography and international networks in general.'

I sighed. 'Well, that's something anyway.'

'What would be interesting, Varg, is if you, in the course of your investigations, either in recent years or earlier, have come across such cases yourself. If you've had any experience of circles who indulge in such matters and you've trodden so close they've felt a need to protect themselves.'

'Protect themselves?'

'Yes. I'm sure it's not in this network's interest that this case should explode the way it has done. All such networks flourish in obscurity and within their own digital horizons. Any unintended revelation from outside threatens exposure, which none of these people want. Someone's making a fortune out of this. The exchange of images is rarely free, and if it is, it won't be long before there's a digital debt collector at your door – and perhaps even a physical one if you choose not to pay. We know that this is a part of the activities of organised crime all over the world, and for this sort of person a life is worth no more than what they can earn on it, even if we're talking about children down to the age of infants.'

'The problem is that I'm struggling with great gaps in my memory, Vidar. Self-induced, I'm afraid.'

'You're sure they were all self-induced? There are enough people whose drinks have been spiked and who wake up the next morning unable to remember anything at all about what happened to them. In nine out of ten cases we're talking rape here, but...' He splayed his hands. 'You don't remember anything like that?'

'You mean someone didn't necessarily set this in motion to hit me now. It was stored for potential use at a later time?'

'Yes. I assume you've never been exposed to any kind of blackmail?'

'If I had been, I would've remembered!'

Suddenly I felt physically ill. My throat constricted, and I found it hard to breathe. Cold sweat appeared on my forehead, between my shoulder blades and under my arms. Inside, a feeling grew that I was on the edge of something, a big black hole it would be dangerous to enter. Nevertheless that was exactly what I had to do.

I had problems focussing on Vidar. Instead I rubbed my eyes frenetically as if to remove not just a speck of dust but a bloody great beam from my vision.

After he had left I lay down on the bench, curled into a foetal position and launched myself into the void.

20

For many of those who don't believe in God and the story of creation as presented in the Bible and other religious sources, the universe we live in is supposed to have started with a gigantic explosion in one of the black holes in outer space, unless the black holes are a result of the same explosion, the so-called Big Bang. As I had understood it scientists still weren't sure what came first, the black hole or the Big Bang, the chicken or the egg. As for me, I had more than enough to get to the bottom of with my own black holes.

Lying on the bench in Bergen Prison, in Åsane, curled up, concentrating harder than I was sure was good for me, I tumbled around in a nightmare darkness, where distorted faces, bare genitals, empty bottles and loud music churned around, some of the faces large and close-up one second, only to be so far away the next that they were hardly visible. Some of the people had names, others were anonymous, and some had masks, black and made of leather, with imperious eyes above crooked noses, surrounded by music that sounded like whip-lashes in the air. Most were adults and white, a few younger ones were dark-skinned; none of them were children. Sometimes the darkness was so immense that it filled my head. At other times the light was so strong I was blinded and woke up the following day snow-blind and with an unpleasant feeling in my body, as though it had been hurled sideways and hadn't met a padded wall anywhere. This was the inheritance of the insane drinking binges, the result of weeks, months and years as a tormented spirit on earth, a lost soul in the midst of life, damned, cursed and forgotten, unseen by the powers of good, attracted by the powers of evil.

Out of the chaos, ultimately, there grew a kind of system to the insanity, with some recurring names, so regular that there was a sort of pattern. I stretched out, swung my legs down to the floor, stood up and walked over to the table. I took my notepad and, after turning to a blank white page, placed it in front of me.

Was it possible to reconstruct a black hole? On a piece of white paper? With no more than scraps of memory left?

I remembered fragments of conversations. 'Dolly! My name's Dolly! How do you want me? Like this – or like this – or like this?' Big, strong, in a variety of poses and with a calculating expression on her face, then she laid me on the floor and sat astride me with her thighs apart. 'Like this!' And then a triumphant shout. 'I've got him, Bønni! Now you can empty his pockets.'

Dolly, Bønni.

'You like them a bit younger, do you? Don't be afraid. Karsten can fix everything: colour, size, age, whatever you want. Schoolgirls? Strict madams? Three in a bed? Four? Bønni will vouch for you. Let's just take a little walk to the bank first. OK?'

Karsten. Bønni.

'Come on, Varg! Karsten'll sort us out something nice. They're lying in their beds like little sylphs just waiting to be taken.'

Karsten?

Some memories were meaningless, with no names and an ending I couldn't make head or tail of. A very young woman with oriental features and a blonde wig served me a green drink, and the next thing I remembered was waking up in a hotel room, stark naked with the taste of rotten grass in my mouth. When I put on the clothes lying on the floor like debris and staggered down to reception, the young ladies behind the counter could barely look at me, and when I insisted on knowing who had paid for the room, they looked at me blankly, flicked fruitlessly through the signing-in book and just shrugged their shoulders. Other people were on the night shift, they said. When I insisted on knowing who, I had a telephone receiver thrust into my hand, and a man in my ear introduced himself as the reception manager. When I repeated my question he said that my friend, the man who had brought

me in late the previous night, had paid way over the odds for the incon-
venience. 'My friend? And what was his name?' He couldn't say. 'Did he
pay with a card?' 'Cash.' 'And what did he look like?' 'Pretty ordinary.'
Afterwards I stood on the pavement looking up at the façade of the
house. I had been there before, on a job, and it was at the bottom of the
list of acceptable accommodation in the town. But what worried me
most was that I couldn't remember anything about how I had ended
up there or with whom. Another black hole, another dark star that had
passed by me, near enough to scorch my skin.

A guy came into my office. I was so drunk that I could barely sit on
the chair behind the desk. Yet I could see him clearly. He sat on the
client chair staring at me. 'They've got pictures, Veum. They're threatening to publish them. Not just to give them to my wife, but put them
on the Net. All my connections! Unless I pay them what they demand.'

'But who are they?'

'There's one called Karsten. One they call Bønni. But there are probably more. And they're threatening me. I'll be ruined if this comes out.'

Karsten. Bønni. A case?

A woman's face, near, close, broad lips, stripes of mascara down her
cheeks, a voice with a foreign accent: 'Skarnes. His name's Skarnes. He's
the devil incarnate. Him and Bønni and Karsten. But there are more.
Many more.'

Skarnes. Bønni. Karsten.

'And you? Your name?'

'Magdalena. The chosen one.'

'Chosen by whom exactly?'

A grimace, as though I have stabbed her with a knife and wriggled it
around. 'Jesus Christ.'

I was somewhere else. A woman passed. She had oriental features
and was wearing a blonde wig. As she caught sight of me she seemed
to be about to smile, but then her face distorted into a mask of terror
and dread. She turned away and walked off quickly as Bønni shoved me
through the room and over to the bar.

Bønni. I was sure of that.

I lay on the floor face down. The voices were distant, muted, as if packed in cotton or because they were talking with their backs to me. 'Talk to Hjalmar. He'll fix it. He's the computer man.'

Hjalmar.

Was it the same Hjalmar? The Hjalmar Hope I had met in Fusa and seen in the car park in Sandsli? But never since. However much I racked my memory no Hjalmar Hope reappeared, except for the first two times. And why should it be him? There were so many Hjalmars, weren't there?

I wrote down the names, one after the other: Karsten, Bønni, Dolly, Skarnes, Magdalena, Hjalmar. And then there was the client who had come to my office. The man who had given me the job, or had he? The man who still had no name.

21

There was a nameless man in my office staring at me. I could see him clearly. He was wearing a coat. A grey coat. White shirt. Tie. A tie with diagonal stripes, grey and white. He had gloves on when he came in, but had put them in his pocket before opening his coat and sitting down.

He was in his fifties, had an oval face, a trimmed blond beard, thinning hair, same colour as his beard. His voice trembled as he said: 'I need your help, Veum.'

I was leaning across the desk and holding on as firmly as I could, as if to a life raft in high seas. It was October, and in recent years it had been a difficult month for me. I had lost Karin in October, and I was reminded I was a year closer to my own death in October. Late in the day though this was, I was as drunk as a penguin, but I grabbed a ballpoint pen and made some notes that the following day would look like incomprehensible hieroglyphics, impossible to decipher even if I were a psychic. But at least I looked reliable, I hoped.

The nameless man had, unless my memory was at fault, something to do with accounts. His wife suffered from arthritis, he told me, so badly that their conjugal life had gradually ceased to exist. A colleague, in whom he had confided, had mediated contact with – he searched for the right word – 'a circle'. Via various forms of communication – email, texts, phone – he had been – again he searched – 'accepted as a member'.

'Member?'

'Yes, it was a club.'

'A club?'

'Yes. Something like that. You paid a sub, but then...' He twitched. 'They wanted more. Much more. Unless...'

Membership clearly brought with it obligations. Demands for supplementary payments were high, and if he didn't pay they threatened to send photos of him to his wife and closest family, and to all his business contacts, about whom they knew everything, photos taken through mirrors in the rooms where the 'erm … club activities' took place. They also threatened to put the photos on the Net, accessible to all and sundry; in brief: demolish everything he had built up and make his life hell.

I had difficulty internalising all the details of what he said. 'Once more … They've got photos of you?'

'Yes.'

'Have you seen them?'

'Yes.'

'I don't suppose you have any of them on you, do you?'

'On me? The first thing I did was to burn them. If Sigrid had seen … if my wife had found them, I don't know what would've happened.'

'Photos with … a woman?'

'With several!'

'I see. And how have you got to pay?'

'Cash. I had to withdraw a shockingly large sum from the bank and wait for further instructions.'

'And you haven't received them yet?'

'No. That's why I'm hoping … to steal a march on them.'

'But who are they?'

'That's what I want you to find out, Veum! I have only some of the names. There's one called Karsten. One they call Bønni. But there are probably more. And they're threatening me. I'll be ruined if this comes out!'

I jotted down the names in capitals, hoping I would be able to decipher them the next day: KARSTEN. BØNNI. MORE.

'But you'll have to be discreet, Veum! This must never get out, and my name mustn't be mentioned. Do you understand?'

I nodded, without being absolutely sure if I was actually nodding.

'What I want you to do is gather together as much evidence as you can against these people, evidence which is solid enough to go to the police with, in the worst-case scenario.'

'To the police?'

'Yes.'

'But why don't you go to the police yourself?'

He looked at me in despair. 'I've been trying to explain that to you. I can't. I don't want my name or my family's name to be mixed up in all of this.'

I must have looked sceptical, because he pulled out his wallet, opened it and laid a big wad of notes on the table, big enough to make a man like me go dizzy. 'I'll pay you handsomely. This is just an advance.'

I eyed the notes. The advance could keep me alive for months. 'OK!'

'But I demand results, Veum. And discretion. Can I rely on that?'

'You can rely on me,' I mumbled, and now it was his turn to look sceptical.

But he overcame his scepticism. From his inside pocket he took a business card, which he placed on the table between us. 'This is where you can find me. Take good care of it. Don't show it to anyone.'

I nodded again, picked up the card and stuffed it deep into the inside pocket of my jacket without casting a glance at what was on it. After a slight pause I picked up the banknotes and they went the same way.

Then he got to his feet. He leaned over my desk. 'There's more where that came from. I'll pay you, Veum. Whatever you ask. If you can find out who these people are and gather the evidence!'

'And if I do,' I said as clearly as I could manage. 'I mean … when I do. Is that when we go to the police?'

He stood studying me for a few seconds. Behind the good-looking exterior I had a sense of another person, someone who knew how to back up his words with actions. 'They'll pay dearly for this, Veum! They'll realise who they've tangled with.'

Afterwards he was gone. I wasn't at all sure when or how, and I couldn't remember us taking leave of each other. I must have fallen asleep over the desk because when I woke up it was past midnight and all I could think of was where the nearest watering hole was and if I could get there before closing time.

22

I didn't remember how I got on their trail. For several weeks I spread the word in every place I went, whether public or private.

There were still some scraps of conversation in my head. 'Just tell them that Veum wants to talk to them.' 'Tell who?' 'Bønni.' 'Bønni who?' 'How the hell do I know! Or Karsten.' 'Karsten Bloody Who?' 'Is his name Karsten Bludihoo?' 'No, I was asking you – who?' 'Oh, "who".' 'What was his surname?' 'I don't know. Just Karsten.'

In a dark corner of a back-street bar, not long before closing time, I sat with a fireworks display in my brain drawing to an end; the intervals between the bigger rockets were longer now.

A woman with broad lips and stripes of mascara down her cheeks leaned over to me, so close that I could feel the soft contours of her breasts on my upper arm, not that any rockets went off as a consequence. 'They've got a hold on me,' she croaked softly, with the hint of a foreign accent.

'A hold on you? Who?'

'Skarnes. His name's Skarnes. He's the devil incarnate. Him and Bønni and Karsten. But there are more. Many more.'

'Say that again. Skarnes…'

'…Bønni and Karsten.'

'And you? What's your name?'

'You can call me Magdalena. The chosen one.'

'Chosen by whom exactly?'

She crossed herself over the plunging neckline and said in English: 'Jesus Christ!'

'And where can I find them?'

'In The Tower.'

'Tower?'

She nodded, drained my glass and asked if I would treat her to another before they closed.

After closing time she showed me some compassion, took me home to a narrow street in Nordnes, where we spent the night in a small bed with flowery linen, as naked as new-born babes, though frisky in a different way.

The next morning, but well into the day, she made some atomic coffee for breakfast. When I asked her what more she could tell me about Skarnes, Bønni and Karsten, she blanched over the wax cloth, looked out to Knøsesmuget and said: 'Who?'

'The people you told me about yesterday. Skarnes, Bønni and Karsten.'

She just shook her head. 'You must have been dreaming. I don't know anyone by those names.'

'Eh?'

She got up from the table, went over to the coffee pot and filled her cup. With her back to me she said: 'Don't ask.'

'You said I'd find them in "The Tower". Which tower?'

She turned suddenly. There were bright red flushes down her neck. 'Don't ask, I said! You can just go! Off with you! I wish I hadn't … I'd been drinking, I didn't know what I was saying, I was fantasising.'

I still wasn't sober, barely into a hangover, but I understood this much: She was frightened. Fear shone from her eyes and her breathing came in strained gasps.

'OK, Magdalena. I'll go. And I'll take all my questions with me.'

Leaving, I crossed Klosteret and cut down the Cort Piil alleyway. The first thing I did on arrival at my office was to write down on my notepad: 'Skarnes. Bønni. Karsten. The Tower.'

A few days later I was frolicking with another woman, first in a beer dive, with British football on the screen above the bartender's head, and then in her flat in Professor Hansteens gate, a well-placed free kick from the football pitch in Møhlenpris. When she said her name was Dolly, I assumed it was a stage name and that she could hardly have got it in Bergen. We had obviously arranged to do a bit of sparring in her ring, because it took her no time at all to fling off most of her clothes and pull my trousers down to my knees, making me lose balance, then she pushed me to the floor and straddled me, as heavy as a walrus. She adopted various seductive poses, holding out her breasts in front of her. 'How do you want me? Like this – or like this – or like this?'

My head whirled, and I barely knew where I was, when I heard the jeering tone in her voice: 'I've got him, Bønni! Now you can help yourself.'

The door to the room had been ajar. Someone came in, went through my clothes and took any cash there might have been – pitifully little, which he made abundantly clear.

Bønni?

'But he's got a bank card here. We'll take him to a cashpoint. Can he stand upright?'

'He could ten minutes ago.'

'But now you've crushed him?'

I felt the pressure on my stomach lighten as she stood up. Behind her I glimpsed a guy of the same proportions, but with him it was more muscle than fat. His head was clean-shaven, and he was dressed for what he was doing: jeans and a dark-brown leather jacket.

'Seems to have survived,' Dolly said, sending me a last glance and waddling out of the room with her clothes hanging from one hand like some extravagant designer creation. With the fingers of her other hand she waved goodbye.

'Goodbye, Dolly,' I mumbled as the man she called Bønni lifted me from the floor and confirmed that I was capable of standing upright.

'Get your trousers on,' he said. 'You look like you need a bit of fresh air.'

'Bønni?' I said. 'You know Karsten, don't you?'

He stared at me. 'Yes? What about it?'

'Actually it was him I wanted to talk to. I asked …' I waved an arm '… Dolly. I asked her if she could … she said she could take me to his place. Up here. But it's only you.'

'What do you want with Karsten?'

'To talk to him.'

'What about?'

'What he's got to offer in terms of…' Again I waved an arm in the direction Dolly had gone. 'That.'

He smirked. 'You didn't get enough?'

'It was too rough.'

'You like them a bit younger, do you? Don't be afraid. Karsten can fix everything: colour, size, age, whatever you want. Schoolgirls? Strict madams? Three in a bed? Four? Bønni will vouch for you. Let's just take a little walk to the bank first. OK?'

'OK,' I repeated, putting on my jacket and holding out my hand for the bank card.

He looked down at my palm. 'I'll look after this for the time being.' He turned round. 'Dolly! We're off.'

She answered something I couldn't hear from somewhere in the flat. He shrugged, grabbed my upper arm and led me out and down to the street. A big, black Audi was waiting for us. He switched off the alarm with the remote, opened the passenger door and shoved me in. I flopped down in the seat. He got in on the driver's side, sat behind the wheel and leaned across me to fasten the safety belt. When he was happy he buckled his own.

'Next stop Danmarksplass,' he mumbled and nodded in its direction. From Professor Hansteens gate he turned into Wolffs gate, where the shale football pitch in Møhlenpris lay deserted and abandoned at this time of day. There weren't many people out walking in Danmarksplass either, where he pulled in opposite the cashpoint in Solheimsgaten. He unbuckled both our belts, got out, came round and collected me, then led me to the cashpoint and inserted the card.

'And now the code,' he said.

'Don't remember,' I said.

He cuffed me round the neck. 'You do. If you don't I'll hit you harder.'

I was still much too drunk to resist. 'Let's try.' I tapped in a four-figure code.

On the screen a message came up: WRONG CODE. TRY AGAIN.

This time he hit me harder. 'Don't be stupid!'

I tried again. WRONG CODE: TRY AGAIN.

This time he grabbed the back of my collar and spun me round. 'Tell me the numbers! If they're wrong I'll beat you to a pulp. Have you got that?'

I nodded frenetically. Then I said the numbers, slowly and with some difficulty, as though I were reading them from a book with tiny writing. He tapped them into the keypad, one by one, and this time the menu came up.

The highest amount he could withdraw was four thousand kroner. He pressed the key, and after some grinding noises from the guts of the machine, eight five-hundred notes fluttered out through its jaws.

He wasn't happy with that, inserted the card again and tapped in the same code number. The process was repeated, but this time he got only four notes.

'What the fuck!' he said. 'What's your credit limit?'

'Credit limit?'

'How much you can take out, for Christ's sake!'

I looked askance from him to the screen. Then I gestured helplessly. 'I suppose that must be it!'

He stared at me with an expression that said he felt like giving me a good beating anyway, but then he changed his mind. 'OK ... let's go then.'

'Where?'

'We're off.'

Once we were strapped in again, he pulled out from the kerb, drove along Michael Krohns gate and down Damgårdsveien. I followed the route as well as I could, though not quite knowing what we were doing.

Damsgårdsveien was undergoing some renovation work. Great parts of the old industrial buildings were going to be replaced with new dwellings, but many of the older houses were still left, several of them long abandoned by their former owners and tenants.

Bønni turned in by one of these. It was a tall industrial building consisting of six storeys. On the pavement in front, I gazed up at the sombre façade. At the very top, behind lowered blinds, something shone dimly, like the light of a UFO landed on a mountain top in the hope that it wouldn't be noticed. A thought struck me: *The Tower? Maybe this is it…*

Bønni brusquely shoved me towards the main entrance, which was locked. He pressed in a code on the pad beside the door, there was a click and he pushed the door open. We entered a drab stairwell, dimly illuminated by the reflection of a neon tube some way up the stairs.

He opened the lift door, thrust me in and tapped the button for the fourth floor. Another door with a coded lock, and when it opened it was as though we had entered a lost version of *One Thousand and One Nights*, complete with scantily clad women, a striking number of them foreign in appearance. The walls were covered with dark-red silk wallpaper, and the muted lighting came from fittings partially hidden behind ceiling mouldings. At the end of the room there was a staffed bar. At various small tables sat well-dressed men aged from their late twenties to their seventies, with glasses in their hands or on the table in front of them, and not a single one without the company of a lady.

'Boss in?'

The bartender nodded, and Bønni carried on, knocked on a mahogany-veneer door, waited for a noise inside, and when he heard it, opened, pushed me into the room and closed the door firmly behind us.

We had walked quickly through the salon outside, but not so quickly that I hadn't recognised a face there. I just couldn't place it.

I stumbled into the room and had to make a grab at the big desk so as not to fall on the floor. It had thick, transparent glass on top, and there weren't many writing implements on it. The walls were varnished in some black, shiny material. Dark-green, heavy velvet curtains were drawn in front of the windows, which normally would have offered a view of Puddefjord and the districts of Møhlenpris and Nygård-shøyden. A sweet, acrid smell of cigar hung over the room, and behind the desk sat a man in a dark suit, with blond hair and regular, almost anonymous, facial features. He observed me through his cool, light-blue eyes as, with studied movements, he lit the cigar he had just poked into his mouth.

'This is the individual who has been going round asking after you,' said Bønni.

The man behind the desk weighed me up. When he spoke there was a clear accent. 'And who are you?'

It was as though my head was gradually returning to its place. 'The name's Veum. Varg Veum.'

Bønni threw my wallet on the table in front of the second man, who opened it and removed one of my cards. He read it carefully, then glanced up at me and nodded. 'Private investigator. Well, well.'

'And you are … Karsten?'

He didn't answer, but said: 'What do you want?'

'To talk to you. But not now. Not … like this.' What I meant was: *Not now, while I'm so rat-arsed.* But I didn't say that.

'But this is your chance. Tomorrow could be too late.'

I sighed and tried to remember. *What is it I wanted? Why have I been asking after him?* The face of my nameless client appeared in my skull somewhere. But how would I explain to him who he was when I didn't even know his name?

'There's a man who owes you money. You've got photos of him.'

He raised his eyebrows mockingly. 'Lots of men owe me money, Veum. I've got photos of lots of men too. You're going to have to give me a peg to hang this on.'

'A peg?'

'A name.'

'Yes, that's the problem.' Unconsciously, I stretched a hand into my inside pocket.

The man I assumed was Karsten motioned to Bønni. At once he was on top of me, grabbing my arm so that it couldn't move and sticking his own hand so deep into my inside pocket that he reached the business card I had put there some days before. Then he let go, stepped forward and passed the card to Karsten.

Karsten threw it a glance, nodded to himself and put it in his own inside pocket with an eloquent look at Bønni. Then he eyed me. 'And what did this man want you to find out?'

I regarded him from under heavy eyelids. 'Find out? I don't remember.' Deep inside my drunken head I realised I had committed a grave error. Nothing to be proud of. Nothing else to do but keep my mouth shut for as long as I could.

'Shall I knock him about, Boss?' I heard behind me.

Karsten sent me a measured gaze. 'Doubt it would help. Just get rid of him. If he can't be a little clearer, we have nothing to talk to him about.'

'And by "get rid of" you mean ... ?'

'By "get rid of" him I mean turf him out. Nothing else. Not this time.'

I stretched out a hand. 'Can I have my wallet back?'

In one sudden move Karsten hurled the wallet towards me. It landed on the floor in front of me, and just bending down and picking it up felt like an effort beyond my powers.

Standing back upright, I said: 'Just get in touch.'

He exchanged a look with Bønni and nodded. Bønni grabbed me by the scruff of the neck, turned me round and we performed a gentle retreat through the dark-red salon. The man I thought I recognised was on his way up a winding staircase to the floor above. He had his arm around the waist of a woman dressed in a scant bra and a kind of raffia skirt. As we passed he looked down and met my gaze.

It wasn't a friendly look, and now I remembered who it was. Sturle Heimark, the ex-policeman I had last bumped into in Fusa late the previous winter.

Then we were in the lift and on our way down. Before getting into the car, I performed the same gesture as up on the fourth floor. I stretched out my hand and said: 'My card.'

'What the hell are you going to do with it? There's nothing on it.'

'My card,' I repeated, a little more impatiently this time.

He took it from his inside pocket and slapped it down into my palm, so hard that it felt as if the sharp edge had cut into me. I closed my hand around it and put it as deep into my inside jacket pocket as I could.

Bønni drove me to the top of Puddefjord Bridge, where he pulled in and dropped me off as though hoping I would jump into the sea. I didn't, but the night turned into morning before I was back in Telthussmuget.

During the subsequent days I expected the anonymous client to ring me at some point to hear what I had found out. It wasn't exactly a conversation I was looking forward to, so in many ways I was relieved that I never heard from him. I had spent the advance, but that didn't make my conscience feel any worse than it already was. Now though, barely a year afterwards, it struck me as strange that he had never contacted me. Perhaps ultimately there had been a reason – a reason that had nothing to do with discretion. A reason I would prefer not to know.

23

On Friday morning I was summoned for another interview at the police station. Vidar Waagenes met me at the entrance and accompanied us upstairs.

'Have they told you what they want to quiz me about?' I asked.

'No.'

The officers who had collected me from Åsane led us into an interview room and one stayed until Hamre and Beatrice Bauge arrived, both in uniform for the occasion. They greeted us politely, but in measured tones; Hamre somewhat downbeat, Bauge tense and ready for action, as though the next step in her career was now within reach.

Hamre had a thick wad of documents with him, Bauge a little laptop, which she opened in front of her and roused from sleep mode. Hamre leafed through the pile of papers until he found the ones he was after. She scrolled down the screen with what I assumed was the same result.

Waagenes sighed loudly. 'Shall we get underway? I have to be in court at one.'

Hamre nodded assent.

Bauge said: 'We'll have to see how far we can get.' She looked at me. 'Depending on how willing the accused is to talk.'

'As long as we have something to talk about,' I said.

'We do, I'm sure.'

'Away we go then,' I said impatiently.

Waagenes placed a hand on my arm, as if to say 'easy now'.

Hamre and Bauge exchanged glances. She said: 'Perhaps you'd like to start?'

Hamre sighed. 'Fine.' From under heavy eyelids he looked at me.

'We'd like to put some names to you, Veum, so that you can explain what your relationship is with these people.'

I nodded. 'OK. Fire away.'

He perched some narrow reading glasses on his nose and held one of the sheets he had located in front of him. 'Mikael Midtbø,' he read.

Everyone looked at me. I looked calmly at him. 'Completely unknown. Never heard of him.'

'No? Living in Frekhaug.'

'He could be living on the moon for all I know. I've never heard the name.'

Bauge tapped away on her keyboard, stroked the mousepad and wrote a bit more. We watched her until she had finished, as though this was some kind of one-woman-show she was presenting.

In the meantime Hamre had selected the next document from his pile. 'Per Haugen.'

I shrugged. 'I met a journalist called Helge Haugen in Førde once. That's as close as I can get.'

'This is a fellow townsman of yours.'

'Bully for him.'

Hamre eyed me despairingly. Bauge was playing her piano keyboard again, but not for as long as last time.

When Hamre took out the last sheet he had selected, a nervousness seemed to come over him. I knew him well enough to realise that this was serious now and I was not immune to a tingle between my shoulder blades.

He smacked his lips silently, then said: 'This guy here then…' He paused, as on cue as an actor. 'Karl Slåtthaug.'

Then he fixed his eyes on me and watched closely. As did Bauge. Even Vidar Waagenes observed me with renewed interest this time.

I allowed the name to sink down into me, until it had reached the bottom. Then I nodded slowly as though only gradually recognising it. 'Yes, him I know about.'

They waited. Hamre said: '"Know about"?'

I nodded. 'I know him, but only peripherally.'

'Ex-colleague, is he?'

I shook my head. 'No. He started at Social Services after I'd finished there.'

'Yes, yes, but in the same line of work. Trained social worker as well, we can see.'

'Indeed! But that doesn't mean we had much to do with each other.'

'No?'

'No! I've not seen Karl Slåtthaug since...' Suddenly I realised I had gone down a blind alley. 'Well, I might perhaps have bumped into him ... last year some time.'

'Bumped into?'

'Yes, bumped into. We had a few beers. Nothing else.'

'How would you explain all the emails he sent you last year?'

'Emails? From Karl Slåtthaug! I don't recall any.'

'Emails with attachments you saved on your machine and – by the look of it – enjoyed at a later opportunity.'

'Emails from Karl Slåtthaug I ... that never happened. I can't remember ever receiving any emails from him. When we said goodbye last autumn ... well ... neither of us expressed any wish to see each other again.'

'Why not?'

I shrugged.

'You had an argument?'

I leaned forward. 'I don't know how much you know about Karl Slåtthaug, but he finished at Social Services for quite different reasons from mine. His name appeared in connection with a case I was investigating...'

'Last year?'

'No, close on ten years ago. And he clearly blamed me for later events.'

Hamre arched his eyebrows. 'Interesting, Veum. Are you suggesting he had a reason to take revenge on you?'

Bauge coughed in reproof, and Hamre glanced in her direction. Then he continued: 'Not that that detracts from your responsibility.'

Waagenes was following with interest now.

'We have only your word that you were … enemies,' Hamre said.

'We weren't enemies. I had nothing to do with him!'

'We've taken note … that you said that. But we have concrete evidence of the opposite.' He tapped his forefinger on the table in front of him, emphasising the significance of what he was saying. 'On your computer, Veum.'

I leaned back and threw up my arms. 'As I've told you … this is simply incomprehensible. For me too, Hamre.'

'For you *too*?'

'Yes. Because surely you don't believe this, do you? That I would…'

He looked at me askance. 'My job isn't about beliefs, Veum. It's about knowledge. And bit by bit we know more and more about what happened.'

'What, for example?'

Bauge intervened. 'We'll come back to that, Veum. Eventually.'

Waagenes spoke up. 'On my client's behalf I'd just like to draw your attention to the fact that we have our own computer expert, who is at present thoroughly examining the copies of both Veum's hard drives we were given by the police – from his home and office computers. Until that work is complete we will reject all alleged evidence based on their contents.'

Beatrice Bauge eyed him with a bitter-sweet smile on her lips. 'Noted, *herr* Waagenes.' She turned to Hamre. 'Anything else, Jakob?'

A spasm seemed to flash across his face as if he didn't like such a young colleague addressing him by his first name. 'No,' he said. 'Not today.'

Bauge opened the door and shouted down the corridor. 'You can take Veum back to Åsane now!'

'You wouldn't like to open the window and use a loud-hailer, would you?' I said.

She tossed her head and walked off with her laptop firmly under her arm.

I turned to Hamre. 'Such a lovely colleague you have, Hamre.'

He didn't answer, just sent a measured nod to Waagenes and me, and left me to the two officers who would accompany me back to Bergen Prison.

'I hope to get Siggen over to see you during the weekend,' Waagenes said before we parted.

'And I hope he'll be of some use,' I answered.

In the prison van no-one said a word. It seemed as if we were on the way to a funeral, and I had a disconcerting sense it was mine.

24

After the incident with the bank card and the hijacked account I had
tried to pull myself together; although the bodged investigation for the
man whose name I didn't even know hadn't exactly bolstered my self-
confidence. I put the aquavit bottle in the office drawer, at the back, and
piled up some unused notepads in front of it, so that it wouldn't roll
forward every time I opened the drawer. I undertook another appraisal
of the pile of bills, once again ordering them according to priority, and
wondered if there was anything I could sell to pay the most urgent
of them. But I couldn't think of a solution. Most of my possessions I
needed, and those I didn't need, nobody would want.

I rang Nils Åkre and asked if he had any cases he could forward on
to me.

'After your success in Fusa?' he replied.

'My God, Nils, that's almost two years ago!'

'Nevertheless…'

Late that November I mixed with bad company again. So bad that
I could scarcely remember where I had been. It didn't get a lot better
when I crawled back on land and the person I met there was Karl Slåtthaug; the only advantage was that he was paying. Bergen's famous Børs
Café was not so far from my office that I needed a map and a compass to
get there, and on that Friday afternoon I sat down at one of the darkest
tables, though still not dark enough for me to be able to sit in peace. I
quickly recognised the man who crossed the floor and stood swaying
by my table, and when he asked if he could buy me a beer a prompter in
my wallet whispered: 'Say yes.'

He thought we had suffered similar fates. 'You and I and Social Services, Varg.'

'You weren't in Social Services when I was there.'

'Later I was. And we all got to hear about it. A living legend,' he grinned. 'You couldn't control your desires, either.'

I felt a chill in my solar plexus. 'What did you just say?'

His gaze flitted from my mouth to my eyes and back again. 'The drug dealer you beat up because he went to bed with one of your girls.'

'She was a client, Karl. Not what I'd call "one of my girls". It was someone I'd taken care of and got back on an even keel, only for her to be destabilised again by some bastard.'

'Whom you killed, right?'

'I beat him up, yes.'

'But later he died.'

'Many years later, yes. But … I had nothing to do with that.'

'I heard a different story.'

This went through me like an electric shock. 'Really? Who from?'

Slåtthaug beckoned a waiter. 'Two more, Svendsen!'

That was when I should have said no, of course. Once again. But the craving was already too strong. 'And an aquavit,' I mumbled.

'And two aquavits!' Slåtthaug called to the waiter, who gave a routine nod by way of return.

'Who from?' I repeated, grabbing his lapels and half pulling him up from his seat.

'Relax, Varg. It's just something I once heard. You know … in our business we meet so many people.'

Later everything came to a head.

At some point he sent me accusatory looks. 'You were the one who got me the boot, Varg. I've never forgiven you.'

'Me?' I thought back. 'I had nothing to do with it.' *Or did I… ?*

It was one of the worst cases I had worked on, and I had to go back ten years in time to locate it. But it was there of course, and I hadn't forgotten.

Karl Slåtthaug had been working at a children's institution, and someone had implied he was giving some of the girls lingering looks, especially the ones approaching sexual maturity. I had been given the job of examining the case more closely by a mother whose daughter was there. It never got as far as specific accusations and it all petered out because of a lack of willingness among the girls to speak. He was better-looking then than he was now, so perhaps they thought they wouldn't be believed. The local Social Services managers decided, however, that he should be moved on, and a few months later he was given his marching orders. I remembered I had made some enquiries with Cathrine Leivestad, another colleague from that time, but all she could say was that the suspicions had been so strong that Slåtthaug had been requested to look around for something else to do. In that sense he was right. This was reminiscent of the way I had been given the boot twenty years before.

At any rate his bank account wasn't empty; the way he was splashing money about, he must have found something to do. When I asked him outright, he looked from side to side before answering. 'I have my connections.'

'Uh-huh?'

'Never mind that though, Varg. Let's have some fun. Let's order a taxi and I'll take you to a place you've never been.'

He was wrong about *that* anyway. Already on the way up Puddefjord Bridge I suspected I knew where we were going. Not long afterwards I was in the lift, making another visit to The Tower, but as a client this time.

I had probably looked a little doubtful on the pavement, but Karl Slåtthaug had gone on about what was awaiting us. 'Come on, Varg! Karsten'll sort us out something nice. They're lying in their beds like little sylphs, just waiting to be taken.' As I continued to hold back he added: 'And what they serve in the bar is tax- and duty-free. But I'm paying! There's more where this comes from.'

In the dark-red room we were received by exotic young girls in the same scanty clothes as last time, but when I insisted on sitting at the bar they gradually lost any interest in me. Karl, on the other hand, disappeared up the winding staircase with one of the youngest girls there, after giving the bartender a blank cheque to serve me whatever I liked.

A woman passed. She had oriental features and was wearing a blonde wig. As she caught sight of me she seemed to be about to smile, but then her face distorted into a mask of terror and dread. She turned away and walked off quickly. For a moment or two I wondered whether I should follow her. However it was my ill-luck that the bartender thought he recognised me, and before I knew what was going on, Bønni loomed up behind me, grabbed me by the shoulders, turned me round and led me through the room. Inside Karsten's office I was dealt a rabbit punch that sent me flying to the floor. The voices were distant and low, as if packed in cotton, or because they were talking with their backs to me. But I had no problem recognising Karsten's voice, and I heard what he said: 'Talk to Hjalmar. He'll fix it. He's the computer man.'

Hjalmar?

'I don't want to see him here. Is that clear? Drop him to the bottom of Puddefjord if you have to.'

Bønni lifted me up and carried me through the salon this time. Far away I heard the giggles from some of the girls. Karl Slåtthaug was on his way down from the upper floor with a ruffled shirt and a confused look on his face. 'What's going on?'

'Your guest's leaving. And I have an absolute ultimatum from Karsten. Bring him here again and you'll lose your membership.'

'OK, OK! I didn't mean to … Let me just … I'll take him. Get me a taxi.'

Karl Slåtthaug stood supporting me until the taxi arrived, so closely that I could smell the scent of cheap perfume on him. 'You should've come up to the first floor, Varg. That's where the action is.'

I mumbled something even I didn't understand, then the taxi came and we scrambled onto the back seat, followed by extremely sceptical looks from the thin, dark-skinned driver. Slåtthaug dropped me off in the market square, but I couldn't bear the thought of walking up the mountainside home. Instead I went to the office, curled up on the floor and slept like a log until late in the morning of the next day. I never heard from Karl Slåtthaug again. The police brought his name up in October of the following year.

25

On Monday morning I had Vidar Waagenes back in my cell, but this time he wasn't alone.

Sigurd Svendsbø was the age I expected a computer expert to be: in his mid-thirties. He moved in a smooth, light-footed way that belied his premature pot belly, undoubtedly a result of too many hours of solitude in front of the screen. His hair was longish, his stubble a couple of days old, and in his left ear he had a small gold ring. Beneath the black leather jacket he wore a red T-shirt emblazoned with EVERQUEST in big, white letters.

When we shook hands I looked at him a second time. 'Haven't we met before?'

'Don't think so. Where would that have been?'

'I've used Siggen for the last ten years, Varg. You might have passed each other going into or out of my office,' Waagenes said. 'I can promise you there aren't any better computer experts in this town.'

Svendsbø smiled weakly, but seemed slightly ill at ease. 'Well, if you've got nothing else to do in your free time.'

'Nothing else? You've got a family, haven't you?'

'Yes, yes, part-time now, though. My night's sleep went up in smoke when they were littl'uns, and then I had to sit in front of the keyboard until daybreak. Some years I felt as if I'd hardly had a wink.'

'Well, now, we have to make the most of our time.' Waagenes walked towards the table in the visitors' room, pulled out a chair for himself, one for Svendsbø on the same side, and motioned towards the other for me. 'Siggen thinks he's on the trail of something, Varg.'

'Really! That sounds promising.'

Svendsbø took a notebook from his inside pocket and looked at me almost guiltily. 'We weren't allowed to bring the computer in.'

Waagenes nodded, displeased. 'The limited access to media.'

'But I made some notes,' Svendsbø continued. 'I still haven't managed to work through all the elements of your hard drives, and I have to admit the police are right on one point. There's a lot of filth on them.' He eyed me as if asking me what I had to say to that.

I shrugged and showed him my bare palms. 'So I've heard. But I didn't put it there and I haven't been on those websites.'

He nodded. 'Your log confirms that, by the way. But that's obvious. If you know a bit about computers you can always edit a log. However, there are always traces left, but then I'd have to go through what's been deleted from your machines and that's such a time-consuming job I haven't been able to get round to it yet.'

'Well, I definitely don't know much about computers, so editing a log's beyond me.'

'Of course, but … for someone who has children himself it hurts me to see what some people can put online. One thing is images, another is video clips, a third is a description of what they've done, what they'd like to do or what they in fact do.'

'And this is open online?'

'No, no. It's rarely open. It happens in closed forums, where you have to be a member and have a personal password to get in. But for … hmm … people like me it's easy enough to pass firewalls and other security measures to get in. You can't bear to look for more than a few minutes though. It simply makes me feel ill.'

'Yes, I'm sure I would've been as well. But … I've never tried.'

'I know, Varg. Vidar says the same. If I'd thought any differently I would've refused to take the job.'

'OK.' I could feel I was becoming more and more impatient. 'Tell me what you've found.'

'Let me first explain to you how this kind of thing is done.'

'Right.'

'I'm sure you know about Trojan horses and spyware.'

'I've heard of them, yes.'

'A rule of thumb is, don't click on any links that don't come from people you know or at least trust. This applies to everything from banks to online shopping or emails sent by close friends.'

'Close friends?'

'Yes, this often happens through back doors. Someone has infected the computer or email account of someone you know and sends an email in his or her name. It might contain, for example, a link to a funny clip you should see, a song you've been recommended or just a link to a website. If you click on the link – if you watch the clip or listen to the song – you've left the door ajar, and you risk being attacked by a hacker, who takes control of your computer.'

'And you think that might have happened in this case?'

'Possibly, yes.'

'But can this person – whoever they are – also put things onto my computer?'

'Yes. They can put software onto your computer – from outside – which means that everything that is transferred from one or several specific addresses isn't opened at once, but is stored there.'

'Such as huge piles of child pornography?'

'Yes.'

'But won't that … Won't it be possible to read on the log that I've never opened these webpages? Or that they've never been opened on these computers?'

'In principle, yes. But don't forget the log can be tampered with, both ways. You might have deleted the addresses of all the webpages you've been on. But – and this is perhaps even more important – hackers can add addresses of pages you *haven't* accessed. How often do you actually check your log?'

'As good as never. Only if I'm searching for a page I've been on and can't remember the address. And that happens very, very rarely.'

'Exactly.'

'But you said there's nothing visible on my log.'

'Yes, that's right. So one possibility is you'd deleted addresses, but I'd be able to tell if you had.'

'I have an even more important question for you. Can you also find out who put all this filth on my computers?'

'That's a more open question. Again it depends on how clever they – the people who did it – have been. If they're skilful amateurs I'll find them soon enough. But if they're pros – who might've been involved in cyber crime – it could be more difficult. But I've got a question for you too, Veum. Do you remember anything from the end of last November?'

'End of last November?'

'Yes.'

I cast around the bare visitors' room as though the answer lay there and thought back. Last November was just after the incident with Karl Slåtthaug and the chaos that came in its wake. I could feel the muscles in my face twitching. 'N-no. I'm afraid I don't.'

He looked at me in surprise. 'Nothing?'

'Well, yes. Of course I remember … something. But either nothing happened – in other words, bleak, grey everyday life – or I was on the juice. The last three or four years have been hard for me to get through, Svendsbø.'

'Call me Siggen. Everyone else does.'

Waagenes turned to Svendsbø. 'Why are you asking, Siggen?'

'Erm…' He looked down at his notes. 'Almost everything that happens on a computer is logged, as you know, either by you or the computer program. By the program, anyway. And as far as I've been able to find out there's none of this material before November 2001. I've even got a date: 27th November. That's when I find the first downloads.'

'27th November,' I repeated.

'Yes, does that mean anything to you?'

I shook my head. 'Nothing. If I'd been able to go to my office I could've checked my calendar. And at home in a drawer I must have last year's appointments book. But I have a nasty feeling we won't find anything there. It was a period when I didn't have much going on, if you understand what I mean.'

'Is all this material dated to around then?' Waagenes asked.

'No,' Svendsbø replied. 'But there's nothing after 1st March 2002. Everything was downloaded over the … one, two, three months between the two dates.' He counted on his fingers to be sure he hadn't missed anything. 'December, January, February.'

Waagenes turned back to me. 'And that doesn't ring any bells, Varg?'

I shook my head. 'I hardly know where I was on Christmas Eve.'

He sent me a despairing look. 'I don't know…'

He was interrupted by a hard knock at the door, which then opened. One of the warders stood in the doorway. 'There's a message from the police. Veum's summoned to an interview.'

Waagenes's face flushed. 'At such short notice?'

'There's been a development, they said. And this is urgent.'

I had a sinking feeling. A development, and it was urgent. That didn't bode well.

'Well, I say! Are you going to transport him there?'

'Yes, we'll take care of that.'

'I'll go there in my car. Warn them not to start the interview before I'm there.'

We got to our feet, all of us.

Svendsbø held up a hand. 'I'm afraid I won't be able to join you. So, see you at the next crossroads. In the meantime you can rely on me. If there's anything to find, I'll find it.'

I grabbed his hand and smiled wanly. 'Thank you.'

Waagenes adopted a positive tone. 'I think we've come a long way already.' He held up a forefinger, like a strict teacher. 'Not a word until I'm there, Varg. Don't let them provoke you.'

'Easier said than done,' I mumbled before following the warder out, where a colleague of his waited with handcuffs, clapped them round my wrists and took me to the waiting vehicle.

For the short time we were outdoors I inhaled deep into my lungs what I could of the fresh air, like at the starting line of a marathon in which I had no hope of achieving a better result than a finish.

26

There was a strange atmosphere around the table as we waited for Waagenes to find a parking spot. From experience I knew it wasn't easy at this time of day.

Beatrice Bauge's mobile vibrated on silent. She checked who wanted to talk to her, made an apologetic gesture to her colleagues and left the room. From the corridor I heard the sound of her voice, less and less clearly as she moved away from us.

Hamre was accompanied by Solheim this time. Neither of them appeared to be in the best frame of mind.

'So how are you killing time, Veum?' Hamre asked.

'Reading and thinking.'

'Reading what?' He leaned forward, interested.

'Books I borrow from the library. Not crime literature though.'

'No?'

'In those books, crimes are solved.'

'Yes, but not straightaway…' He attempted a little smile, without much sincerity, and I answered with a shrug.

'So what do you think about then?'

'Bit of everything, I'm afraid.'

'Anything you'd like to share with us?'

'Not until Waagenes is here.'

He sighed. 'OK, fine.'

Hamre had a briefcase in front of him. Solheim had an open laptop, but he wasn't looking at it. Beatrice Bauge returned. She glanced at her watch impatiently but said nothing. She also had a laptop open, but, unlike Solheim, she stared intensively at the screen, scrolled down and wrote nothing. Not yet.

After around a quarter of an hour Vidar Waagenes arrived, suitably breathless to make a credible impression. 'Apologies. I had to go to the rear car park. There was nothing free around here.'

'We're ready to begin then,' Beatrice Bauge declared in business-like fashion.

Waagenes nodded and checked with me. 'OK with you, Varg?'

'I have no choice, do I.'

'No, you don't.' Bauge looked at Hamre. 'Would you like to get the ball rolling?'

Hamre glanced down, rubbed his hands as if they had got cold waiting, nodded and cleared his throat. Then he leaned forward and directed his gaze at me.

'In cases such as these, Veum,' he began, 'we have various categories of sex offenders.'

He paused for dramatic effect. I watched him without saying a word.

'We're talking about an international network here, and it's obvious that the person sitting in Norway and watching abuse on the screen that has taken place in, say, Brazil, is not as guilty as the real abuser. Nor if the assault took place in Askøy, Sotra or any other place around here.'

After another pause he continued: 'There are also various categories within the group of viewers, if I can call them that. Some of them are passive and do nothing else. Others choose to share the experience and send the material on – either to someone he or she knows or a network of which they are a member.'

I motioned with my head to say that this was obvious. *Get to the point, Hamre!*

'Among the actual abusers there are also categories, but now it is difficult to keep a cool head. We're talking about abuse of children, Veum, some of them infants, others pre-sexual maturity, though still children. Obviously most people would react with greater revulsion to the rape of a six-month-old baby than the rape of a thirteen- or fourteen-year-old girl.'

His mouth fell open as if he were swimming and needed extra oxygen to continue. 'How safe can any small child feel in a world populated by wolves? There are children out there being abused by their own parents, Veum! By uncles and aunts, not to mention grandfathers! Some are abused by siblings, others by close friends of the family, even by girls babysitting for them. There seem to be no limits!'

The room had gone quiet. Hamre's face was a blotchy red and I could feel my cheeks were flushed too.

He held up one hand and counted on his fingers. 'Someone is supplying these children, unless they're already there inside the house's four walls. Someone is organising this abuse; someone is participating actively; and there is someone, often a spouse, turning a blind eye and pretending not to know. Various categories deserving of various degrees of punishment. Any legal practitioner can tell you that.' He glared at Waagenes and then Bauge, both the representatives of the law in the room.

Then he fixed his eyes on me again. 'And which category do you belong to, Veum?'

I returned his gaze, without giving an inch. 'I've told you before and I'll tell you again: none of them! I haven't even opened a webpage with that kind of content!'

'No? But we know better.'

'Vidar … Waagenes and I have just come from a meeting with a computer expert who's told us that this kind of material can be sent to any computer with no-one any the wiser!'

'I can imagine.' His scar glistened angrily. 'But not in this case, Veum. We have stronger evidence than that.'

'Oh, yes. And what is that, might I ask?'

'You'll find out, and pretty quickly.'

Hamre opened the briefcase and took out five A4 sheets, which he placed in front of him face down. 'Let me show you some print-outs we have from your computers, Veum. There are identical copies to the one you had at home and the one in your office. And so as to be absolutely clear: this is only a small selection. There are many more where these come from.'

He flicked the pieces of paper over so that the picture was face up, cast a revulsion-filled glance at them and pushed them across the table, where they lay like an unusually bad hand of poker on the table in front of me.

Technically they were poor pictures, but the content was clear enough to see, and it didn't take me long to glance through them.

The girl was the same in all the photos. I guessed her age would be around eight to ten. We were both naked. In one of the pictures I was lying with an ecstatic expression on my face and my head between her legs. In another I was kneeling before her while her mouth hung open. In a third I was spread across her with my arms out like a fallen angel. But what created the greatest impact was the despair shining from her face as she stared at the photographer and begged for help.

I sat gawping, feeling myself freeze on the inside. For the first time since I had been arrested I could feel I was on shaky ground. A new feeling seized me, a fear that I had repressed these acts, that I had in fact performed them, but my brain refused to register them.

None of the others said a word. The triumph I read in Beatrice Bauge's eyes was unbearable. Hamre and Solheim stared, jaws set. Waagenes didn't look as shocked as I felt.

Suddenly my stomach turned, I uttered something like a grunt and got up from my chair holding my mouth. 'I'm going to be sick!'

Hamre jumped up. 'Not here. Bjarne! Take him out!'

Sick rose in my throat in sour-tasting spasms. Solheim grabbed me under the shoulder, led me out of the room, some way down the corridor and into a men's toilet with a urinal and two cubicles. The vomit was already squeezing between my fingers, and when I fell to my knees in front of the porcelain bowl it was like a deluge breaking free, and I spewed in long, convulsed retches, as though my body were being torn apart.

In the end I staggered to my feet again, my stomach and solar plexus still in cramp, but already empty of the little food I had eaten over the last few days. What came up now was acrid, acidic gastric juice, straight from the source.

Far away I heard the ringing of a mobile phone and Solheim

answering. 'What? Just a minute. I can't hear...' The door slammed behind him.

I stumbled out of the cubicle and looked at myself in the mirror above the sink. A ghostly face stared back. I turned on the cold-water tap, held my hands under it and rinsed my face, then rubbed it as hard as I could.

I pulled a paper towel from a dispenser and dried my face. Then I stood motionless. Solheim still hadn't returned.

I opened the door a fraction. Now I could hear his voice through an open door from one of the nearby offices.

Without a second thought I stepped into the corridor, walked in the opposite direction of the interview room, past at least two more office doors, opened the stairwell door, crossed the landing and ran down the steps. The civilian employee in reception barely looked up as I passed.

On the terrace outside the police station I glanced left and right. The sudden daylight blinded me and in shock I realised that outside everything was as before, as though nothing had happened. Over there was what for some years had been the Nye Folkets Hus – the community centre. Over there was the sixteenth-century Rådstuen, where the town council held its meetings; and over there, Småstrandgaten with the malls, shops, buses and cars.

I walked down from the terrace, turned into Domkirkegaten and headed towards the corner of Østre Skostredet. It was only after I had rounded it that I broke into a run.

27

Of one thing I was certain. Within a few minutes every single police officer in Bergen would be on the lookout for me, and as, by and large, the police patrol in cars nowadays, not on foot, the safest place to go was where it was difficult to drive a vehicle.

From Østre Skostredet I turned up Skostredet towards Kong Oscars gate. Between Lille Øvregate and Skansen there was a network of alleyways and narrow streets, and I walked briskly – so as not to attract too much attention in an area that invited petty crime from junkies and other strays on the streets – taking the shortest route. Around one of the corners in Nedre Fjellsmug, invisible to passers-by in Lille Øvergate, I stood panting as I weighed up my situation.

My escape had been spontaneous and without any form of a plan. Now I was on the street wearing the clothes I stood up in – trousers, shirt and jacket, but without a coat. I had no phone, no money and no bank card. Almost sixty years old, I had no close friends. The ones I'd had were either dead or had cut me off years ago. Thomas, Mari and little Jakob lived in Oslo and had more than enough to cope with; Beate, if she was bothered, was in Stavanger with her new partner, Regine. The only person I had was Sølvi.

After her husband was killed coming up to a year ago now, Sølvi had run their business from the office in Bredsgården, where she was to be found for most of the working week. My sole hope was to get in touch with her, but I wasn't certain if the police had latched onto the relationship between us. Vidar Waagenes knew about it, but how had he reacted to my sudden exit? Would he have handed over the information he had to the police or would he have maintained the oath of confidentiality in this case as well? I had to trust him, and if I knew him well, he wouldn't have said a word.

Accordingly, I would have to get from Nedre Fjellsmug to Bredsgården without being seen; and as it was broad daylight, September
and a long time before darkness fell I would have to take some risks.
Yet I couldn't move too far up Telthussmuget, because they would certainly have a lookout there: Moses Meland or some other experienced
undercover officer.

I flitted through the alleys, past Det Lille Kaffekompaniet, where
the scent of freshly ground coffee made my nostrils quiver. I quickly
crossed Vetrlidsallmenningen and nipped into Langeveien. There I
hugged the wall on the right while keeping an eye on Fjellgaten opposite, where Telthussmuget culminated. No-one spoke to me, no-one
shouted out. I turned down Forstandersmuget, glanced right and left
before crossing Nikolaikirkeallmenningen, where the church had once
stood, and not long afterwards I was at the top of Wesenbergsmuget,
which arched round in an attractive curve to Øvregaten, right behind
Bryggen.

I still felt I was on very shaky ground. Fear of the consequences of
what I had done lay like a rock in my chest, blocking my breathing and
making me gasp for air, even when I was standing still.

I followed the long alley down. It tapered gradually to the narrow
opening onto Øvregaten. I poked my head out and discreetly observed
both sides before scurrying across, running down the steps and taking
the cobbled path to the right of the old potato warehouse at the top
of Bredsgården. Now it was only a short way to the narrow passage-
way with the classic wooden floor leading right down to the pavement
on the outside of Bryggen. Halfway down, I ran up to the staircase to
the walkway off the first floor, followed it down to the building facing
the street, knocked on the door bearing their sign, Bringeland Papir &
Kontor, opened it and darted in.

She swivelled round on her chair with a frightened expression in
her eyes before she saw who it was. Then she got up and her expression
changed from surprise to a nervous smile and thence to one large question mark. 'Varg! Have they let you go?'

She came over, embraced me and held me close.

I hugged her, put my mouth in her hair by her ear and mumbled: 'No, I did a runner.'

For a moment it was as though she hadn't understood what I was saying. Then I felt her stiffen in my arms. She pulled away from me and searched my face. 'What! You escaped?'

I nodded, and gulped. 'I couldn't stick … It was just too awful. Do you know what they're accusing me of?'

She nodded, and her eyes had something hesitant, almost wary in them. 'I couldn't believe it when … your solicitor rang.' She carefully extricated herself from my arms. 'I think … I've known you for only six months. How well can you know another person?'

I eyed her in disbelief. 'But you can't believe … after all, you've seen me with Helene. I've been on my own with her.' I could hear as I said this I was getting deeper into something that might work against my intentions. 'I could never … You must believe me, Sølvi. With my background in Child Welfare. If there's one thing that is holy for me – holier than parental rights, holier than laws and rules and regulations – it is the inviolability of children. The abuse of children, that's the most disgusting crime imaginable.'

I gripped her shoulders and pulled her to me. She didn't resist. 'I'm innocent, Sølvi! Someone has dumped a load of filth on my computer and the police are convinced it's me …'

'But who would … who could do such a thing to another person?'

'In a line of work like mine … you inevitably acquire enemies.'

'But you have to tell the police!'

'I have done.'

'But you can't just run off like this. They must be out looking for you!'

'You can be sure of that. They didn't contact you while I was inside, did they?'

'No. Waagenes asked if he could give my name to them, but I told him not to. He said there was a possibility he might use me in your defence, and I said go ahead, if it was necessary. I talked about Helene and how well you got on together and how I had no cause for suspicion whatsoever. He said fine, he would contact me later, he was only ringing to send me your love after visiting you … in prison.'

I walked to the window and looked out. The traffic along Bryggen was moving as it always had done for the last fifty years. Just more slowly because of the heavy-goods vehicles after the Fløyfjell Tunnel was opened in 1988. On the other side of Vågen lay the domain of children and families, Nordnes, where even the rebuilt areas after the war were beginning to represent the 'old days', as if they had always been like that.

'What are you going to do, Varg?' she asked from behind me.

I tore myself away from the window and turned to her again. 'I need help.'

She agreed. 'I'll do what I can, but … I don't think you can stay with us, can you?'

'No, no. That would be much too unsafe, and furthermore impractical, bearing in mind that I have to find out what happened.'

'You don't mean investigate, do you?'

'What else? I can't sit on my hands until the police find me. And they will do, in the end. And I don't want to leave the country.'

'Listen … I'm looking after a flat for a friend, up in Hans Hauges gate. You can have her key.'

'For how long?'

'She's in Italy for at least two more weeks.'

'But I need…' I stirred uneasily. 'I'll give you back whatever you lend me as soon as I … But first and foremost I need a phone. Buy me a cheap one in your name and a stack of phone cards.'

She nodded.

'And then … if you could help me … could you rent a car?'

She viewed me with scepticism. 'You could borrow mine, but I really need it myself, living as far out as I do, and with Helene…'

'Yes, I know.'

'But that's fine. I've got money in the bank, so I can lend you whatever you need.' For the first time in the conversation she put on a wry smile. 'You're not one of these con men we hear about in Swedish pop songs, are you, Varg?'

'If I were, I would've run off with your money before.'

'Oh, don't be so sure I would've been fooled so easily.'

Suddenly the phone rang on her desk. We exchanged glances. I motioned for her to answer it. Before she lifted the receiver I said: 'If anyone asks after me...' I gestured silence.

'Bringeland Papir & Kontor. You're talking to Sølvi.'

She listened to the speaker and mouthed to me: '*Waagenes.*'

I repeated my gesture, first with a finger to my mouth, then a flat hand: *Not a word.*

She kept a straight face and pretended to be horrified when he told her I had run off. 'What! But where? Surely the police will be looking for him?' After his answer she sent me an affirmative nod, not that it came as any surprise to me. 'No, no, not a word. I assume he hasn't got a phone anyway?' He said a little more. 'Yes, I can imagine ... Yes, if he gets in contact of course I'll ... Yes, yes. But keep me informed if you hear anything ... Yes. Thank you. Bye.'

She rang off. 'There's been one heck of a rumpus.'

For the first time I grinned, although my lips felt a bit stiff. In my mind's eye I could visualise the bollocking Solheim must have got when he returned to the interview room with the news that the bird had flown. They won't have spared his feelings when they found out, neither Hamre nor Bauge, I thought.

'What are you going to do, Varg? I have to pick up Helene from school, but I can pop back this evening. I just have to ring for someone to babysit Helene. You can have Lisbeth's flat key. I'll tell you how to ... Oh, there is one thing, by the way. She's got a cat.'

'What?'

'That's why I've got the key. It's an indoor cat, but naturally she needs food and care, so I drop by at least once a day. You're not allergic, are you?'

'Not to cats or anything else, to my knowledge.'

'I think she's friendly. You've just got to let her get used to you and then...'

I sighed. 'That is the least of my problems right now, Sølvi.'

'Her name's Madonna, if you feel like a chat.'

'Let's see how chatty she is.'

She gave me the key and explained to me where the house was in Hans Hauges gate and which floor the flat was on.

'See you this evening. I'll try to get hold of a phone, but I'm afraid the car will have to wait until tomorrow.'

I thanked her and cast a final glance around, as though the shelves on the walls with envelopes of varying sizes, packets of photocopy paper and other office equipment represented a form of everyday life I could only dream of returning to, in the near future at any rate. Then I opened the door and cautiously stepped back into reality.

28

They hadn't used his middle name when they christened the street in 1911, but it was called after the lay preacher, Hans Nielsen Hauge. The street was like an inspired sermon – rising in pitch at both ends – and the buildings on it were what Bergensians called 'chimney houses' because they burned down so quickly if they caught fire. But at the southern end of the street new blocks of flats had been erected, as late as the end of the 1980s, when the Salvation Army also took up residence there.

The flat Sølvi's friend owned was on the northern part of the street, in a classic 'chimney house'. I unlocked the main entrance, then the door to the flat on the first floor. Once inside I breathed a sigh of relief. I hadn't seen any police cars on the way up from Bryggen. The manning of the police station on an ordinary Monday, just before shifts changed, can't have been at its most impressive.

I inhaled the unfamiliar smell of a flat containing an animal. A grey-and-black striped cat slunk through a half-open door at the end of the hall. In the doorway she stood weighing me up with her green eyes until she decided this wasn't very interesting and turned round, back to whence she had come, with all the innate arrogance cats possess.

I followed and entered what transpired was the sitting room. It was pleasantly furnished with what some might call feminine taste, dominated by light colours, a large number of cushions on the corner sofa and a wide selection of potted plants – above all orchids – on the broad window sills. The pictures on the walls were within the same colour spectrum, some of them sun-drenched fields of flowers, others more abstract, though less inviting. The corner sofa consisted of a three-seater and a two-seater in a rust-red hue with lighter diagonal stripes, like light

June drizzle. The shorter wall was dominated by a large bookcase with an unsystematised mixture of dog-eared paperbacks and leather-bound classics, the spines so creased that they had either been read many times or bought from an antiquarian bookshop. A modest stereo and a small portable TV suggested she preferred books to music and television, and I understood why she and Sølvi were such good friends that Sølvi was her first choice to look after her pet while she was away.

Madonna had crept into a basket under the window and in front of the radiator. She peered up at me and her whiskers quivered as if to inform me that she was following everything that I did. In the hall I had passed a box of sand where she did her business and, walking into the kitchen, I saw a bowl of water and one of cat food, which she still hadn't eaten.

In a kitchen cupboard I found some tea. I filled the kettle and put it on the stove to heat while I quickly acquainted myself with the rest of the flat. There were two rooms, a kitchen and a small bathroom with space for a shower cabinet in one corner. The bedroom faced the back-yard, and the bed was covered with light-blue linen. On the bedside table there was a pile of books and from the clock radio on a dresser along one wall the time gleamed at me in red figures: 14.45.

I established there was a back door from the kitchen leading to a fire escape down into the backyard, in case a sudden retreat became necessary from here as well.

There was a strange stillness in the flat. No sounds from the neighbours and very little traffic in Hans Hauges gate, so there was little more than a distant rumble outside.

When the water had boiled I made myself a cup of tea, fetched the phone directory from the hall and sat down by one of the sitting-room windows, where the daylight was strong enough to read by. While waiting for Sølvi I could at least see what I might be able to find out in this way.

The notepad I had been using in prison was in my inside pocket. I started leafing through it, jotting down all the relevant names on a blank page and trawling through the directory.

Fusa had its own section in the alphabetical part at the back. There I found both Nora Nedstrand and Svein Olav Kaspersen. Sturle Heimark wasn't registered. I couldn't find his name in the Bergen section either, which made me put two lines under his name and a question mark beside it on the list. In Bergen I found Hjalmar Hope, with an address in Georgenes Verft, the newly built housing project on the tip of the Nordnes peninsula.

I also found three of my fellow accused. Mikael Midtbø had an address in Frekhaug, which Hamre had mentioned during the interview a few days ago. Per Haugen lived in Flaktveit in Åsane and Karl Slåtthaug in Landås with a Strimmelen address.

It tormented me that there was a name missing from the list. The man who had commissioned me to find Karsten, Bønni and the circle that was obviously a gentlemen's club on the top floor of a disused industrial building in Solheimsviken. How on earth could I discover his name, now, almost a year later? The only other link I had with the circle was Karl Slåtthaug, and being accused of the same depravity as me, he must now be behind bars.

Karsten and Bønni were first names, so it was a waste of time looking for them. Bønni was almost certainly Bjørn, in Bergensian parlance, but knowing that didn't help me get much further in my investigation.

The last name I found was Siggen, whom I would definitely be contacting. Sigurd Svendsbø lived in Skytterveien, a little way out of Sandviken. So they were all nicely dispersed over the whole Bergen region, and there was no doubt that if I was going to have any chance at all to carry out any kind of investigation I would be utterly dependent on a car. In which case I would have to rely on Sølvi. And then it struck me I should have asked her if she had a laptop spare as well, but I doubted she did. It was beginning to look as if I would have to rely on the old methods; the phone directory had been a loyal and resolute assistant for so many years.

In the kitchen there was a little radio. I went in and switched it on to hear if there was anything about my escape on the news. There wasn't. Madonna came out, went to her bowl without even giving me a second glance, munched some of the dry biscuits and lapped some water. Nevertheless, I had a suspicion she had primarily come in to see what I was up to. When I bent down to pat her she wriggled away and darted back into the sitting room. After an inspection of the corners she returned to her basket and made herself comfortable again.

I threw myself onto the sofa, closed my eyes and let my mind wander. It wasn't particularly enjoyable. I was in a precarious situation. The police were hunting for me, but, for now at least, only in the more obvious places. As yet I had no money, no mobile phone and no car. I barely even had a plan. All I had was a list of names retrieved from a corrupted memory, through mists of booze and abandon over far too long, where other unexploded bombs could be waiting to go off. And when I started investigating I would have to keep as low a profile as possible to avoid being caught.

Finally I dozed off. When the doorbell rang I jumped into the air and was on my feet as Madonna poked her head out of the basket and subjected me to a green stare. I stumbled into the hall to the intercom. I lifted it without speaking.

Her voice was low and questioning. 'Varg?'

I breathed out, but didn't answer. I pressed the button that opened the door downstairs, left the front door of the flat ajar and through the crack saw her rushing up the stairs as her eyes sought mine in the doorway. As soon as she was inside I closed the door and twisted the handle. For a moment we stood looking at each other, like two refugees who had escaped by a hair's breadth from being taken prisoner. She put down the heavy shopping bags she was carrying. Then she cuddled up close to me; I put my arms around her and we held each other tight as though this was all that could help us against what had happened.

Then she freed herself. 'Is everything alright?'

'Madonna hasn't clawed me anyway,' I said. 'Not even when I dozed off and she had the opportunity.'

She nodded to the bags. 'I brought along some food and clothes. I think they'll fit although they're not exactly tailor-made for you.'

Familiar with the layout of the flat, she hung up the black jacket in the hall wardrobe. She was wearing a black-and-white blouse and a black skirt, as if to show that she was still in mourning. She walked ahead of me into the sitting room and looked around in the gloom. I glanced at my watch. It was five minutes to eight and only the street illumination let light into the room.

She walked to the window and took hold of one curtain. 'We can draw them. I don't have any contact with the neighbours, so I doubt anyone will react if we switch on the lights.'

'Sure?'

She nodded, drew the curtains and switched on a steel standard lamp in the corner between the three-seater sofa and the two-seater, then bent down and ran a hand along Madonna's back. The cat stood up at once and rubbed against her calf to demonstrate with the utmost clarity that she made a distinction between people.

Sølvi had been to the hall to bring in the bags. Now it was time to unpack. She pulled out a bottle of wine, a lettuce, a packet of tagliatelle, some minced meat and a jar of pasta sauce. 'I assumed you were hungry.'

'Haven't had a bite since breakfast.'

She lifted out a black peaked cap with red letters on the front: *Berkley. Catch more fish.* 'Thought perhaps you might need something to hide under.'

'Smart thinking,' I nodded, and tried it on. 'Yours?'

She smiled sadly. 'Left behind by Nils, but I don't think he ever wore it. Probably one he was given.'

'I'll take it as a good omen. That I'll get a bite, I mean.'

Then she took out the new phone and the little pile of cards. 'I hope you can work this out by yourself.'

I held it in my hand and cast a superficial glance at it. 'Let's hope so. You don't have a spare laptop by any chance, do you?'

'No. Should I buy one as well?'

I hesitated. 'Let's see how things go during the first few days.'

She looked around. 'I think Lisbeth's got a broadband connection. She took her laptop with her of course. Come to the kitchen with me so that we can talk while we cook.'

There was no doubt that she had been here before. She took out the frying pan, a saucepan and the other equipment she needed and started cooking. 'You can open the wine,' she said as she rinsed the lettuce in the sink.

There wasn't much to talk about actually. I told her what it had been like in the week or so since I had been arrested and once again asserted that I was one hundred percent innocent of the accusations.

She just shook her head, as though this was a summary of events from a world she could hardly imagine. 'There must be lots of sick people out there.'

'Sadly, there are.'

While she continued cooking I sorted out the phone, inserted the SIM card that came with it, registered it in her name and put in the first phone card. Afterwards I tapped in the phone numbers I had in my head, but there weren't many of those. The others I found with the help of the directory. Before the food was on the table it was ready to be used.

I had found the mobile and landline numbers of Vidar Waagenes in the directory. I hesitated, then I tapped in his number. After three rings a woman's voice answered. 'Yes?'

'Hello. Is Vidar at home?'

'Who's ringing?' she said cautiously.

'It's … Varg.'

'Just a moment.'

Two seconds later Waagenes was on the line. 'Varg! Where are you? What on earth happened?'

'I was ill.'

'I can understand that, but throwing up is one thing. It's quite another to run away from the police. You can imagine the dressing-down Solheim got when he returned with his news.'

'Yes.'

'As your solicitor I can offer you only one piece of advice: Hand yourself in at a police station. The sooner, the better.'

'I'm up against it here, Vidar. Someone has set a trap for me. I didn't even know I'd walked into it and … you heard yourself what Siggen said. With the help of modern technology they've created such strong evidence that I haven't a hope!'

'The pictures told their own story, Varg.'

'Did you get copies of them?'

'Yes, Hamre gave me the ones he had, but I haven't got them here. They're in my office safe.'

'Go back and study them carefully then. I can't even remember them being taken. I can't tell you anything about them. Believe me – I've had some terrible blackouts over the last few years.'

'Do you mean that someone fabricated this evidence to trap you?'

'Yes. I haven't a bloody clue whether it's me in those pictures or they've put my head on someone else's body with Photoshop or whatever it's called.'

'But it's still the police's job to get to the bottom of this matter, Varg. How do you think you're going to be able to crack it on your own? With the police looking for you, to boot?'

'Well, how serious is this? Are they going public with it?'

'Not yet. I persuaded them to do a local search for you first. After all, you're not accused of murder. There's no reason to believe you're a danger to the public.'

Oh, yes, I am! To some of them, I said to myself. *If I catch them*. To him I just said: 'No. So, in other words…'

'They'll keep an eye on the places you usually go – home, office – not twenty-four hours a day, I suppose, but I wouldn't recommend you go anywhere near them.'

'What about … Sølvi?'

'Is that where you are now?'

'…No, but … do they know about her?'

'I haven't said a word at any rate.'

'Don't say anything, if they ask.'

'They already have.'

'…Thank you. Cut me some slack for a few days, Vidar. Either the police catch me, in which case I'll have to rely on you again. Or else I'll find something out. But I know time is short.'

'The phone you're ringing from ...'

'New, registered in someone else's name.'

'You've rung my private number. I hope my line isn't being tapped. This case isn't so serious that they would get a warrant to go so far. I hope not anyway.'

'It isn't so serious? It's the worst abuse of children we can imagine.'

'Yes, yes,' he said quickly. 'I didn't mean it like that, naturally. Your running away, *that's* not so serious. They're probably fairly confident they'll pick you up. It's not so easy to stay hidden in the modern world. We leave trails wherever we go, whether we want to or not.'

Sølvi appeared in the kitchen doorway and signalled that the food was ready.

'Can you read my number on your phone, Vidar?'

'Yes, I've already noted it.'

'Call me if anything comes up I need to know. If not, I'll call you.'

'I have to repeat my appeal to you to hand yourself in. You have to trust the police.'

'Right now I don't even trust myself.'

He sighed. 'Well, be careful then, Varg. You may be moving into dangerous territory.'

'I know. Thank you. Talk soon. Bye.'

I rang off and went to the kitchen, where Sølvi had set the table for us both. I filled the glasses, we clinked without a word and tasted the wine. It lay on the palate, bitter-sweet, a little tart, but not so tart that rowan berries picked fresh from the tree in September came to mind.

There were two things that had dragged me out of the swamp since March. One was the job I had been given and had resolved in the days it lasted. The other was meeting Sølvi and the relationship that had grown between us. Even though it was still at an early stage, it was enough for me to fasten the top back on the spirits and be able to enjoy the taste of a good glass of wine or two again without drowning it in aquavit for dessert. Still, there were days when I struggled with temperance, but then I put on my trainers and headed for Mount Fløyen or Isdalen Valley at such a speed that the drink I wanted most when I arrived home was water.

Even now, with uncertainty and fear bubbling away inside me, I was able to close my eyes, have another sip and let the wine roll around my mouth, then put the glass down and tackle the food instead.

After we had eaten we rinsed the plates and cutlery, took our glasses and sat down on the sofa, close to each other. Madonna observed us from her basket with a condescending expression, as though she knew what we were up to.

'I don't like it, Varg. I would feel happier if you'd handed yourself in to the police and let them deal with the case.'

'That was what Waagenes thought too. But I have to find out more under my own steam. All I have to go on is a handful of names, some not even complete, and the least I have to be able to give the police is who they are and where they can find them.'

'But you're all on your own … out there.'

'I'm used to that. And I have you up my sleeve.'

She looked at her watch. 'I have to be home by twelve. How are you fixed for bed linen?'

'We can have a look.'

We went into the bedroom. She folded back the duvet. 'Looks nice and clean,' she said, turning to me. She stood up and kissed me lightly on the mouth and began to undo my shirt.

We made love as if it were for the very last time. Afterwards the sheet was off the mattress on one side and the duvet on the floor. I lay on my back with Sølvi beside me, one thigh over my legs, as if to keep me in place. But I had no plans to flee from here, not until I was forced to.

At half an hour before midnight I accompanied her to the door. She said: 'I'll be round early tomorrow with a rental car.'

I nodded. 'Get one of the most common makes. Preferably a Toyota, so that all I have to do is get behind the wheel.'

'And I'll bring some cash.'

'You'll get it all back with interest.'

'I've already had the interest,' she said, stroking my cheek.

Another little kiss, a quick hug and she was gone.

I didn't sleep much that night. Whenever I did drop off I woke with a start, ready to rush through the back door if someone was coming in. But no-one came. A couple of times I noticed that Madonna was in the room, making sure I was still there, but she left again without a sound.

At half past seven, while the town was coming to life, I got up. I switched on the radio and listened to the local news. Nothing about me. Immediately after nine o'clock my phone rang. It was Sølvi. She was in a Toyota Corolla round the corner in Jens Rolfsens gate.

I got dressed, put the cap on my head, pulled it well down over my forehead and went out to meet her.

When we were both in the car she looked at me earnestly. 'I'm scared, Varg. I don't like this.'

'I don't, either. But…' I grinned wryly. '…A man's gotta do what a man's gotta do.'

'I've lost one husband like this. I don't want to lose another.'

'I understand. But I don't have any other option. It is as it is.'

'And where are you going to start?'

'I reckon I should go to Fusa first.'

'Fusa?'

'To see if any of my old enemies are still there.'

She leaned forward, put her arms around my neck and her mouth against my cheek. 'Don't take any risks! Promise me that…'

I nodded and promised, but behind her back I had my fingers crossed, at least mentally.

After she had got out of the car, waved goodbye and walked down to Nye Sandviksvei to follow it to Bryggen, I sat in the car with a worse conscience than I'd had for as long as I could remember. Then she was round the corner and I could think about something else.

The first thing I did was to ring the insurance company in Fyllingsdalen and ask after Nils Åkre. He'd retired, said the receptionist.

'What! When was that?'

'Oh, before the summer. But I can put you through to someone else.'

'Thank you, but this is … private. I'll ring him at home then.'

'You can try,' the woman said grouchily. 'But I think they're in Spain most of the year. He was last time I spoke to him anyway.'

'Have you got his telephone number down there?'

'No, I'm sorry.'

With that we concluded our conversation. Not long afterwards I was driving towards Åsane, on my way round Samnanger municipality to Fusa. Avoiding the ferry. The fewer electronic trails, the better; that was my motto. I could only guess at what awaited me in Fusa.

29

I drove through Åsane as demurely as a parish priest on his way to the first funeral of the day. The speed limit was as if written on stone tablets in front of me, and I adhered to it rigorously. What I feared most was a random police check. I doubted the police had set up any roadblocks to stop me leaving town, but you always have to be on the lookout for the traffic police. They were on you with their speed guns when you least expected them.

Even outside built-up areas it was important not to exceed the speed limit, to the great irritation of the motorists behind me. This led to frequent overtaking on the E16 between Arna and Trengereid, until I turned off for Samnanger, where there wasn't so much traffic. After passing Tysse I breathed more easily. The police station in Fusa had more than enough to do solving crosswords.

There were few visible changes on the stretch from Eikelandsosen and beyond in the time that had passed since I was last there. The Nedstrand Fishing Equipment building looked even more run-down than before, and there was no sign of any activity.

I turned into Nora Nedstrand's drive and parked at the side. The big Mitsubishi Outlander was stowed away tidily in the garage and there was light in several of the windows.

I got out of my car, kept the cap on and stared rigidly at the large windows on the first floor to see if anyone had reacted to my arrival. But I saw nothing. In front of the house I hesitated for another second, then pressed the bell and heard the characteristic ding-dong inside.

With the door half open she stopped and looked at me through the gap.

Nora Nedstrand had changed noticeably since I was last here. It was as though she had shrunk, but not because she had been on a single-minded diet; more that somehow the air had gone out of her. Her colour scheme was new too. She was wearing a grey sweater and dark-blue, baggy jeans and her red hair had gone white, not because of acute despair, probably, but because she had stopped dyeing it.

The look in her eyes was weary and dejected.

'My name's Veum. I don't know if you remember me?'

'Yes, I do.' She started to close the door.

I employed the salesman's trick and put a foot in the crack. 'Wait! I have to talk to you.'

'We've got nothing to talk about.'

'Oh, yes, we do. I'm looking for Sturle.'

'He isn't here.'

'No, but—'

She interrupted me. 'And I have you to thank for that. It was you who put the police onto him.'

'Yes, but … Can't we sit down and have a chat?'

'We can do that here. I don't want you inside my house.'

'I see, but won't you come outside? Talking like this…'

'Right then!' She came out onto the step, closed the door hard behind her and stared at me. 'What is it you want, actually?'

'As I said, I was looking for Sturle.'

'He's moved,' she said, her voice cracking. 'He left a few weeks after you last came here with all your accusations.'

'I didn't accuse anyone! I asked some questions, in connection with Knut Kaspersen's death. You yourself admitted you had a close relationship with him.'

'Close relationship! We'd known each other since we were kids. We didn't have any relationship.'

'The way you spoke about him suggested you were … good friends.'

'Knut worked with my husband, Oliver, and as adults it was in that context we met. There was no relationship, I keep telling you.'

'Your husband took his own life.'

'Yes, he did, but that has nothing to do with it.'

'What was the reason then?'

Her cheeks puffed out as though she were pumping herself up to give me an earful. 'Is it possible for any human being to answer that question? He didn't leave a letter, but … I had a feeling that … He had been low, but that was probably because they were having problems with the fish farm. There had been an infestation of lice and they had to kill all the salmon. It was an economic catastrophe, and it was only Knut's hard work in the following years that overcame it. When he died the finances were back on an even keel.'

'And afterwards?'

'Svein Olav's running the farm now, but … I don't know. I don't think it's much to shout about.'

'Back to … So you think he took his life because business was going so badly?'

'Acute depression, the doctor said. Oliver had been to see him for some medicine. I found the prescription in his bedside table. The priest said the same, as if that were any consolation.'

'But Knut … helped you?'

'Knut was a support initially, yes. But then Sturle appeared and everything changed.'

'How did you meet?'

'Sturle and I?' For a brief moment there was a ray of light in her face, before it clouded over again. 'He was visiting some acquaintances in a cabin close by, not far from Vinnes. Mutual acquaintances, I should add.'

'And then you got together?'

'Yes.' Her lips tightened, as though she didn't want to say any more.

'And how did Knut react to that?'

'Knut? I think he was the same. You mustn't imagine … If you're trying to construct some kind of love triangle here, you can forget it. We were all adults. Sturle was retired.'

'You sold your share of the salmon farm when your husband died and bought a flat in Spain with the money?'

'Yes, we were down there more and more often, in the heat. It did us good.'

'But the weekend Knut died, Sturle was back here.'

Her face flushed dark. 'He was not! He was in Madrid at a football match! Nothing else was ever … Not even the police could be bothered to check.'

'No?'

'No.'

'So why did you two split up?'

'Because you came here and brought all of this up. Because … the seeds of doubt you sowed were enough to start a quarrel.'

'So you had your doubts too?'

'I had to ask him and … I found…'

'You found what? The plane ticket proving he'd been back here after all?'

Her eyes darkened. 'Yes, I did! I asked him about it, but … he exploded. He said he wouldn't stand for me … I could just go to hell, he said, and as for you…' She paused.

'Yes. Me?'

'He'd take care of you, he said. And then he packed his bags, only a few days after the Chief of Police had been here and said they were shelving the case unless anything new came up. Then he glared at me and said: "See! It wasn't me!" And then he left.'

'But you were sitting on the proof he'd been here that day, weren't you. What did you do with it? Did you contact the police?'

'No.'

'Why not?'

She shrugged. 'I wasn't interested in any more trouble.'

'But you still have it?'

She nodded. 'In a safe place.'

I observed her, unsure how to tackle this. 'And since then?'

'Since then I haven't heard a word from him.' She took a deep breath, with a strange sob, and turned away so that I wouldn't see the tears in her eyes.

I shifted my weight from one foot to the other. 'So you don't know where he is then?'

'I assume he's in Bergen.'

'You haven't tried to contact him?'

She tossed her head. 'No, I haven't.' But she seemed to be full of regret.

'It might not be too late,' I said gently. 'You've got his telephone number, I suppose.'

'No. It's secret. But if you…'

'Yes?'

'If you find out where he lives … I'd like to talk to him, once more.'

'Perhaps we should do it together?'

She appeared uncertain. 'Together?'

'Yes.'

We measured each other with our eyes.

Then she shrugged her shoulders. 'Well … maybe. And now you have to go.'

I nodded. 'See you again perhaps, Nora.'

'I am not Nora to you! You can call me *fru* Nedstrand.'

'*Fru* Nedstrand.'

She sniffled, tossed her head again, turned and walked to the door. I made no attempt to hold her back, and when she slammed the door it was as if she had marked a definitive full stop to any conversations we might have had, from now till all eternity. But she shouldn't feel too sure. I was convinced we had a deal, a thousand years from today or perhaps as soon as tomorrow.

30

While I was in the area I used the opportunity to examine the fish farm as well. Svein Olav Kaspersen had already asserted two and a half years ago that he didn't talk to the police, so I could feel fairly safe in his company if I bumped into him.

There was a car parked in front of the old workshop building; not the blue van, but a red Ford Escort from the mid-90s. The first thing I noticed was that the CCTV camera over the entrance was gone. The second was that one of the windows on the first floor was smashed, and no-one had bothered to do any more than nail a piece of chipboard on the inside. Walking round the house I noticed the camera there was gone too.

I passed the white house where Knut Kaspersen had lived. It looked exactly as it had done the previous time I was there, but it was dark and locked and uninhabited, from what I could see. The flower beds were overgrown and neglected, and an atmosphere of abandonment hung over the whole property.

I followed the path down to the sea, but slowed up when I caught sight of Svein Olav walking along the gangway by an open-net pen with a plastic bucket in each hand. He did the same, and as we approached a point in the middle, on the smooth rocks beside the sea, it was like a classic western with two cowboys preparing for a duel at dawn. We stopped some metres apart. He put down both buckets to have his hands free for his six-shooter.

'Busy, Svein Olav?'

He mumbled something I didn't catch.

'But the business up there is finished?'

'Th-thanks to you!'

'Were you charged?'

'Charged? Didn't even have to file a waiver of prosecution!'

'So why didn't you just carry on then?'

'The bottom had fallen through. Besides … with the Chief of Police hovering around…'

'Yes, but … are you still working with Hjalmar Hope?'

'Not any more. He's gone to Bergen.'

Him too, I thought.

With a little grin he added: 'But he said he'd sort you out.'

Another one. The queue outside my office would be long with that kind of creditor too.

'I remember the last time we spoke, Svein Olav, you said that the weekend your uncle died, your neighbour up there, Sturle Heimark, was back from Spain.'

He stared at me with a furrow between his eyebrows. 'Yeah?'

'Did you meet him yourself?'

'Heimark? Nope, but I saw him!'

'And where were you?'

'Where was I? I was here!' He corrected himself. 'Well, not here. At home.'

'And where's home?'

'Near Vinnes.'

'And how could you see Heimark if you were there?'

'I wasn't there the whole time, was I.'

'No, you were here.'

'Right! For a while. Up at the store. I saw him from there.'

'On his way from the sea then?'

He hesitated. 'Yeah, I think so.'

'And your uncle. Did you see him that day?'

'… Might've done. Can't rightly say.'

'I think you can. You didn't go to sea with your uncle that evening, did you?'

'I did not! Why are you askin'? You don't believe that … that I…?'

I watched him. I didn't know. But one thing was certain. Sturle

Heimark had been here and he couldn't get much further from a football stadium than this.

Svein Olav glared at me. 'I reckon you should go now, Veum.'

'So you remember my name, do you?'

'I know where your office is too!'

'Yes, I had a suspicion you did. But you're not much good with computers, are you, Svein Olav?'

He didn't answer. I saw him clench his fists as if considering whether to use them. But he decided against it.

'Good luck with the farm then. Safer than computers, don't you think?'

'That's none of your business. You clear off! You're trespassin'.'

'And if I don't, you'll ring the police, will you?'

He grimaced, then he bent down, grabbed the two plastic buckets, turned his back on me and headed towards a farm building.

I went back to my car with a sense that I might have set some wheels in motion. There were at least two people I would very much like to get in contact with, even if it would prove dangerous to my health. One was Sturle Heimark. The other was Hjalmar Hope. And so there was only one place to go. Back to Bergen.

31

Twice in the course of the return journey I passed a police car. The first time was on the road between Arna and Vågsbotn, where I drove through a radar speed trap well under the limit and without being stopped. The second was on the motorway through Åsane towards Eidsvåg. A police car was alongside me for a while and involuntarily I felt beads of sweat break out between my shoulder blades. Then they switched on the blue lights and shot forward, heading for Bergen, where they disappeared down Glaskar Tunnel. I breathed a sigh of relief. It wasn't me they were after this time either.

I turned up one of the side streets off Hans Hauges gate and parked. I let myself in and went up to the flat. Everything was calm and peaceful, just as I had left it.

It was like a refuge, a place of freedom in the life of an unfree, wandering monk, a Francis of Assisi with the authorities at his heels. But precisely for this reason it was impossible for me to settle there. I had to steal a march on the authorities, before they caught up with me, and so I had to try and trace Sturle Heimark and Hjalmar Hope, among others. In addition, I had to see what I could find out about the people working at what a woman who called herself Magdalena had referred to as The Tower, and who Karsten, Bønni and my anonymous client were. I had seen Sturle Heimark in The Tower and someone had mentioned that a Hjalmar was a dab hand with computers. Was this Hjalmar Hope or a completely different Hjalmar? But, most important of all, who had made the pictures Hamre showed me and placed them on my hard drives? And what the hell was I doing in those pictures if it really was me?

I called Vidar Waagenes. He sounded busy, as always. 'On my way to court, Varg. Have you come to your senses?'

'I'm still free at any rate. Have you heard anything from our friends in Allehelgens gate?'

'They're on the lookout for you. You can be sure of that. They haven't contacted me.'

'Svendsbø – is he someone I can trust?'

'What do you mean?'

'I'm thinking about contacting him. Is there any danger he'll report me to the police?'

'I doubt it. Siggen's first obligations are to me. But…'

'Have you got his mobile number?'

'Just a moment.' He was back at once. I noted down the number and while I was writing he said: 'I have to be off. Talk later, Varg.'

'OK, thanks.'

I dialled the number.

'Svendsbø here.'

'Hi Siggen. This is Veum. I don't know if you've heard, but—'

'Yes, I have. I'm not sure how clever that was, but…'

'You've seen the photos on my computer, haven't you?'

'Yes, I had no choice.'

'I can assure you … they have nothing to do with me. Either they're … manipulated – faked by Photoshop or whatever the bloody software is called – or else there's something wrong with me.'

'I hear what you say.'

'I could do with a chat. Can we meet?'

'I live in Skytterveien. It might be advantageous if I have my computer equipment handy?'

'Maybe.'

I could see Skytterveien in my mind's eye. It was a cul-de-sac. If I parked there I could only escape on foot. But I would have to take some risks and Waagenes had said I could trust him.

'Can I come now, right away?'

'That's fine. It's the top one of the low blocks. You'll see my name by the bells outside.'

I didn't lose a second and just over twenty minutes later I was there.

Skytterveien nestled idyllically between the rocks at the front of the forested hill west of Munkebotn. The blocks of flats stood on the plain beyond the detached houses in Sølvberget, and to get a view as good as the one they had there, you would have to climb up the only high-rise building there was. I took a risk and left my car in a housing co-op space. As I closed the car door and locked it, I heard the sound of children playing at the edge of the wood, in the local kindergarten. Svendbø's flat was in the line of low blocks beneath the high-rise. Across the street was a community centre, which emphasised the social atmosphere in this area, an inheritance of the loyalty and solidarity in the 50s and 60s, when the patch was being built.

I found the name as instructed and rang the bell. Svendsbø was wearing a different T-shirt this time. It was black with red letters on: CRYSIS 3. He showed me into the flat, through the sitting room and into what was perhaps meant to be a bedroom. In one corner there was, in fact, a sofa bed. The rest of the room reminded me of a control room in a computer centre with several screens, consoles, keyboards, external hard drives, a couple of printers, a scanner and various pieces of equipment I struggled to identify.

Svendsbø stared at me intensely as if to interpret the impression it was all making on me. I nodded and said: 'Impressive.'

'It's been my hobby ever since I was in my teens.'

'And you make a living from this?'

'Better now than when I was employed actually. There are enough customers out there needing an independent consultant in this field.'

'I obviously needed one myself.'

He nodded. 'Yes, you certainly needed a higher threshold and a more solid firewall.'

'Is it really so easy to get into other people's computers?'

'If you don't take the correct precautions, it is. Or if you're stupid enough to click on a link that initially might look innocuous, but in fact hides a bomb. "Logic bombs" they're called in the trade, and there are enough examples of them, from the Christmas card worm that brought

IBM to its knees fifteen years ago to the hackers who infiltrated the Pentagon and other central operation rooms.'

'I'm a dwarf by comparison then.'

'And fast asleep, I would say.'

'Well … But when we met yesterday morning you said you were on the trail of the people who could have planted this material.'

'Yes, come over here.'

He led me to one of the computers, sat down on the office chair and pointed to another next to him. He connected an external hard drive, which he then opened on the screen in front of him. He pressed a couple more keys and at once I recognised my own email account.

I jerked back.

He laughed. 'Yes, as you can see, I can read all the emails you've sent and received…' he scrolled through '…over the last year. You don't tidy up much, I note.'

'Well…'

'And here we have the so-called deleted elements. There's quite a bit from several years back. You must have forgotten the command: "Remove deleted elements"?'

'No, I sometimes find things there that I can still use.'

'Then it's better to archive them. Never mind. This is just kids' stuff.' He clicked onto some webpages I didn't recognise at all, where numbers and letters in the strangest combinations flickered past. 'We're into the operating system now, Varg, and from here we can go in a variety of directions. With the right commands it's also possible to get into the guts of your system, putting it crudely, and read the small print there – unless it's been properly hidden. In which case you often need a pass-word. But with the right software … if I let it whir away for a while it frequently gets through, unless they – the people who commit this kind of cyber crime – have used a very personal password, but they seldom do. Accessibility inside the network is important for them.'

I nodded slowly, trying to follow his lecture.

'In short. I've got into this area and I've found several IP addresses that have been in your machine without your clicking on them.'

'Oh, yes?'

'But now I have to go into hidden catalogues to find out who these addresses are registered to. Here we go up a notch in class. Some people don't know how to put obstacles in the way. You, amongst others. All you have to do is get into Telenor's registration lists, or some other operator's; it's not that difficult, let me tell you. This is probably how the police worked, maybe with a court order in their pockets. So, in this case, Telenor let them see the lists. I've found the other three here who were charged along with you – Midtbø, Haugen and Slåtthaug.' He looked at me. 'You've contacted Slåtthaug before, by the way. His name was on your contact list, but I didn't see any messages, not even among the deleted emails.'

'Really? But that's so long ago it must have been completely deleted. At least ten years.'

He nodded. 'In addition, there's someone who's computer-literate enough to hide their address or operate under a false flag. There are also the Norwegian Data Protection Authority rules; they set limits for how long a log can be accessible, but you can get round these too, if you take a few short-cuts.'

'And is there someone like that ... working on my log?'

He puffed out his lips and blew, in a way which made him resemble a fish in an aquarium. 'There is, Varg. And I haven't cracked the codes yet.'

'But you're on the case?'

'You can be sure of that. It's Vidar's top priority.'

'Another thing, Siggen. Do you know someone called Hjalmar Hope?'

Once again he made a fish-face, as if signalling this was someone he didn't like. 'Yeees ... but I wouldn't count him as one of my best friends. Do you suspect he may have something to do with this?'

'Would that surprise you?'

'Not really. He's in the trade, if I can put it like that, but he's not one of the best. He's been involved in some shady stuff as well. I think he was a partner in a company in Samnanger, or around there, that was on the police radar a few years back.'

'That's right. In Fusa. The very same.'

'The last time I saw him he was with SH Data.'

A tingle ran down my back. 'SH Data in Sandsli?'

'That's them. I've worked for them too on a consultant basis, but Hjalmar Hope is employed there, as far as I know.'

'Hm. Did you know someone else working there, one ... Åsne Clausen?'

For a moment he looked a little disconcerted. 'Åsne? Yes, but she's ... dead.'

'Yes, I know.'

'So she can't have had anything to do with this.'

'No, no. I was just making connections ... as you brought up SH Data. I had a job a few years ago that involved them as well.'

'She had a son who was a computer whiz by the way.'

'Yes, I think I've heard that before.'

'I remember she talked about it ... It must have been the only time I ever talked to her about anything personal.'

'But he's very young, isn't he?'

He shrugged. 'Haven't a clue. As I said, I had nothing else to do with her, so ... Nor with Hjalmar Hope, for that matter.' He turned back to the screen. 'Do you think he could have had something to do with this?' A couple of taps on the keyboard revealed the unpleasant images. First one, then two more, finally even more.

I slid back in the roller chair. 'This is just too awful!'

He turned to me. A bitterness seemed to have him in its grip. 'Yes? I say the same. People like that should burn in hell, if it exists!'

'They should be punished at any rate ... and stopped before they get that far.'

I saw my expression on the screen, ecstatic, as I moved up between the little girl's slender thighs. I saw myself slumped over her and the desperation on her face. 'Can you find out if these images have been doctored?'

He nodded. 'I've checked. They haven't.'

'They haven't!? What do you mean?'

'The light, the resolution, photo-technical details. This is you, Veum, and there's no manipulation.'

'But you...' My mouth was suddenly dry. 'You can't believe that ... I can't remember anything about this at all! If it was me I must've been completely paralytic.'

His expression was more pitiless now. 'As if that's any excuse! It's still you lying there.'

'What about ... the other photos? It's not only these ones, is it.'

'You want to see the whole collection?'

'I don't want to, no, but...'

He tapped on the keyboard and an apparently endless stream of images appeared on the screen. He flicked through them and I noticed some were magnified. It was like being shown around a cabinet of horrors. The photos I was in were trivial compared with those of other children ... and adults. I had to turn away from the screen so many times.

He stared at me without a scrap of sympathy. 'Strong stuff, eh?'

My voice was a croak when I answered: 'This is just so awful! What goes on in the heads of these people?'

'Selfish, brutal abuse of power, coupled with the sickest sexuality.'

'But...' I pointed to the screen. 'They aren't Norwegian, all these photos, are they?'

'It's hard to say. As you yourself know, arrests have been made in a number of countries, and many of these images have crossed national boundaries. Perhaps only the ones of you were taken in Norway.'

'Yes, because I reacted to ... Many of the children have dark skins. Some are completely black, others lighter-skinned, but there are no white children – except for...'

'Who knows what goes on in Norwegian reception centres, Veum? Have you seen the statistics of children who go missing from places like that?'

I nodded. 'Yes, I know. But ... my God!' I looked around the hi-tech bedroom. 'You said yesterday that you had children yourself...'

He smiled wryly. 'And you can't see any signs of them? I can show you the children's room, if you're in any doubt.' He motioned to the wall behind us. 'But like so many others I'm only a part-time father. The mother I lived with found someone else, moved to another part of the country, and here I am.'

'I know the situation, even if it's a few years ago now.' I pointed at the photos on the screen. 'I assure you ... this has nothing whatsoever to do with ... I remember none of this. But I'll get to the bottom of it whatever it may cost. And one of the people I intend to speak to is Hjalmar Hope. Do the names Bønni and Karsten mean anything to you?'

'Not in this context. But we've all known a Bønni at some point in our lives. It must be one of the most common nicknames in Bergen.'

'Of course. What about Sturle Heimark?'

'The policeman?'

'Yes, but he's retired now.'

He still had reservations. 'I remember him contacting me a few times for information. He was responsible for parts of the police computer-training scheme.'

'That's him.'

'I talked to him on the phone, that's all. And I went to the police station to give a couple of lectures that he arranged.'

'Could I ask you a favour?'

He waited for me to go on, without revealing any great goodwill.

'Sturle Heimark is also someone I'd like to talk to. He's supposed to be living in Bergen, but I have no idea where and he clearly has a secret phone number. With all the equipment you have, can you find his address?'

This time he didn't make a fish-face but something more akin to a hamster's. He showed his front teeth, smacked his lips and turned back to the computer. He unhooked my hard drive and went onto one of his own programs.

While waiting for the result of his search he tapped his fingers on the desk beside him. He pressed a few more keys, then he nodded. 'Let's see ... I've got a mobile number.'

I leaned forward and made a note.

'And let me see now ... Here's an address. But of course I don't know if he's living there.'

I gazed at the screen and copied it down. Strandgaten with a three-figure number. So it was a long way out. 'At least that gives me something to check.'

'Then ...'

'Yes, I won't take up any more of your time. But let me know if you come across anything.' I wrote down the number of my new mobile, tore the page out of my notepad and gave it to him. He placed it on his desk without a glance.

On the way out I caught a glimpse of the room next door. There were two bunk beds with brightly coloured linen on, big posters on the wall, bookshelves, Lego boxes and toy chests. It struck me, like a reflection of myself almost thirty years before, that nothing was sadder than a divorced father with a room full of toys and no-one in there, apart from a few times a month. No-one laughing and playing. No-one complaining and crying.

A checkpoint hadn't been set up in Skytterveien. I managed to get down Helleveien again without any great problems. From there I chose the right-hand entrance to Fløyfjell Tunnel, the quickest route to Sandsli and SH Data.

32

As I parked outside the building where SH Data had its offices, just before the end of the working day, I had a strange sense of déjà vu. I had been there before, around two years ago. Then it had been Åsne Clausen I was waiting for; this time it was someone different.

I found the SH Data number thanks to the mobile phone directory and rang it. When a woman's voice chirruped an answer, I asked to speak to Hjalmar Hope.

'One moment please,' she said, and I rang off. So he was definitely there.

Sitting and waiting in a car park gives you time to reflect. In a way I felt comfortable and safe. The car Sølvi had hired didn't differ greatly from any of those around, and it would take a lot for the police to find me here. If anyone passed I would raise the mobile to my ear and pretend I was in the middle of a conversation, in case they should wonder why I was just sitting there. In a way I was also outside the daily life of the town. It would soon be thirty years since I'd had a regular job with a monthly salary. True, the working week had been hard to keep within limits, but if I had to go out at night or travel to Copenhagen to bring someone home, at least I was paid overtime and a daily allowance. As a private investigator I was happy when clients paid up after the case was over. All too often I was left with the advance and a string of unpaid invoices. I had never done my own debt collection and that was obvious from my accounts.

In life's accounts I hadn't done a great deal better, not that I had the energy to reflect on that right now. I had quite different and far more urgent problems to deal with.

I had the car radio on. The traffic was gridlocked, as usual at this time of day. That made life difficult for those picking up children from the kindergarten, but easier for those on a surveillance job. It wasn't easy to evade detection in the traffic between Sandsli and Bergen town centre in the midst of the rush hour.

The number of people coming out of the business centre increased as the clock on my dashboard approached five, but it was more like half past when Hjalmar Hope walked through the main entrance. I recognised him at once and slumped lower in my seat to hide behind the steering wheel.

He wasn't alone. With him was someone I had no problem recognising either. It was Sturle Heimark. They chatted all the way to a dark-blue Audi. Hope got in behind the wheel, and Heimark sat beside him. I had killed two birds with one stone, but I still had no idea what it meant.

When they exited the car park I neatly slipped in behind them. Once again I had the sensation I was reliving something I had experienced before. Hope followed the queue down past the Lagunen Shopping Centre, through Troldhaug Tunnel, along Fritz Riebers vei towards Fjøsanger, where the idyllic beaches along Lake Nordås were replaced by a commanding motorway and from there into the even more congested Fjøsangervei road. At Danmarksplass it was as though the town's combined car parks were spewing out exhaust for their own pleasure, and movement at the crossroads appeared to be what militarists call a 'gradual advance'. I sneaked past two cars behind them before the traffic clogged up as we approached the lights at Bystasjonen Shopping Centre.

We crawled through the centre and out towards Nordnes. At Tollbodallmenningen Hope pulled to the side. I turned into the car park in the middle of the wide road and sat watching. They talked for a few minutes. Then Heimark got out of the car. He bent down and said a few words to Hope before raising a hand to his forehead, slamming the door and stepping onto the pavement. Hope pulled away from the kerb and turned towards Nordnesgaten, while Heimark rounded the corner into Strandgaten. That tallied with the address we had found at Siggen's.

Again I tailed him, but now it was harder not to be noticed. There weren't so many cars on the streets. Most people had returned home and were already tucking into their evening meal.

But I had a suspicion I knew where Hope was going, as his home address was Georgenes Verft. To get there by car entailed quite a detour, so while he continued down Haugeveien, I parked by the cross-roads with Galgebakken and walked from there down to Georgenes Verft, where I sat by the entrance to the USF arts venue. There had been a sardine factory here once, where my mother had worked in her younger days. I had often been to the jazz nights there, and I was always reminded of my mother as I leaned against one of the pillars in the Sardinen club, listening to cool jazz and thinking that at one time this had been the United Sardine Factories. The original Georgenes Verft ship-yards had been further inland, but the housing project had moved the name out here.

Hjalmar Hope's dark Audi suddenly appeared in front of me, and I quickly set off, just in time to see him disappear into the garage complex under the new blocks of flats. I reached the drive in front as his car entered and the garage door automatically closed behind him.

I walked along the path between the blocks, keeping a sharp eye on the fronts to see if lights came on anywhere. After some minutes I spotted a light going on in a flat in one of the furthest blocks with an entrance at the back. I walked over and, sure enough, there was his name by the bell.

I rang and waited.

When he opened up he recognised me at once. But he didn't react fast enough.

'Hi Hjalmar,' I said. 'Long time, no see.' I shoved him into the flat, followed through quickly and slammed the door after me.

33

I manhandled Hjalmar Hope through the hall into the sitting room.

It was a modern, streamlined apartment, furnished in minimalist style and about as personal as a furniture catalogue. Through the window we could see between the blocks outside and across Puddefjord towards the old U-boat pens the Germans had built during the war and which to all appearances would be standing there on doomsday.

Despite being several decades younger than me, Hope put up surprisingly little resistance. He had a handful more flab on him than when I had last met him and hardly belonged to those with a membership card for the nearest fitness studio. If he did it lay unused in his wallet. His dark hair was a touch thicker round the ears and a somewhat premature double chin had made his face less distinct. But the dark suit and the white shirt, open at the neck, still placed him in the employed camp, though with an income based on commission rather than a fixed salary.

I thrust him down onto his steel-grey, brushed-nickel-framed sofa and stood over him in a pose I had borrowed from Humphrey Bogart, a man I was sure he had never heard of.

'What the hell do you want?' he said, looking up at me, eyes wide.

'Do you remember me?'

His gaze shifted to the side. Then it returned, and he nodded. 'I remember you alright, but what the hell are you doing here?'

'Your fish business in Fusa went belly up, literally. I went there earlier today and had a chat with your partner, Svein Olav.'

'The salmon farm was more suitable for Svein Olav than … the other venture, yes.'

'But you're still in the computer industry, I see. You're a dab hand at computers, I heard someone say.'

He glared at me while waiting for me to go on.

'SH Data. What do you do there?'

'Is that any of your business?'

'Did you know Åsne Clausen?'

He seemed to be caught off guard. 'Åsne? Yes, but she's…'

'Yes, she's dead. Absolutely correct. Did you have anything to do with that?'

He flew into a rage. 'What the hell are you trying to say? That I had something to do with … I barely knew her. That was right after I started there, and she … took her own life, they said.'

'And the reason for it?'

'Was private. Something to do with her husband. What do I know?'

'But you know Karsten?'

His eyes widened and the tip of a tongue darted out and licked his lips, like a small reptile that had an existence of its own in his mouth. 'Bruno?'

'Yes.' I could feel myself becoming unsure. *Bruno?*

'Only peripherally. I gave him a hand a few times, with their computer system, when they set up.'

I tried to look as if I knew more than I did. 'And then?'

He shrugged. 'Afterwards they've managed on their own, I assume. Why are you asking? That had nothing to do with SH Data.'

'Bønni, do you know him?'

He had started to regain control. 'Tell me, what are you after? Why have you come here asking me all these meaningless questions? I've a good mind to ring the police.'

'Svein Olav said you don't ring the cops.'

He snorted. 'Svein Olav!'

'He's not the only person you're in contact with in Fusa.'

'Oh, no?' Again he was on his guard.

'It's less than half an hour since I saw you drop off Sturle Heimark in Tollbodallmenningen.'

Silence. On Puddefjord the express passenger boat *Snarveien* passed on its way from Sukkerhus Wharf to Kleppestø on the island of Askøy.

In Laksevåg the street lights had come on. It was past seven o'clock now and darkness was settling over the town.

'What are you two up to?'

He chewed his lips as if to keep the reptile inside. 'We have … erm … common interests.'

'And they are…?'

'He's pretty hot on computers too. We're running and developing a project.'

'A computer project?'

'You could put it like that.'

'He's a former police officer.'

'Yes, so what? Because you're retired doesn't mean you're not allowed to work. That's precisely…' He bit his lip.

'That's precisely why you contacted him?'

He didn't answer.

I went for a bold move. 'You know the police still have him on their radar after the suspicious death in Fusa, don't you?'

'Suspicious? What the hell are you talking about now?'

'Svein Olav brought it to my attention at the time. Sturle Heimark was back home on a lightning visit the weekend his uncle, Knut Kaspersen, died.'

There was some violent churning of his jaw muscles, as though the little reptile was trying to get out. 'Svein Olav should just shut his gob!'

'But he won't, you see. Perhaps you should send him a greeting like the one I received in March the year I dropped in on you.'

For a second or two I saw a glint of triumph in his eyes, as if the memory of it pleased him. Then he came back down to earth. 'A greeting?' he said with the most innocent of expressions. 'I'm not quite with you there…'

Suddenly there was a ring from his inside pocket: a syncopated blip-blop I had never heard before. He kept eye contact and took out his phone, the very latest model. He looked at the display. 'Talk of the devil. Sturle Heimark. Shall I answer it?'

Before he could make a move the ringing stopped.

I hesitated. Then I said: 'Is it you who put the filth on my computer?'

He looked up at me in surprise. 'What filth?'

'You know what I'm talking about.'

'No, I don't. Honestly…'

His phone beeped twice, also a kind of two-step syncopation. He opened the message and read the display. He glanced up at me. 'But perhaps this is the answer.'

Before I could react he had deftly tapped in a response to the message. He had a little smile on his face now. 'So the police are after you, are they, Veum?'

'Heimark sent the message, did he?'

The smile changed to a smirk. 'He still has his contacts…'

Another message blip-blopped in. This time I reacted. I leaned forward, got my left arm under his chin and forced his head back as I grabbed the hand holding the phone. He tried to wriggle free and held the phone tight, but I managed to grasp it from him.

I moved away and looked at the unfamiliar display. The whole message was visible at the bottom, beside a message symbol: *Keep him there. I've rung the police.*

'Shit!'

I met his eyes. And a huge grin. Between the shiny teeth the little pink reptile head protruded again.

He stood up and held out his hand. 'Give it to me!'

'I'm taking it with me,' I answered, and stuffed it into my pocket. Then I strode across the room to the balcony door facing the path. I opened the door and poked out my head.

I could hear sirens from the district around Skottegaten and Strange-hagen. Hjalmar Hope grabbed my arm and squeezed, trying to drag me back in. I turned, pulled him towards me, sank my knee in his flabby stomach and freed my arm. With a whimper he slumped to the floor in front of me.

Then I was through his flat and outside at the back again. I quickly got my bearings. Behind the building, steps went up the steep moun-tainside to Nordnes Park and Nordnes School. As I ran up the steps in long strides I saw the reflection of blue lights from the area between USF and Georgenes Verft.

Hjalmar Hope was on his feet and I could hear him shouting from the balcony at the front: 'Here! Here!' Unless I was much mistaken his biggest worry was that I had run off with his phone. I continued my escape to higher ground.

34

With the taste of blood in my mouth I ran up the last stretch to Nordnes
Park. At the top I stood panting and listening for signs that someone
was following me. But I didn't stop for long. I quickly cut down through
the old elementary school and what had once been the Seamen's Insti-
tute. I came out in Haugeveien and at the top of Tollbodallmenningen
I stopped to check my surroundings.

I was in the area where I grew up now, and even as I was making my
escape, images and associations flickered through my brain. As a child
we had heard stories about people having to go 'underground' during
the German occupation and groping their way around in the darkness.
This was roughly how I felt now. In the town that was mine I was an
outlaw. I didn't have to watch out for the Gestapo, but it would have
been very inconvenient to be hauled into the police station before I had
made some progress towards finding any answers.

Not far from where I was standing lived Sturle Heimark, but he was
the last person I wanted to call on now. I found the messages between
him and Hjalmar Hope on the phone I was holding.

The first one read: *The police are after V. Veum. Charged with possession of child porn.*

Hope's reply was brief: *He's here.*

And then Heimark's response: *Keep him there. I've rung the police.*

Relieved to have been a step ahead of them, I put the phone in my
pocket. From my own phone, I called Sølvi.

'Varg! Where are you?'

'In Nordnes with the police hard on my heels. Can you come into town?'

'I'm on my way. I've organised childcare, but … What do you want
me to do?'

'Drive along C.Sundts gate, turn into Strandgaten by Tollbodall-menningen...' I racked my brain. 'Park in front of Nykirken so that I can see you from Nykirkeallmenningen. I'll come down when the coast is clear. But if there are lots of police in the streets near the centre flash your lights three times before you switch off the engine. OK?'

She sounded doubtful. 'This is crazy, Varg. It's as if we're in a film!'

'A very bad film, if you ask me. Are you coming?'

'Yes, yes, of course.'

We rang off and I kept walking.

At the corner of Nordnesveien and Nykirkeallmenningen I stood waiting, ears pricked, eyes peeled. There were no sirens to be heard, no blue lights to be seen. I hoped they were concentrating their efforts around USF, along Skottegaten and in Georgenes Verft. From here I had good avenues of escape in several directions, but it would be better to see them before they saw me because I wouldn't have much chance against a fresh recruit from police college.

While I was waiting I switched on Hjalmar Hope's phone again. It obviously wasn't secured with any form of code. I went through his contacts list and there I found Svein Olav, Sturle H and Bruno K. Was Karsten a surname then? That should make it easier to search for him. None of the other names was familiar, apart from one: Severin C. Wasn't Åsne Clausen's son called Severin? As far as I could remember ... yes, he was.

In Strandgaten a dark-grey Volvo S40 that I recognised as Sølvi's pulled into the kerb by the western exit of Nykirken Church. I watched carefully. She didn't flash her lights; in fact she switched off the engine as soon as she parked.

In my childhood the section of the timber buildings around Schrødersmuget that had survived the explosion of the Dutch ship loaded with explosives in 1944 was still standing to the north of Toll-bodallmenningen. I had classmates who lived there. But those houses were gone now, replaced by blocks of flats in around 1960. I strode alongside them now, down to the corner of Strandgaten, looked right and left, crossed the street and got into the back seat of Sølvi's car.

'Hi. Thanks!'

'Are you going to stay there?'

'I'll duck down when we move off so that no-one can see me.'

She rolled her eyes, a clear sign that she still didn't like the film I had persuaded her to join me in. But she started the car and moved towards the centre.

'Did you see any police?'

'One car passed, but it seemed to be going up towards Klosteret.'

As we passed the church I lay down flat on the back seat and stayed like that until we were out of the market square and on our way through Bryggen. Only then did I dare to sit up again.

'And the rental car?' she asked.

'I'll have to go back for it later. It's in Haugeveien.'

She turned into Sandbrugaten, past Mariakirken and up Nye Sandviksvei. Halfway up Hans Hauges gate she found a parking space. The street was deserted. There was nothing to suggest that anyone had found out where I was hiding. A couple of minutes later we were in the flat. We drew the curtains and switched on the lights. Madonna darted out to see who was visiting this time, confirmed to her approval that it was Sølvi and carried on into the kitchen for some food.

When Sølvi returned she looked at me with concern. 'How long do you think you can avoid the police?'

'I have no idea. For as long as possible.'

'Have you made any progress?'

'A few names have cropped up, which I'll have to investigate.'

'I've brought my laptop with me. You can have it until this is all over.' She looked around. 'I think Lisbeth's broadband connection is here somewhere.'

I nodded towards the corner sofa. 'There it is.'

'By the way … Helene's got a sleepover with a friend from her class, so I can … stay here.'

I instantly pulled her close. 'Then we'll have to try not to spend the whole night on the internet.'

'No … shall I make some food while you get online?'

'What's your password?'

'It's not very original: *Helene1992*.'

She kissed me lightly on the mouth before going to the hall and collecting her laptop and a plastic carrier bag full of food. While she went to the kitchen, I connected up, clicked on Internet Explorer and began to search.

There were several hits for Bruno Karsten, but none that told me anything more than that he was involved in a number of companies, either on the board or as a general manager. On the tax list he was recorded as earning between three and four hundred thousand kroner a year, and his net worth was zero. Which told me that he belonged to those who had learned the tricks. There were no interviews with him and I couldn't find an address or a telephone number for him.

It was impossible to search for Bønni, but there was another name that stuck in my memory. *Skarnes*. The first search revealed only a town in Hedmark. I refined the search: *Skarnes Bergen*, but that didn't produce a relevant answer either. When I enlarged the geographical area to *Skarnes Hordaland*, there were more hits, but only one of them referred to a person. Someone called Ole Skarnes had a postal address of Lepsøy in the municipality of Os. He was the only one I found, and when I searched the name there were no further personal details and no photos. In the recesses of my mind I could hear the echo of a woman's voice: 'Skarnes. His name's Skarnes. He's the devil incarnate. Him and Bønni and Karsten. But there are more. Many more.'

Skarnes. Bønni. Karsten.

'And you? Your name?'

'Magdalena. The chosen one.' I made a note of the name and address on the list of people I ought to investigate further.

I deliberated. Then I delved for references to Severin Clausen. Despite his youthful years there were several hits. 'Fifteen-year-old Severin Clausen's favourite subject is computers' was the first I found. The article said that computer technology was the optional subject Severin liked best, and the teacher praised the young student, whose grade was a consistent A. 'A future computer expert' was the verdict of the journalist behind the feature. Another hit told readers that

Severin (16) had created his own computer game, which he wanted to present to the top game companies in the hope of having it launched internationally. There was no follow-up article to say whether he had succeeded in his venture. There were several articles saying more or less the same. He appeared in a couple of photos from The Gathering, a five-day computer party in Hamar, Easter 2001. I had a strong feeling that I should try and contact Severin (now seventeen?), if for no other reason than to ask him what his connection with Hjalmar Hope was.

A search for his father, Nicolai S. Clausen, produced a large number of hits, and also several photos, largely in connection with press conferences or other business initiatives in the media. On the tax list he was recorded as earning just over a million kroner and had a net wealth of several million kroner.

The next targets were my three co-accused: Mikael Midtbø, Per Haugen and Karl Slåtthaug.

Mikael Midtbø was the youngest, thirty-seven years old with an address in Frekhaug. Beyond that, there was nothing on the Net. Per Haugen was seventy years old according to an article from two years ago in *Bergensavisen*, where he was among a random selection of Bergensians asked whether they had any comments regarding the proposed staging of the Winter Olympics in Bergen and Voss. He had no comment to make other than 'By then I'll be dead, so I don't have an opinion'. He was described as being a completely anonymous-looking elderly gentleman. I couldn't remember ever having seen him before. Beyond that, there was nothing of interest.

Karl Slåtthaug had been more active in the media. He appeared in various contexts, as a chief fundraiser for many charitable purposes, mostly street children, in Eastern European countries and South America. He had written papers on the debate about child welfare and the importance of having a full provision of institutions in this area, both public and private. In addition, he was committed to environmental issues, both in the controversy surrounding wind turbine farms, which he supported, and drilling for oil in the Barents Sea which he opposed.

There was nothing about the case that led to him being given the boot from Social Services, naturally enough. It happened before news coverage had managed to spread fully across the Net. But it stuck in my mind like glue, and it occurred to me that perhaps I ought to take a trip out to the children's institution he had been obliged to leave and see if anyone was more willing to discuss the case now than they had been at the time. Cathrine Leivestad would be the key person to contact.

I didn't get a great deal further because I was invited into the kitchen to taste a bouillabaisse, which in fact contained only two of the six pre-scribed types of fish – one red, one white – in addition to an abundance of vegetables.

'Shall we pick up the car this evening?' Sølvi asked, standing with an as yet unopened bottle of white wine in her hand.

'Probably wise to wait until tomorrow morning,' I said.

She smiled, unscrewed the top and filled the glasses, which were already on the table.

Later we didn't spend much time in front of the screen.

35

The following morning we got up early and Sølvi drove me to Nordnes. She dropped me where she had picked me up, and while she drove around the tip of Nordnes and along Haugeveien to check if there was any obvious surveillance of the rental car, I walked up to Fredriksbergs-gaten, which rose behind what was left of the old church hall. I waited until she called me on her phone and confirmed she couldn't see anything suspicious around the parked car.

'I'll risk it then. Thanks.'

'Good luck, Varg. And do be careful.'

We rang off, I put my phone in my inside pocket and walked with wary step up to Haugeveien, got into the car after a quick recce, sat down and started the engine. No-one jumped out of the bushes like a jack-in-a-box and, much relieved, I drove down Haugeveien and crossed Klosteret.

In my head I already had a plan for the day. I had spoken to Cathrine Leivestad and she had said she was willing to accompany me to the institution in Olsvik where Karl Slåtthaug had worked. We'd do this after 'my worst meeting' was over, from two o'clock onwards.

The initial visit on my agenda was probably the most dangerous. I hoped it would be less so early in the day, bearing in mind their activities, than in the evening.

As far as I could remember, I had been to The Tower twice before – taken the first time by a man they called Bønni, the second by Karl Slåtthaug. I hadn't driven there either time, but I knew to a fairly high degree of accuracy where it was. I didn't have much trouble finding it: along the stretch between Puddefjord Bridge and Solsheimviken and right down to the sea. The heralded renovation of the buildings along

Damgårdsveien still hadn't materialised properly. The six-storey-high, once white, now dirty-grey, industrial edifice stood like a last outpost to modernisation, totally dark and without any signs of life.

I sat parked at a reasonable distance from the old entrance, surveying it. From the nearby building site came the sounds of excavators, jackhammers and noisy generators. From the abandoned building there wasn't so much as a groan.

At length I got out of the car and walked over. The entrance was closed, locked. The combination lock beside the door had been removed. Bits of cable hung from a hole in the wall. All the signs were that the business had either collapsed or moved to another locality.

A gate in the fencing beside the building stood ajar. I opened it and went inside. A disused quayside no-one had bothered to keep tidy was covered with all manner of scrap, everything from toilet bowls to what looked like snowploughs, in sharp contrast to the sleek buildings of the Hi-Tech Centre on the opposite side of the narrow arm of the fjord.

At the back of the building there was a fire escape all the way up to the fourth floor. I walked over and shook it to see how stable it was. It was dark brown with rust, but there was nothing to suggest that it couldn't bear weight. Without a moment's hesitation, I climbed up.

The door to the fire escape on the fourth floor was locked. I peeped into the crack. The lock mechanism was not so advanced that it would resist a multi-tool penknife. I was glad I had found one in the kitchen drawer in Hans Hauges gate and had been prescient enough to bring it along. I took the knife from my pocket and tried my luck. The lock gave way with a little click. I moved backwards and pulled the door towards me. I swiftly stepped inside and closed the door behind me.

I was in a rear corridor, where an internal staircase led up to the fifth floor. I opened the door ahead and came into what from the previous time I had been here I remembered as the bar. Now the room had been stripped of everything that could be removed in terms of the interior and furniture. All that was left was a worn floor covering and the same dark-red silk wallpaper, which seemed even more forlorn now that the rest of room was a ruin.

I crossed the room and entered what had been Bruno Karsten's office. All that was left here was the view of Møhlenpris and Nygårdsparken. All the equipment had been removed; all the furniture was gone. The rats had left the sinking ship, and from the look of the place it would take a forensics officer to find a clue of any use in there.

I walked back to the bar and up the spiral staircase to the floor above. At the top they hadn't been quite so thorough. What once had been a kind of loft was divided into cubicles, five on each side. Some of them had been stripped bare, but in a couple there were stinking mattresses left on the floor like abandoned life rafts after a shipwreck. Open gaps in the walls revealed where two-way mirrors had been mounted. I went from cubicle to cubicle and let my eye wander high and low in the hope of finding anything that could lead me further in the hunt for Bruno Karsten and Bønni. All I found were a couple of telephone numbers scratched into the wall with no names beside them. I noted the numbers and went back down to the fifth floor.

In the abandoned office I stood gazing across the fjord to Nygårdsparken. Many of my most secure contacts in the town's underworld had their fixed abodes there, at least when they were broke. On the other hand, the police were often there too, in uniform and plain clothes. It was a risk, but I didn't have a lot of options. There was every reason to suggest this was where I had to go this time as well, in the hunt for the birds that had flown The Tower.

36

There weren't many trees left in Allégaten. Only the name was a memento of the legendary Nygårdsallee, laid in the 1700s. The very last linden trees had been pulled up by the roots when the big Natural Science building was erected in the 1970s, an edifice that had gone down in the town's history as a fundamental error of judgement.

I parked the car in the shadow of this and cut up to Nygårdsparken via the steps at the top of Stromgaten. On Flagghaugen, Flag Hill, it wasn't long before Little Lasse appeared from the bushes, nervously smoking a rollie that contained more ingredients than tobacco.

'What the fuck, Veum? I hardly recognised you under that.' He pointed to the cap, which I had pulled down well over my forehead again.

'My new disguise, Lasse.'

'Haven't I told you not to visit me here?'

'You're never at home.'

'I don't have a home any more,' he grimaced.

'Exactly.' I slipped a hand inside my jacket. 'But I have a private donation for you if we could go for a little stroll and chat.'

'Fine,' he said, turning all 1.85 metres of his lanky frame in the direction of the lower parts of the park, down towards Thormøhlens gate and the bird pond there.

I noticed that he made no comment about my being on the run. Which meant, I presumed, that the news of my serious charge and the fact that I was being looked for by the police hadn't yet reached Nygårdsparken. Actually that was not so surprising. People who dabbled in child pornography online were mainly lone wolves who sat masturbating in front of their computers, with no direct link to professional criminals such as those Little Lasse obviously consorted with, because of his drug addiction.

We passed *Dawn Breaking*, Sophus Madsen's sensual female figure in bronze surrounded by abundant rhododendrons. She was hiding her face in shame as if she had been caught red-handed behaving inappropriately, hardly something she would have been alone doing in these parts. I pointed across the fjord to The Tower, which could just be glimpsed behind Mjellem & Karlsen's shipyard, the quarter's cornerstone industry, which barely a month ago was declared bankrupt by the new owner – the financial scandal of the year in Bergen.

I glanced at Little Lasse: 'Do you know what was going on there?'

'In Laksevåg?'

'Can you see the tall building to the right of Mjellem? With big windows facing the fjord on the fourth floor.'

'Oh, yes. That one. Nope. No idea.'

'Does the name Bruno Karsten mean anything to you?'

We had reached the bottom of the hill now and turned towards the first of the small, arched bridges over the pond.

'Bruno? Nope. But I've heard of someone called Karsten.'

'Oh, yes?'

'Originally German, but with a Norwegian mother, apparently. Classic Mr Big. Finances everything from drug deliveries to the likes of us ...' He tossed his head in the direction of Flagghaugen to illustrate what he meant. 'And takes most of the profit himself. Probably runs loads of other dodgy stuff too. I've never met him. No idea what he looks like.'

'And Karsten's the surname?'

'Yes, I think so.'

'Have you any idea where I can find him?'

'Nope. As far as I know, he lives in Germany. He only comes up here on business. When something has to be sorted.'

'Where in Germany?'

'Hamburg, I heard. It's a seafaring town like Bergen used to be. Lots of steady contacts from those times, in all areas of life. From die Reeperbahn to das Hotel Vier Jahreszeiten, if I can put it like that.'

'Wow. I'm impressed, Lasse. You can speak German, too.'

'I went to sea for some years in my youth as well, when it was the thing to do. We only saw the best hotels in Hamburg from the outside, but we went window shopping in the Reeperbahn, didn't we.'

Some glimpses of my youth as a deck boy on MS Bolero in the early 60s appeared in my head, but I forced them back down. 'Who are his contacts in town then?'

He rolled his shoulders. 'He's got a network, I s'pose; but as I said … I've never been in contact with it, apart from indirectly perhaps.' Again he eyed Flagghaugen longingly.

'What about prostitution? Trafficking?'

He shrugged.

'Child porn?'

His eyes glinted. 'Aha! Is that where you're going? The case that was in the news last week?'

'For example.'

'Nope. Not my sphere of interest.' He clenched his right fist and held it in the air in front of us. 'If I caught one of the men dealing in that kind of thing, I'd flatten him. I can promise you that … They don't have such a nice time when they end up behind bars. They're the lowest of the low, worse than rapists. Children are sacred, Veum! Even for the likes of us.'

I nodded, a bit stiffly. 'I think most of us would react like that.' I waited before feeding him the next name. 'Do you know if anyone from the circle around Karsten is called Bønni?'

He repeated almost verbatim what Siggen had told me the day before. 'We've all known a Bønni or two in our younger days, haven't we, Varg?'

'True…'

'But I wonder. A strong guy. A thug, is he the sort you're after?'

'That could be him, yes.'

'I think I've heard him talked about in connection with the German. Collects debts, punishes welches, you know…'

'Bingo; that sounds like him. Do you know what his name is?'

'Hårkløv. Bjørn Hårkløv. Comes from a gangster background in

Fyllingsdalen, in the 1980s. Ask your pals in the police. They must have him on their records.'

'I'll think about it.'

'Do you think he still lives there?'

'In Fyllingsdalen?'

We had walked all the way around the pond now, and he pointed to Puddefjord again. 'Through the tunnel, on the other side.'

'I know where Fyllingsdalen is, Lasse.'

He grinned. 'Just wanted to be sure.' He discreetly held out a hand. 'You mentioned a donation.'

I took out a few hundred-kroner notes and gave them to him. And who was going to pay the bill this time, other than good old Veum? I just had to close my eyes and hope there was light at the end of the tunnel, and it hadn't been walled up because it hadn't been used for many years. And that someone was standing there, handing out alms for the deserving needy, among them fallen private investigators from Bergen.

I accompanied Lasse back up to the brow of the hill. Now he had enough money to fill his hash pipe for the night or whatever he was on at the moment. I strolled back to the car, got in and took out my phone.

While waiting for two o'clock and Cathrine Leivestad to arrive I examined the list of telephone numbers I had written beside the name of Bruno Karsten. I rang them one after the other, from the top of the list down. With a couple of them there was an answerphone message saying the company no longer existed. With a couple of others there was an engaged signal, even after repeated attempts. Only one produced a living person – a cool, neutral woman's voice speaking Swedish. But when I asked for Bruno Karsten, she just answered: 'Who?' I repeated the name, and she said: 'We don't have anyone here by that name. And we never have had … What did you say his name was?' 'Bruno Karsten.' 'Not here.' 'Really?' 'No. Goodbye.'

Then I took out the telephone numbers I had found etched in the walls of the abandoned rooms in Damgårdsveien. I rang both of them. The first was an answerphone message asking me to leave my number and saying they would call back. I didn't. The second was a woman's voice, in very broken Norwegian, but I gathered that she was offering original Thai massage in cosy surroundings. I noted the address and said I would think about it. If nothing else, it was conveniently close, not so far from Hans Hauges gate. Besides … if she had oriental features and a blonde wig, I might well have a chat with her anyway. She was on the list.

It occurred to me that there was another number I had promised to ring. I dialled the number of Nora Nedstrand. When she answered I told her I had found out where Sturle Heimark lived and, in addition, I had his telephone number. She thanked me curtly, but before she had a chance to hang up I raised my voice: 'But Nora … *fru* Nedstrand! Perhaps it would be safer if we called on him together?'

'Why?'

'If he really did do what you fear, then … it's better if there are two of us.'

'I see. I'll ring him first and make an arrangement.'

'Fine, but for God's sake … don't say I'll be with you.'

'Why not?'

'That simply wouldn't be smart.'

'No, I suppose not,' she said in a tone that sounded disgruntled. 'I'll ring you when I've arranged something with him.'

'Fine.'

There were no more on the list, for the time being. When it was two o'clock I called Cathrine. We agreed I would pick her up at the southern end of Nygårdsgaten, directly behind Sankt Jakob Kirke in Lars Hilles gate. Twenty minutes later we were on our way to Olsvik.

37

Cathrine Leivestad had been in Child Welfare for what used to qualify as half a lifetime. With the ages people lived to now it hardly constituted more than a third, but despite that, it was enough to give her a long row of gold stars in my Sunday-school book. She was your classic battler, who had stood up for children and their rights throughout her career, and this was reflected in her lean features, the bitter, compressed lips and the disillusioned eyes with which she confronted her work. In the society around her people were more interested in building motorways and shopping malls than talking about the proper care of children from difficult backgrounds or children in general.

When we passed an oncoming police car she noticed I pulled my cap down further over my forehead and seemed to duck behind the wheel. 'Tell me, Varg. Have the police got a bone to pick with you at the moment?'

I flashed her a sidelong glance. 'You won't want to hear, Cathrine.'

'Try me.'

I explained the situation to her and while I was talking I noticed her staring intensely at me from the passenger seat, her mouth agape, but she didn't say anything.

At length she commented: 'And you're moving around like this in broad daylight, taking a risk?'

'I have to clear my name! And the car's rented to someone else.'

'And Karl Slåtthaug's inside for … for the same?'

'Yes. That's why I'd like to go and see the institution that gave him the boot. You know yourself how vulnerable children are in reception centres for asylum seekers and similar places.'

'Yes, sadly. It's a problem no-one seems to take seriously enough

– neither the police nor politicians. On this issue you could say most people prefer to turn a blind eye. See no evil, hear no evil and speak no evil, or at least nothing that can affect the image of the idyll.'

We were out of Lyderhorn Tunnel and soon afterwards branched off for Olsvik. Gradually we gained height and had a view of Askøy Island, then, following Cathrine's instructions, I turned off.

Olsvik International Children's Home, known to Norwegian professionals as OIB, resided in a magnificent white timber building down by the sea; originally a summer house belonging to a prominent Bergen family who had roots in Olsvik. The house and estate were bequeathed in the early 1980s, and the OIB was established there in 1989, after a substantial rebuild. The purpose was to offer aid to refugee orphans, in close co-operation with Child Welfare and other authorities. But whenever they had free capacity they also helped the local Social Services with places for Norwegian children, and it was one of these that led to Karl Slåtthaug's fall in the 1990s.

We parked alongside the fence around the estate, opened the gate and followed the gravel path to the house. The family's old tennis court to the east had been converted into a shale pitch for ball games, parts of the garden were covered with climbing frames, swings and other recreational equipment, but the stately old front entrance – up a staircase and through a green double-door of manor proportions – had been retained.

On the pitch five or six boys aged twelve to thirteen were playing football. On one of the swings sat a dark-skinned girl barely more than seven or eight, being pushed by a couple of other girls maybe a year or so older.

None of them took any notice of Cathrine and me when we arrived, but I was aware they were following us from the corners of their eyes, never quite sure what a visit from outside might forebode.

'Did you warn them we were coming?'

'No, no. As I said on the phone earlier today, they're used to random checks. For them this is routine.'

'Who's in charge here?'

'The director for the last few years has been someone called Maria Nystøl, a well-organised woman of … our age.'

I smiled wryly. 'Your age or mine?'

'Mine then.'

'Just turned fifty, in other words?'

She tossed her fair hair. 'Varg, I've grown out of flattery. I definitely wouldn't say "just turned".'

'Well …'

Cathrine opened the door, and we entered what had been the hall of the old summer house, with open doors into several day-rooms and a broad staircase up to the first floor and whatever was there. We heard some people talking somewhere, but couldn't see anyone. From a half-open door to the right came the clink of cutlery and crockery. We smelt something that might have been the meal of the day, although I wasn't quite able to identify what was on the menu. A sign on a door to the left told us where the office was. Cathrine knocked, waited for a moment, opened and went in.

What they called the office, containing a sofa and three armchairs, also might have functioned as a practical little meeting room. On the walls there were shelves of various case-files and books, primarily legal, many different bilingual dictionaries and some more general reference works, including the Bergen Lexicon and the Vestland Atlas. The only picture had a classic Sunday-school motif: two children playing on the edge of a precipice and an angel making sure they didn't fall. The picture also had a title: 'No-one in danger is so safe'.

Along one wall, with the light coming in from the west-facing window, there was a little desk, and the woman sitting at it had turned to us as we entered. She recognised Cathrine, rose to her feet and gave a stiff smile. When she spoke I could hear a slight accent. 'Oh, hi, have you come to visit me?'

Cathrine nodded. The woman looked at me. Her hair was dark, and it was combed back into a short ponytail at her neck, so tightly that her face seemed to be stretched taut over her pronounced cheekbones and sharp nose. Only the full, sensual lips stood out.

'This is … a colleague of mine,' Cathrine said, not giving too much away.

I held out my hand. 'Varg Veum.'

'Maria Nystøl.'

She met my gaze, unable, quite, to hide what she was feeling. It was as though a visible quiver was running through her, and her hand trembled as she grasped mine. We had met before, but neither of us betrayed the fact with so much as a single word.

She turned to Cathrine and sighed. 'How can I help you?'

Cathrine glanced at me, and Maria Nystøl was forced to look at me again.

'This concerns a very serious case.'

'I see.'

'Were you here when Karl Slåtthaug was taken on?'

She eyed Cathrine. 'Goodness me, won't we ever be rid of this?' To me she said: 'Yes, I was here then, but I wasn't the director. That … was someone else. But he had to go as well when the business with Karl happened.'

'And what did happen?'

'Nothing that I know of!'

'No?'

Cathrine said: 'Nothing was documented, no.'

Maria Nystøl's cheeks flushed up. 'But Child Welfare took their decision and had him moved!'

'We can't take any risks with children.'

'And today he's in prison, accused with some others in a big child-porn case,' I said.

Maria Nystøl gawped at me, open-mouthed. 'What! There are others?'

I could feel Cathrine's ironic gaze on me, as if to say: *And here's another of them.* But I said: 'Yes, I don't know any more than that. At any rate, he's locked up while the investigation is ongoing.'

She had turned pale, but still there was a flush of irritation high on her cheeks. 'I can't believe it.'

'No? Did you know him well, Slåtthaug?'

'Well, it depends what you mean. We were colleagues. We both worked at the same level then. We had similar shifts; those of us who were here during the day were responsible for keeping the children busy – organising teaching for those who needed it. And then there were occasional night shifts.'

'There must have been several of you?'

'No, we usually work alone. But some of the others are on call and can be rung if need be. It's very rare anything happens.'

'No children that just disappear?'

'Just disappear! What do you mean?'

'Actually, it's a well-known phenomenon. Cathrine and I were talking about it on the way here. About how many children disappear from institutions like this every single year, many of them without trace and without ever reappearing.'

'We register all the children who live here! No-one disappears without us … knowing.'

'Knowing? What do you mean by that?'

She rolled her eyes. 'By that I mean they are picked up by the author-ities and transferred to other institutions, or the parents turn up so the family can be reunited. And some of them are sent abroad when they reach sixteen, to the country that first received them.'

'No other unexpected disappearances?'

She almost spat the answer at me. 'No! Never.'

I glanced at Cathrine. 'And proper controls are in place here?'

She shrugged. 'To the extent that we're sent the paperwork, yes.'

The two women stared at each other and I had a strong sense of mutual mistrust.

Then we were interrupted by the main door bursting open and the hall being filled with loud wails. Maria Nystøl glared at us and hurried out. We followed and stood in the doorway watching.

It was the girl we had seen on the swing, who must have fallen off. She was holding one arm and howling at the top of her voice, while the two girls who had pushed her were both talking at once, in falsetto, tears streaming from their eyes as well. Maria pulled the injured girl to her and held her tight, then released her and felt her arm. More screams.

Maria demonstrated with her own arm. 'Do this. Stretch it out.'

The girl stretched out her arm, still sobbing uncontrollably.

Maria spread out her fingers. 'Let me see. You do the same.'

The girl did the same and her sobbing slowly began to subside.

Maria hugged her again. 'There's nothing broken. It was just painful, Yasmin. Come…' She stood up, took her hand and smiled at the other two girls. 'Let's go and visit Margit in the kitchen and see if she has something nice for us.'

They went to the door across the hall. The scene was drawing to a close. Only Yasmin was emitting the occasional sob, but she willingly followed Maria to the kitchen.

Immediately afterwards Maria Nystøl returned. 'Sorry. This happens all the time. There's something every single day.' She looked through her office door to the window. 'Mostly on the football pitch. Or climbing trees or some such activity.'

We stood in the hall.

'Was there anything else you wanted?'

Cathrine and I exchanged glances.

I turned back to Maria Nystøl, and caught her eye. 'Did you have any contact with Slåtthaug after he finished here?'

'No. Never. We were just colleagues, as I said.'

'Yes, but you must have a life outside this?'

Again I sensed electricity go through her. For a second or two she looked away. Then her eye contact was back. 'Yes; so? Don't we all?'

'Yes.'

Then silence.

In the end Cathrine cleared her throat. 'Right, I think we'll be off.' She smiled wanly at Maria Nystøl. 'It looks like everything's in order here. You know where you can find us if there is anything.'

Maria wore a vinegary smile. 'Yes, I know.'

We nodded goodbye. As I was about to close the front door behind us I turned and looked back into the hall. Maria was standing where we had left her. When I met her eyes this time, she was unable to hold her emotions in check any longer. I saw the tears and her mouth spreading in what might have been a form of pain-filled ecstasy, as I seemed to remember I had seen once before.

I had kissed that mouth and we had gone to bed together. But her hair had been down and loose, her dress tight and short, and she had been beyond intoxication and fear. 'You can call me Magdalena,' she had said then. 'The chosen one.'

38

It was almost five o'clock when I dropped off Cathrine in Jonas Lie vei in Kronstad, where she lived with her husband, their children having grown up and moved out. I thanked her for helping me.

On the way back I had asked her if she knew any more about this Maria Nystøl, but she had said no. 'It's a private institution, Varg, so we haven't been colleagues, both working for the state.'

'So you have no idea about her background? Family and so on?'

'No.'

From Jonas Lie vei I continued towards Haukeland Hospital and from there down to Årstadveien and back to the centre. It struck me that I wasn't far from another unpleasant memory with computer connections. Coming out of Kalvedalsveien I turned into Kalfarlien and parked by the kerb in front of the white house where I had observed Åsne Clausen nearly two years ago. When I had attended her funeral her husband had threatened to destroy me, and the look I had received from her son, Severin, was still seared on my memory. But the name Severin had also been on the contact list in Hjalmar Hope's phone, and that alone was enough reason for me to attempt to have a few words with him.

There was a light on in the upstairs windows, and through one of them I could see a person who resembled his father, Nicolai Clausen, moving back and forth in what I had previously assumed was the kitchen. Yet there was something that made me hesitate. He was moving slowly and with a stoop, like an old man.

It was drizzling as I got out of the car, still wearing the cap pulled well down over my face, almost like a protective mask. I opened the gate, went up the steps and followed the gravel path to the house. The similarity with the magnificent summer residence that had been taken over by OIB struck me, although this building was considerably more modest in size.

The front door was on the north of the building. I pressed the doorbell and heard it ring indoors somewhere. After a while I heard the pad of footsteps, the door was opened a fraction and what had once been Nicolai Clausen stared out at me, dull-eyed. Gradually he seemed to recognise me, and a quiet glow grew in his eyes that hadn't been there from the outset.

'V-Veum?' he said in a way that suggested it was a name he had difficulty swallowing.

I nodded. 'May I come in?'

He stared at me in disbelief. 'In here?'

'In fact, I have to insist.'

At once he stepped back and opened the door a fraction more, as a signal that I could enter. There was no resistance left in him. I followed him into the house with a sense of entering a mausoleum, where all signs of life had long since been purged.

Nicolai Clausen had become an old man in the course of the two years that had passed since we last met. His dark hair had gone grey, or else he had stopped dyeing it, and it lay flat on his scalp with no hint of a wave. Deep furrows were scored in his face, but what made the greatest impression was the matt sheen in his eyes and the stoop, as though he were carrying something very heavy no-one else could see. The man who had earlier radiated aggressive masculinity was reduced to a cardboard cut-out it would be easy to blow over.

I followed him into the kitchen, where he was preparing what looked like a very basic dinner: a ready-made meal to put into the oven. The table was set for two and on the worktop there was a jug of water and two glasses.

Nicolai Clausen went to the other end of the room, turned and leaned back against the worktop. He was unable to raise his eyes higher than my chin when he said: 'Åsne's death deprived me of the will to live.'

I nodded. 'Yes, it came as a shock to me too.'

He didn't answer, just stared morosely into space.

'You blamed me then.'

He moved his gaze upwards and in some way took in the whole of my face, then dropped his head again. 'Yes, but … I was to blame. I was guilty … of the betrayal.' He gulped several times before carrying on. 'She betrayed me, too, though.'

'Well, that's what you commissioned me to find out, however unwilling I was to take the job. But I never reached that conclusion.'

'No, but I did.'

'On the other hand … she did show me a pile of photos – taken in London, she said – of you and a selection of women on the town. And at least one of the photos was … quite intimate.'

He sent me a bitter look. 'She showed them to me too, of course. She'd got someone to tail me many times when I was in London. And that was the result. All I had to offer in return were my suspicions.'

I felt my mouth go dry. 'Oh? But why did she decide … to take her life?'

For an instant it was as though I saw the man I had seen two years previously. He straightened up and a gleam of light and beauty shone through him. 'Åsne was a very special woman. She was talented, gifted … but also extremely sensitive.'

'I see. I had a different impression of her, though. She appeared to be both determined and dynamic – which showing us the photos emphasised. She seemed as far from being a suicide candidate as you could imagine.'

He turned pensive. 'She had two sides perhaps. What you saw was the genes from her father and his family.'

'Kåre Kronstad?'

'Yes, but I … I saw the other side too. And when this conflict arose – me with my suspicions, her with these photos – everything seemed to collapse around us and a chasm grew between us, so big and deep that … for Åsne it was too much to bear.'

'Oh? Did she admit anything?'

'Anything?'

'Yes, that she'd had a relationship.'

He started to shrink again. 'Yes ... she must have had a relationship. But she wouldn't admit it. She didn't deny it either, she just changed the subject. To me and my affairs.'

'What I don't understand, Clausen, is this: If you had such a beautiful, sensitive wife, whom you describe in such positive terms, how come you betrayed her ... not just once, but many times? And with, from what I could gather from the photos, what were classic escort women, perhaps a better class of prostitute. There was nothing to suggest any kind of romantic relationship. Or ... am I wrong?'

'No,' he mumbled, and looked down. 'It was a flaw in my character. I couldn't bear the thought of going out alone. When the conferences were over and the last evening flight had left, I rang one of the phone numbers you find online all over the world and booked – yes, you're right – an escort. They were great girls, to look at and talk to, and sometimes that was all we did. Had a few drinks, chatted and I found her a taxi. But on other occasions ... there was a little more.'

'Mhm. And Åsne obviously suspected this, as she hired a private investigator and had these shots taken.'

Again his eyes moved upwards. 'But I wasn't mistaken either! She had someone else. In the end, she admitted it.'

'Oh, yes?'

'And once she had these photos ... she decided to leave me.'

I had started to get an unpleasant feeling about where this was going. 'Oh, yes,' I repeated, with even more force this time. 'And why didn't she?'

'She did, Veum! She left us all.'

'Who was the man?'

'I don't know.'

'Why didn't she just go to him?'

He didn't answer.

I stood watching him. What wasn't he telling me? 'Please, Clausen. How did Åsne actually commit suicide?'

He stared at the window, where our reflections had become even clearer, as night was falling now. Something halfway between a sigh and a sob escaped him. 'She … she hanged herself.' He looked at the ceiling. 'Here. On the first floor.'

Involuntarily I followed his gaze, as though the mirror image of a hanged woman would be visible on the white ceiling.

'And there was never any doubt?'

'Doubt?'

'The police didn't investigate further?'

He looked at me blankly, as though he didn't understand what I was asking.

Impatiently, I said: 'Who found her?'

Suddenly the front door opened and there was the sound of footsteps outside. A youthful voice said: 'Hello?'

Neither of us answered, but seconds later he was in the doorway. For the second time in my life I was standing face to face with Severin Clausen, and when he made eye contact and saw who I was, he didn't seem to have changed his opinion about me from when we had last met.

39

'What the hell are you doing here?' he snapped, then turned to his father and repeated the question. 'What the hell's he doing here?'

Nicolai Clausen made a vague gesture with his hand. 'He wanted ... to talk.'

'Talk! And you let him in?'

He turned back to me. Severin Clausen was as gangly as the last time I had seen him and wore large glasses a good way down his narrow nose. His hair was blond and reminded me of his mother's; his face was long and dotted with pimples. He seemed older than his seventeen years, but his clothes were youthful enough: a red T-shirt and blue jeans. 'You just get out! We have nothing to talk to you about.'

I tried to look as sympathetic as I could, and at first that wasn't so very difficult. 'I know you're distraught about what happened, Severin, but...'

He interrupted me. 'Distraught!' His whole body was convulsed with anger, and he came towards me. 'I found her!' He pointed to the ceiling. 'Up there! Found my own mother hanging from a beam. And it was your fault!'

'No, it wasn't, now you listen to me ... I had a job to do for your father, but it was finished. I had nothing to do with later events.'

'You took the photos in London, didn't you?'

'Eh? No, no, no!' I half turned to Nicolai Clausen. 'Your father can corroborate that! I had nothing to do with that.'

Severin followed my eyes.

Nicolai Clausen looked as undecided as he had when I arrived. 'No, I can't.' Then, all of a sudden his expression changed and he regarded me with a new gravity. 'What! Was it you who took those photos?'

'My God!' I opened my palms in a gesture of defiance. 'You commissioned me, Clausen, because of your suspicions. Until that moment I'd never heard of you or your wife, and the photos had been taken a long time before then!'

'Yes…' He reverted to his previous, slightly confused expression. 'I suppose they had.'

'But you tailed her here in Bergen!' Severin retorted.

'Yes. I'll admit that, but it was a total fiasco. She – your mother – spotted me and told me to stop what I was doing. But then she called on me a few days later and placed the photos of your father and his … girlfriends … on my desk. From then I had nothing more to do with the matter. The rest was a discussion between her and your father, and I know nothing about what was said between them, and nor do I take any responsibility for it.'

'So you don't know who she was with, either?'

I splayed my hands. 'How would I know that?'

He blinked behind the thick lenses. 'If I ever get hold of him…' He didn't complete the sentence. Then he turned back to his father. The looks they exchanged weren't very affectionate, at least not on Severin's side.

'I loved her,' Nicolai Clausen said lamely. 'I realised too late, but I … She was everything in my life and after she … passed on … it was a black hole. My ability to work. Money. Business. It all just evaporated.'

'What happened?' I asked.

Clausen looked at me vacantly.

'He got the big E!' Severin said.

'The big E?'

'The elbow, from Grandad. Grandad bought him out and side-lined him. He's been sitting there with his jaw drooping ever since.'

'Severin,' his father whimpered.

'You're pathetic!' Severin said. 'If it hadn't been for you, she'd still be here.'

Clausen looked down. 'Well…'

Severin's lips quivered as he turned back to me. 'I came home from school that day, but there was no-one at home, no-one I could see. No-one in the kitchen and no messages. For some reason I went up to the first floor. As though on some intuition. I don't know. And … there she was, hanging, at the top of the stairs, with a tipped stool under her. I ran up, grabbed her legs and lifted her, but she didn't react and I took the stool…' His voice broke. 'Put it underneath her, got up and unhitched the noose around her neck so that I could carry her down and lay her on the floor, but … it was too late. I knew at once. The staring eyes. The rank smell of … Ugh! I'll never forget it, not if I live to be a hundred.'

I nodded. Then I ventured: 'And I understood from your father … there was never any doubt that it was suicide? No-one else could have done it, could they?'

His blank eyes went from me to his father. 'Him, you mean?'

'Him or someone else?'

He had gone so pale that the red pimples on his face stood out even more than usual. 'No,' he said. 'No-one ever considered that.'

Nicolai Clausen tried once again to stand up straight. 'There was never any talk of … anything like that. She chose to do … what she did. End of story. The guilty party is here.'

The son's eyes flashed. 'And if there's a hell you'll burn forever!'

I faced Severin again. 'What happened afterwards?'

He removed his glasses, took out a tissue and started to clean his glasses as if that would help him to see backwards in time. When he put them on again he met my gaze, more composed now. 'I tried to ring him. But of course he was busy. So I rang Grandad instead, and he came and … sorted everything.'

'Sorted everything?'

'Yes, he rang the doctor we normally use and later he spoke to someone he knew in the police.'

'Aha. You don't remember any names?'

'Dr Hermansen.'

'I meant in the police.'

'No. Grandad knows so many officers.'

'But they came to examine the scene?'

He looked at his father. 'No ... it wasn't necessary. Grandad told them what had happened and that was it.'

I made a mental note of another name on my list, in bold: *Kåre Kronstad.*

Then I addressed Clausen again. 'Did you try to find out who he was, this other man in her life?'

'There was nothing to find.'

'What do you mean?'

He shrugged and threw up his arms in one movement.

'Weren't there any clues, among her papers, on her phone?' I looked at the son. 'Her computer?'

'I often wondered,' Clausen mumbled. 'Perhaps he was at her funeral. Perhaps he was among those accompanying her to the grave?'

'A colleague?'

He shrugged. 'But ... I have to finish cooking so that we can eat.'

I turned back to Severin. 'I hear you're a bit of a computer whiz.'

He scowled at me. 'Yes?'

'Did your mother get you started on that?'

He answered sullenly: 'Yes. Probably.'

'You went to work with her sometimes, I imagine?'

'When I was smaller, yes. She and someone called Ruth. They shared an office and Ruth taught me quite a bit. More than Mum actually.'

'What's the rest of Ruth's name?'

'Olsen.'

Another one to have a chat with, I thought.

'Does the name Hjalmar Hope mean anything to you?'

He eyed me suspiciously. 'Yes. What about it?'

'You're on his phone contact list, I ... found out.' I glanced at Clausen. He was interested in what we were discussing, I noticed.

'Right. He's ... I mean he *was* one of Mum's colleagues. He helped me a little with ... something I'm developing.'

'The computer game I read about on the Net?'

'Yes, he's got contacts. He offered to help me get it launched.'

'For a tiny commission, I take it?'

He shrugged. 'Surely that's not so unreasonable?'

'So that's how you know him?'

'Yes. How else?'

'Well … he's got so many irons in the fire, good old Hjalmar has – so I gather.'

'Irons in the fire?'

'Just an expression.'

He seemed more irritable now. 'Were there any other questions?'

'Not now.'

'Then I think you should do as the old boy said. Get out so that we can have something to eat.'

Clausen nodded in agreement. 'Yes. And high time too.'

I looked from one to the other. Right now I thought it fairly improbable that either of these two would have hacked my computer and left child porn there. To all outward appearances they had more than enough to deal with as it was. I didn't envy them the atmosphere they would have over dinner, today as on all other days since Åsne Clausen had left them for good and in the most definitive way possible. Whether she had done it by her own hand I was not at all sure, but for the moment that was not my major focus, so I let it drop. There were enough ghosts in the room as it was.

I thanked them. Neither of them escorted me to the door. Nor did I hear a single word before I closed the door behind me. I walked down to the car and flicked through my mental notepad. What now? Sturle Heimark perhaps?

But I was getting hungry. I postponed a possible visit to Sturle Heimark until later in the evening and drove via Leitet and Skansen to Hans Hauges gate. As I turned from Bakkegaten into the street I slammed on the brakes.

I pulled into the kerb, switched off the engine and ducked behind the steering wheel to hide my silhouette against the lighting behind me.

There was a police car with its lights on in front of the house where I had spent the night. Two uniformed officers were talking to a woman by the front entrance. It was hard not to recognise her. It was Sølvi.

40

Unsure what to do, I sat staring at what was going on. Had they tracked me down already? Surely Sølvi wouldn't have informed on me?

From this distance it was impossible to interpret what was being said, but it looked as if the officers were satisfied with what Sølvi was telling them. They said polite goodbyes, got in their car and drove towards me. I ducked down to the floor as though searching for something I had lost. I saw their headlights sweep past and heard the sound of the engine. I only ventured to poke my head up when it was totally quiet.

I scanned the pavement. It was empty. Sølvi had either gone inside or returned home. I took out my phone and called her.

She answered at once. 'Hi.'

'It's me. What was all that about?'

'Where are you? Did you see?'

'At the end of the street.'

'Well, it turns out that some neighbours had noticed that there were lights on in the flat and as they thought Lisbeth was away they rang the police. I happened to be coming here when I saw them, but it gave me a shock.'

'Same here. Did you manage to put their minds at rest?'

'Yes, I told them about the cat and that I popped in every day to feed her. I said I might've forgotten to switch off the light yesterday.'

'And they didn't ask about me?'

'Not at all. I'd guess they were thinking along the lines of a burglar. Are you coming over?'

'Yes.'

We hung up, I parked properly and set off across the street. I quickly unlocked the door, took the steps two at a time and slipped inside the door, which she had left ajar.

She met me in the gloom of the hallway and at once I saw there was something wrong. The way she looked at me, the lack of a smile, told me something had happened.

I shut the door behind me, walked towards her and held her shoulders. She stared up at me with an expression on her face as though she no longer knew who I was.

'What is it, Sølvi? Has something happened?'

She nodded. 'Yes.' Then she gently freed herself from my hands. 'Come with me into the sitting room. There's something I have to show you.'

Once inside, Madonna stuck her head up from the basket and appraised me with her green eyes, in a Cleopatra-like pose, aristocratic and distant. On the coffee table lay a C4 brown envelope and with a sinking feeling I realised what was in store for me.

'Sit down, Varg,' she said, motioning towards the sofa. She sat down on the chair opposite and reached forward for the envelope. I saw her name and address on the front, typewritten on a sticker.

She was pale when she pulled the now familiar photos out of the envelope.

'Don't believe your eyes, Sølvi! That's not me.'

Her voice was tremulous. 'It's not you? I can see it is!'

'I told you right at the outset. This is material someone has planted. Either it's touched up or...'

'Touched up? This is you in the photos!'

'But just look at them.'

'Don't you think I have?'

'Look properly.'

She placed the five photos on the table in front of us and bent over them with an expression on her face as if she were being forced to examine a putrescent animal.

'Can't you see? First of all, I have my eyes closed in all of them, and that isn't out of bloody ecstasy. It's because I'm unconscious. Someone has slipped me a Mickey and placed me in this situation without my knowing.'

She raised her face and looked at me, still sceptical.

'Look at that one, for example. At the top. My hair isn't visible because someone's holding onto it to keep my face upright for people to recognise me. I couldn't do that to a child, Sølvi. You have to believe me.'

The scepticism was beginning to fade in her eyes. 'I want to, Varg! But you have to understand … it looks absolutely genuine!'

'That's what the police thought too,' I said bitterly. 'Is it any wonder I had to go out and spew up when they showed me these?'

'And this child…' She placed her finger on the photo where the desperate child's face was in focus. 'It's not someone you know, is it?'

'Not at all!'

Suddenly her eyes flooded with tears. And a sob came from her throat. 'You have to understand, Varg! I was so frightened. Naturally I thought of Helene and that you might've done … the same to her.'

I leaned across the table and grasped her hands firmly. 'Hand on heart, Sølvi. This is an impossibility. It has never happened. Surely she would've said if it had? If even you don't trust me, I have no-one left to rely on any more!'

She got up from the chair, came round the table and plumped down on the sofa beside me. Then she cuddled up to me, laid her face against my neck and cried silent tears. 'I was so frightened,' she repeated. 'So very, very frightened.'

I let her cry. Once more Madonna raised her head and sent me an accusatory stare because I had made her surrogate mother weep so bitterly. She was on the point of launching herself at my face and leaving her claw marks on it.

While Sølvi cried I studied the light-brown envelope. It had stamps on and a postmark. Her name and address were correct and precise, with the postal code and everything. That concerned me even more. Who the hell had found out about this? Who knew about our relationship apart from Vidar Waagenes? The same person who had hacked my hard drive and gained access to my emails? Or someone else?

After her crying subsided she carefully extricated herself, straightened up, stretched and kissed me on the mouth. 'Sorry, Varg. I didn't mean to … But you have to concede they do look genuine, and how could I have not been taken in?' With renewed anger she added: 'This must be pure, unmitigated evil on the part of the man or men behind this. They must really wish you ill.'

'Yes,' I said. 'No doubt about that.'

'What did you do to them?'

'If I knew that I'd be closer to an answer.'

'Oh? Have you found out anything?'

'Impossible to say.' I gave her a quick summary of the day's events, from the abandoned tower, via the conversation with Little Lasse and the visit to OIB with Cathrine Leivestad.

'Who's that?'

'An ex-colleague from Child Welfare.'

'Right.'

For a moment I wondered if she was jealous. 'She's trustworthy. And there's another woman I have to talk to again.'

'And that is?'

'She called herself Magdalena last time I met her.' And I hastened to add: 'Several years ago. She's a director at OIB. Actually her name's Maria Nystøl.'

'And when do you want to talk to her?'

'Perhaps this evening. How long can you stay?'

'I can't stop over tonight.' She looked at her watch. 'Actually I have to be getting home as soon as possible. Helene's with a friend. I just had to talk to you because of … those.' She motioned towards the envelope and the photos.

'Take them with you and keep them somewhere safe. You never know. There may be fingerprints or other clues on them. I'll keep this.' I separated the photo of the young girl's face from the others. 'In case she should turn up in real life, as it were.'

She nodded, gathered the photos together and put them back in the envelope.

I followed her into the hall and we fleetingly kissed goodbye.

'Let's stay in touch,' I said.

She smiled with tears in her eyes. Then she was gone, and the door was closed quickly behind her.

I went into the sitting room and directed a triumphant gaze at Madonna. 'You're going to have to put up with me for a while longer, my little friend,' I said aloud.

But she didn't even bother to raise her head this time, just showed me the back of her neck: thin and narrow and aloof.

41

Knøsesmuget is a long, narrow street and stretches from Klostergaten, across Skottegaten, right down to St Hansstredet, binding the whole of the western side of the Nordnes peninsula, like a piece of twine around an unexpected present.

It had stopped raining at around ten that night, when I rang the bell of the white house midway along the alley where Maria Nystøl lived. I saw the blinds in the right-hand window stir. Immediately afterwards I heard a safety chain being lifted inside, the door was opened and Maria invited me in with a less than friendly toss of the head. As soon as I was inside she banged the door shut, and she didn't give me a hug either. I had experienced much warmer welcomes elsewhere. Before we did anything she made sure to lock up thoroughly.

'I guessed you'd make a reappearance,' she said. Her hair wasn't as tightly combed back as earlier in the day, but she was dressed in tight blue jeans and a dark-brown jumper with the contours of her white bra visible, shining through the pattern. Her mouth suggested a sullen, dejected state of mind, which in a way reminded me of the Brigitte Bardot films of my youth.

With another toss of her head she showed me into the sitting room, which was behind the blinds facing the alley. I wasn't sure, but as far as I could remember, we had been in only the bedroom and the kitchen the last time I was here. The room was pleasantly furnished, with well-worn furniture, suggesting that she would probably have bought it second-hand rather than new. There were no bookshelves in the room, and the pictures on the wall were the kind you bought in an interior-design store, exhibiting no more of her personal taste than a predilection for black and green contrasts separated by a red stripe. There was a TV in one corner of the room and, on the table, a bottle of red wine and a half-full glass.

'Would you like some wine?'

'No, thank you. I'm driving.'

She paused. Then she said: 'You weren't so abstinent the last time you were here.'

I smiled stiffly. 'No. I was pretty plastered, as far as I remember.'

She scowled at me. 'You can say that again.'

She plumped down in one chair and indicated with her head that I should sit in the other.

'But I do remember a little more,' I said, sitting down. 'And I thought you wouldn't perhaps want us to discuss it while Cathrine was present.'

She chewed her lip and mumbled: 'No. Yes.'

'The script says you're supposed to say: No, I wouldn't. Yes, not while Cathrine was present.'

'What do you want?'

'When I left here, hungover, that morning about a year ago I recall noting something down in the office. "Skarnes, Bønni, Karsten, The Tower", I wrote. I was wondering if you could tell me what I meant by it.'

She swallowed and gave me a blank look. 'What you meant?'

'Or what *you* meant. After all it was you who'd been talking about them the night before.'

She glanced longingly at the half-full glass. 'You shouldn't take any notice of what I was babbling on about that night. You weren't the only one who had drunk too much. All I wanted from you was a shoulder to lean on and some … warmth.'

'Don't take any notice? It's one thing you straying off the straight and narrow with …' I patted my chest '…and quite another that since then I've had confirmed at least three of those names you mentioned. I've been to The Tower. I've met Bønni and Karsten. And I remember very clearly what you confided to me that night. "They've got a hold on me," you said. What did you mean by that?'

'I was babbling, I told you!' Now she was unable to resist any longer. She reached out a hand, grabbed the glass, drained it, poured herself another and banged the bottle hard down on the table. 'It was because you said you were … a private investigator. I thought it would make me interesting, didn't I.' With a disdainful pout she added: 'And obviously it did. Even now, a year later.'

'What hold have they got on you?' I persisted. 'As you still feel you have to protect them.'

She pinched her lips together.

'I can hear you have a slight accent. Where do you actually come from?'

'That's none of your business.'

'But you've got a Norwegian surname. Divorced maybe?'

She shrugged. 'Maybe.'

'Do you know Bruno Karsten from Germany, in other words?'

Her jaw dropped. Then she pulled herself together, raised her glass to her mouth and took another swig, but not so much this time. 'I don't know any Bruno Karsten.'

'Really?'

'No!'

Our eyes were locked.

'Then you're forcing me to speculate.'

Even though she was pressing her lips together she couldn't hide their sensual curves. However, she resolutely kept her mouth shut.

'What they've got on you must be pretty rock solid. If I were to draw my own conclusions they would be harsh, you being such an elegant, attractive woman. You've been a prostitute, perhaps in Germany. Bruno Karsten knew you from those days … or recognised you. In the position you'd reached in this country it wasn't hard for him to apply some additional pressure on you, perhaps even force you to help him with what he was doing. And that, Maria, is criminality on a large scale. Prostitution, cyber crime, almost certainly the distribution and selling of drugs as well.'

'How would I be able to help him?' she whispered.

'Right. You remember him now, do you? Bruno Karsten?'

Once again she didn't answer.

'With the access you had to children who may or may not have been registered? At any rate not as anything more than numbers in a list of stats. Earlier today we talked about hidden statistics, about the children who just disappear without any further investigation because there are no relatives who notice they're missing and because some of those whose responsibility the children are – let me put this politely – are disloyal servants.'

She jumped up with such force that the wine glass went flying and spilt the contents across the table, where they lay like a lake of thin blood.

'What are you accusing me of? Selling children to the devil?'

I stood up to avoid any form of aerial attack. 'You're getting warmer, Maria. The devil, yes. The last time we met you accorded Skarnes in particular that same epithet. He was the devil himself, you said. In the same breath as Bønni and Karsten. So who is he?'

She was panting now. 'You've got no bloody idea what you're talking about!'

'Ole Skarnes? Is it him?'

She went so white that for a moment I thought she was going to faint. Then she slumped back down in the chair, grabbed the over-turned glass, recharged it and took another large swig. 'I don't know any Skarnes,' she said, repeating her earlier mantra.

'No, of course you don't,' I retorted, warily sitting back down as well. I stared at the bottle of red wine. It looked so tempting, but I managed to repress my desires. I had to keep my head as clear as possible.

'Listen, Maria. I know about The Tower. By the way, it's empty now. The building's going to be demolished. I know about Bruno Karsten. I know that Bønni was his right-hand man and, to be blunt, his low-life sidekick, here in Bergen. I'll find out about Skarnes as well. But I can promise you one thing: If you don't start opening up about what you know you won't be in that job of yours in Olsvik for very long. I'll make sure of that. But the choice is yours.' I gestured with both hands. 'All you have to do is talk.'

She was slumped over the table now, staring into her red wine as though reading her cheerless future in the dregs. Her jaw muscles were grinding away and I could see her fighting with herself.

Then she raised her chin. In a thin voice she said: 'And if I talk you won't say anything … to the office?'

I eyed her intently. 'That depends on how serious it is what you tell me. I can't promise anything. But the alternative is certain. If you don't tell me anything I'll contact Cathrine as soon as she's back at work tomorrow.'

She swallowed hard. 'You were right for the most part. Yes, I'm from Germany. Yes, I have a background as a … prostitute. Not on the street though.' Again she made a pout I was gradually beginning to recognise. 'Escort, prostitute, call it what you will. And, yes, I knew Bruno Karsten from those days. But it was a long time ago! Almost fifteen years.' She paused as though immersing herself in thoughts of how quickly the time had passed or whatever was bothering her now.

'But what brought you to Norway?'

The same pout followed by three words: 'The usual. Love.'

'A *herr* Nystøl?'

She nodded. 'He was a client at a hotel in Hamburg who fell in love with me so deeply, he said, that he wanted to take me to Norway and draw a line under what I was and what I'd been doing for years. However, it transpired that after a couple of years of marriage he couldn't live up to his promise. My past was like a barrier between us and we agreed to go our separate ways, like … good friends.'

'No children?'

'No.'

'And then Bruno Karsten turned up again?'

'No, no. That was only a few years ago. I studied social work, got a job in Olsvik, first as an employee, the last two years as a director. Then I met Bruno – quite by chance – one night in town, at a restaurant with colleagues. He used his charm and I was unable to keep my workplace a secret from him, and he … found me. Then the nightmare started.'

'Which means?'

'He wanted me to hustle again.'

'Work as a prostitute?'

'Yes. I was the best, he said. He promised me money. Big bucks. But I refused. And then he threatened to tell Child Welfare what I'd been doing in Germany. In the end…' her voice became a whisper behind her wine glass '…I gave in, several times. Exclusive clients.'

'Exclusive?'

'International businessmen. Politicians. So-called celebrities. People obsessed with discretion.'

'And they found that with Karsten?' I sent her a sceptical look.

'They thought they had anyway.'

'But … you're a grown woman. I would've thought they'd prefer slightly younger girls.'

'Of course. But some like…' a muted smile flickered '…mature wine.'

'Some even prefer very young girls.'

She sought eye contact again. 'Yes, I know! But … not through me.'

'Can you vouch for that? You've never let any of your girls into that market?'

'Never!' She held her left breast. 'Hand on heart.'

'What about Karl Slåtthaug?'

'That was before my time.'

'You were colleagues, you said earlier today.'

'Yes, before he had to stop.'

'But he also had contact with this world. I know that.'

'With Bruno?'

'Yes. At least he frequented The Tower, and at the moment…'

'Yes? What were you going to say?'

'At the moment he's in prison, one of the accused in the big child-porn case.'

'Yes, you said, earlier today.' She gazed darkly into middle distance. Then she shifted her gaze back to me. 'But I never did anything like that. You have to believe me.'

I sighed. 'Right. There's one name we have to return to: Skarnes. What was it that made you call him a devil?'

A grimace flitted across her face. 'He was a punter. The kind that

grows in stature only by making others seem small, if you know what
I mean.'

'Violence?'

She nodded. 'Yes, and other repugnant stuff. He liked to debase the
girls he bought in the most revolting way. I was in the shower for half an
hour after I'd been with him, and many times I had to throw up.'

'Ole Skarnes?'

She barely moved her head in confirmation.

'And where can I find him?'

She shrugged. 'No idea. I met him at a hotel whenever we met.'

'But why did you mention his name alongside Karsten's and Bønni's?
Was he part of the network?'

'Yes, that was my understanding. He never paid when we were
together. I was part of his reward, he said. He called me his bonus.' She
gulped down another large swig of wine.

'Reward for what?'

'How can I know?' Suddenly she changed her approach. She licked
her lips and smiled wearily. 'But I'd rather be your bonus, Varg.'

I stood up. 'I don't think so, Maria.'

She got to her feet and came round the table, slightly unsteady on
her pins already. She advanced on me, grabbed my jacket and pressed
her body against mine. A strong smell of red wine came off her, drowning whatever perfume she might have been wearing. 'You know what I
can do with a man. Don't you remember?'

My face flushed. 'To be frank, I … Only fragments.'

But that was only partially true. I remembered her well enough for
my most private parts to remind me. In bed she had been up and down,
round and about; being with her had been like a session in a tumble
dryer except that I had no idea how long the programme had been set
for.

I freed myself and walked towards the door. 'I'll take you at your
word, Maria. But if I find out you've kept something from me I'll be
back. Or I'll call.'

I took out a biro, wrote down my telephone number on a sheet in my notepad, tore it out and gave it to her. 'Call me on this number if you should remember something.'

She nodded, without a word, without making any more amorous sallies. As I left she accompanied me out, and when the door closed I heard the sound of the safety chain being drawn. No-one would be welcome here for the rest of the day.

42

Back in Hans Hauges gate, I had another little surprise waiting for me. Madonna came into the hallway to greet me, and while I was hanging up my coat and cap, she rubbed against my trouser leg ingratiatingly. Then she walked ahead of me into the kitchen and I soon saw the reason for the charm offensive. Her plate was empty.

I filled it to the brim, poured water in the bowl beside it and went back into the sitting room while she pounced on the food. After I had started the computer to search for Ole Skarnes she followed me in, jumped onto the sofa and pressed against me again as if to thank me for the food. Surprised, I took my fingers off the keyboard and stroked her neck. Then she lay down in my lap, rolled onto her back and spread her legs like the most brazen Madonna I had met for a long time. After quite a lot of pats and strokes she pronounced herself sated, got up, stretched sensually, slunk past me across the floor and into her basket. Before finding a comfortable position, perhaps for the night, she sent me a last look, as though I had finally been accepted as part of the family. For some reason this made me feel like a new man and no longer an outlaw.

I continued my search on the computer. This time I had more luck. I tried another search under Ole Skarnes and his name appeared in connection with something called Bjørna Fjord Accountancy A/S, with an address in Sandsli. Ole Skarnes was the director. I jotted down his address and phone number and started another search. Looking for Bønni, or Bjørn Hårkløv, as Little Lasse had said, I found a specific address in Fyllingsdalen and a mobile phone number. I scribbled both down on my notepad.

I didn't get much further. I had a quick shower and went to bed. Another poor night's sleep followed. I dreamt I was on the run, and again and again was on the verge of getting caught, but escaped by being ejected out of the dream, with such force that I nearly ended up on the floor.

The following day one of the first things I did was ring Sigurd Svendsbø. He didn't sound completely awake when he answered, so I assumed he had been up longer than me with his computers.

'Siggen? Veum here.'

'Oh, hi,' he grunted.

'I was wondering if you could check a couple of names for me. If you can get into some systems that are not accessible to everyone.'

'Should be possible,' he said, his voice still croaky.

'One name is Ole Skarnes. He might well be a central figure in this case. I think he's a director in a company called Bjørna Fjord Accountancy. There were some IP addresses you hadn't identified, weren't there?'

'Yes, a couple.'

'He might be one of them. Can you get onto police records?'

'Doubtful.'

'See if you can find anything about a Bjørn Hårkløv, known as Bønni.'

'Just a mo, Veum. I have to find something to write with.' I waited, and soon afterwards he was back. 'Now I'll take notes. The first was … ?'

'Ole Skarnes. The second Bjørn Hårkløv.'

'Great. This might take a little time, but I'll call you. Any news otherwise?'

'No breakthrough, but I'm onto something, I think.'

'And you've managed to avoid the cops so far, I can hear.'

'Yes.'

Afterwards I rang Vidar Waagenes. However, he sounded quite irritable. 'What's going on, Varg? I hope you know what you're doing. Every hour you spend at large will be seen in a negative light when we end up in court.'

'Even if I have a few tasty titbits?'

He couldn't keep the sarcasm out of his voice. 'You have found some, have you?'

'Not yet.'

'If you're just tapping in the dark, you might as well hand yourself in.' He raised his voice. 'I mean it!'

'Give me a day or two, if they don't ambush me first.'

'If you're hauled in it will look even worse for you.'

'Ole Skarnes, does that name ring any bells?'

'…Ole Skarnes? Never heard of him. But I'll make a note. Has he got anything to do with the case?'

'Maybe. Then there's a Mr Big with a German background: Bruno Karsten. He's definitely involved.'

'Involved in putting this material on your hard drives?'

'Let's call it … contiguous criminality.'

'Contiguous criminality?' Again the sarcasm was more than clear. 'That's a new concept. Let me write it down for future use. In court.' He repeated it slowly as if copying it syllable by syllable: 'Con-ti-gu-ous cri-mi-nal-ity.'

'Cyber crime, prostitution, distributing and selling narco. A nice number for a defence lawyer, maybe?'

'Noted, Varg.'

'Have you already had Bjørn as a client?'

'Hårkløv? No, I don't think so.'

'Bønni to friends, if he has any.'

'In which case I'm not in his circle of acquaintances.'

'But do you have access to criminal records? Can you find out if he has any convictions?'

He hesitated. 'Possibly. How important is it?'

'Closest associate of Bruno Karsten.'

He sighed audibly. 'Listen, Varg. I know you're searching for well-trodden paths inside all kinds of criminality. But if this is really something an outsider has put on your hard drives…'

'It is!'

'Fine. But what I wanted to say was this: In that case perhaps you ought to be looking further afield than inside normal criminal milieus.'

'I already am.'

'Anything you want to share with me?'

'...No. But you said you would check out a colleague of yours, regarding Åsne Clausen and her death.'

'Yes. Well ... he didn't have a lot to tell me. Her father, Kåre Kronstad, seemed to put a lid on anything connected with the private side of the case. Not only that, he barged into his son-in-law's company and took it over.'

'Yes, any reason for that?'

'It's said that Nicolai Clausen broke down completely after the suicide. He couldn't take care of the day-to-day running, and as Kronstad also had financial interests in the company he took responsibility for almost everything.'

'You're a lawyer. Tell me, wouldn't a suicide automatically trigger some form of police investigation?'

'In principle, yes. An autopsy at any rate. But if you have the right connections and can add gravitas to what you say, which you expect Kåre Kronstad would be able to do, it's not that certain it will be taken *so* seriously. I mean, if no-one suggests it might be a criminal act; and, obviously, the police have their hands full with other cases.'

'Thanks for telling me. We know all about that. Have you heard anything from them?'

'From the police?'

'Yes.'

'They've rung a couple of times to ask if I've been in contact with you, but I don't have a sense that they've prioritised the hunt for you. I suppose they assume you'll appear at some point, voluntarily or not.'

'I see.'

'The next time I think I should answer that I *have* heard from you.'

'Sure?'

'In my profession I have a rule: Honesty is the best policy. Don't you agree?'

'Situations can arise where a tiny white lie can be appropriate. Don't tell me, as a lawyer, that you haven't come across them.'

'Well...'

'Can you ring me if you find out anything about the names I gave you?'

'I'll see what I have time for, Varg. I have other clients as well, you know.'

'More important than me?'

'Everyone deserves some attention.'

'And honesty is the best policy. Thank you. I'll be hearing from you, will I?'

'Certainly.'

We hung up. While we were talking, someone else had been trying to contact me. I recognised the number. It was Nora Nedstrand. I rang back, and she replied almost at once, as though she had been sitting with the phone in her hand.

'Yes?'

'Veum here.'

She got straight to the point. 'I've arranged to meet Sturle. He's expecting me at twelve o' clock. I'll be leaving at any moment.'

'OK. Did you say … You didn't mention my name, did you?'

'… No.'

'Then I'll meet you outside where he lives.'

'Right,' she said, and rang off without wasting any time on pleasantries.

I looked at my watch. Half past nine. I had two and a half hours. I leaned back against the sofa, took my notepad and slowly flicked through it.

There were some almost invisible links between the cases I had tried to retrieve from oblivion. Between Sturle Heimark and Hjalmar Hope there was an obvious connection. What was more, I had seen Heimark in The Tower. I had been there with Karl Slåtthaug, who had a connection with Maria Nystøl, the children's home in Olsvik and – again – the main man behind The Tower, Bruno Karsten. When I had been lying on the floor of Karsten's office, they had talked above me about a Hjalmar. 'Talk to Hjalmar. He'll fix it. He's the computer man.'

Was it a coincidence or was it the same Hjalmar? I had seen Sturle

Heimark and Hjalmar Hope in the car park outside the building containing SH Data. Hjalmar Hope had been a colleague of Åsne Clausen's,
I had been told by her son, and he had helped Severin to develop his
computer game. So there was a clear link there too. Could Hjalmar
Hope have been Åsne's secret friend?

I had noted down the name of another of her colleagues there, Ruth
Olsen. I would very much like to have a chat with her. But top of the list
was Sturle Heimark, and I would be meeting him with Nora Nedstrand
at twelve.

So far there were two deaths in these interconnected cases; three
if I included the suicide of Oliver Nedstrand in the mid-90s. Knut
Kaspersen had drowned in Fusa Fjord in February 2000, and Åsne
Clausen had taken her own life in November of the same year. Many
murders were disguised as accidents, and a suicide could easily be the
result of a helping hand, so long as the circumstances didn't invite a
closer examination. But I was only on the fringe of these cases, at any
rate the one in Fusa. And even in Åsne Clausen's case it was only in the
heads of Nicolai and Severin that I was a central factor in the sequence of
events that led to the tragic conclusion. So why would anyone consider
it important to blame me in the way they had done so convincingly?
There had to be something behind all this.

Computer skills were clearly a key feature and so far Sturle Heimark,
Hjalmar Hope and Severin Clausen had stood out as being on the front
line. Of these three, Heimark was the oldest and therefore the one in
whom you would initially have least suspected such expertise. Another
reason to try and wheedle something out of him.

But Heimark was a hard nut to crack. As an ex-policeman he would
be physically capable of defending himself, very probably mentally as
well, and he had already tried once to get his former colleagues to take
me in. He was bound to make another attempt, given half a chance. Still,
that was my next move, with or without any help from Nora Nedstrand.

I gave Madonna another portion of food, filled her bowl with water
and received a long, friendly miaaaaaouw in gratitude. When leaving,
I quickly closed the door and with the most natural expression in the

world walked the short distance to the next street and around the corner, where I got into the car, started it up and once again drove 'home' to Nordnes.

43

The block where Sturle Heimark lived was in the part of Strandgaten that most reminded me of a provincial street in Siberia: a façade of concrete down both sides, built at the end of the 1950s when the council authorities responsible must have been on a study tour of Murmansk to find some architectural inspiration. Here the Russians had definitely won the Cold War.

It was half past eleven when I found an empty space to park in the vicinity. I put enough coins in the meter to stay for two hours. To check I was in the right place, I strolled over to see if his name was on the list by the doorbells. It was, in discreet, hand-written letters. Then I walked back to the car, got in and waited for Nora Nedstrand to show up.

The big, dark-grey Mitsubishi Outlander rounded the corner from Tollbodallmenningen at a few minutes past twelve. She found a free parking spot and fed the meter. The traffic wardens, it seemed, would have to look elsewhere for their prey today. I kept a wary eye open to check she didn't have anyone following her, but no suspicious cars appeared. I hoped she wasn't even aware that the police were after me, and I had to trust that she hadn't told Heimark who she was coming with.

She scrutinised the house numbers as she moved in my direction, and when she was close I got out of the car and met her on the pavement. She gave a start as though she hadn't been expecting to see me.

'Hi,' she said dourly.

'Hi. What did he say when you rang?'

'He seemed a trifle surprised … and pretty annoyed. But when I said I had something important to tell him he agreed to meet me today.'

I motioned to the door. 'I hope he's waiting for you then.'

She pushed the door, but it was locked. Then she rang the bell and stood waiting for a response from the nearby intercom.

It came, concise and to the point: 'Yes.'

'It's me. Nora.'

The reply was a buzz from the lock. I pushed the door and held it open for her. An information board inside told us that S. Heimark lived on the third floor. We took the lift up without exchanging many words. She seemed quite nervous, and I didn't feel on top form myself, if anyone had cared to ask.

On the third floor his door was anonymous, the only one without a nameplate. I took up a position beside the door, on the edge of the stairs. As if to show how little interest he had in this visit, she had to ring the bell here too.

As he opened the door I quickly stepped forward, put a foot inside and forced my way in before her. When he saw me he tried to close the door in my face, but I was in the hall before he could stop me. Nora didn't move, as though frightened what might happen.

'Veum?' he barked, trying to puff himself up in front of me.

'Disappointed you didn't have me nabbed the other day?'

'I already knew.'

'Good contact with your old colleagues, I can hear.'

'Good enough for this at any rate.' He turned to Nora. 'What the hell are you playing at? Have you joined forces with the likes of him?'

Her face was a blotchy red, her eyes were filling. 'He … he … forced me!'

'And how did he know you were coming here?'

'I … We…'

'A deal, eh?'

I advanced further into the hall. 'Come in, Nora. He'll have to listen to what you have to say.'

For a second or two I saw uncertainty spread across his face. 'Tell me now. What do you have to say?'

'I think you know, Heimark,' I said. 'Let's go and sit in the lounge and discuss it together.'

'I have nothing left to say to you, Veum! You know that.'

'I don't know that! After what you did when I was at Hjalmar Hope's we have a lot left to discuss – about Bruno Karsten, about The Tower, about Hope and lots more, so it would be a wise move to invite us in. If you don't I might ring the police this time and tell them where they can find a murderer.'

'Murderer!' he snorted. But he stepped aside and gestured to Nora to come in.

They gave each other a wide berth, avoiding contact, and he slammed the door hard after her. Then he turned and waved us brusquely into what was apparently the lounge.

It looked like the headquarters of a confirmed bachelor with no other interests in life than beer and football. There was a television in the corner of the room. The furniture was plain and sparse: four chairs in the same style and a battered coffee table in the middle. No pictures on the walls. No bookshelves. A plastic crate of empty beer bottles in one corner, a coffee cup and a Thermos stained brown on the table by one of the chairs. The TV was on, but with the volume down. The screen showed a football match between two teams with striped shirts, in which most of the players looked like South Americans.

I nodded towards the TV. 'Establishing another alibi?'

He glowered at me, as though ready to pummel me with his bare fists. But he restrained himself. It wasn't a foregone conclusion that he was the strongest boy in the class after all. I would know how to give a good account of myself anyway.

He faced Nora. 'Have you been talking to him about that bloody ticket again?'

She blinked and looked petrified. 'C-can we … can I sit down?'

He pointed fiercely at one chair. She slumped into it as though on the point of keeling over. He remained on his feet. So I did the same.

She looked up at us like a naughty schoolchild called in to talk to both the headmaster and deputy head.

'Well,' I said in an attempt to take the lead. 'She had to admit she found your plane ticket and she still has it. It can be documented that you were in Norway the weekend Knut Kaspersen died as a result of a drowning accident … ostensibly, as Svein Olav put it when I was there a couple of years ago.'

'Ostensibly? Ask Svein Olav yourself how ostensible it was.'

'Svein Olav? Do you mean to say…?'

'Keep me out of this! I might've been there for a very different reason from the one you assumed.'

'Oh, yes? And that would be…?'

'Nothing to do with you.'

'I know that you and Hjalmar Hope are in cahoots. Were you then too?'

'You can keep Hjalmar Hope out of this.'

'Him too? But I have to talk to Svein Olav?'

A sudden protracted sob came from Nora. 'I know it was you, Sturle!'

We both turned to her.

'You said so the first time you met him. The fu … I can't even repeat what you said. The fu … homo, you called him.'

'Knut…?' I started to say.

But he was quicker, irascible, as I had seen him before. 'But he was! You could see it from miles off. But you never realised, Nora. You're blind to … that sort of thing. Why do you think your husband hanged himself? Eh? He was frightened someone would discover what he and his business partner were up to. They were partners in all senses.'

She was shaking as she burst out: 'Oliver? And Knut!'

'Svein Olav stumbled across them, although he was only a boy then. He told Hjalmar.'

'Told him what?'

'What Uncle and your husband were up to in the boat shed once when he was there. He wasn't very interested in you. You told me that time and time again. You had only the one child as well!'

'No, that … Oh, Jesus!' She hid her face in her hands, and her whole body shook with long, painful sobs. Neither of us made a move to console her.

I said: 'So that was the motive for the ... accident? Sexual discrimination. A poor gay man who wasn't allowed to live his life in the village like any other person?'

'Motive? Accident? In that case, it must have been Svein Olav. He was the type to react like that.'

'So what was so important about what you and Hjalmar were doing that you had to come all the way up from Spain?'

'That's none—'

'Yes, I've got the point. You're a computer man, I've heard.'

'Yes.' He looked daggers at me.

'Was it an urgent matter that brought you home?'

He didn't answer, just sent me a laconic look.

'And you still meet, I see.' I decided to take a leap into the unknown. 'Did you and Hjalmar put this filth on my computers?'

He grinned malevolently. 'Yes, I heard about that, Veum. Funny business. Clever people, obviously. But perhaps that's the way you are, as you like homos so much ... ?'

'You know Bruno Karsten, don't you.'

'Who?'

'And Bønni.'

'No.'

'You're forgetting I saw you in The Tower once.'

'So? It was a closed club. I was there as a client. Footloose and fancy-free. Who could deny me that?'

Nora had removed her hands from her face. Now she was following what we were saying.

'Ex-policeman out having fun, at the other end of the scale?'

'And why were you there?' he retorted. 'You were after a slice of the action too, I assume.'

'What sort of place was it?' she asked unexpectedly.

I eyeballed Sturle Heimark and answered bluntly: 'A whorehouse. Where your ex-partner was a client, he says.'

'And you too,' he countered in kind.

Her face went grey. With her white hair, this made her look much older than she actually was, a shadow of the exuberant woman I remembered from the first meeting.

'I think this is how we should play it, Nora,' I said. 'When we leave this luxury apartment you go to the police station and produce your trump card. If you can also give them the plane ticket, they have an ace. Our mutual friend here will have to get himself the best lawyer he can find.'

Heimark sneered at me. 'I don't even need the best, Veum. This is just rubbish from beginning to end. You have no idea what you're talking about.' He turned to Nora. 'And to you I have only one thing to say. If you follow his advice it'll be all the worse for you. I'll sue straightaway for defamation of character and slander, if that's what you want. And you'll never see me again, until we meet in court, that is. Understood?'

She nodded, mute, but I could see that what he had said had shaken her, and I saw my visit to the police station going up in smoke. 'Will you come with me?' she said, looking at me.

Heimark smirked.

'No, I … not today. There's something else I have to investigate. But outside on the street I'll give you the name of the officer you should speak to. I can guarantee they'll give you all the attention you need.'

Heimark snorted, but didn't comment.

'And as for you,' I said, turning to face him again. 'If you ring any of your former colleagues after we've gone I recommend you hand yourself in. I'll be gone from Nordnes faster than they can take the lift down to the police garage.'

But I didn't like the way he watched us as we left. He didn't seem particularly concerned, and in his eyes I saw a glint of triumph, as though he had several more cards up his sleeve than the one I had advised Nora to play. Did he in fact have the best hand when all was said and done?

Downstairs, I gave her the names of Atle Helleve and Annemette Bergesen and advised her to ask for them by name at the police station. As she walked to her car she seemed rather confused, and I still wasn't sure she would go ahead and do it.

I got into my car and took the shortest route out of the district, to be on the safe side. But no road barriers had been set up this time, either. There wasn't so much as a sniff of a police car.

44

It was stupid to drive all the way to Sandsli without checking before-hand. After passing Danmarksplass, I turned down Kanalveien and into a car park in front of one of the businesses. From there I called SH Data in Sandsli and asked if Hjalmar Hope was in. He was, but by the time the nice receptionist had put me through I had rung off. Then I continued my journey.

Once again I parked outside the big company block in Sandsli, but this time I went a step further and entered through the main entrance in the longer wall facing the car park. It was a large, modern building with a lot of glass in the façade. Inside, there was a central atrium, which rose to the top. Along the shorter wall in the entrance there was a board showing all the companies who had offices there: close on twenty alto-gether. There was a solicitors' and a couple of accountancy firms on the list, but most were businesses connected with either IT or North Sea oil. I noticed one of the companies: Bjørna Fjord Accountancy A/S. That, I knew, was the firm where a man called Ole Skarnes was regis-tered as the director. Chance? Maybe, maybe not.

A Securitas guard sat in a glass box, observing me with some sus-picion. SH Data had its offices on the third floor. To access the lift I needed an electronic card, apparently, so I used the stairs instead. That meant I wouldn't get into the firm directly when I reached the top, but I would be on the internal balcony that ran around the whole atrium on every floor as an emergency exit. I had to talk into a loudspeaker beside the thick glass door to the open-plan offices. A beautiful, well-dressed blonde in her late twenties was sitting at a desk opposite the door and she answered when I pressed the button.

'I have an appointment with Hjalmar Hope,' I lied, and she looked up quickly before pressing a door-opener and letting me in.

SH Data must have been doing well. In the large, light rooms I counted somewhere between twenty and thirty employees, all at work in front of their respective computers – some desktops, most laptops. The colours of the interior were light-grey and white, which made for an efficient though cool effect.

I stopped by the beautiful blonde, who looked up at me over the top of her large, black glasses and said in a friendly voice: 'I've already told Hjalmar he has a visitor. Have you been here before?'

'No.'

I scanned the desks and at some distance I saw Hjalmar Hope coming towards us, at a slower pace when he realised who his visitor was.

I smiled at the receptionist and walked towards him. I met Hjalmar Hope about midway in the central aisle. 'Hi, Hjalmar. I remembered there were a couple of things I hadn't discussed with you last time we met. We were interrupted suddenly, as you may recall. Have you got a room where we can talk undisturbed, or should we do it here in full view, child porn and all?'

He raised a finger to tell me to keep my voice down. After looking around, he tossed his head backwards. 'We can find a little room behind here. But I haven't got much time for this, Veum.'

'Very stupid of Sturle Heimark to set the police on me, by the way.'

He didn't answer; he stopped in front of a door to a glass box, where I supposed everyone could see in, but no-one could hear anything. We entered, he closed the door and showed me to a table in an interior that was so simple it could have served as an interview room at a police station. We both sat down warily as though neither of us had any great desire to have this conversation.

'We've nothing left to discuss, Veum. I've spoken to Sturle. The police are after you, and I'm already tempted to call them now.'

'I wouldn't do that if I were you, Hope. Then you'll have to tell them about your connections with Bruno Karsten while you're at it.'

His face stiffened. 'I explained to you last time we met. I was helping them with an operating system.'

'We're talking about organised crime here, Hope. You have a problem there, I can promise you that. And what about the fatal accident in Fusa two and a half years ago?'

He rolled his eyes. 'Eh? What the hell are you talking about?'

'It's now documented that your good friend and partner, Sturle Heimark, was in Norway the weekend Knut Kaspersen died, even if he kept claiming he was in Spain.'

'Fine! So what?'

'You told me last time that you were working on a project together. Perhaps you were at that time as well?'

'And if we were, what would that have to do with the death of some salmon farmer?'

'Do you like women, Hope?'

He seemed to lose his temper. 'Do I like women? What the hell do you mean by that?'

I held his eyes. 'What I said. Do you like women or are you a bit … ?' After a short pause I added: 'Like Uncle Knut?'

'Uncle Knut?'

'Kaspersen.'

His face was flushed. 'What the hell are you talking about? Can we put an end to this nonsense now?'

There were two ways to make people open up. One was to gain their trust. That wouldn't work in this scenario. The other was to carpet-bomb them with questions from all sides of the case, in the hope that confusion would cause them to give something away. I attacked from a new angle. 'You must have received an invitation to The Tower as well, didn't you, like all Bruno Karsten's collaborators.'

'The Tower?'

'Bar, club and brothel in Solheimsviken. Don't pretend you don't know it. Bønni and Karsten talked about you when I was there.'

'When you …' He deliberated. 'OK. No, I've never been there, Veum, neither as a guest nor anything else.'

'Because there were only girls?'

'Are you starting on that again? I didn't go there because I didn't want to. I don't do … that sort of thing.'

'No? Tell that to the police when you explain to them why you helped Bruno Karsten with their computers.'

He leaned back and stared at the ceiling with a despairing expression. 'That was a job, Veum!'

I pointed through the glass wall to the room outside. 'Are you registered officially here?'

'…Well, no.' Then he hastened to add: 'Sometimes I offer my services on a private basis too.'

'Of course. A combination of "on a private basis" and organised crime, that's exactly the kind of case the police love to investigate.'

'Get to the point, Veum! What do you actually want?'

'I want an answer to two questions, Hope. The first is this: What sort of project was it you and Heimark were working on?'

'That's none of your business. That's between Heimark and me.'

'That doesn't wash. If what Heimark says is correct, he came expressly to Norway the weekend that Knut Kaspersen died. Expressly because of the project you were working on, I would hazard a guess. Were Data Protection getting too close? Did you need help from an experienced policeman to cover your traces? And what was the project to do with? Fraud? Child porn? Something else? And why did you have to kill Knut Kaspersen?'

He threw up his arms in frustration and stared at the ceiling as though someone were there he could appeal to. 'How many times do I have to tell you? We did not kill Knut Kaspersen!'

'No … but someone did?'

'Ask Svein Olav. Maybe you'll get an answer then.'

'I've asked him.'

'And what did he say?'

I decided on a bold manoeuvre, one not in the Highway Code. 'He said it was you two.'

'Us!' He stood up and shouted so loudly that some people outside the glass box looked in our direction. 'The bloody idiot! Is he trying to blame us? Who gained from the death?'

'Well … I suppose he did, perhaps.'

'Not just perhaps. He was so keen he would've given his right hand to be part of the project Sturle and I had going. Keeping his uncle under water until he drowned would have been child's play by comparison. He came to us and wanted to be in on the project. That would be his investment, if you like. A loan with the salmon farm as security. But I didn't want to have anything to do with him.'

'And why not?'

'First, he didn't have a clue about what we were doing. Sturle and I were the computer experts. Besides, what we were doing in the old factory went completely belly up, and whose fault was that, I wonder?' He glared at me. 'Then we had the police at the door, but even then he couldn't contain himself. He sent a couple of his pals to town to beat you up. As if that would do any good.'

'It didn't.'

'After that I refused to have anything more to do with him. Sturle and I took the whole project with us and went back to Bergen, leaving him there with that salmon farm of his.'

I was making a mental note of everything he said. 'In other words … Svein Olav killed his uncle to inherit the salmon farm and join in what you and Heimark had set up; and he did this the same weekend Heimark was on a lightning visit from Spain … ?'

Hope gestured furiously. 'The guy was a complete fool to do this the same weekend as Sturle was in Norway … to help me.'

'And he knew that before?'

Hope looked away. 'No. But he was told in no uncertain terms when we found out.'

'He told you he'd done it?'

'We saw through him. He wasn't hard to figure out.'

'He managed to keep it concealed from the police anyway.'

'Sturle gave him some tips.'

'You feel very secure about all of this, I can see, from the way you're talking so freely. You've just implicated yourself as an accessory to murder, Hope.'

'Accessory? I'm no bloody accessory. We saw through him, I'm telling you. And that's a very different matter.'

'Not in my book.'

'Prove it, Veum. Aren't you in enough trouble as it is? This will be my word against yours. I understand they have cast-iron proof against you.'

'So you know that, do you? That's the second question I wanted to ask you. Was it you two who put that filth on my computers?'

He leaned back with an expression that reminded me of the one Sturle Heimark had been wearing when Nora and I left him a little more than an hour ago. 'No, Veum. I didn't have that pleasure, however much I would've liked to assist. And you can get every IT expert in the world to search as thoroughly as you like. Sturle told me all about it.' He grinned. 'You're in a real fix, Veum.' He took a phone from his inside pocket and held it up.

'You've got a new one, I see.'

His face clouded over. 'Yes, you owe me one. Can I have it now – this minute? If not, I'll report you for theft as well, now that I'm going to talk to the police anyway.'

I got up. 'You won't talk to anyone, Hope. You're in a fix yourself, as I've already tried to explain to you. You'd better keep a bloody low profile now, and if you come anywhere near this case I'm investigating one more time, it'll be me calling them…' I pointed to his phone. 'Deal?'

He flipped the lid of the phone shut and put it in his inside pocket. 'I'll think about it. But I'm making no promises.' After a slight pause he added: 'Are you going now?'

'Not quite. Åsne Clausen, how well did you know her?'

'Åsne?' Suddenly he became serious. 'Well, what can I say? We were colleagues, as far as that went. I'd just started here when she … Well, you know, of course, as you're asking.'

'You'd just started?'

'Yes, a few months before.'

'So you weren't especially … close?'

He arched his eyebrows, ironically. 'Close? My understanding was you don't think I'm particularly interested in women.'

'So you are?'

'Åsne was a competent colleague, but she was well and truly married, and I didn't have a competitive tender, if I can put it like that.'

'You helped her son, I understand.'

'Severin – yes, I did.' He nodded. 'He's a real talent. He presented an idea he had for a computer game, which really does have something going for it. It's ambitious too. An ecological game, in fact. Climate change. How to stop the polar icecap melting and prevent the sea from rising. It might not sound very sexy, but it has broad global appeal, I think.'

'And your contribution?'

'Well…' He shrugged. 'I can help him adapt it, set it up commercially, for example.'

'But through Severin you must have had some contact with Åsne as well?'

'No, no. This was, broadly speaking, after … she passed on. But it was through her we got to know each other, I'll admit that.'

'And would you say he's good with computers?'

'Good? Fantastic, I would say, bearing in mind his age. But … well, he is the coming generation. Soon we'll be obsolete, those of us over thirty as well.' He looked at the clock impatiently. 'Have we finished now?'

I nodded, and we left the little glass box with me feeling I had achieved not much more than a possible clarification of the Fusa mystery.

He didn't accompany me to the exit and we left each other in the middle of the room without so much as a nod. However, I didn't actually leave. I stopped by the smiling receptionist and asked: 'Tell me … is there a Ruth Olsen who works here?'

'Yes, there is.'

'Would it be possible to have a little chat with her too perhaps?'

'I'll find out,' she said, reaching for the telephone.

45

Ruth Olsen turned out to be a stocky little woman, elegantly dressed in black trousers and a red blouse that matched the bright red of her glasses. She moved in a rather lissom, sensual way, which immediately made quite an impression on me. I could feel myself reacting spontaneously, at the corners of my mouth and in a couple of other places.

She looked at me standing by the reception desk with raised eyebrows. 'Yes? I'm Ruth Olsen.'

'Varg Veum,' I said, not raising my voice any more than necessary. 'I was wondering if you had the time to answer a couple of questions.'

'What about?'

I lowered my voice a further notch. 'I'm, erm, a private investigator. It's about Åsne Clausen.'

The little smile playing on her mouth vanished, and she regarded me with visible scepticism. 'I don't know if I ...'

'It won't take long.'

She clenched her lips together.

'It was her son, Severin, who gave me your name.'

'Severin?' She looked surprised. 'Well, then ... you'd better come with me.'

Her workstation was by a computer in a corner of the room, with a view of the copse at the back of the building. Her desk was tidy and organised. There were a few writing implements in a holder, and facing her chair there was a little frame with a photo of what I assumed from a quick glimpse was her child. Beside the screen lay a writing pad, on which she had made some notes.

She pulled an extra chair over to the desk and motioned me to sit there, as she took a seat behind the desk.

She observed me. 'Private investigator? What does that mean?'

'I investigate criminal cases.'

'Yes, I understand that much, but … it'll soon be two years ago since Åsne … passed away. Who has any interest in investigating that case now?'

'I'm not able to say. But Severin said you and Åsne had been colleagues.'

'Well, we shared this corner.' She pointed to the adjacent desk, which was obviously occupied by someone else who wasn't present now. 'But we were no more than colleagues.'

'No?'

'No. So if you're after something from her private life you've come to the wrong person.'

'I see. But … you must've had some sense of – what shall I say? – her personality. Did it come as a surprise to you that she took her own life?'

Her mouth quivered. 'Yes, of course. Don't such things always come as a shock?'

'Not always. She showed no signs of … depression? Annoyance, something tormenting her?'

'If she had a bad conscience about anything, she hid it well.'

I was a little taken aback by the way she expressed that. 'Bad conscience? Have you anything in mind?'

'No, no! I just … Forget it. I didn't … express myself very well.'

'So you never met outside work?'

'No.' She paused, then added: 'We did meet outside under the auspices of work, of course, but that was the whole gang of us.'

'Her husband, did you ever meet him?'

'Only on that kind of occasion. Sometimes partners came, and I said hello to him. Not that he made much of an impression.'

'But you often met Severin?'

'Yes.' Her face softened. 'He's an unusually gifted boy, especially in what we do: IT; programming. He has a great career ahead of him, of that I am sure.'

'Really?'

'He came to work sometimes with Åsne, and if she was busy I showed him the odd thing or two. Not that it was necessary actually. He was very quick to pick everything up, and since then he's gone stratospheric, literally. Put the youngster in front of a screen and he's in another world for the rest of the day.'

'You've got children yourself, I can hear.'

'Yes.' She spontaneously reached out and turned the photo round so that I could see better. 'Two girls.'

I cast another glance. The smaller of the two girls had a beaming smile, the other was far more cautious.

For a moment I seemed to go giddy, and I was struck by a feeling so strong that I feared I might pass out where I was sitting. I had to force myself to look away.

'Herdis and Bente,' I heard her voice say, as through cotton, from a great distance.

But it didn't help, regardless of how far away I turned. The face of the older girl was seared into the hard drive of my brain, and I had no difficulty recognising her. It was the face of the child who was staring at the photographer with such despair while I lay on top of her in one of the photos Hamre had shown me and which Sølvi had received through the post.

46

Afterwards I barely remembered how I had found my way out. I hadn't been in a position to ask a single question about the two girls. All I had managed to stammer was that there was something else I had to research and could I contact her later? She had been nonplussed and repeated what she had already said, that she had never known Åsne Clausen well enough to have anything to say, but at least she gave me her phone number so that I could ring her at any time, if need be.

'You don't need to accompany me home,' I burbled finally.

'Home?'

'Out, I mean.'

'Well, you can see where you have to go from here, so…'

The look she sent me as we parted told me it wasn't very likely she would be giving me any investigative jobs, if she ever needed one. I was on the interior balcony before I was able to collect myself enough to check my phone to see if any messages had come in while I had been in SH Data.

There weren't any. But there was one more visit I had to make in the building.

Still quite agitated, I walked down the stairs to the main floor and stood by the information board. I hadn't been seeing things. Bjørna Fjord Accountancy *was* on the first floor.

Before I went up again I stood deep in thought, still observed by the Securitas guard in the glass box. So as not to attract too much attention I looked at my watch and pretended I was checking my diary before I slowly walked back towards the stairs.

In my mind there was no doubt. It was Ruth Olsen's daughter who had been in the photograph. And Ruth had been a colleague of Åsne

Clausen, who took her own life – if she hadn't been killed, that is – almost two years before. Ruth and Åsne had both been colleagues of Hjalmar Hope, who was still my main suspect with regard to a possible hacking of my hard drives. But what had Siggen said? These photos could be dated back to the end of November 2001, so less than a year ago? Hadn't he mentioned a specific date as well? 27th November?

The date rang a bell somewhere. 27th November 2000, so the year before; wasn't that the day I went to Åsne's funeral? Was there a connection, which was now further reinforced by what I had seen in Ruth Olsen's office? How old was her daughter? Eight or nine? Younger? Or older?

More and more leads were pointing to SH Data, and now there was another one. The hitherto extremely anonymous Ole Skarnes ran an accountancy firm with an office in the same building. It was, as yet, impossible to say whether this was the Ole Skarnes Maria Nystøl had called 'the devil incarnate'.

I felt a tingle of unease as I made my way along the balcony around to the opposite side of the atrium. I wasn't at all sure that Hjalmar Hope hadn't alerted the police to my whereabouts. And what about the Securitas guard in the vestibule? Did the internal network the police had also include people like him?

Bjørna Fjord Accountancy had a very nondescript sign by the door, with no names of owners or employees. The door itself was solid wood, so there was no way of peeping in. But when I tried it, it opened.

I entered a much smaller room than that occupied by SH Data. As far as I could see, the total area had to be about a twentieth the size of where I had just been. Behind a desk sat a young woman leafing through a magazine while chewing energetically at whatever it was she had in her mouth. She barely looked up after I closed the door firmly and coughed several times.

'Yes?' she said, with no interest.

'Is Ole Skarnes in?'

She appeared to need time to consider the question. Then she looked towards the end of the room, where there was a door in a full-height partition with one and a half metres of wall and a window section of matt-texture glass to make it difficult for people to see in.

'Yes, I s'pose he is.'

'Could I have a word with him?'

She pouted as if to suggest she would think about it. At length she said: 'What was the name?'

'Veum.'

She inclined her head, pressed an intercom button and lifted the receiver so that only she could hear what was said. 'Someone's asking after you: Veum, or something like that.'

She looked at me and I nodded confirmation.

From behind the glass I glimpsed a figure half rise, a dark silhouette against the window behind him. I didn't have a decent view of him, but, judging from his pose, he was standing with the intercom phone in his hand as well.

'Yes,' said the obliging young lady, shifting the chewing gum to the other side of her mouth. 'I'll tell him. Yes.' She put down the receiver and appraised me from under heavily mascaraed eyelids. 'If you could give him five minutes, he'll be able to receive you, he said.'

Again I felt my nerves tingle. Five minutes – what for? To call the police? Speak to someone he was in cahoots with: Bruno Karsten or Bjørn Hårkløv, if Maria Nystøl was to be believed? Or just finish what he was doing?

'Been working here long?' I said to make conversation.

'Eh?'

'I was just wondering if you'd been working here long.'

She took out her mobile and looked at it to see what the time was. 'Since nine o'clock.'

'Yes, but I meant … in general.'

She rolled her eyes. 'Are you hard of hearing? Since nine. I'm temping, if you understand what I mean.'

I could actually work that one out. 'Right, so the permanent person's off ill?'

'Ill? He can't afford any permanent staff any more. The whole company's on the verge of bankruptcy. And that's after being married to one of Bergen's richest women.'

'Really? I didn't know that. Who is it?'

'Sigrid Kronstad. The sister of Kåre Kronstad. Between them they inherited one of the biggest fortunes ever seen in Bergen. But she kicked him out, of course.'

'Skarnes? Why?'

'Well, I dunno. At work they said he had lots of affairs. But he hasn't tried it on with me!' She seemed a little disappointed.

Once again I made a mental note of Kåre Kronstad. Then I went on: 'In other words, the upshot is that Skarnes is – to use your phrase – on the verge of bankruptcy.'

She nodded enthusiastically, as if to emphasise how funny she thought it was. 'He has to pay up front to get anyone to sit here. But they take care of that in the office of course.'

'Which office?'

'Busy Business. Ever heard of them?'

'No, actually I haven't.'

'That's who I work for.'

'And you've never been here before?'

'Never been here and hope I never come back. He's an...' She mouthed the well-known Bergensian version of a swear word: '... asshole.'

'I understand.'

'I very much doubt you do.' Now she was pointing to a couple of chairs and a shelf of magazines along the opposite wall. 'You can sit over there.' She turned back to her own reading material, in which she was engrossed within seconds.

I did as she said, went over to the magazines and flicked through them. None looked particularly interesting. Subject-wise there was a choice between finance and cars, but I was too restless to give either of them a chance right now. I sat on the edge of the chair, still feeling that I was trapped if he had called someone.

The next few minutes seemed like years. It was as though problems were piling up whichever way I turned. The information I had gathered was complicating the picture and I was no nearer an answer; more the opposite.

I sat flicking listlessly through a car magazine while keeping an eye on the glass pane between Ole Skarnes and me. I saw him get up and come towards the door, still a blurred silhouette against the window behind him. He stopped for an instant and peered through one of the stripes in the glass, but it still wasn't possible to identify who he was.

Then the door opened. He stood there, met my eye and said with measured enthusiasm in his voice. 'Veum? Come in.'

The receptionist watched me with complete indifference as I passed her. But this was the day's second massive surprise for me. The nameless individual who had visited my office a year ago now had a name.

47

I followed Ole Skarnes into his office. He closed the door behind us, pulled a chair from the wall and placed it by the desk before taking a seat himself, a mirror image of how we had been in my office the previous year. But the situation was different at any rate. I was stone-cold sober, and at the outset he appeared to have everything under control.

He was wearing a plain, grey suit, a white shirt and a rust-red tie with a pattern of white trumpet lilies. He had a well-groomed little beard and his thin hair was cut close to his scalp on both sides. On top he was bald. He had narrow, indiscernible lips and his mouth was pinched as he observed me with his back to the daylight, like an expert interrogator ready to spring into action.

In fact it was him who set the ball rolling. 'What the bloody hell are you doing here, Veum?'

'You remember me?'

'Of course. But I never heard anything from you, so…' His shoulders twitched. 'Have you come to pay me back my money perhaps?'

'What money?'

He raised his voice. 'The advance I gave you and which you never invoiced me for.'

'I didn't make a note of your name.'

'I gave you my card, but you didn't seem to be up to par, to put it mildly, so if you've spent it I won't exactly be surprised. However, that makes it all the stranger that you're here.'

'Your name came up, in a particular context.'

'Oh, yes?'

'Did you manage to sort out your problems then?'

He held the mask, but I sensed movement behind it. He took a deep breath before answering on the exhalation: 'What problems?'

I leaned forwards a tad. 'You're right that I wasn't up to par, as you put it, at that time. But let me sum up: Someone had taken compromising pictures of you, which they threatened to make public in various ways if you didn't pay them an … insurance fee, perhaps we can call it?'

He looked at me from his wax mask, without answering.

'You were supposed to pay in cash, I seem to remember.' I raised my voice to underline an important point. 'And if you didn't do what they said, they threatened to send the photos to your wife and release compromising material online.'

He still didn't say anything.

'And it sounds as if they succeeded with their intentions.'

'Sounds?'

I tossed my head backwards. 'The girl out there told me you were on the verge of bankruptcy. You can barely pay for a part-time receptionist and you have to pay in advance for their services.'

His face slowly reddened. The look he sent to the glass partition behind me didn't bode well for a happy outcome of Miss Chewing Gum's temping. He bit his lower lip. 'Right. Things have gone downhill a touch since you and I last met. It was in fact to prevent this I visited you at the time.'

'You asked me to find out who was behind it all. I've done that now even if it's taken me a year. Are you still interested in the result of my investigations?'

'You were supposed to find out who they were and you were supposed to gather proof for me. Are you telling me you have both now: names and proof?'

'At least I know who they are.'

'But …' He stroked his beard pensively. 'First off I'd like to know … You said my name had come up in a particular context.'

'Yes. Are you interested in hearing which?'

'To a degree, yes.'

'You're known to be a man with particular sexual predilections.'

Again his face darkened. 'Known for ... what do you mean? And which predilections, if I might ask?'

'If you visit prostitutes you soon have a name, Skarnes. You soon have a reputation. Especially if you're someone they have to be wary of.'

His jaw muscles had started grinding now. It was as though I could see his teeth gnashing and he was taking slow, controlled inhalations through his nostrils now. 'Reputation?' he forced out.

'And you didn't pay, either. It was a bonus, you said. And so there is a choice of conclusions: Either you had a bonus agreement with Karsten and the others, or that was the reason they went after you.'

He eyed me from the other side of the desk as though he no longer knew where I was going.

'At any rate it was Karsten and Bønni you engaged me to find, and I repeat: Are you still interested in the result?'

He stared blankly at me as though it was no longer of any significance. 'Yes? No?'

'Let's hear what you have to say, Veum.'

I studied him. He was a cold fish, and I didn't know for certain where I was with him. As a matter of form, I took out my notepad and leafed through it. 'Karsten is Bruno Karsten: German businessman with interests in Norway, so to speak. Dubious dealings of various kinds. Bønni is the nickname of Bjørn Hårkløv: He does Karsten's dirty work. They used to run a place called The Tower. That was probably the club I think you told me about, where they'd taken photos of you through two-way mirrors. The same photos they used to blackmail you with later. Am I right?'

He sighed and made a vague movement with his head. He seemed almost weary of it all when he said: 'So? What do you want from me, Veum? The fee for finally doing your job, one year late?'

'Can you afford it?'

He opened and closed his mouth a couple of times, then found the right words. 'I doubt your fee is that high.'

'Don't count on it. I remember something you said, Skarnes, as you were leaving that time. If you found out who these people were, they'd pay dearly. They'd realise who they'd tangled with. But you knew who they were if you got prostitutes as a bonus from them.'

Suddenly he raised his voice as if I'd pressed a hidden button. 'There's no-one I despise more than them!'

'Who?'

'The whores! Selling themselves for next to nothing. Debasing themselves for a pittance. Doing whatever they're asked.' A wolfish smile crossed his lips. 'There's nothing I like better than forcing them to do whatever I want and then afterwards – when they want payment – giving them nothing! Just leaving them there like the tarted-up clowns they are.'

I could feel the pressure building up inside me. 'OK, so when you called it a bonus it was just a bluff, in other words?' He didn't answer and I carried on. 'But you didn't answer my question. You knew who they were, both Karsten and Bønni?'

'I knew their names, yes. But that wasn't what interested me most. I wanted proof, I told you. Proof I could use to stop them doing what they did anyway.' He glowered at me ferociously. 'And it was your fault, Veum! You didn't do the job I asked you to do and instead…' His voice barely carried now. 'Instead they sent the damned photos to … Sigrid, my wife.'

'And the result was…?'

He looked around, pointed to the reception. 'You can see. These are the pitiful remains of my little empire.'

'Based on your spouse's fortune.'

'Yes, indeed. Could I help it if my wife had a fortune and was willing to invest in what I was doing? She was no businesswoman herself. She'd inherited the money.'

'Kåre Kronstad's sister.'

He was taken aback. 'Yes? So what? One of the town's most prominent families and then … Can you imagine how it feels to be shown the door by people like that?' He didn't wait for an answer. 'No, you can't, Veum! No-one else can, apart from the person who's been through the experience.'

We sat looking at each other. I still didn't know where I was with him. There was a cold impenetrability about him, and I had an unpleasant feeling he was holding something back; something he didn't want to talk about.

'But you made peace with Karsten and Bønni in the end?'

He gulped. 'We came to an arrangement, yes. When there was no more cash…'

'You still paid for their services – or was it really a bonus? If so, for what?'

'Don't even bloody think about it, Veum!'

'I'll think about what I like.'

He leaned forward. 'In which case, I warn you. Those guys aren't exactly nice. Tread on their toes and they'll bite.'

'Noted,' I said, trying to appear bolder than I felt. Then I changed my approach. 'This building. Lots of companies under one roof. Do you know any of the other people working here?'

'Know them? Not many. Why do you ask?'

'Hjalmar Hope, for example?'

He shook his head. 'No.'

'Sure?'

'Yes, Veum. Quite sure.'

'And Åsne Clausen?'

'… She's dead.'

'Exactly. And you knew her of course?'

'Yes, she was Sigrid's niece, as you know. Besides, I did her husband's accounts.'

'Right! And things are going as badly for him as they are for you at the moment, aren't they.'

'Clausen's withdrawn. It's his father-in-law running the business now.'

'Kåre Kronstad. Your ex-father-in-law.'

'Indeed. And so what?'

'You still do his accounts?'

'For Clausen? No. They've replaced me.'

'I understand. Did you ever meet the son – Severin?'

'Only briefly. At the odd family gathering.'

'What about Ruth Olsen, a colleague of Åsne Clausen's?'

'I never had any contact with Åsne outside the family. I did the accounts for her husband, Veum. That was all.'

'Perhaps we should talk a bit about your wife again. Are you divorced or still only separated?'

'Is that any of your concern?'

'There was no mercy shown when she received the photos in the post?'

'Mercy? In the Kronstad family? They don't give you anything for free. I can tell you that for nothing.'

'So you're left high and dry, in other words?'

He glared at me. 'I've lost most of my clientele. The house was hers. The car belonged to her. The mountain cabin in Geilo. All I was left with was the summer house, because that came from our family.'

'The summer house? That's on Lepsøy, isn't it?'

He half confirmed this with a movement of his head.

'So that's why you moved there?'

He sighed. 'I co-own it with my sister. Was there anything else, Veum?'

'To all intents and purposes you're a free man. You can visit whom-ever you like?'

'Now you've lost me.'

'But … you don't fear anyone any more. You don't owe Karsten and Bønni anything. You don't need me.' I went for the jugular. 'You won't pay for sex. So, I suppose you prefer those who make no demands?'

His smile was cold. 'Who don't make any demands? Yes, naturally, that's the best.'

'Because they're young, I mean, and now I'm talking about children, Skarnes! Someone I spoke to called you a devil. Perhaps she saw the real you more clearly than anyone else?'

'Maybe, Veum. Have you any proof for these allegations?'

'Not yet. But I might have soon … and then I'll be back.'

'You do that.'

'And I won't be alone.'

'Who will you have with you? Bønni perhaps?'

'The police,' I said with a stern glare.

But I wasn't able to break him down that way, either. He was past the stage where he allowed his feelings to run away with him. Although a second or two later his eyes roamed, as though I had caught him *in flagrante*, or at least mentally.

We didn't get a lot further. I stood up. He stayed seated behind the desk without moving. He didn't say he would like to see me again, but I didn't promise he wouldn't.

In reception I smiled wryly at the young woman. 'Have a nice day,' I said without giving her the slightest inkling of what was awaiting her when Ole Skarnes called her into his office, not long from now. Afterwards it struck me that I ought to have warned her. If she wasn't careful he might reveal the devil in him.

The Securitas guard watched me long after I had left the building, but no-one was waiting for me outside, and the car was where I had left it, without even a ticket under a windscreen wiper. No-one had anything to tell me, next to nothing to sell.

I sat in the car more confused than at any point so far. I had never experienced a case with so many loose threads. There were too many leads to follow and they went in every conceivable direction, so far with only one common denominator that I could see: Hjalmar Hope.

He had been involved in what happened in Fusa. He was connected with Sturle Heimark. He had worked for Bruno Karsten and on his own shady activities. He had been a colleague of Åsne Clausen's. At her workplace one of the faces from the repugnant child-porn photos had appeared on her colleague Ruth Olsen's desk. In the same building Ole Skarnes had an office, a man Maria Magdalena – to use her other name – had called 'the devil incarnate', and who, in addition, had been the accountant for Åsne's husband, Nicolai, and the brother-in-law of her father, Kåre Kronstad. The connections were chaotic and without any discernible pattern, and of all these people, who the hell – if anyone

– would have been interested in planting all the filth on my hard drives in November, almost one year before?

The most dangerous lead of them all was the one that led to Bruno Karsten. The way there passed through Bjørn Hårkløv, also known as Bønni. That was where I should go now. But there was another name that had cropped up so frequently perhaps it was time to pay him a visit as well. A call to the shipping company produced the information that Kåre Kronstad was working from home today. With the help of directory enquiries I found out where that was. It turned out to be in the direction I was going anyway. There was no reason to hesitate. I drove there straight from Sandsli.

48

Kåre Kronstad lived in one of the big detached houses set back from the road between Paradis and Hop, where life would have been better before the new motorway was built alongside Lake Nordås and an invisible wall of dust and exhaust fumes rose between them and the water.

I parked the car by the hedge surrounding the property and walked over to the large wrought-iron gate. Working from home was obviously a relative concept, but Kåre Kronstad had probably reached an age now when he could allow himself a day off occasionally while others ruled the empire for him. At any rate he was easily recognisable as he raked the leaves on the extensive lawn leading up to the elegant house built in brick and designed by a 1920s architect who knew his stuff. When I opened the gate and stepped inside he straightened up and, under an apple tree with the rake in his hand, waited for me to approach.

Kåre Kronstad was someone most people in Bergen knew, if nothing else through articles in the newspapers. He came from one of the town's best families and had inherited a considerable fortune from his parents when they died in a car accident in the late 1950s. He established the shipping line around 1960 and, although in the early years he stood in the shadow of Bergen's biggest line, he had piloted his ships safely through both calm and stormy weather, performed sensible manoeuvres and emerged a winner in most of his ventures. He was a small, stocky bundle of energy, dark-haired in boyhood photos, now with quite a thick silvery mane, combed back from his high, sun-tanned forehead. His eyes were blue and sharp from where he was watching me, dressed in grey working clothes with a lightweight white shirt flapping outside his trousers.

Once there, I said who I was, what I did and proffered a hand.

He viewed it sceptically as though not sure what to do with it. But then he decided and gave me a fleeting but firm handshake. 'Kåre Kronstad,' he said, and I nodded.

When he continued it transpired he was old-school: 'And what may I do for you, sir?' It was many years since anyone had addressed me so formally, but then I don't usually move in those circles. For all I knew, it still came naturally to Kåre Kronstad.

'This is about … your daughter's death, nearly two years ago.'

He gave me a fierce look, but his face remained impassive. 'In what connection, might I ask?'

'Some doubt has arisen surrounding the cause of death.'

He straightened up further, which added even more gravitas to his words. It wasn't difficult to see that Kåre Kronstad was a man who was used to being listened to and he didn't often meet opposition. From the end of a boardroom table he had total control down both flanks, and it would take great courage to reject anything he proposed. 'Cause of death?' he repeated in a tone suggesting he didn't understand what I was saying.

'Yes, whether it really was suicide or whether … she was the victim of a crime.'

For a few seconds he scrutinised my face in a way I had hardly ever experienced. What he could see there I had no idea, but he nodded towards the house and said: 'Come with me and we'll discuss this there.'

'Thank you.'

With determined step he guided me to the well-maintained building, parts of which were covered with ivy, not that it was necessary to hide any of the magnificent edifice. The large, varnished front door made of a dark, reddish-brown wood was unlocked. He opened it and led me through a sombre hallway with brown panelled walls and dark floor-tiles to a living room with huge paintings on the walls, well-nourished green plants, Persian carpets on the floor and panoramic windows facing Lake Nordås. Outside, the cloud cover was opening to reveal a picture of grey and blue, and some scattered rays of sun angling down onto the choppy waters. From there he headed through a side door to a room where the smell of several generations of cigar-smokers permeated the walls of what he termed with impeccable accuracy 'the smoking room'.

He showed me to a small coffee table with well-worn though also well-maintained leather furniture, went to a corner cabinet and half turned in my direction. 'Can I offer you anything?'

'No, thank you. I'm driving.'

'A glass of soda water maybe?'

'Yes, please.'

He mixed soda water with whisky for himself, put the glasses on a small tray and came back to me, put it down on the coffee table, placed some black mats under the glasses, but refrained from tasting his drink until a suitable time had passed. I took a quick swig, so quick that the carbon dioxide went up my nose and made me sneeze.

'Your good health,' Kåre Kronstad said. Then he leaned back in his chair, raised his hands, steepled his fingers and looked directly at me again. 'Now I'd like to hear what's on your mind, *herr* Veum.'

'Yes … The thing is … Well, about two years ago I was commissioned to do a job by your son-in-law, Nicolai Clausen.' As he didn't make any comment I continued: 'He wanted me to follow your daughter because he suspected she was having … erm … an affair.' Still no perceptible response. 'But your daughter happened to spot me, and I was forced to relinquish the job. After a few days she visited me in my office and placed solid evidence before me proving the contrary. By which I mean … proof that her husband had been out with other women, predominantly in London, and at least in one case in a blatantly intimate manner.'

'This I already know,' he said, ice-cold. 'Continue.'

I could feel my back getting wet. Kåre Kronstad had natural authority, which made him an exacting conversational partner if you weren't clear-headed and concise enough. 'You may imagine my horror when, a month later, I read news of her death in the newspaper.'

'You were not alone.'

'No.' After a short pause I carried on: 'Now, in connection with another case I'm … well … investigating, I've had to contact your son-in-law and grandchild, Severin. My understanding is that it was Severin who found her when he came home from school and that he, not being able to get in touch with his father, rang you for help.'

'That is correct.'

'But when you arrived your daughter had already been lifted down.'

'Yes. Severin had, naturally enough, done what he could to save her. He had laid her on the floor, but he soon realised – as I did too when I saw her – that all hope was gone. Åsne was dead. There was nothing more we could do.' With a deep sigh he showed for the first time during the conversation a vestige of emotion.

'And it was you who took care of what happened later?'

'Yes, I made the necessary arrangements. I rang our GP, Dr Hermansen, and he came at once. But he, too, was unable to do much more than confirm it was too late.'

'What happened then?'

'What happened then?' he repeated. 'What do you mean?'

'I mean … did everyone take it for granted that it was suicide? Did no-one contact the police?'

Once again he scrutinised my face. Again it was as though he were weighing up where I stood and what I was actually after. Then, once again, he took a decision. 'Listen to me, Veum.'

I nodded to indicate I was all ears.

'My wife, Ingrid, took her own life when Åsne was very small.'

'I'm sorry to hear that. I didn't know.'

'A tragedy, of course. And … If you only knew how difficult it was, erm, in our circles. Not only was I alone with a small girl, who hadn't started school yet, but I had to live with … people talking, their looks … well, I'm sure you can imagine. The press was reserved and discreet in those times, although I doubt they would be now, and I couldn't bear the thought of yet another scandal in the family. Accordingly I did whatever I could for the whole affair to be handled with maximum discretion. Dr Hermansen wrote the death certificate and signed it. I rang a connection I had in the police – high up, I may say – and we quickly agreed that this was a personal tragedy and not the basis of a police investigation.'

'And that's where it finished?'

'That's where it finished.'

'And what do you personally believe? Did you have a suspicion there may be more to it?'

Again I noted a hint of temperament in him. He exclaimed: 'You mean she might … might not have done it herself?'

'Yes.'

He stared into the distance. 'As her mother had chosen that route so many years ago I assumed Åsne had inherited her propensity and she was placed in a situation where the pressures she was exposed to led to her doing what she did.'

'How close were you to your daughter, *herr* Kronstad?'

'We were respectful. As I was left alone with her so early in life we had to have help with many practical matters, so she grew up with nannies and others who gave us some assistance while I … well, I had my own business to see to. But I never remarried. There was never another Ingrid. I have stayed true and concentrated one hundred percent on business.'

'Too much perhaps?'

'What do you mean?'

'Well … my impression, the little confrontation with Åsne, told me … She definitely wasn't the suicidal type in my eyes.'

'No?'

'No. So let me ask you another question. How is your relationship with your son-in-law, *herr* Kronstad?'

His face visibly hardened. 'At the moment as good as non-existent. My blaming him for what Åsne … for what happened to Åsne … wasn't ungrounded.'

'Did she tell you what she'd discovered?'

'No, no. Not a word. She was probably too proud. But after her death I called Nicolai over for a conversation. Incidentally, he was severely affected by the situation. Crushed and incapable of maintaining his position in the company, it's worth mentioning. I pressed him, and after some insistence on my part he was forced to admit what he had done. Then there was no alternative. Within a short time I had bought him out, taken control and contacted my solicitor, so now the primary heir is Severin and no-one else.'

'Right.' I hesitated. 'When I spoke to your son-in-law yesterday, he claimed that … he said that Åsne had admitted she had someone else. But he didn't know who it was.'

He eyed me. 'I see. And?'

'Let me put the question this way: Is it conceivable that Nicolai Clausen might have taken Åsne's life?'

'With what he had on his conscience? I very much doubt he was capable of it.'

'Then there's the man whose identity we don't know. The man she was having an affair with.'

'Says Nicolai!' he interjected.

'Yes, says Nicolai, but nevertheless. There are other indications that suggest that may have been how it was. But as long as we're unable to identify this person we can't count on anything being one hundred percent certain. What if this man had a wife? Could jealousy be a possible motive in the case?'

'Motive … for murder?'

'Yes.'

He stared at me. Then he leaned forwards a fraction in the big leather chair. 'Let me be clear, *herr* Veum. If in the course of your enquiries you come across anything at all that may inform us of the truth of what happened to Åsne on that unfortunate day in November 2000 and you ensure the guilty party appears in court, I'll pay whatever you demand as a fee. You have my word on that!'

'Thank you very much. But I can't guarantee anything. For the moment, this is only a hypothesis, and barely that.'

'I understand. But, as I said, you have my word.'

I had Kåre Kronstad's word. In Bergen you can't sit prettier than that.

But if I was to have any hope of earning some money the prerequisite was that I had a result.

And it was still a long way off.

At length I came to the second matter that had been on my mind since my trip to Sandsli. 'Earlier today I dropped by your ex-brother-in-law, *herr* Kronstad.'

His expression hardened. 'My ex-brother-in-law? Are you referring to Ole Skarnes?'

'Yes.'

'What the hell have you got to do with him?'

'My understanding is that it's over between your sister and him.'

'You can bet your bottom dollar it is. The swine got what he deserved. Sigrid, my sister, suffers from severe arthritis and naturally she's limited in what she can do in life. We have to accept that a man has his needs, but to lay yourself open in the way that Ole did, there is no excuse for that. Not in our circles. I can assure you of that. My sister will never be the same again and she did the only thing she could when she showed him the door. I have supported her to the hilt and so have all our friends. The man is *persona non grata* among everyone with a voice in this town.'

'A fate worse than death, in other words?'

He pursed his lips without saying any more on the matter. We drained our glasses, and after a few final remarks he accompanied me back to the steps outside. Before I had passed through the wrought-iron gate he had resumed his raking, as resolute in his physical labours as in the whole of his manner. You don't get in Kåre Kronstad's way whether you are an autumn leaf on the grass, a brother-in-law on the razzle or a passing private investigator.

49

The next name on my list was Bjørn Hårkløv. The address I had for him was in Fyllingsdalen. It was a low block of flats in Dag Hammarskjølds vei. I drove into the car park between the houses and found a bay marked 'Guests'. I got out and walked over to the block where he lived. By the doorbell to one of the flats there was no name. Judging by the layout it had to be on the second floor, on the right. I took a few steps back and peered up. There was a light on in what could have been the kitchen or bedroom; it was hard to tell as a pale blind was drawn to avert prying eyes.

I got back in the car, unsure what to do. Inexorably, time was pressing, like an impatient customer in the annual sales queue as the door opens. Whenever I passed a police car I instinctively ducked as far down behind the wheel as I could and afterwards pulled my cap even further over my forehead. With every minute that passed I was getting closer and closer to the time when I could avoid them no longer and would be hauled in to face the higher authorities. Before then I needed better cards in my hand than the incomplete pile of Tarot cards I felt I had now, in which the devil was playing his game as he felt fit, and death was the surest winner.

Letting time take care of itself, I took out my phone and rang Sigurd Svendsbø.

He seemed breathless when he answered, and in the background I could hear the sound of traffic. 'Yes?'

'Siggen? Veum here.'

'Oh, hi. I'm sorry but I haven't found out any more about the two people you mentioned.'

'Actually, I've met Ole Skarnes.'

'Can you repeat that? I'm in the street and can't hear.'

I raised my voice. 'I've met Ole Skarnes.' I explained the link quickly. 'But I'm still interested in anything you can find about him.'

'OK.'

'And Bjørn Hårkløv … I'm just outside the house where I'm told he lives, but whether he's there at this time of day I …'

I stopped in mid-speech, because at that moment someone I instantly recognised by his own robust person as Bønni came out of the front door. I sank lower in the seat and said quickly to Svendsbø: 'He's coming out. I'll ring you later. Bye.'

'OK, bye.'

I pressed 'off' and stuffed the phone in my inside pocket as I watched Bjørn Hårkløv, dressed in a black leather jacket and dark trousers, make a beeline for the row of parked cars in the bays reserved for residents. He took out his car key, and the lights of a grey, two-door Audi blinked orange. If you didn't have many friends, it was the perfect car. He scanned round, but didn't stop at me, then got in and started up. On the main road, he turned left, into Bergen. After a suitable lapse of time I followed.

It was Thursday afternoon and the traffic from Bergen to Fyllings-dalen was getting heavier. In our lane through the tunnel the flow was lighter, but halfway up Puddefjord Bridge it slowed, so much so that I had time to reflect. What if the traffic stopped as it often did at this time? What if an officer in a patrol car saw me, or Hårkløv recognised me in his rear-view mirror? Did I have any escape options other than on foot or head first into the fjord? There was nothing else I could do but stay on his tail and hope for the best.

Through Nygård Tunnel he moved into the lane for the town centre, and I did the same, at an appropriate distance. He drove over the limit and the distance increased. I kept to the prescribed sixty kph shown on the traffic signs. The quickest route through Bergen centre had obviously been designed by a drunk: great arcs so as not to fall into Lake Lungegård. Past Grieg Hall, he moved into the left lane again, to switch to the right after the intersection with Christies gate and into Vaskerelven.

The closer we came to Nordnes, the more I had a nagging sense I knew where he was going. I was right. He drove to Klosteret and was lucky and found a spot to park there. I had to drive a fair way up Haugeveien before I found a gap, jumped out and ran down towards Klosteret, just in time to see him turn into Knøsesmuget. I loped after him, trying not to attract too much attention, reached the corner and tentatively poked my head round while he was waiting outside the door of the house where Maria Nystøl lived. The door opened, he forced it in and entered, but I couldn't see who was inside. Then the door was slammed after him.

Once again I stood dithering. What did Hårkløv want with Maria? A little bonus as well? Or something more brutal? Had they found out that I had been to her house – and if so, from whom?

There was still some daylight and if I wanted to risk waiting until he had finished I would have to find somewhere else to stand – in a suitable basement entrance or by the corner to Søndre Munkelivsgate.

I walked slowly down through the alleyway, keeping to the wall on her side, turning my face away as I passed her windows, but pricking up my ears, in case I could hear something from inside. But there was nothing.

A weekday-afternoon atmosphere seemed to have settled over this area. People were making their way home from work; some just passed on their way, others let themselves into their houses, some had crying children, others heavy plastic bags from the nearest supermarket. Many registered my presence with suspicious looks, which made me feel even more uneasy.

I chose to continue all the way down to the corner of Skottegaten. This was when I needed a cigarette, of course, so that I could light a reassuring fag and stand on the corner, forced to breathe in fresh air, as all the country's smokers had been, gradually. But I had neither the habit nor the accessories and decided instead to keep looking impatiently at my watch as though waiting for someone.

I felt a strong sense of unease in my body. I already knew that there was a link between Maria Nystøl, Bruno Karsten and Bjørn Hårkløv.

For that reason I shouldn't be surprised at Hårkløv's appearance at her home. But did this visit have anything to do with my enquiries over the last few days, or was it something he did from time to time, as one of his regular chores?

I looked at my watch impatiently. It was twenty minutes since he went in. How long should I wait before I made a move? I wasn't sure how easy it was to get into the house from the back. If there was access it would be from the parallel street, Claus Frimanns gate, but the passages from the side were probably closed to non-residents.

I checked my watch again. I gave them ten minutes. If he hadn't appeared by then I would have to make a move.

For the second time that day I was saved by the bell. The ten minutes were almost up when the door opened and Bjørn Hårkløv came rushing out of the house. He slammed the door behind him, then cast a glance – first up the alley, then down – and in doing so gave me time to sneak into Søndre Munkelivsgate, beneath the back gardens behind the Community Centre in Klosteret. I waited there long enough to be sure he hadn't seen me. When I cautiously made my way back into Knøsesmuget, it was empty.

Then I had another decision to make: Should I dart back and try to tail him again or should I see how Maria was? I was perhaps already too late for the former as my car was parked further away than his and I would risk being seen if I ran in that direction. The latter would perhaps turn out to be more useful.

I walked up to her house and pressed my fingers against the door. I remembered how well she had locked up the previous time I was there. Now it was open. I had a nasty feeling all was not well. Not at all well.

I stepped inside, closed the door and called her name: 'Maria!'

No-one answered.

I went in further and called again: 'Hello! Maria?'

As I still didn't get an answer I opened the door to the sitting-room, where we had been the evening before.

'Oh, bloody hell!'

She lay in a strangely painful position, squeezed between the table and the sofa, face down on the floor, her legs spread and a backside naked in what might have been an inviting pose had it not been for the dried blood between her thighs and the uncontrolled twitching of her body, as though she were dreaming. Beside her were big tufts of dark hair, a pair of torn cord trousers, a blouse and the underwear that had been ripped off her. From her came a smell of blood and sperm, and when I pushed the table away and leaned forward, she weakly raised her head and tried to look at me. 'Not again, please,' she mumbled before seeming to lose consciousness.

I grabbed a blanket from the sofa and covered her, then shoved the table further away and gingerly drew her along the floor, where I laid her on her side and made sure her airways were free. Her face was in a terrible state. She had congealed blood under her nose and around her mouth and big swellings on one cheek and her chin.

I patted her other cheek gently. 'Maria! Can you hear me?'

Her eyelids flickered and she opened her eyes. Her eyes roamed. When she spotted me she gave a start and burst out: 'No! I'm not going to say anything! I won't say…' Again she closed her eyes.

'Maria!' I leaned over her. 'It's me. Varg. I didn't do this.'

'No, it was Bønni.'

'I know. But why? Did he say why?'

Her eyelids flickered again, and she seemed to be trying to raise herself with her forearms. 'Not supposed to say anything. I'd said too much. Next time…'

'Next time…?'

'They'll kill me, he said.' She gasped for air and her whole body twitched. Then she burst into hysterical weeping. 'Don't say anything, Varg,' she managed to force out between sobs. 'Don't say anything to the po … to the police!'

I tried to console her by stroking her dishevelled hair. In many places I could feel swellings on the scalp and there were bald patches where tufts had been torn out. 'You need help, Maria. We have to get you to A&E – or get someone here.'

She opened her eyes wide and turned her face to me for the first time. 'No, Varg! Don't! They'll report this to the p ... to the po ... You mustn't! I can manage. I always manage. I've experienced worse. Don't forget what I was.' With a bitter expression she added: 'What I am!'

'But ... he raped you. They can find his DNA. He'll go to prison, Maria! For a long time.'

She sobbed long and hard before answering. 'He might do, yes. Maybe. But not Karsten. And he can send other thugs. He's behind this. I don't want to die! I want to live.'

'But...'

'Don't try and persuade me.' At once she sat up, pulled the blanket around her and looked me in the eye. 'I mean it, Varg. He beat me up. He raped me. But I'm not seriously injured. He didn't break anything. I'm owed some holiday I can use until I ...' she raised a hand to her face '... look better. With make-up anyway.'

'And he did this because someone had told them you'd spoken to me?'

She nodded.

'And you hadn't told them yourself?'

Once again she opened her eyes wide. 'Of *course* not!'

I observed her. 'Well, now you've received the punishment...'

'W-what do you mean?'

'You can tell me the rest.'

'The rest?'

'What you omitted to tell me last time. About the children.'

She met my stare, at first with defiance, then a kind of shame; and in the end her eyes filled with tears. She gasped for breath and turned her head from side to side, as though I were holding her and she were trying to squirm out of my grip.

'They blackmailed you, didn't they. Because of what you told me last time, about your background in Germany.'

A mask of grey despair descended over her face as she nodded, against her will, again as though I were holding her neck and twisting her head this way and that.

'You filtered children out of the system. Those who were orphans or didn't have anyone to look after them. This happens in dozens of Norwegian asylum centres every single year. We know that, but for some reason we can't stop it. And why? Because children are not significant? Because children don't write in the newspapers and scream when others are bad to them? Because children are used to doing what adults say? Otherwise they're hit. Because, because, because?'

She just stared at me, mute.

'And you sent them to Bruno Karsten and his network, where they were passed on, I imagine, to the abusers who exist everywhere, from the top of society to the bottom, but all with the same aim: "Grab a helpless child and do with them as you like."' I seemed to hear a guitar solo and the psalm in my head: *No-one in danger can be so safe as God's little flock of children …*

The fury I felt inside must have been reflected on my face, because she pulled away from me with horror-stricken eyes. 'Please, Varg! Please don't do that!'

'Just admit that this is what was going on!'

She nodded, even more against her will this time. I barely understood what she was saying when she whispered it: 'Yes, but I resisted as much as I could. They had to force me … every single time.'

'Like this …?' I pointed, first to her face, then to her lower body. 'This?'

She sighed. 'N-no, not as bad. It was enough for them to mention … all the things they could do, how easily I would lose my job if they made a phone call to the right people.' A shudder went through her. 'Don't you think I thought it was terrible? Don't you think I felt for them, for the poor children? I took extra special care of them when they returned.'

'What! They returned?'

'Y-yes. Not all of them. Some disappeared for ever. But many came back.'

A suspicion was aroused in me. 'And were taken out again, several times, maybe?'

She chewed her lips and looked away. 'No.'

'Look at me, Maria!'

She slowly turned back. 'Not several times.'

'They didn't come back several times?'

'No. The next time they disappeared for good.' She added quickly: 'The few who were involved.'

'Into the network? Into organised prostitution? To other countries?'

She looked at me with despair in her eyes. 'Maybe. Oh, I wish I could…'

'Could what?'

'Undo what was done!'

I sat looking at her, gripped by a mixture of depression and fury, a feeling of total helplessness against systematised evil; an evil that befell the weakest of all – child refugees. But, and I didn't want to forget this, also Norwegian children. Local children. Ruth Olsen's daughter, for example. That made me go on. 'You gave them foreign children, Maria. What do you know about Norwegian children in the same situation?'

'The Norwegian children we have are only here for a short time, to relieve other centres. I've never … They've never taken these children. The controls are too stringent.'

'That's the only reason?'

She opened her mouth to say something, but caught herself.

'You took extra-special care of them when they came back, you said. Did they tell you what they'd experienced?'

She shook her head. 'No, never. Many of them were traumatised enough beforehand and … I think they'd already repressed it.'

'And they certainly wouldn't've got any better by being treated in that way by someone they trusted.' I could feel the contempt I felt flowing from my mouth. 'I damn well feel like beating you up myself, Maria!'

She looked at me with a cowed expression. 'Do it then! Just hit me! Beat me black and blue! It won't change the reality.'

I heaved a sigh. 'No. I suppose it won't.' I cast an eye over the super-ficially cosy room where only the battered and bruised woman, the torn clothes and the scattered furniture told a different story. 'You know I can go to the police with what you've told me, Maria. You know I only have to lift a phone and you've lost any work with children for ever and a day. And I'm bloody tempted to do that.'

She said nothing.

'But I'm not going to, for the moment. On one condition: I want names from you and I want them now.'

She nodded distractedly, looking out of the window, as though fearing that Hårkløv, Karsten or someone else were standing outside and listening.

'I've got Bønni. Bjørn Hårkløv, if you didn't know. Bruno Karsten as well. The last time I was here you mentioned Ole Skarnes. But as your client. Was he also involved in this?'

Her eyes were glassy, and her voice was strangely distant as she answered. 'Yes. He had fantasies … They forced me to … I had to bring one of the girls back here. Once I had to meet him and he was supposed to be a Gestapo officer and we were … a mother and child fleeing. Only he could help us, but we had to … be at his service. Both of us. It was disgusting, Varg! I spewed like a drunk afterwards.'

'And the girl?'

'They took her with them. I couldn't … I wasn't allowed to see her again.'

'Who took her with them?'

'Skarnes and Bønni.'

'And she never returned?'

'Never.'

I had been to bed with this woman, but I knew from where I was sitting that I would never be able to do so again, if the opportunity arose. But in some way she was a victim, too. There were others who should be punished more severely and I swore to myself there and then that I wouldn't rest until I had done everything in my power to achieve this.

Before leaving I asked her once more if I shouldn't ring for medical assistance. Again she refused, and I went on my way without any further attempts to provide care. She would have to be alone with her pain – external and internal. I had other people to see before the day was done.

50

Hårkløv's car was long gone. My rental car was waiting contentedly for me without any greetings from a traffic warden.

I took a risk and drove straight back to Fyllingsdalen. But there wasn't a car where Hårkløv's had stood earlier in the day. I had no idea where he might be. True, I did have his mobile number, but if I rang him he was hardly going to tell me where he was, and I would perhaps lose the element of surprise.

I sat considering my next move. I took out my notepad and read through my last notes. I had underlined two details. One was the fact that Ruth Olsen's elder daughter, Herdis, had been in one of the same photos as me, whatever that meant. The second was that the man whose name was being mentioned with ever greater frequency, Ole Skarnes, had been the accountant for Nicolai Clausen. And Clausen's late wife, Åsne, had been a colleague of Ruth Olsen's, with offices in the same building as Ole Skarnes. This was the thread I most wanted to unravel. Another went from Maria to Hårkløv and on to Karsten. And then there was the woman with oriental features and a blonde wig who kept appearing in my brain. Would it be possible to track her down, and if so, what did she have to tell me, assuming I could make her talk?

The worst of the rush hour was over when I emerged from Nygård Tunnel again and got into the lane for the town centre. But this time I turned right in front of the library, passed the railway station and headed for Kalfaret and Clausen's flat.

The light shone in the kitchen this time as well and dimly from what had to be the sitting room. I recalled the unpleasant conclusion of the conversation on the previous occasion and felt less than cocky as I, cap over my forehead and lapels turned up, approached the house yet again and rang the bell.

Nicolai Clausen opened the door as before. He regarded me briefly from the doorway, dark bags under his eyes and apparently suffering from the latter stages of sleep deprivation.

'There's a new development, Clausen. May I come in?'

He didn't have the energy to attempt a protest, stumbled to one side and let me in. I closed the door and he walked ahead of me into the kitchen, as before. On the worktop there were two portions of a ready-made meal called Mother's Meatballs, not as yet elevated to their impending state of magnificence but waiting to be put in the microwave and perhaps the homecoming of his son.

Neither of us sat down.

Clausen automatically turned to me. 'What's this about now?'

'Let me get straight to the point: Ole Skarnes.'

His eyes were lifeless. 'Oh, yes?' Then something appeared to rouse him into life. 'You don't mean … It wasn't him who was … ?'

'Who was … ?'

'Åsne's lover?'

The thought hadn't actually struck me, and I had to let it do a quick circuit around my brain before I answered. 'I doubt it. It's true he comes across as immoral, but he was her uncle after all, through marriage.'

He seemed to let that sink in. But made no comment.

'He's your accountant, I understand?'

'Not any more. The family disowned him.'

'So I believe.'

'Indeed.'

'What about Ruth Olsen?'

He still didn't look interested. 'Who's that?'

'A colleague of yours – of Åsne's, rather. Severin mentioned her yesterday when I was here.'

'I didn't know any of her colleagues.'

'No?'

He tried to stand erect to remind me of what he had once been. 'I was much too busy with my own concerns.'

'You never went to her workplace?'

'No.'

'Never at any socials? Such as … Christmas parties, work outings, that sort of thing?'

'Only occasionally. I wasn't interested.'

No, there were two things that had interested him: earning as much money as possible and going out with escorts abroad. A new idea occurred to me: perhaps not only abroad? 'Bruno Karsten. Do you know him?'

'Who?'

'Bruno Karsten, German … let's call him a businessman, shall we. He has a stable of the kind of girl you used to like going out with. Yes, here in Bergen.'

There was another glint of the old personality in his eyes. 'I never did anything like that here! You have to understand that.'

'Well. Once you've acquired certain habits…'

'Nothing like that happened here, and I've never heard the name you mentioned.'

'Not even in a business context?'

'No.'

'This Ruth Olsen has a daughter called Herdis. I suppose you haven't met her, either?'

He heaved a sigh. 'Severin never brings anyone home, if that's what you're thinking.'

'Actually I'm not. She's too young for that.' I tilted my head towards the two meals. 'He's not home yet?'

'No, but I'm expecting him.'

'Let me give you a prompt, Clausen. And I'd like to ask you to think carefully before you answer.'

'Alright.' He gave me an enquiring look.

'This is the prompt.' I raised my voice and stressed every syllable clearly. Child por-no-gra-phy.'

This time I got a spontaneous reaction. His jaw dropped and he gawped for several long seconds before he could close his mouth. His face went grey and he swayed in front of me. Then he groped along the worktop behind him until he found a chair and slumped down. With an expression on his face as if I had walloped him in the stomach, he looked up at me. In a low whisper he said: 'Have you found that out?'

I nodded, keeping a close watch on him.

'Åsne found out…'

'That you…?'

'Me?' He seemed puzzled. 'She was waiting up for me one night when I came back home. Severin was out, at the cinema or something. She grabbed me as soon as I entered.' He formed two claws with his hands. '"Come here," she said. "Come and see what you've done…" And then she dragged me into Severin's room and started up his computer. Well, don't ask me how she'd found his password, but she had, and after a few taps on the keyboard she opened some webpages – some pictures – well, I was left flabbergasted. I could barely believe it was true.'

'Really?'

'I…' His eyes searched around the room. 'I suppose I'm a man with some experience. Mind you, Veum, with mature women who knew what they were doing. I could never have … This was children, right down to … kindergarten age! And Severin was looking at this in the evening while we thought he was doing school work, other things, but not … nothing like this!'

His despair seemed genuine; I had to give him that.

'Then she turned to me and the tongue-lashing began. "Can you see now what you've done? This is your genes! He got this from you!" And she attacked me, physically. She clenched her fists and pummelled me. I had to grab her wrists and hold her still. It was desperate, but she wouldn't calm down. "I'll never forgive you," she said. "Never! Not for as long as I live!" The following day she took her own life.'

'The following day?'

'Yes.'

'So you think … You reckon that's the straw that broke the camel's back – her finding this … material … on her son's computer?'

'I have no idea. But it must've reinforced … what she was already feeling.' He added bitterly: 'So perhaps I'm not the only one to blame in this matter.'

'What did he say?'

'Who? Severin?'

'Yes. You must've confronted him with it, I suppose?'

He looked away. '...No. I've never said a word to him.'

'No?'

'Perhaps she was right. He had it from me. Another character flaw. Then ... why should I make life harder for him? It was bad enough as it was. I preferred to carry the burden myself.'

'But ... does he still have this material on his computer?'

He shrugged. 'I have no idea. Probably.'

'Doesn't that worry you? As a father, I mean.'

He had sunk back into his basic posture – a mixture of resignation and total apathy. 'I don't know.'

'I'll have to talk to him.'

'No! This was meant for ... your ears only. I was ... You took me by surprise. I don't know how you found out.'

'Computers are never safe, Clausen. Åsne found the password. Others can get in.'

'But ... please don't say it was me ... that I told you. Don't say I knew! Don't make him believe it was his fault that she...'

'We don't know that, do we.'

'No. It was still mostly mine though.'

'I mean ... do we know she took her own life, Clausen?'

He eyed me in puzzlement. 'Do we know?'

'What actually happened that day?'

'What happened?'

'Severin came home from school and found his mother dead. She was hanging from a beam in the ceiling, he said, but he lifted her down before anyone else came. As such, we have only his word for it that that was how it happened.'

He moved his lips silently before he could find the right words. 'You don't mean ... Severin...?' However, he was unable to complete the sentence.

'Let's imagine he came back from school. His mother confronted him with what she'd found on his computer, and the confrontation turned so nasty that he ... resorted to violence against his mother.'

'But ... all the signs are that she'd hanged herself.'

'All? Who took the responsibility to organise an investigation? Your father-in-law, Kåre Kronstad? Dr Hermansen? The police didn't even come to the crime scene, if we can call it that. I'd call that side of the matter a scandal. You didn't even let them investigate your wife's death, Clausen!'

'I ... I didn't realise.'

'Didn't realise? Let me ask you one more thing: Where were you that day? How come Severin couldn't contact you on the phone?'

His eyes went walkabout. 'I ... don't remember. At a meeting, I imagine.'

'Don't remember! You find out your wife's dead and you don't even remember where you were when you found out?'

'I do remember when I found out. Alice, my secretary, said he'd been trying to contact me; Severin, that is.'

'And she couldn't contact you, either? Where were you actually? On your way from home after killing her?'

Once again his jaw dropped. Now it took him even more time to pull himself together, but he didn't quite manage to close his mouth. He stared at me as though he no longer knew who I was. 'Killed her? What are you talking about?'

'You say you had a confrontation because of what she found on Severin's computer. If that confrontation spilled over into what she'd found out about you and your activities abroad, perhaps that was enough for things to turn nasty and end in ... a fatal outcome.'

Still he appeared curiously unengaged, as though what I was accusing him of somehow didn't concern him personally. And perhaps it didn't. For the present it was impossible to say anything certain, and the credit for that undoubtedly went to his influential father-in-law.

'Kåre Kronstad. What's your relationship with him like, Clausen?'

He didn't need long to answer that. 'We don't talk any more.'

'He wouldn't have put himself out to protect you, would he?'

He shook his head. 'No. Hardly.'

'Would he have protected Severin, do you think, if he thought it was him who ... had laid hands on his own mother?'

'Laid hands on?'

'Killed her, then!'

He stared into space. 'Kåre Kronstad idolised his daughter. I don't think he would've forgiven anyone if he'd heard anything of that kind.'

'Sure?'

He hesitated once again. 'You can never be sure with ... my father-in-law. But...' He shrugged his shoulders and didn't complete this reasoning either.

I couldn't help but feel a sort of sympathy for him. Nicolai S. Clausen hadn't got off scot-free. He had been punished by fate; life had struck him a blow, and he was so changed from the man I had met around two years ago he was scarcely recognisable.

I looked at my watch. 'When are you expecting him home?'

'Severin? Any moment.'

'I need to have a few words with him as well.'

'Not here.'

'OK. I'll wait outside.'

He shrugged and glanced at the door.

'Bon appetit,' I said, angling my head at Mother's Meatballs. He stared at the two portions without responding. I found my own way out.

51

Night had begun to fall when I got back into the car. I kept an eye on the road – in both directions; but Severin came from Kalvedalsveien this time too. With the same laziness as most of the pupils of his generation, he had probably caught the bus for two stops to avoid walking up the hill to Kalfarveien.

When he was level with the car I opened the door and stepped onto the narrow pavement, right in front of him. He gave a start, but when he saw who it was, he recovered and adopted the same aggressive attitude as on the previous day.

'You again? What do you bloody want now?'

'To talk to you.'

'We've got nothing to talk about.'

'We have.'

'What about?'

'About what's on your computer.'

'What's …' He came to a halt. Then he flushed a deep red – so red that the pimples became almost invisible. 'Have you hacked my computer?'

'Not me.'

'Who then?' His eyes strayed to the house. 'It wasn't … ?'

'You know yourself how vulnerable a computer is. There's always a back door for a trained hacker.'

'And that's you?'

'It could be someone I know.'

He chewed on that, still red-faced, but now perhaps with unease as much as annoyance. 'And what did you find there?'

'I think you know. And you're over the age of criminal responsibility, so when the police get to hear of this …'

'The police? My computer's none of their fucking business!'

'Oh, no? Are you following the news at the moment? Several people have been arrested for the illegal distribution and possession of … yes, you know what it's about. Child pornography.'

His face crumpled and he gasped for breath. 'You'll have to prove it was me who downloaded it!'

'Of course. Because someone else could have done it, couldn't they.'

He sneered. 'Every idiot knows that. With the right know-how you can download all the shit in the world onto someone's computer, especially if there's some muppet clicking on every link that appears on the screen.'

It struck me that, if nothing else, we had an actual defence witness here for Vidar Waagenes; someone who could confirm our theory. I instantly modified my tone. 'Do you think someone could've hacked your computer too?'

'Yes,' he answered sullenly, but not quite as convincingly as I would have liked. 'If there's anything on it, that is.'

'You surfers … I suppose you have lots of contacts on the Net?'

'Of course. You meet more interesting people than … here, for example.' To emphasise this he pointed at me first, then circled round to take in the whole neighbourhood.

'So you might also discover a network that offers you that kind of image, for example.'

He didn't answer.

'A face that you recognise can even appear on such webpages. There are enough young girls who bitterly regret sending private photos to a boyfriend who then becomes an ex with plenty of ammo for revenge.'

'I've heard of that,' he said, still as sullen.

'Did you ever meet the daughters of your mother's colleague, Ruth Olsen?'

His eyes flitted about. 'Yes, a couple of times.'

'You never saw either of them on these webpages?'

'Eh! Herdis? Or … I can't remember the name of the other one.'

'Herdis, yes.'

Now his face had gone purple again, and he scanned the surroundings as though wondering if he would be able to do a runner. I
straightened up to make it clear that, if he did, I would do everything in
my power to stop him.

'But she's just a little girl!' His nostrils quivered and I could read him
like an open book. There was one good old-fashioned axiom: Nothing
was better than someone you knew turning up in contexts such as these.
The taste of forbidden fruit was even more powerful in such cases. 'I
haven't been on any webpages like that, I'm telling you.'

'But Herdis mentioned you at once when I broached the subject.'

He met my gaze, as defiant as only a teenager can be.

'How do you think your mother would've reacted if she'd found out?'

'My mother! She never saw it! It was just … something I happened
to see. While I was surfing.' Immediately he realised that he had given
himself away. I watched his face close. He pursed his lips tight as if he
would never open them again.

'Exactly. Something you happened to see while you were surfing.
What if your mother or your father found out? What if your mother
recognised Herdis on your computer? What if she confronted you with
this?'

'Confronted? She never said…'

'The day you came from school, for example. The day you say you
found her dead.'

He blanched. 'The day I … I say … she was dead?' Slowly, he took
in what I was insinuating. Then his face cracked and there was a massive
explosion. Tears streamed from his eyes and he barked at me. 'She was
hanging from the beam! I lifted her down to help her. But it was too
late! She was dead! It wasn't me who … She was dead when I arrived!
She was!'

I watched him. The reaction seemed genuine, as genuine as you
could expect from such a young person.

'But it's not certain it was suicide, Severin. Someone else could've
hung her from the beam after killing her.'

He stared at me with big, tear-filled eyes. 'What? Someone else?

… Who?' Instinctively his gaze strayed to the house I had just left, as though he was being drawn there by the same thoughts I'd had myself less than half an hour ago. 'You don't mean…?'

'I don't mean anything, Severin. Now I think you should go home, have something to eat with your father and forget this. If you have any information at all, I suggest you go to the police.'

'The police?'

'Yes, I assume you still have this material on your computer?'

He looked away without answering.

'Then you should be aware that, if the police track you down, it would be to your great cost.'

He just gaped at me. Then he peeled away, as if expecting me to hold him back. But I had no such intentions. I stepped aside to show that he could go home to Mother's Meatballs, however wretched they might be.

I got back in the car and sat watching him until he had let himself in. In the rear-view mirror I saw a patrol car racing up Kalvedalsveien with wailing sirens and blue lights. To be on the safe side, I waited a few more minutes, then started up and continued on my far more laborious patrol to where it was I was going.

52

Madonna met me in the hallway. She subjected me to a critical examination, as if to say: 'What sort of time do you call this? How long do I have to wait?' Nevertheless she came over and stroked her fur against my trouser leg, as though wanting to tell me something.

I followed her into the kitchen, replenished her dish and water bowl, and she rubbed my hand in gratitude before I had a chance to take it away. With a satisfied purr from somewhere inside her slim, muscular body, she swooped on the dish, and I stood up, put the packet of cat food on the worktop and observed her for a while. In many ways it seemed to be a perfect life, so long as someone came to fill her dish for her. I almost envied her.

I went into the sitting room and logged onto the computer. While I was waiting for it to start up I thought about the photos Sølvi had received in the post. I took out the one she had left behind, and there was no doubt: This was the same child I had seen in Ruth Olsen's office. This was a clue I couldn't let pass. On the other hand, this was one of the shots where it wasn't clear that it was me in the picture unless you knew.

I put the photo on the table in front of me, placed my fingertips against my temples, hoping this would open some hatches into my memory, and I concentrated as hard as I could. Surely there had to be a scrap of recall after being in such a pose? Or had I experienced it as so humiliating and so distant from me that my brain's own defence mechanisms had cut in and brought the iron curtain down for good between me and what had happened?

God knows how many times I had gone over the dark years in my attempts to pinpoint the most likely course of events, but this time, once more I was brought to a halt by the woman with the oriental features and the blonde wig. Somewhere in Bergen she had served me a green drink that must have had a substantial dose of an anaesthetic in it, because the next thing I remembered was waking up in a hotel room where I was afterwards told that I had been brought during the night by a friend whose name no-one had made a note of. I thought I had seen the same woman in The Tower when I went there with Karl Slåtthaug; and later, on one of the walls there, I had found the telephone number of a woman who spoke Norwegian with a foreign accent and also offered Thai massage in what she called 'cosy surroundings'. The room where she worked was a few blocks away from Hans Hauges gate, so I decided to try there before doing anything else.

The screen had gone black again, so I pressed a key. I looked for the address of Ruth Olsen. She lived in Breistølen, as high up the mountainside as you can get from Sandviken, a dream for people who swore by panoramic views, but a nightmare for drivers in the fire service. But could I risk visiting her? What if I met her daughter and she recognised me? The very thought of it made my insides shrivel. There had to be a better solution.

I dialled the number of the Thai massage parlour nearby. The same voice answered. I used one of my oldest pseudonyms, introducing myself as Finn Wolf and asking if there was any chance of an appointment, preferably this evening. She cooed in a charming way and said she could take me in about an hour, at 'nineteen hundred hours'.

'Do you require anything special?' she added.

'Yes, I do,' I said, without a word of a lie. *Anything special? Well, the truth, for example?*

'See you later,' she said, and rang off.

Madonna had come in from the kitchen. Unbidden, she jumped up on the sofa, curled up beside me, stretched her neck so that her head was lying half on my thigh and then rolled onto her back in an undisguised request to be stroked, an offer which I met absent-mindedly while dialling Sølvi's number on my phone.

She was giving Helene a hand with her maths. I could have done with the same myself on frequent occasions. She sounded quite distracted too, but at least I managed to tell her that I was still free and was informed that the police hadn't been to her door yet. She hadn't even heard from Vidar Waagenes. Everything was strangely calm, she said. 'The calm before the storm,' I commented, but when I heard the sharp intake of breath I regretted my comment and said I hadn't meant it like that. Then I gave her a short résumé of where I had been and whom I had spoken to, without going into any detail about the physical state of Maria Nystøl or the danger of being confronted by Bjørn Hårkløv in the near future. She apologised that she would not be able to come and visit me that evening, because of Helene, but I replied – as indeed was the truth – that I would be out anyway. She finished with a verbal kiss and hug, and I was left with the phone in my hand and an urgent desire for a little more than that when we saw each other again.

I still couldn't rid myself of the idea that the situation was worrying. Who had sent the revolting photos to her in the post? And what about Helene, who was the same age as the girls in the photos? I didn't like this at all. Perhaps I should drop everything, drive to Morvik and sit by their front door as a bodyguard? But then who would clear my name?

I went into the kitchen, cut myself a few slices of bread, found some cheese and ham in the fridge, poured a glass of milk and sat down at the table. After eating this simple meal I said a polite goodbye to Madonna and set off – if not all the way to Thailand, then to one of the country's outposts; one that was about as far from home as it was possible to be and which boasted a range of activities that in some cases were definitely of the more dubious variety.

53

The entrance was via a basement in a side street down towards Skute-viken. I noticed a little CCTV camera mounted out of reach on the wall above. The window was covered inside by a purple velvet curtain. The door was locked and I had to ring a doorbell to get in.

I stood with my cap pulled well down over my eyes, my hand to my mouth and my head angled as though thinking. After somewhere between twenty and thirty seconds a voice came from the intercom above the bell. 'Yes?'

'We have an appointment at seven.'

'Welcome!'

The lock buzzed. I pushed the door and accepted the invitation. I stepped straight into a small reception area. I heard delicate oriental string music coming from a sound system, and in the air there was an exotic perfume of essential oils. A curtain of the same material as in the window stirred, and out from a back room came a petite woman dressed in a loose white tunic and matching baggy trousers, oriental in appearance with lustrous, raven-black hair gathered in a ponytail.

As so often before meeting people with a different skin colour I was struck by a kind of race blindness, where all individuals of the same race looked more or less the same. Even though I tried to see her with a blonde wig it was hard for me to say if this was the woman. But when I took off my cap and showed her my face I could see she recognised me, and a mixture of fear and horror spread across her beautiful face. She instinctively retreated a few steps while looking around – for what? A weapon? A phone? Something else?

I followed her. 'Don't be frightened. I just want to talk to you. I won't do anything to you.' I reached into my inside pocket. 'I can pay.'

Her eyes were dark brown and almond-shaped. I saw big, pearl-sized drops on her forehead and smelt a strong scent of lemon, rosemary and something else, more indefinable. She gulped and stared at me with widened, nervous eyes.

'I can see you recognise me.'

The muscles around her jaw moved. I saw her body tense and I kept an eye on her legs. For all I knew, she had mastered a martial art I had barely heard the name of. 'Yes, I … I've seen you before.'

'But then you were wearing a blonde wig.'

She nodded slowly.

'Your work outfit?'

She moved her lips, but without saying anything.

'We met at a bar, and I was … drunk. You gave me a green drink and I don't remember anything else.'

She inclined her head.

'Who told you to give me that drink?'

'Wh-who?'

'Yes.'

A barely audible sigh escaped her. 'I can't say.'

'You have to say! If you don't, I'll call the police.'

'No! Not police! They send me out!'

'It's best you answer my questions then,' I said, a little rougher than I liked.

From my inside pocket I took the print-out of the photo Sølvi had received in the post. I unfolded it and held it in front of her. She lifted her hands to her face, held them over her mouth as if to hold back a scream and opened her eyes wide. She looked from the picture up at me and back again.

'Seen this before?'

She shook her head vigorously. 'No, no! I no see. It horrible.'

'Never seen the little girl before?'

'No, no! I never see! She … She look … Norwegian?'

'But the man on top of her is me.'

'You?' Now her horror was mixed with a form of disgust, and she repeated the word, spat it out: 'You!'

'But I'm unconscious. And I'm fairly sure that's because someone served me a green drink with some very effective knockout drops in.' I leaned forwards. 'The police would be very interested to hear more about that!'

'But I no know! I only ... I only have to give it. The drink. Afterwards they take you in back room and I no know what happen then. I have many ... to look after.'

'Many people to serve the same drinks?'

'No, more to look after.'

'As in The Tower?'

She was lost. '"The Tower"?'

'The rooms in Solheimsviken. They're abandoned now. And you saw me there again ... not long after.'

She nodded briefly, with twitches, as though she had symptoms of Parkinsons.

'Let me repeat the question: Who told you to serve me the drink?'

She looked at me in desperation. 'You promise not say I tell you?'

I put my hand on my heart. 'I promise.'

She hesitated still, then answered. 'You know him who run bar.'

'Who was that?'

'They just call him Johnny. But it was German who own it.'

'The German? Bruno Karsten?'

'We ... girls. We call him just German.'

'But it was Karsten? The same man as in The Tower?'

She nodded. 'Yes.'

My head was buzzing. 'Karsten told you to?'

'No, no.'

'Johnny?'

'No, they know Johnny, I tell you.'

I gesticulated impatiently. 'Get to the point! Who told you ... I've already asked you lots of times.'

'I know only one of them.'

'OK. And that was ... ?'

'His name ...'

'Yes! I'm waiting.' I took out my phone and held it in front of her. 'I'm calling the police now if you don't—'

'Ole.'

The cat was out of the bag. 'Ole. And the surname?'

'I not sure. I think maybe … Garnes.'

'Skarnes by any chance?'

'Yes. I not sure. But you not say. He can be … brutal.'

'So I've heard. We're talking about the same man. But you said … Were there two?'

'Yes. Second man.'

'Yes?'

'He younger. And I not know his name. I never see him before and never since.'

'Do you know who Bønni is?'

'Yes, yes.' She nodded, again with a frightened expression. 'It not him.'

'No. What did he look like?'

'I … Very normal. Quite long hair, maybe. Not shave. Look like a … I not like way he look at me, like he want … He like Skarnes. Disgusting.'

Brutal. Disgusting. There was no end to the compliments good old Ole Skarnes was showered with.

I was about to say something when I heard a sound from the door. I turned round in time to see the door being opened from outside; a large man came in with a bunch of keys in one hand and a baseball bat in the other. The Thai woman let out a little scream.

It was Bjørn Hårkløv, and he grinned unpleasantly as he swung the bat in front of him. 'Thought there was no camera in here, did you, Veum? Eh? Think we don't take care of our girls? You made a mistake there, man. Terrible mistake.'

54

I looked around.

If this had been twenty years ago I would probably have tried to spar with him for a round, but exposing myself to anything of this kind now, had to be considered an extreme sport. I couldn't ring the police either, which I had done the last time I was in a similar situation.

Bjørn Hårkløv stood in front of me, legs akimbo. He swung the baseball bat threateningly in the space between us: flat thwacks into his hand, ominously close to my face.

I moved backwards while keeping an eye on the Thai woman.

'What the fuck are you after?' he barked at me. 'Didn't you get enough the last time we had you in for treatment?'

'Have we met before?'

For a moment he was at a loss. 'Eh? It's true you were legless both times, but…' Again he swung the bat in front of me. 'This time you won't forget.'

I had backed into the wall now. I couldn't go any further. 'Listen, Hårkløv, let's talk!'

He smirked. 'So you know my name?'

'I know your name. I know where you live. I know who you work for. And I'm not alone.'

'Not alone…?'

'Not alone in knowing. If I don't return from here unharmed there'll be others who will move heaven and earth, here and in Hamburg, to catch you and your paymaster, Bruno Karsten. That much I can promise you.'

I watched that enter his skull, slowly and laboriously, but it did sink in after a while. It was how it always was. Big muscles; tiny brain. Exceptions were rare. It didn't even have anything to do with anabolic steroids.

'And who might that be?'

'What about powerful rivals for the same market?'

'Oh, yes? Give me one name, Veum. Give me more!' He swatted the air with the bat to add emphasis to what he was saying.

'Are you stupid? Do you think I'd risk their lives? These are my employers we're talking about.'

That was a language he understood. Nonetheless he became more explicit: 'You're risking your life.'

I met his eyes. They were hard, grey and pitiless. I recalled how Maria Nystøl had looked after he had been to her house, and I felt a mixture of fury and fear growing inside me.

I glanced sideways. The Thai woman had retreated behind the little counter. On it was the only movable item in the room, which looked to be a card-payment machine. It wouldn't do much more than bruise his forehead if I reached for it.

He followed my eyes and read my thoughts. Then he grinned and advanced. The first blow I saw coming and I managed to avoid it. The next hit me between the shoulder and neck and made me gasp with pain. I bowed down and charged at his stomach with my head. That meant he had no room to swing the bat for the next blow. Instead he grabbed my head and tried to twist it round. I clenched my fists and pounded his body. He groaned, but appeared unaffected. The grip on my head became even stronger. I decided to let my body follow the direction he was twisting and, arcing over to the left, I thrust up my elbow and hit him where I had hoped: right under the chin.

He gave an angry groan. For an instant he relaxed his grip and I fell onto the floor. I made a run for the door, pulled it open and threw myself out. He caught up with me by the steps, but now we were outside and I yelled as loudly as I could, an inarticulate scream, but articulate enough to echo around the walls. Windows were opened and many people further up the street stopped what they were doing and reacted.

Hårkløv grabbed my legs and tried to drag me back down the steps, but I kicked out and managed to break free.

I saw many of the people around us already had their phones out. I guessed the police would soon be on their way. I felt no inclination to wait to receive them, so I ran up to Nye Sandviksvei, rounded the corner and went on up to Hans Hauges gate, where I had left the car.

Below Nye Sandviksvei I could already hear the sirens. I jumped into the car. I had at least one more call to make this evening, although I wasn't much looking forward to it. The first visit was to Breistølen and Ruth Olsen, if she was at home. It was no more than a five-minute drive from where I was. I pulled out, drove down into Nye Sandviksvei and straight up, afterwards.

Breistølen was a cul-de-sac and I wasn't going to risk getting trapped there. I parked in Fjellveien and walked the last bit. On arriving at the right address I stood on the step, uneasy. What if Herdis opened the door? Would she recognise me? Would she give a scream of fear and horror? Or had she, like me, repressed the experience, as far as that was possible?

I pulled my cap down over my face as far as I could, hoping that, in the worst-case scenario, she wouldn't recognise me at once. Then I rang the bell. But I hadn't needed to worry. It wasn't Herdis who opened the door. It was Hjalmar Hope.

55

For a few seconds we stood staring at each other.

When we finally started to speak, we did so at the same time. The only difference lay in the expletives we used.

'What the hell are you doing here?' I asked.

'What the fuck are you doing here?' he said.

'I could ask you the same question,' I said, but he didn't take the point.

Ruth Olsen appeared behind him. 'Who is it, Hjalmar?'

I poked my head in. 'It's me. Veum. I have something I'd like to show you.'

'Really?'

'Be warned,' Hjalmar said.

She glanced from one to the other of us.

'This man's wanted by the police.'

'Yes, but I'm innocent!' I said. 'Someone…' I paused. I didn't want to say too much with Hjalmar around.

He glowered at me.

I pointed to him. 'What's he doing here?'

She straightened up. 'Hjalmar's … a friend.'

'And colleague.'

'That too, but since my divorce … he's been a good support.' The look she sent him was more affectionate than I would really have liked.

Hope made a show of putting an arm around her shoulder and pulling her close. She didn't seem to object. 'Veum thinks I'm not that way inclined, Ruth.'

She looked at him in surprise. 'Not that way inclined?'

'He thinks I'm a bit…' He made the classic limp-wrist gesture.

'Oh?' She glanced from him to me with a glint in her eye. 'I can confirm the opposite to be true, Veum. Not that it's any of your business, of course,' she added.

I could feel all sorts of thoughts churning round my brain. I mumbled: 'Well … I'd like to have a few words with you. Alone.'

Her expression was sceptical, but she seemed to be grasping the gravity of the situation. She realised I had something important to tell her. 'Well then … you'd better come in.'

'Ruth,' said Hope in an insistent tone.

'Yes?'

'We can do this in the hallway as far as I'm concerned,' I chipped in. 'And it won't take long. But not with him present.'

Hope glared at me, as though considering whether to launch a physical assault. But he didn't feel confident enough of the result this time either. At any rate, he didn't attack.

She nodded. 'Come in.'

We were together in a narrow hallway, unpleasantly close to one another, so she stepped aside and nodded to Hjalmar. 'Go back to Herdis. She's going to bed soon anyway.'

This was a stab to the heart, but I said nothing.

'Right.' He looked extremely hesitant, but made for a door that was slightly open at the back of the hall. Through the crack came the sound of a TV.

'And close the door after you,' I said.

He was on his way but spun round as if to launch himself at me. 'You don't tell me what to do!'

'Maybe not,' I said. 'But you're doing it anyway.'

Ruth nodded reassuringly to him. 'Just do it, Hjalmar, so we can get this over with.'

He glared from me to her and back again. Then he turned, walked to the door and closed it without a loud bang. There was matt glass in the door, and through it I heard a high-pitched voice ask something. I looked across, nervous. She could come out at any moment, and the big question was still: Would she recognise me?

'So?' Ruth said impatiently. 'What was it you wanted?'

I shifted my gaze from the door to her. 'Is that your daughter inside?'

'Yes, Herdis. Bente's already asleep.' When I didn't react she continued speaking: 'Yes? Get to the point!'

'... This is a very unpleasant matter.'

She started to become ill at ease. 'Unpleasant, what do you mean?'

'Has Herdis ... Has either of your daughters ever said she's been subjected to any kind of ... abuse?'

Her mouth fell open. 'What?' Her eyes widened. 'Abuse? What are you talking about?'

'You're divorced. What was the reason for the divorce?'

'The reason? We were incompatible, simple as that. We had quite different interests, it turned out. Too late, of course. But ... you don't mean ... that my husband ... ?'

'Mm. Was there ever any suspicion of that?'

'That wasn't why we split up. If I'd had the slightest suspicion I would've gone to the police of course!'

'So why did you split up?' I said in a low voice, almost as an afterthought.

She locked her eyes on me and straightened up with the same lissom sensuality I remembered from the last time we met. 'That has absolutely nothing to do with you. We grew apart. I did what I could but ... in the end I gave up.'

'Not enough sex, quite simply.'

'He was no longer interested.'

'But Hjalmar Hope is?'

'Yes, Veum. In fact, he is.'

'How long have you been together?' When she didn't answer at once, I continued: 'The reason I ask is this: How far can you trust him?'

She paled visibly. 'Hjalmar!' She turned to the matt-glass window. 'You don't mean ... ? I refuse to believe that. He and the girls are the best friends in the world. He's a great guy.'

In a flash I saw myself from the same perspective, with Sølvi and Helene. How far did it extend actually – the trust women had in their friends and lovers? Too far?

'Now you'll have to produce some tangible evidence, Veum. This is making me ... I'm beginning to panic.' She looked as if she were about to rush into the sitting room, wrap her arms around her daughter and protect her against all the evil in the world, from now to all eternity.

'I have to show you something, Ruth.'

I took out the crumpled envelope from my inside pocket. I opened it and took out the picture of the child I was sure was Herdis and of the man I was unfortunately equally sure had to be me. Then I held it up to her.

She stared at it. At first she clearly couldn't believe her eyes. She blinked hard, as if to make the picture disappear from her retina. Then she clutched at her mouth and breathed in sharply. I hunched my shoulders in instinctive defence against the scream I knew would come, but when it did it was mute. It was no more than a pained groan from between compressed lips, as though she were holding everything back: the scream, the fear, the fury. Tears sprang from her eyes, and she swayed in front of me.

When I grabbed her around the shoulders she fought her way free from me, without taking her eyes off the photo for a second.

'Herdis,' she croaked. 'This isn't true. This can't be ...'

'You knew nothing about this?'

She looked at me as if I were speaking a language she didn't understand. 'Know? It's come as a complete shock. We have to ... I have to go to the police with this.'

'They already know.'

Slowly she began to click. 'Are we talking about ... what's been in the papers recently? The child-pornography ring?'

I nodded. 'Do you know anything about it?'

'Know?'

'Well, I mean ... could your ex have been involved? Could Hope be involved?'

She opened and closed her mouth, still staring at me in disbelief. 'I ...' She snatched the photo and studied it, with an intensity that made her face quiver.

Without any warning the sitting-room door opened. 'Mamma?'

We both looked in her direction. Herdis was standing in the doorway wearing beige tights and a red jumper. She was pale and had freckles over her nose and cheeks. I had no difficulty recognising her from the photo Ruth Olsen was holding in her hand and the one in her office.

'Are you coming, Mamma?'

She just sent me a fleeting glance.

Her mother, with a sudden tenderness in her voice, said: 'Yes, I'm coming, darling, I just have to...'

The little girl looked at me again. I could see wonderment gradually growing in her eyes, as though she were asking herself if this was someone she knew or had perhaps seen before. Once again I braced myself for the scream I expected, but it didn't come this time, either.

'I'm coming, Herdis,' Ruth said.

'I'll be off then,' I said.

'OK.'

She turned back to me as the daughter watched us.

'I need the name of your ex-husband, Ruth.'

She looked at me, still visibly shaken. 'I'll give it to the police. I'm going to ring this very minute.' Before I could say another word she leaned past me and opened the door. 'Now go.'

'OK, I'm on my way.' I made a move. 'But when you ring the police...'

'Yes?'

'Don't tell them it was me who gave you this.' I indicated the photo she was holding.

'Why not?'

I didn't answer, just shrugged my shoulders and left. I ran to the car and drove off as fast as I could before she managed to warn them. I needed more hours of freedom. As many as possible.

56

I was at the bottom of Helgesens gate when I heard the sirens. As I took a right into Nye Sandviksvei, a patrol car appeared behind me and turned into Helgesens gate, blue lights swirling. I carried on, but without going up Bakkegaten to the flat in Hans Hauges gate. I was going further this time.

I pulled in where Åsne Clausen had confronted me one unpleasant October evening almost two years before. There were two names I was concentrating on now. One was Hjalmar Hope. From my notepad I found the phone number of Svein Olav Kaspersen and keyed it in.

He answered after a few rings. 'Y-yeah?'

'Svein Olav? Veum here.'

'Whaddya want?'

The rejection in his voice was clear, so before he could switch off, I said quickly: 'I've been speaking to Hjalmar.'

'Really.'

'He says you killed your uncle two years ago.'

Silence.

'Are you there?'

'What was that?'

'Hjalmar said you killed your uncle to inherit the salmon farm so that you could get a loan and join him and Sturle Heimark on their computer project.'

'Lies!' he shouted down the phone. 'Lies, all of it!'

'But because you knew nothing about computers and were a loose cannon anyway, he broke off contact. They went to Bergen and continued their work there, while you were left – if not holding the baby, then at least with your uncle's death on your conscience.'

'He was lying! To cover his back.'

'Cover his back?'

'It was … Oh, Jesus, this makes my blood boil!'

'Just tell me how this all fits together, Svein Olav.' I wished I was in Fusa, face to face with him. There was a substantial risk of him hanging up at any minute.

'Uncle came to see me one night I was on the computer, and before I could switch it off … In short, he found out what Hjalmar and Heimark were up to. I'm not sure what you know, but it was child porn of the worst kind. He was steaming. He threatened to report us to the cops.'

He was breathing heavily down the phone. I pressed him. 'Yes?'

'I had to tell Hjalmar of course. He went berserk. He called Heimark, who was in Spain, and managed to get him to come, just for a day, to sort it out.'

'And how did he do that?'

'No idea! But that night Uncle Knut drowned.'

'So Sturle Heimark killed your uncle because he was threatening to report you to the police?'

'Yes!' His voice was husky. 'I asked Hjalmar afterwards how it'd been done, but he just said I shouldn't bother my head about it.'

'And then Heimark went back to Spain.'

'Yes, and they didn't find Uncle until Tuesday.'

'Drowned, with no external signs of violence.'

'Yes, but…'

'Yes?'

'I'm sure they were in it together.'

'Sturle Heimark and Hjalmar Hope?'

'Yes.'

I cursed myself for not having any means of recording this. For the time being I would have to trust that he would repeat this when the police came knocking again.

'And it never occurred to you to report them?'

'No, it … didn't.'

'Nor after they went to Bergen?'

'No. Of course it was terrible. I thought about Uncle and what happened to him. What his opinion of us must've been at the time.'

'Yes.'

After a brief pause came a hesitant: 'And what's gonna happen now?'

'I don't know. If I were you I'd write down what you've told me, with as much detail as possible, and the best you can do is to contact the police, voluntarily.'

'We never talk—'

'Yes, I know. You never talk to the police, but now and then it's actually worth the effort. Good luck, Svein Olav.' I thanked him for being so honest and we rang off.

While we had been talking I had heard several beeps telling me someone was trying to contact me. I looked at the display. I recognised the number. It was Sølvi.

I called her back at once.

She sounded distraught. 'Varg! Where are you?'

'What…?'

'In the flat?'

'No, I—'

'The police have been here and I had to tell them where you … about the flat. They threatened to take me with them and put Helene in an institution, temporarily, but…'

'I see, but how did they find out …? Not many people know about you and me.'

'I have no idea. They were just here, at the door, all of a sudden. Helene had gone to bed, luckily. They were polite enough, but very determined, and as I said … I can't risk losing my child, Varg!'

'No, no, of course not. It won't happen. Relax. Good job you called. I won't go back to the flat.'

'I don't know how long I can keep this up, Varg. This hasn't been a normal year, by any stretch of the imagination.'

'It'll soon be over. More and more pieces are falling into place.'

'But where are you? It's gone ten o'clock.'

'I … Promise me one thing, Sølvi. I have one last visit to make. If you don't hear from me before midnight, call the police.'

'Midnight! But what should I say?'

'Say I've been in touch and they have to come at once to…' I hesitated. Could they have put a tap on her phone? Surely not so quickly. They would need a warrant to do that, wouldn't they?

'To … where?'

'A man called Ole Skarnes. Postal address, Lepsøy.' I gave her the exact address I had found online.

'Ole Skarnes?'

'Yes.'

'But … Oh, please be careful, Varg! I can't lose … not another, in such a short time. Can't you take someone with you?'

'Who would that be? This isn't so dangerous, Sølvi. I know what's waiting for me.'

After a little more chatting, we hung up. I sat back and asked myself the ineluctable question: Well, what was I going to do now? Did I know what was waiting for me? There was only one way to find out.

57

I stared through the windscreen without starting up the engine. I had to admit she had set off a chain reaction in me. Perhaps I shouldn't go there alone. Perhaps it would be safer if I had someone with me. But who?

There wasn't a great selection to choose from. Then I had an idea. I found Sigurd Svendsbø's phone number. When he answered I didn't waste time: 'Svendsbø? Veum here. I need some help. Are you free this evening to go on a little expedition?'

He sounded very sceptical. 'An expedition?'

'There's a man I have to visit – one of the men behind all this online porn mess I've ended up in; but I need help from someone who knows how such things can be done. Someone who can give me the support I need if he tries to talk his way out of it.'

He was still hesitant. 'I don't know … Have you spoken to Waagenes about this?'

'He'll say no. But you've got children yourself … Give me a chance to expose these bastards, once and for all.'

'OK. Can you pick me up?'

'I'm already on my way.'

Ten minutes later I was in Skytterveien. He was standing by the kerb waiting for me, wearing a dark-blue tracksuit and trainers, as though just going out for a run.

I opened the car door and let him in.

He glanced at me. 'Who are we going to visit?'

'One of the men I asked you to check out for me: Ole Skarnes.'

'And how far away is that?'

'Lepsøy.'

'Hope it won't take all night.'

'You've got other things planned?'

'I'm still trying to crack some of the codes in your case, Veum, so don't blame me if we're late now.'

'No, no.'

On the way to Lepsøy I filled him in on the details as well as I could. He made no comments, just grunted and made occasional other noises to show he was following.

Midway between Osøyro and Halhjem I turned off to Bruarøy and Lepsøy. The last stretch to the island of Lepsøy was in pitch black with dense forest on both sides of the road until, after some sudden bends near a bay, we came to an illuminated greenhouse and the last narrow bridge over to the furthest islands by Bjørna Fjord. There I stopped the car and switched on the internal light to check my notes for Skarnes's address. After a couple of wrong turns and fruitless checks of names on post boxes I ended up by a spur road into the forest.

I turned in there and parked in front of a building that was more like a country mansion than a house. A car was parked in the drive – a dark-green Mazda 323; tired paintwork and at least ten years old.

'Here?' said Sigurd Svendsbø, still as sceptical.

'Looks like it,' I replied.

Light shone from some windows behind drawn blinds. When I stepped out of the car I saw that someone had made a narrow opening between two of the slats in one to see out. As we moved towards what I presumed was the front door, the opening closed, like an oyster trapping its prey. I went first; Svendsbø was a couple of steps behind.

There was no bell by the door and no nameplate, but I heard the sound of footsteps inside and the door opened as we arrived. Ole Skarnes appeared in the doorway.

'Veum?' he said. 'I wondered who it was, appearing at this time of night.'

'Yes, but this is urgent.'

'Really? I thought we'd finished talking.'

'Not quite.'

He shifted his gaze to Svendsbø. 'And who is this?'

'A consultant.'

Svendsbø mumbled his name behind me.

Skarnes directed his attention back to me. He was dressed in casual clothes, for being at home: a dark-grey V-neck sweater over a white shirt and comfortable, dark-brown cord trousers. On his feet he wore tartan slippers. 'Well … you'd better come in then.'

We followed him in through an L-shaped wood-panelled hallway with hooks on the walls, largely hung with leisure wear, and beneath them a pair of sea boots, some trainers and several pairs of town shoes. From there we went into the living room, the interior also influenced by the Norwegian tradition of sturdy cabins, with a selection of landscape paintings and a few handwoven rugs on the walls. Large windows faced what was probably the sea, but all I could see was dark, towering pine trees.

The furniture stood in stark contrast to the rest: a big, comfortable leather suite and a dining table with slim, elegant chairs. In a corner of the room was a mute TV. On the coffee table was a folded newspaper beside a half-full glass of cognac and a coffee cup.

'Can I offer you something? A glass of cognac?'

'I'm driving,' I said. 'But…' I turned to Svendsbø.

'No, thank you,' he said.

Skarnes shrugged. 'Well, I won't force you. Anything else? Coffee? Mineral water?'

'Coffee if you have any on the go. If not, a glass of water's fine.'

'No, no. I've got some coffee. And … ?' He raised his eyebrows ironically. 'The consultant?'

'Coffee's fine,' Svendsbø said.

'Have a seat in the meantime.'

He waited until we had sat down before he went through a semi-open door. Through the crack, in the dim light, I caught a glimpse of a worktop. Soon afterwards he returned with a silver Thermos jug and two coffee cups that matched the one on the table.

While he poured the coffee, I said: 'You live here permanently I understood last time we spoke?'

'Yes, after I was left on my own I moved out here for good. I own it with my sister. We used to keep it as a country house.'

'So that's why you call your firm Bjørna Fjord Accountancy?'

'Yes, it reminds me of this place every single day.'

He sat down on the other side of the table, took his glass and warmed the cognac in his hand, without tasting it, as a reminder of what we were missing. 'I'm sure you haven't come here at this time of night to exchange small talk?'

'No. But I'm fairly sure you know what this is about. You're not so stupid.'

His face tautened. 'Then I suggest you get to the point; the sooner the better.'

'Firstly, an image of you is beginning to emerge that is becoming more and more unpleasant to swallow, the more I hear. We mentioned it this morning as well. Your brutality to women. Your view of prostitutes. But now that will have to wait. Abuse of children is quite a different matter and in my eyes even more serious.'

He just sat listening, glass of cognac in hand, glazed eyes, not batting an eyelid.

'One of your … A woman told me about an incident in which she had to perform with a small child, as mother and child fleeing from the Gestapo; she told me what you did to them.' I could feel the fury rising inside me again. 'The girl disappeared. What the hell happened to her? Can you answer me that?'

He shrugged. 'That's an unsubstantiated allegation. I have no idea what you're talking about.'

'No, of course not. But you'll have to explain yourself to the police later, you can be sure of that. There are many more than me with your name on their notepads. Just don't imagine you're going to get out of this.'

His skin went pink and his expression became even more dogged. His nostrils flared – another sign he was ready to defend himself, come what may.

I glanced at Svendsbø. I could see he was following every word. I took a deep breath. 'With regard to me personally: What made you contact me at the outset?'

He made a vague gesture with his hand. 'You were in the phone directory. I took advice. But you were hopeless.'

'Not so hopeless that I don't remember the job. You were being blackmailed, you said. You wanted to know who was behind it, and you wanted to find some proof against them. But you must have bloody known already. You were in league with them.'

'I was not! There was no link.'

'No? But you'd been in The Tower – that place in Solheimsviken.'

'As a client, yes. And I paid for it. That's why I went to you.'

I scrutinised him. 'But then you found out who they were anyway, without my help.'

'Yes.'

'How?'

He looked down in his glass. For the first time in the conversation he seemed to be tempted to have a taste. But he looked up again, without succumbing to the temptation. 'That's got nothing to do with you, Veum.'

'Well … Now listen to something that really is to do with me. You made a woman, whose name we both know, serve me a drink laced with knockout drops, from a bar run by a guy called Johnny. While I was unconscious you and someone else carried me out and transported me to a place where you took some very compromising photos with an under-age girl. Photos which you put on my hard drives together with a load of other material of the same variety. Right?'

'I put stuff on your computer?'

'Svendsbø here can document how that's done. He's demonstrated it for me.'

'Really?' He glanced at Svendsbø before refocussing on me. There was a glint of jeering in his eyes. 'I cannot fathom where you get these stories from, Veum.'

'No? I'm wondering what made you put this filth on my computers. What the hell had I done to you?'

'What you'd done? I wouldn't be bloody here if it weren't for you.'

'Here? What do you mean?'

'I explained the situation to you earlier today. I'm on the verge of bankruptcy. My wife kicked me out and turned off the taps to the money she's sitting on. In a few days I'll lose all of my customers, and my damned brother-in-law's going to make sure I never get a customer from his circle again. And here I sit, on my uppers, in an old summer house, without a krone to my name in the bank! All because you couldn't keep your mouth shut. You blabbed to Karsten and his crowd who had put you on his trail, with the result that they sent my wife the awful photos.' He was getting really steamed up. 'All of this because you were such a damned inept private detective, Veum!'

'Exactly. So it's about money now as well, is it? You've made me the scapegoat for the fix you've got yourself into?'

'If you'd found the people as I asked you to, I could've … taken countermeasures.'

'Countermeasures?'

'Yes.'

I opened my palms. 'So it's my fault, is it? Doesn't that sound absolutely absurd to you? Because I didn't complete the job you gave me?'

'Besides, I wasn't the only person who bore you a grudge.'

'No, exactly. As far as I can see, you're no computer expert, either. Who was in it with you?'

He just glared at me, without answering.

'I've got a witness, Skarnes!'

'A whore!' he spat. 'About as credible as a chimp.'

'So you know what I'm talking about, do you? You know who it is?'

He sent me a withering look. 'I know as much as I want to know. But you can tell these stories to the marines.'

'I'll find out.'

'Find out what exactly?'

'Who the other man was.'

'Well, good luck to you, I say. Was there anything else?' He made a show of looking at his watch.

Then we heard the sound of a car outside. Skarnes looked towards the window with a concerned expression on his face. 'Now what the hell is that? If you've tipped off the police, it'll be all the worse for you, Veum!'

'I haven't...'

He stood up and walked to the window, opened a gap between the slats, like when we arrived, and leaned forwards. I stood up too. As did Svendsbø. Outside, car doors slammed – first one, then another. Skarnes let go of the slats, turned round and glanced suspiciously at both of us. Then he left the room, went through the hallway and opened the front door.

I glanced at Svendsbø. He seemed uneasy. I said: 'Relax. This'll be fine.' But my words didn't seem to convince him.

Now we could hear loud voices coming from the hall, until Skarnes was shoved firmly into the living room, and the two new guests followed him in. For one charged moment we stood there almost like on the stage: Skarnes, Svendsbø, me and the two new arrivals: Hjalmar Hope and Sturle Heimark.

'Look what the cat's brought in,' I said. 'A belated welcome, I suppose I should say.'

'Shut your mouth, Veum!' Heimark snapped.

'That won't be easy,' I answered.

58

'What the hell do you want?' Skarnes barked. 'You can't just force your way in like that!'

'We do as we like,' Heimark said.

Hope eyeballed Svendsbø, who had taken a few steps to the side. 'Don't you try anything!'

Skarnes followed his stare. 'Do you two know each other?'

'All too well, I'm afraid.'

'They're in the same line of work,' I said.

'I told you to keep your gob shut!' Heimark yelled at me.

I held my hands up in defence. 'I told you it wouldn't be easy.'

Heimark looked around. Then he said brusquely: 'Sit down, all of you.'

No-one did as he said.

'That means you as well, Veum.'

'I'm fine as I am.'

Heimark took two long strides over to Skarnes, placed two hands on his chest and shoved him backwards into the chair where he had been sitting. Svendsbø retreated until he had his back to the wall and couldn't go any further. Hope followed him with an expression on his face suggesting it would be a pleasure to knock him down.

Skarnes snarled from his chair: 'Alright, the whole lot of you, what do you want?'

Heimark glanced at me. 'Looks like the party's already started. Have you got a cognac for me?'

Skarnes motioned towards the cabinet, where there were bottles and glasses. 'Help yourself.'

Heimark walked over. 'Hjalmar's driving, but ... Veum?'

'I am too.'

'Sure?'

He looked at Svendsbø. 'And you?'

Svendsbø shook his head, not taking his eyes off Hope for a second.

Heimark selected a glass and, after studying the label with an expression of acknowledgement, poured himself a generous portion of the reddish-brown liquid. 'One of my favourites, too,' he mumbled.

Hope said impatiently: 'Shall we get to the point?'

Heimark gave the impression of being in total control and having all the time in the world. 'Perhaps we should hear what these guys have got on the agenda first.'

'I have so much to discuss with you two,' I said.

'Oh, yes?'

'Knut Kaspersen's death, for example.'

That hit home. Both Heimark and Hope focussed all their attention on me. Skarnes and Svendsbø followed suit.

'I've been talking to Svein Olav, you see, and he had a very different version of events from the one you gave me. If he follows my advice he'll be talking to the police tomorrow.'

Heimark and Hope exchanged glances. Heimark said: 'We can come back to this later.'

'Oh, yes? Why? Now that we're all gathered here.'

'It has nothing to do with what we have to say to those two!' He waved a hand at Skarnes and Svendsbø.

Hope reached inside his jacket and pulled out the same piece of paper I had given Ruth Olsen a few hours earlier. 'No, this is what this is about,' he said, unfolding the print-out in front of Svendsbø, in his face. 'Seen this girl before, have you?'

Svendsbø opened his mouth, not to say something, but the way a fish gasps for air when it is tossed on land.

Hope turned away, crossed the room, stood in front of Skarnes and showed him the same picture. 'And you? Do you recognise this?'

Skarnes retained his composure. He eyed the photo stiffly. 'So? I've seen far worse.'

'Yes, you probably have!' growled Hope. 'You and all your bloody paedo ring!'

Skarnes pointed at me. 'He's the man in the photo!'

Hope spun round to face me, then turned back to Skarnes. 'I know.'

I looked straight at Skarnes. 'So you admit it, do you?' I said. 'In front of two witnesses. You set this up and put the filth onto my hard drives.'

'He wasn't alone,' Hope said. 'That asshole was in it with him.'

I stared in the direction he was pointing, at Svendsbø. 'You! What was your connection with Skarnes?'

Svendsbø was all at sixes and sevens. 'I … I hacked into the same system.'

'The same system? Do you mean … ?'

'They knew each other. They belong to the same network,' Hope said.

'What network?' I said.

'I did not!' Svendsbø said quickly.

'Hjalmar…' Heimark intervened.

But Hope carried on: 'The whole damned paedo ring!' He turned back to Skarnes. 'Don't you realise we're sitting on the register? We didn't set up your system for nothing, you know. Anonymity was guaranteed.'

'Guaranteed!' Skarnes snorted. 'What about those in prison?'

'They didn't pay! They're up to their necks in their own shit. But we've got you registered, every single one of you bastards.'

'You haven't got me registered!' said Svendsbø. 'No bloody chance.'

'Maybe not. You're a smart arse. You know all the tricks. But don't feel too cocky. Perhaps there's a back door to your IP address as well. If we contact the police anonymously they'll have so much to do there won't be time for anything else from now to the New Year!'

'Hjalmar,' Heimark said. 'We've got witnesses here, for Christ's sake!' He pointed to me.

Hope eyed me. 'I don't give a shit. He's one of them.'

'I am not! I was doped! It's not me you can see in the photo, I was unconscious, a dummy placed there. I know nothing about it.'

'If so, that's your problem.'

'But now I know what you were arguing about in Fusa. You and Heimark were developing a computer system that would to a large extent anonymise people carrying out all sorts of cyber crime. I imagine that's the job you had with Bruno Karsten & Co. And when Svein Olav's uncle found out what you were up to and threatened to expose you, you called in Heimark from Spain to tidy up because you weren't man enough to do it yourself.'

Heimark approached me with his fists raised. 'Now you just shut up, Veum!'

I stepped back, but raised my arms and clenched my fists. 'You just try it!'

'Veum's not the main culprit here, Sturle.' Again Hope turned to Skarnes. He held the print-out in his face and pointed to it. 'This is the daughter of a ...' his voice actually cracked '... close friend of ours.'

'Really?' Skarnes snapped, his head raised as if ready to strike from his chair. 'Then you'd be better off talking to her father than me, wouldn't you.'

'The hell I would. Why do you think we've come here?'

He turned away from Skarnes again, and we all followed his gaze. Pressed flat against the wall, with the expression of a hunted animal, Sigurd Svendsbø stared back at us. Siggen to friends. But he didn't have many now. Not in this room anyway.

59

It was as if a flock of angels had passed through the room, at least one with a face averted in shame.

I looked at Svendsbø. 'So you're Ruth's ex-husband.'

Hope left Skarnes and stood in front of Svendsbø once again. 'Your own daughter. What the hell goes on in the heads of your sort?'

'Your sort would never understand!' retorted Svendsbø.

'Accessibility is the key here,' I mumbled.

'I just can't imagine what a lovely woman like Ruth could see in you,' Hope went on, and for a moment I seemed to forget what Hope himself had been clearly exposed as. Not only did he profit from filth, but he had been an accessory to a murder to allow him to continue wallowing in that filth.

Svendsbø looked at him with an expression of injury, as though he were the victim here and not one of the baddies.

I raised my voice and said: 'You're all bloody involved in this.'

All four locked their eyes on me. Skarnes still seemed the least concerned. Heimark was as aggressive as always. Svendsbø looked at me as though it had only occurred to him now that I was in the photo, as though it hadn't been him who photographed his own daughter at the session. Hope was lurching between aggression and despair: the aggression directed at Svendsbø and me; the despair at the situation he was in. But what worried me most was how I would get out of this unscathed.

I held up a hand and raised an index finger. 'First of all. There's a widespread international network that shares child porn, in which at least two of you are directly involved as consumers and suppliers of material.' I pointed to Skarnes and Svendsbø. 'And you two…' I shifted my finger to Heimark and Hope. '…You two weren't any better. You

developed a system together, and as for you...' Now I was pointing at
Heimark. '...You knew your way around computers as well. And did
you arrange the security as well? Were you the security regulator and
the executioner? Did you see all this as a way of securing your old age?'

'I was not a fucking executioner!'

'You ex-colleagues will let you know about that. At any rate you
contributed with useful expertise, whether it was you or Hope who
performed the act.'

Hope sent a reflex nod to Heimark, but without saying anything.
There was an evil glint in Skarnes's eyes. My gaze was focussed on
Heimark. I considered him to be the most dangerous of the trio.

'In a way, though, this is just the backdrop here. You're all involved in
extensive co-operation with what I would call organised crime, represented by *herr* Bruno Karsten and *herr* Bjorn Hårkløv, who is known to
most simply as Bønni. You, Hope, supplied them with computer expertise – when not working at SH Data. I can't rule out the possibility that
Karsten and his network also had some interest in the distribution of child
pornography. He and Hårkløv had a contact on the inside – at least one –
of an asylum reception centre for child refugees, which regularly supplied
children for this filth and out-and-out prostitution. And you, Skarnes, you
and Svendsbø here, were punters – at the brothel in Solheimsviken, also
known as The Tower, and of other services, such as the Gestapo role play
we were talking about before these gentlemen turned up.'

'I never went to The Tower!' Svendsbø shouted angrily.

'No? But you had no hesitation in taking your own daughter to at
least one porn special. Didn't you have any conscience? Didn't you consider how she would feel? Or was she doped up, like me?'

He looked down. 'She was given a good dose of Valium. She remembers nothing.'

'No? Not even on the hard drive at the back of her head? On her
internal retina? You can be sure she does. She remembers alright, con-
sciously or unconsciously.'

'And it wasn't like that! It was him; he forced me into it!' He pointed
at Skarnes.

'Forced you to do what?'

'To take her along. Herdis. When we were going to nail you. If I hadn't, he would've told Ruth what I was doing and I'd have lost access.'

'Wouldn't have made any difference, would it? You'd taken photos of her before anyway. The ones online.'

He was desperate. 'Right, but he put them online. As far as I was concerned, they were only meant for him.'

I shook my head. 'I really don't understand people like you. I'm damned if I do.'

Hjalmar Hope stamped on the floor, a physical consequence of the impatience that was boiling over into desperation. 'So what the fuck do we do? Are we going to stand around listening to this guy's prattle, or are we going to do something?'

'What precisely?' said Ole Skarnes, with a gleam of sadistic expectation in his eyes.

They exchanged glances, all equally at a loss, it seemed.

But I was still alive and kicking. 'Didn't you come here to settle a score with Svendsbø, Hope? You're Ruth's shining knight, aren't you?'

Hope turned back to Svendsbø. 'She got a real shock when she saw the photo, Siggen. She tried to ring you, but put the phone down before you answered.'

Svendsbø reached inside his jacket. 'Yes, I saw she'd been trying.'

'I said I'd talk to you. But when I got to Skytterveien you were already on your way … here.'

'You followed us?' I said.

'For long enough to know where you were going anyway.'

'And then you called Big Daddy because you didn't dare come out here on your own.'

Heimark approached me with his fists raised again. 'Veum!' he said in an admonitory tone.

'There's some unrest in the camp, I can see.'

Ole Skarnes smirked.

Svendsbø said: 'You lot don't understand anything. None of you! You don't understand what it's like to live with…'

He stopped in the middle and shot a look at the window. Outside, we heard the sound of at least two cars screaming to a halt in the drive. We all stared.

Heimark was the first to react. He ran to the window, pushed up a slat and peered out. 'Oh, shit!' he exclaimed, half turning. 'It's the police.'

'What!' said Hope, looking at the door as though he expected stormtroopers to come piling in on cue. Even Ole Skarnes looked as if he had finally lost his composure and got up from his chair.

Svendsbø looked around. Then he ran across the room and legged it through the door to the kitchen. A second later a door was heard slamming outside.

I didn't hesitate for long, either. I followed him through the kitchen to the back door, tore it open and threw myself into the darkness. I soon got my bearings. A path led through the forest at the back. At the front of the house I could hear car doors shutting and some quick commands being given. However, I set off after Svendsbø into the forest.

60

It was pitch black. A wind had blown up and above my head the tall trees swayed and bent. As I scurried along the narrow path through the wood, low-hanging branches whipped into my face and I had difficulty finding my bearings. In the distance I heard the roar of breakers. Bjørna Fjord was growling like a bear in the autumn night.

A couple of times I came to a halt and listened. I heard the sounds of someone crashing through the wood ahead of me. I might have been getting on in age, but Svendsbø had spent the best part of his life in front of a computer screen, and I considered myself at least as fit as him.

Occasionally clearings opened in the forest, and now I could clearly glimpse the fjord ahead. On a hill to the right of us were some darkened buildings, probably other summer houses, and suddenly we were on a lawn with berry bushes planted at the edge.

I could see him in front of me now. He was running in a way I thought I had seen before – jig-like with arms circling. He was at the far end of the lawn, where he unhooked a gate in the fence and continued through another copse towards the sea. I set off again.

He hadn't closed the gate after him, and I could see I was catching him up. He crossed another open area and took a right, where the path ended in a concrete walkway towards the furthest rocks. The sea was foamy-white here and the surf towered into the air. Svendsbø slipped on the concrete and almost fell but regained his balance. I moved along it with more circumspection. As far as I could see, he was caught in a trap.

The walkway ended in a little platform between some smooth, shiny rocks. At the sea-edge I saw a narrow, concrete construction clearly silhouetted against the greyish-black fjord. It reminded me of a pulpit

where the devil himself could scream his imprecations to a gathering
of shipwrecked ghosts. As I approached I caught sight of steps leading
up to an opening in the middle, like an entrance to the sea. At once I
realised it had to be the base of a diving tower, with two boards, the top
one around five metres high. But the boards had gone and it was obviously a long time since the tower had been used.

I caught up with Svendsbø as he was hesitating between which way
he should go: over the slippery rocks on the land side of the walkway
or out to the diving board. I threw myself at him, grabbed his shoulder
and twisted him round. He tried to free himself and we both toppled
over onto the platform as the sea-spray rose around us like the froth of
two sea-animals engaged in a fight of life and death.

I had hold of one arm and with a violent jerk I turned him round
and pushed him so that he was lying face down on the concrete base. I
held him in a half-nelson, with my knee in the small of his back, and I
leaned over.

'Lie still! Do you hear me? Or else I'll break your arm.'

He groaned aloud. 'OK, OK.'

I relaxed my grip but didn't let go. 'Where the hell were you going?'

He raised his face, wet with sea water. He stared across the fjord.
'Out there.'

'Into the sea? You're not going anywhere until you've made a state-
ment to the police.'

'To the police?'

'So that I get my name cleared once and for all.'

'You don't deserve it.'

'Don't I? What have I ever done to you?'

He twisted his head half-round to look me in the eye. He groaned
aloud, but this time it wasn't with pain but despair.

I tried to straighten up, but was still gripping his wrist. 'Do you admit
it was you who put that filth into my computers?'

He didn't answer and I pushed up his arm.

'Yes, yes!' he yelled.

'And it was you who sent the pictures to Sølvi, wasn't it?'

'Yes. It was me.'

'What on earth was Waagenes thinking of when he employed you as an expert?'

'That's what I am, for Christ's sake. I had done jobs for him before. Getting this particular job too was a gift, nothing less.'

'Because you'd already hacked my machines?'

He tried to nod. 'Yes.'

'How did you get in?'

'For a man like me it was easy. I got you to answer an email that on the surface was from a friend of yours. You opened a link and were caught in a trap, like so many before you.'

'I can't have been sober.'

'Probably not,' he sneered. 'Otherwise you wouldn't have opened the link, would you.'

'But you still haven't told me why.'

'It was Skarnes's idea. I'd helped him with computer matters before, and we'd shared quite a few – erm, you know – pics. But the idea was that they would lie there like a time bomb in case the police got into the system. Or a bomb we could detonate ourselves if we felt the time was ripe. The important thing was to play with the power it gave us … over you. We both felt we had a score to settle with you.'

'Skarnes because of the money and a kind of revenge. But you? What the hell have I ever done to you? I didn't even know who you were until Waagenes brought you in.'

'No? I even tried to give you a clue when we first met Waagenes. But you were too stupid to understand.'

'Understand what?'

Another breaker crashed onto the rock and soaked us in salt water. I almost lost my grip on Svendsbø. I held him tighter, to have something to hold onto if for nothing else.

'Ow!' he yelled. 'You're breaking my bloody arm!'

'Understand what?' I repeated, even louder this time.

'Deep down I wanted you to know what you were doing penance for.'

'Penance? Me?'

'The date I told you about – when the files were put into your computer.'

At once I remembered: 'Åsne Clausen's funeral. A year to the day.' The last piece of the puzzle fell into place. 'That was where I knew you from. Your way of walking. But from a distance. It was you walking with Åsne from the office to the car park that time I tailed her two years ago.'

Again he tried to turn his head round completely to see me. 'But she caught sight of you and, on her way to my place, she got out of her car and spoke to you.'

'On her way to Skytterveien. Exactly. You were her secret friend.'

'Secret friend? I loved her. She was the first woman who had been able to free me from the hell that was my life – this sick attraction I had for children.'

My head spun. Then the pieces came together and I saw the shape of what had happened with greater clarity. 'But this computer system of Hope & Co's wasn't as secure as they claimed. Hackers could get in, and that's precisely what Severin did.'

He stared at me, silent, boundless despair in his eyes.

I continued. 'And because his mother was a computer expert she hacked into his machine and was shocked by what she found. Among other things, a picture of Herdis, whom she recognised. Was that what happened? Did she contact you about it?'

'Yes,' he groaned. 'She rang me early in the morning and told me to go over… I'd never been to her house, but she said she was alone. At first I thought … But she dragged me into Severin's room, showed me the pictures and afterwards … she asked me if I knew anything about it. I thought initially that Severin had taken the pictures himself, but then … I couldn't keep my mouth shut. I had to admit it. Deep down, I hoped she would understand, that she would take it as a positive – that it was her who had got me out of this way of thinking. I tried to explain to her that it was someone else – Skarnes – who had forced me to put the pictures online. But she didn't understand. She went straight for my throat. I had to understand, she said. She would have to tell Ruth.

Perhaps report it to the police. She was hysterical! In the end she physically attacked me.'

'So you would maintain it was self-defence? You killed her by accident? And to disguise it you hung her from a beam so that it would look like suicide?'

'It was an accident! I would never have dreamt of...'

'And you were lucky because her father was so determined to cover up what everyone thought it was: suicide. But you knew better. You've known all the time.'

'That was why I tried to bring the date to your attention. It was a kind of penance as well. Actually I wanted someone to know. Because no-one can prove a thing!'

'But I still don't understand why you wanted to target me.'

'I've already told you. It was Skarnes who suggested your name. And I recognised it of course. Åsne was out of her mind when she came to my place after scuppering the job you were doing for her husband. She was convinced he would use whatever you found against her in a divorce case. And a lot of what went on in her family was also about money.'

'I know all about that. So you regarded yourself more as an assistant?'

'Something like that. But it was you and the husband from hell who had put her in the mental state she was in. That was why she reacted so violently to what she found on Severin's computer. You have to understand ... I loved her! It was her who ... It was her who had laid to rest the demons inside me. It was her who had shown me what real love could be.'

I listened to what he said, then I couldn't restrain myself: 'You mean ... as opposed to inflicting abuse on your own children? And others?'

He recoiled, as if I had hit him. 'No-one can understand ... how it feels to be like that. It's not what you want for yourself. It's what you're compelled to do.' He mumbled something I didn't catch.

'What did you say?'

'Even to those nearest to you,' he shouted as another breaker crashed over us.

I never found out if it was the breaker that did it or it was a moment's inattention on my part. All of a sudden he tore himself free from my grip and arched his back with such power that I was thrown backwards and left clinging onto the slippery rocks so as not to be swept into the sea. He staggered to his feet and stumbled forwards, crossing the narrow top of a rock over to the base of the diving tower that rose above us. Inside the entrance to the tall structure he turned, holding his hands against both sides to stay upright.

I called his name. He stood motionless, as though he hadn't heard.

Then my phone rang. Without taking my eyes off him, I pressed the answer button and held the phone to my ear. 'Yes?'

'Varg?' It was Sølvi. 'Is everything OK?'

'...Yes. I'm OK, but...'

'I couldn't wait until midnight. Have the police arrived?'

'Yes, but I'm not there any longer. I'm ... down by the sea.'

'What's going on?'

I stood staring. One moment he was there, the next he was gone.

'Nooo!' I shouted.

'Varg! What's going on?'

Without answering, I stuffed the phone back in my inside pocket and charged forwards. I crossed the same narrow part of the rock he had passed less than a minute ago. I sprinted up the steps and stood in the entrance staring down at the foaming breakers, out to the white-crested sea. He was already gone. There was no sign of any life, only the dark water billowing in and out, back and forth, like time itself, forever in remorseless motion.

I didn't move. Another cascade of water crashed in and covered me as I clung onto the concrete base around me with all my strength. When it was over I scrambled back onto land and was a good distance along the walkway before I stopped and peered into the darkness, as though expecting him to emerge from the depths like a merman and come roaring towards me, on the back of a shark.

I took out my phone again and re-established the connection.

She answered at once. 'What was that, Varg? What happened?' She sounded hysterical.

'I lost a witness, Sølvi. Perhaps the most important one.'

'What! Who was it?'

'I'll tell you later. I have to ring Waagenes. But everything'll be alright now. Don't worry.' I hoped I made it sound more convincing than I felt.

Before returning to the summer house up by the main road, I rang Waagenes and woke him from his beauty sleep. Which he fully deserved, bearing in mind how careless he had been with the experts in his employ. Quickly, I brought him up-to-date with events. He said I should hand myself in to the police, and I answered that that was what I was going to do. He would meet me at the police station, he added. Many thanks, I said, but I had expected nothing less.

Then I slowly set off back through the forest. I wasn't looking forward to the coming days, but in my heart of hearts I was sure they would accept my explanation. Perhaps they would even engage some other experts to examine Svendsbø's computers to see if any revealing clues could be found there, no matter how well he had tried to cover his traces. And then I had a little to tell them about the scoundrels I hoped they already had in irons. But still some big-time crooks would go free, as always. There was a long way to go with that aspect of the case.

Before entering the forest I turned for a final time and gazed at the abandoned concrete pulpit. Another breaker crashed over the rocks, but no-one was riding on the crest of the waves. He was gone for ever. Swallowed up by the sea.

Other titles from the Varg Veum series,
available from Orenda Books

'A NORWEGIAN
CHANDLER'
JO NESBØ

'STAALESEN IS ONE OF
MY VERY FAVOURITE
SCANDINAVIAN AUTHORS
AND THIS IS A SERIES
WITH VERY SHARP TEETH'
IAN RANKIN

GUNNAR
STAALESEN

WE SHALL
INHERIT
THE WIND

INTERNATIONAL BESTSELLER

'STAALESEN IS ONE OF
MY VERY FAVOURITE
SCANDINAVIAN AUTHORS
AND THIS IS A SERIES
WITH VERY SHARP TEETH'
IAN RANKIN

'A NORWEGIAN
CHANDLER'
JO NESBØ

GUNNAR
STAALESEN

WHERE ROSES
NEVER DIE

INTERNATIONAL BESTSELLER – OVER 2 MILLION COPIES SOLD